Maggie Mason is a pseudonym of author Mary Wood. Mary began her career by self-publishing on Kindle where many of her sagas reached number one in genre. She was spotted by Pan Macmillan and to date has written many books for them under her own name, with more to come.

Mary continues to be proud to write for Pan Macmillan, but is now equally proud and thrilled to take up a second career with Sphere under the name of Maggie Mason.

Born the thirteenth child of fifteen children, Mary describes her childhood as poor, but rich in love. She was educated at St Peter's RC School in Hinckley and at Hinckley College for Further Education, where she was taught shorthand and typing.

Mary retired from working for the National Probation Service in 2009, when she took up full time writing, something she'd always dreamed of doing. She follows in the footsteps of her great-grandmother, Dora Langlois, who was an acclaimed author, playwright and actress in the late nineteenth–early twentieth century.

It was her work with the Probation Service that gives Mary's writing its grittiness and her need to tell it how it is, which takes her readers on an emotional journey to the heart of issues.

Maggie MASON

Blackpool Evacuee

SPHERE

First published in Great Britain in 2018 by Sphere

1 3 5 7 9 10 8 6 4 2

Lyrics to 'We'll Meet Again' on p308 © Ross Parker and Hughie Charles.

A CIP catalogue record for this book is available from the British Library.

ISBN 978-0-7515-7318-3

Typeset in Bembo by Hewer Text UK Ltd, Edinburgh
Printed and bound in Great Britain by Clays Ltd, Elcograf S.p.A.

Papers used by Sphere are from well-managed forests
and other responsible sources.

Sphere
An imprint of
Little, Brown Book Group
Carmelite House
50 Victoria Embankment
London
EC4Y 0DZ

An Hachette UK Company
www.hachette.co.uk

www.littlebrown.co.uk

To the memory of my dear mother and father-in-law, Edith and Jim Wood, who spent so many happy holidays in Blackpool and sparked my initial interest in the town.

The love you showered your family with lives on today.

PART ONE

1940

AN ISLAND IN PERIL

CHAPTER ONE

Julia and Clara
Fears and Memories

Julia's stomach muscles clenched. The letter her beautiful Clara had handed her when she'd come in from school meant the end of their life together for the foreseeable future – maybe for ever! *Oh God, no. No, not that.*

Wanting to say no, no one was going to part her from her daughter, the fear of what the Germans would do when they invaded – for it was certain now that they would – gave her the knowledge that she must take her Clara to the quayside the next day.

The letter said that the boats would board at 9 a.m. and leave Guernsey by 11 a.m. Beneath that was a list of what they were allowed to take with them. The list of items was small. Her daughter was to leave her and go into someone else's care, with so few of her belongings.

Pacing this one room that was their home, in the attic of Rose Cottage Boarding House, didn't help. Neither did Clara's tears, or her pleas.

'Don't make me go, Mum, please don't let me go. Everyone says that the newspapers said that parents would have a choice. I'm almost fourteen, they can't *make* me go.'

Taking her sobbing child into her arms, Julia looked towards the open window. The lovely June day was marred by the sound of bombs in the distance growing louder and louder. Wisps of smoke drifted by, carried across the Channel by the wind.

The Germans were beating the British on the beaches of France. Cherbourg, just thirty miles away, had been bombarded with shells and bombs for days now, and whereas on a clear day the port and houses could be seen, now the town was a red glow of fire, from which belched a black cloud of smoke.

Her world, as she knew it, was under threat. Not that it was a happy place for her anyway, shunned as she was by most of the islanders on account of being an unmarried mother, and having to bear seeing her daughter ostracised – but it was home.

Julia sighed as she thought of how few friends Clara had and how she suffered name-calling and the humiliation of being left out of whatever her peers were planning. She was never asked to parties, or even just to muck around on the beach. Yes, they were lonely, she and Clara. But being together made them happy and they made the most of their lot even though it wasn't much.

This room and the leftovers from the food prepared for the guests, plus a meagre wage which just kept them afloat was given grudgingly by Ida Philips, the sour-faced woman who owned the boarding house. In exchange she expected Julia to be at her beck and call day and night – scrubbing down the kitchen at nearly midnight, and then up with the crowing of the cockerel at dawn to cook breakfast. Then there were the dishes to wash, the beds to make, the piddle pots to empty and the whole house to be cleaned.

Often, tired to the bones of her, the tears would stream down Julia's face for no particular reason, but mostly when she thought of her parents, and how, instead of protecting her and standing by her, they had left the island soon after the tragedy that had taken her fiancé Tim and his father.

They couldn't take the shame of having an unmarried, pregnant daughter and had gone to live in Germany where her mother had an elderly uncle. Julia had rarely heard from them since, though they had often been on her mind. Despite her mother's coldness towards her, she missed them and worried about them, asking herself over and over how they were faring since Hitler's uprising. Had they been imprisoned, as foreign nationals were in Britain?

Being left alone to face her grief and the fear of losing her child had devastated Julia. Her mother had given her one option. Julia must travel to Britain, go into the convent that her mother had written to, then once her child had been born and taken away, she could join them in Germany and help her mother to care for her uncle.

But Tim's mother, Winnie, had come to the rescue. Not able to take her in at that time, after her own life had been devastated, she did all she could to save her grandchild from being taken from them. She paid for a room for Julia in this boarding house, and for the medical care she needed. After the birth, Ida Philips had offered her this job and this room and it had seemed like the answer to Julia's prayers. Although trained as a nurse, she'd lost her job and knew that she wouldn't be accepted back at the hospital where she'd worked.

Taking Ida's offer had meant she could stay near to Winnie and yet not be completely reliant on her. Winnie had never known the extent of the work that Julia did. *Poor Winnie. How will she take the news that Clara must go away?*

Clara broke into her thoughts as if reading them. 'What about Granny? I can't leave Granny.'

No answer to this would come – only guilt at the course Julia knew she had to take. She had to stay strong. She had to let her daughter go to safety.

'Mum! I said what about Granny?'

Taking a deep breath, Julia spoke the necessary lie. 'Granny will want you to go. She will know that it is the best thing for you, darling.'

Inside, Julia knew that Winnie would crumble. But what could she do?

If it was possible for a fear of a different kind to penetrate what was already holding Julia in its grip, it did now. The worry she'd felt lately for Winnie surfaced, and tightened her throat. A tiny little lady, with hardly any meat on her bones, Winnie had lost weight lately, weight she couldn't afford to lose, and her cheeks had become hollow. Always she insisted that she was all right and that her frequent trips to the doctor were because her arthritis was bothering her more than it should, but Julia had her own thoughts on what was truly wrong with Winnie. During her nursing days she had seen similar symptoms many times. Cancer. The dreaded, incurable disease. This was borne out by the yellow tinge of Winnie's skin, and finding her, on several occasions, doubled up in agony with pains in her stomach.

Guiding Clara to the chair, Julia glanced at the photo in the frame that stood on the mantelpiece. Two beautiful, smiling faces looked back at her. Hers and her beloved Tim's. Happy faces. Young and in love, and just a week away from getting married.

Rhoda, Julia's best friend at the time, who had scarcely spoken to her since Tim's death, had accompanied her to the dock to see Tim off on a fishing trip with his dad. Rhoda had been given a box camera for Christmas a few months before, and had taken the photo. How happy the three of them had been.

Excited about the wedding, Julia and Rhoda had made their way to Mrs Robins's house after they'd seen Tim off. Rhoda was to be bridesmaid and they needed a final fitting of their frocks. They had loved the swirling, satin gowns – Julia's a dazzling white and Rhoda's a cerise pink. They'd twirled around and giggled at Mrs Robins's antics as she'd tried to make them stand still. With a dozen pins sticking out from her mouth, Mrs Robins had only been able make grunting noises as she'd reached out for them.

The trip they'd seen Tim off on was going to be the last father and son, who shared a love of fishing, were to have before the wedding. *But only the last for now, not for ever and ever. Oh, Tim . . . Tim.*

Her legs gave way and Julia slumped on to the arm of the chair. Softly stroking Clara's dark hair, her heart jolted as her child looked up at her. She was so like Tim. She had his pale blue, wide eyes, his curls, his nose. And yet, others often said that Clara looked like Julia too, with her own dark curly hair. Though her eyes were brown, and her nose smaller, it was her full lips and even teeth that Clara had inherited.

The combination of herself and Tim had endowed Clara with a beauty that was emerging more and more as she approached womanhood. Though Julia was glad that, so far, Clara had shown no sign of developing in the same way as her.

Slim, with a tiny waist and hips, Julia hated how her breasts were larger than average and attracted unwanted attention. Because of them and her situation, men leered at her when they thought their wives weren't looking, deepening the distrust and disdain that the island women had towards her.

Always she wore loose-fitting blouses with the buttons done up to her neck and flowing skirts, rather than the pencil-slim ones that were the fashion. The last thing she wanted was the kind of attention she received. It made her feel dirty, and as if men thought that she was easy with her favours. Some had even whispered to her that she must miss what she'd had with Tim, and hinted that they could step in and look after her in that way.

Nothing could have been further from the truth. She and Tim had only ever experienced one fumbling, bumbling encounter. Both had been embarrassed, and sorry it had ever happened. It had been a month before the sea had claimed Tim and his dad, luring them out by its calmness, then whipping up into a sudden storm, churning and tossing their little boat so that they were unable to fight its insurmountable power. Julia shuddered. Often she'd stood on the shore when the sea had been in this mood, imagining how terrified Tim and his dad must have been.

Her mind closed down to these thoughts and visited instead the uncomfortable moment when Clara had been conceived. She and Tim had taken a picnic to Le Portelet, a beach in the Forest area in the south of Guernsey, inaccessible by land. They'd borrowed a boat from a friend of Tim's father who had a boat house at Petit Bot, a shoreline from which you could swim to Le Portelet. They'd loaded the boat with their picnic basket. Le Portelet beach had been deserted when they'd arrived.

They'd spent a blissful afternoon, swimming, playing in the waves, chasing each other and rolling in the sand, enjoying the taste and feel of their near-naked bodies entwined together – until Tim's kisses had become more demanding.

Always when this happened, one of them had been able to call a halt, or cause a distraction, but that afternoon Julia had found herself yielding to the feelings that swept over her as Tim's hand explored her body. A yearning for more had burned inside her, and she hadn't resisted.

Tim had hastily climbed on her, his eagerness making him clumsy. Coming to her senses, she'd tried to stop it happening. 'No, Tim, not that.'

'Yes, Jules. Yes. We have to.'

She'd felt an uncomfortable pain, and then Tim had moaned loudly and rolled off her. After a moment, he'd apologised. 'I shouldn't have done that. I'm sorry. Oh, Jules, it all went wrong. It'll be better than that, I promise. I was too excited, I – it came to an end too quickly. I'm sorry. I promise that next time . . .'

She'd put her hands over her ears, her distress filling her. 'There'll not be a next time!'

'Jules!'

'I – I mean until we're wed. Promise me. Promise you'll stop groping me and everything until after we're wed. I don't want to . . . I . . . '

'Oh, Jules, I'm sorry, but you wanted . . . '

'I know, I'm not blaming you. I just wish we hadn't.'

As the voices replayed in her head, Julia once more heard Tim's sob. They'd clung together, each taking the blame, promising not to let it happen again, until their tears had turned to laughter as Tim had said, 'The problem is, I need the practice, I've never done it before.' And she had said, 'I have to agree with that.' A silly exchange, but one that had lightened the moment, and led them back to the easy companionship they'd always enjoyed.

Clara's sobbing penetrated the place Julia had allowed herself to drift to. Slipping off the arm of the chair, she knelt in front of her daughter. 'Oh, my darling, I – I don't know what to say, or do. I don't think we have any choice.'

'We do, Mum, we do! You can say no! You can! Stop shaking your head!'

'Clara, listen to me. The Germans are coming. They will occupy our island. We will all have to do exactly as they say. Everything will be different. You . . . and I . . . we will be forced . . . Oh, I can't bear it. Oh, Clara, they say that the German soldiers rape all the young women . . . yes, you too. The tales are of girls of eleven years of age being forced to have sex with them.'

Clara's white face pulled Julia up. In her anguish she'd said more than she'd intended. No mother should first mention the sexual act in such a brutal way, let alone when it was about the forcible taking by ruthless soldiers. 'I'm sorry, my darling. I'm sorry. I had to tell you the truth of it, I – I had to.'

'But what about you, Mum? Will you be safe?'

Everything Julia had tried not to think about crowded in on her. No, she wouldn't be safe. A shudder ripped through her, making her tremble, but she wouldn't let in the truth of what might happen to her.

'Come with me, Mum. Please. Lots of folk are leaving. Granny could come too. Please, Mum.'

The mention of Winnie tore at Julia. Winnie was the reason that she couldn't go. Both needed her, the young and the old. But the young one, Clara, was strong. She would mourn, and weep, and be afraid and alone, but in the depth of her she had a strength she could call upon. The old one, Winnie, had been strong, but now, after years of standing by them, she needed Julia to prop her up. To see her through what Julia knew in her heart were her last months.

With these thoughts, her mind was made up. She had no choice. She had to let the young one go. She had to stay and do her duty by the old one.

The next day, feeling tired after her tears had kept her awake for most of the night, Clara clutched at the small suitcase that her granny had found for her in her attic room.

Crowds jostled her, pushing her and her mother out of the way as they scrambled for the dockside. One woman spat in their path.

'Don't do that. We're as good as you are!'

'Hush, Clara.'

'Why, Mum? Why? Why do you stand for it?'

'For the sake of peace, darling. And you are best to do the same. You'll be away from them soon.'

'I don't want to be. I want to stay here, and I want them to accept us. We are a part of them. You and your father were born here, as were generations of our family.' The anger that Clara had often felt, both at the rejection she and her mother suffered and the acceptance of it that her mother displayed, came to the fore. A scream formed in her that she wanted to let loose, telling them all that none of them were any better than her or her mother. But the scream caught in her throat and she had to swallow hard so as not to burst into tears.

Clinging onto her mother's hand as if she was a small child again, Clara clamped her lips together. Ahead of them, her classmates were filing onto a boat that didn't look big enough to take them all. Another boat was moored alongside. Clara could see the young children and their mothers boarding this one. *Maybe there won't be any room on either for me.* With this thought, she felt glad of those in the crowd who deliberately prevented her and her mother from making progress towards the quayside and a hope entered her, compounded by the sound of a bell ringing out from the first boat and a voice shouting, 'No more. Get back. Another boat will come tomorrow.'

Clara smiled and moved closer to her mother as she watched a sailor unwind the anchor before jumping aboard. The boat began to slowly manoeuvre out of the dock to shouts and yells of, 'Stop, take one more, please!' And others declaring that they would pay, whatever it took.

As Clara and her mother walked back towards home, the island that had been familiar in every way took on the mantle of a strange, unwelcome place. Abandoned cars, some with their doors still open and their engines running, littered the roads leading to the dock. Dogs and cats roamed around, looking lost, hungry and tired. Some of the cottages had wide open doors. Bunches of keys dangled from keyholes.

Only the noise of those returning, not having secured a place on the boats, stopped Clara's beloved Guernsey from seeming to be a deserted island.

'Shall we go and see Granny?'

'No. That's not a good idea, Clara. We can't put her through the pain of saying goodbye to you again. Let her think that you have gone. That way, she can begin to get used to the idea.'

Will she ever do that? Will Granny forget me and carry on as if I never existed? The lump in her throat finally broke. Tears wet her cheeks. She'd heard folk speak of a broken heart – now Clara felt certain that she knew how that felt. Because her heart hurt. Fear engulfed her, but it didn't take precedence over the pain of loss she felt.

Her world was coming to an end. She didn't know how long it would take to happen, but she knew that nothing would be the same ever again from the moment there was a space on a boat that would take her far away.

Feeling her mother's arm tighten around her gave her no comfort. There was no comfort to be had. Tomorrow, or the next day, everything would be lost.

CHAPTER TWO

Julia
The Sorrow of Parting

Julia clung on to Clara the next morning, oblivious to the rain soaking her and the wind stinging her calves and whipping her shawl from around her shoulders.

Clara's sobs shook her body. Julia had no words that could help them.

Without warning, someone jerked them apart. 'Come on. Get on with it. You're lucky that there's one place left on the boat for you. Not that you deserve it.'

Julia's heart stung to hear this. She wanted to rip the woman's hair out strand by strand, and scream at her, but she just called out to Clara: 'Write, darling. Write as soon as you're settled. Let me have your address.'

Clara looked back at her, pain and fear painted on her face.

'It'll be all right, darling. You'll be back, or I'll come for you, I promise.'

The woman shoved Clara forward. 'Hurry up, will you?'

It was too much for Julia. Her agony clouded her judgement. She rushed forward. 'Can't you be civil to her? Can't you see how terrified she is? Please show her some kindness. Please!'

'Scum don't deserve kindness. Now get off with you. I thought you'd be relieved. Everyone knows where the Germans will get their favours. Well, you won't have anything stopping you with this one out of your way, will you, harlot?'

The breath caught in Julia's lungs. Her hand came up, but before she could strike out a strong pair of arms grasped her. 'None of that. Showing your true colours, eh? And in front of your child as she has to face the wide world. Shame on you.'

The stinking breath of Constable Ferrington wafted into Julia's open mouth as she gasped from the pain of his over-zealous restraint. 'Let me go. Let me say goodbye to my daughter. *Clara! Clara!*'

But it was too late. Clara was lost in the midst of the pushing crowd, all jostling for position, hoping for a place on the boat.

Julia's body folded, only to jolt back upright as the shock of the Constable's hand squeezing her breast brought her wits back to her. 'Don't!' The word was a snarl rather than a plea.

'Getting choosy, are we? You'd do well to keep in with the likes of me. I could protect you and give you pleasure while I'm doing so.'

The words were whispered. His face so close that moisture from his mouth dampened her ear. Repulsion trembled through her. 'Let me go. I'll never go with you, never! I'd prefer to be raped by a German soldier than lie with you!'

'Ah, that's your thinking, is it? Collaboration? Well, I'll be watching your every move, and if I get whiff of it, I'll be the one to personally tar and feather you, girl.'

'That's not what I meant. Please let me go. If you've an ounce of decency, you'd let me look out to sea and wave to my daughter.'

'So you can show that you care? Ha, I don't think so. You won't play ball with me, so I'm going to show you how it will be if you step out of line, my girl. I'm arresting you for assault.'

'But, I never—'

'Oh yes, you did. I witnessed it with my own eyes. You lifted your hand to Mrs Lister, with intent on striking her. And you kicked my shin when I tried to apprehend you — offences that will get you three months behind bars.'

Horror clung to every fibre of Julia's being. Her lips moved but no words came out. The agony of the policeman's hold increased as he hauled her away. Out of the corner of her eye she caught a glimpse of the disappearing boat, carrying her Clara away from her. Despair crowded in on her.

Thrown roughly into a cell, Julia sat on the stone slab in a daze. The stench made her heave. Bile rose in her throat and she swallowed hard, choking on the vile-tasting acid. *How did this happen? How did I come to be here? And my Clara gone . . . gone. Oh, dear God, help me.*

A scuttling sound had her heart jumping. Looking down she saw a rat, as big as a kitten, coming towards her feet. Pulling them up underneath her, she cringed away, pressing her body into the mildew-ridden brick wall. Water dripped onto her head, but she dared not move. Cold seeped into her, making her shiver. Warm salty tears trickled into the corner of her mouth. Never had she felt so wretched.

Hours later a key clanked in the lock, waking Julia from a slumber she hadn't been aware of falling into. Voices drifted to her as if disembodied and coming from a nothing space.

'I tell you, I can't release her. She is a criminal awaiting a court appearance tomorrow.'

'Well, I am disputing your right to hold my client overnight. I've asked you, and you have no evidence, other than your word, and that has been brought into question many times, when you have been found to be vindictive. I believe you are being so on this occasion.'

'Mrs Lister is a witness—'

'Oh, I don't think so. She won't stand up for you. As much as she is bigoted against Miss Portman, when I sought her out, she had no intention of helping you in this prosecution. Have you forgotten that you prosecuted her son for relieving himself in a public place, when she begged you to let him off with a warning?'

There was a silence. Julia held her breath. She knew the voice of the man challenging the constable. Mr Vale was the local solicitor and had a distinctive, high pitch to his tone. But why was he here defending her? Winnie! Dear Winnie. Of course. Tim's father had been a partner of Mr Vale's. Tim himself had been training with them after he had come back to the island from university in London.

Winnie would have heard that Julia had been arrested, and would have sent for Mr Vale's help.

The cell door swung open. 'Get yourself out of here. The charges against you have been dropped. But I meant what I said, I'll be watching your every move, once the Germans get here. You won't be able to step within an inch of a soldier before I have you for collaboration.'

'I doubt that, Ferrington. I doubt you will even have a job, as the Germans will rule everything, including law and order. I'd make yourself scarce, if I were you. There's a few on the island who bear a grudge against you. And some of them would take great delight in getting you into hot water with the invaders.'

Even in the dim light, Julia saw the constable's face drain of colour.

'Come along, Julia, I'm to deliver you to Winnie. She is waiting for you.'

Julia followed Mr Vale, leaving a stunned constable standing with his mouth slack as she spoke up. 'And I will be putting in a complaint about you, for one. You fondled me when you held me restrained.' The words came out in a calm way that she didn't feel. They surprised her as much as they did the two men.

Mr Vale coughed. 'Is that right? Well, we'll discuss that further. You'll be hearing from me in due course, Ferrington.'

Outside, Mr Vale took Julia's arm and leaned towards her. 'Even if he did, my dear, I don't see such a charge standing, so maybe you are best to forget it.'

Infuriated, Julia didn't reply. She knew how it was. Women didn't stand a chance in such a case. It would either be considered that it was she who had tempted the man beyond endurance, or in her case, that she deserved all she got.

They drove in silence, but for Julia it wasn't a comfortable one. The pressure that Mr Vale had put on her arm had been more familiar than guiding, and his words had been spoken in a tone, and in such close proximity, that suggested intimacy rather than legal advice.

This behaviour was repeated when they reached Winnie's. Mr Vale once more leaned towards her. 'I'd like you to know that I have always felt sorry for you, and wanted to protect you in some way, but my standing prevented me from doing so. Such a pity that you and Tim didn't wait until your wedding. I thought more of Tim than to take you down before the nuptials. And in not waiting, you saddled yourself, and made yourself untouchable. A great pity.'

'I didn't saddle myself, Mr Vale. Clara has been my world. I wouldn't have been without her. She is a part of Tim that I still have. I wouldn't have changed anything.'

'I'm sure you wouldn't, my dear, but, you know, if things had been different I would have asked for your hand after Tim died. I have always had feelings for you.'

Something snapped in Julia. 'Feelings? You've shunned me more than most. You'd cross the street rather than look at me. That doesn't speak of someone with *feelings*!'

Again, he coughed. 'I had no choice, but I do now. I'm leaving the island. I can't bear to stay. I'd like you to leave too, and meet up with me in London where no one knows about you.'

'What! Can you hear yourself? You are insulting me with every word you utter. I wouldn't go with you if you were the last man alive! I thank you for getting me out of custody and getting the charges against me dropped, but I'm getting out of the car now, and I don't care if I never see you again.'

His hand curled around her arm. 'Don't be stupid. I'm offering you something you would never get in a lifetime of trying. I want you, Julia. It's an ache in me that I've lived with for a long time. I want you, and I'm going to have you.'

His words shocked Julia to the core. 'Let go of me.'

The thought of him touching her repulsed her. A portly man, he was a good fifteen years older than her thirty-five years, and smarmy. Yes, that's what she'd term him now. Having always thought of him as an upstanding gentleman, and accepting his shunning of her, he had now diminished in her eyes.

Her skin crawled as she saw the depth of his lust in his misted eyes. 'Please let me go, Mr Vale. What you ask can never happen.'

His grip tightened. 'It must, and it will.' His mouth was wet at the corners, and his breath came in heavy gasping movements.

Julia's stomach churned. 'Let me go, or I'll scream.'

His hand loosened its grip on her, but didn't entirely let go. Instead he slid it downwards until it was in her lap. His fingers curled and dug into her groin. Rigid now with fear and repulsion, Julia couldn't speak or try to stop his progress. His hand began to move, rubbing her between her legs. 'There, you like that, don't you?'

'No! Let me out of here! Please, please stop.' The door handle didn't yield to her desperate attempts to grapple with it. She looked up and down the deserted street. It seemed every living soul had abandoned the island. She was alone.

Alone and trapped in this car. If she moved, Mr Vale would have more of an advantage over her.

He was leaning closer to her now. She could feel his gasping breath on her cheek and taste the faint trace of pipe tobacco that emanated from him. Her mouth dried.

It was when she felt his hand on her bare thigh and his lips nuzzling her breast through her blouse that she reacted, rather than pleaded. Grabbing his thick blond hair, she yanked his head backwards. 'Stop! Leave me alone. How dare you touch me? Let me out of the car, you beast!'

Shock had him staring at her as if she was an alien being. 'I . . . I'm sorry. Forgive me. I . . . I got carried away. I shouldn't have. Please forgive me. I love you, Julia. I want you to be my wife. Now that you are rid of your brat, there is nothing stopping us. Like I say, we can go where no one knows about you, I'll—'

'Shut up! *Shut up!* Stop talking. Let me out of here. Let me out!'

Looking around once more, Julia was relieved to see Winnie's curtain pulled aside and Winnie glaring out.

'Winnie's there, she can see you. Let me out now and I won't say a word about what you have done. But if you don't, I'll tell everyone.'

Mr Vale shot back in his seat. For a moment he did nothing. Then he calmly leaned over her. 'You could have got out at any time, harlot! It was you who locked the car door with your elbow. I cannot lock it from this side. I thought by doing so you were giving me an invitation. I should keep your mouth shut, if I were you. You think you've had it uncomfortable on this island until now – well, that's nothing to what

21

you'll experience if you breathe a word. And one other thing. Now that I have come out from under the spell you sought to put me under with your sexual advances, I wouldn't touch you with a barge pole. Get out! Get out!'

On legs that didn't feel as though they would hold her, Julia staggered up the drive to the house. Winnie opened the door. 'Oh, Julia, dear girl. What was happening? What was Vale doing?'

Afraid that she would not be believed, Julia lied. 'He was just comforting me, the whole experience has been awful. I'm so worn out.'

'Come and sit down, my dear. I want to talk to you.'

Listening to Winnie, all thoughts of the horror of what she had been through over the last day left Julia's mind and instead it screamed at her: *Winnie is dying. No! Oh, no, dear God, don't let that happen!*

Even though she had guessed this was the case, she wasn't prepared for hearing the truth of it spoken. But now, as she held the woman who had been more than a mother to her over the last thirteen years or so, the shock of facing losing her wouldn't sink in.

'I'll look after you, Winnie. I won't leave you.'

'No, Julia, you must do as I say.'

'But how can I leave you?'

'You have to. You won't be safe here. You've heard the tales of what might happen to the women on the island. You are more than a target. The islanders will make sure of that. And then call you a collaborator and God knows what will happen to you then.'

This Julia knew to be true.

'I should have done this before, but I, like us all, had buried my head in the sand. I thought it would blow over, that our mainland army would protect us, not leave us out on a limb for the Germans to walk all over. We are a pawn in a much bigger game. It wasn't until two days ago when you told me that Clara was going, and now she has actually gone, that I woke up and knew that I must do something.'

'But, to go into a nursing home. Oh, Winnie, no. You must let me stay to look after you.'

'No. I have it all arranged. I went to my doctor this morning, and he telephoned the nuns. They are willing to take me in. I only have months, maybe weeks, left. Please, please, Julia, take the money I'm offering you, and escape. There's two hundred pounds. More than enough to pay for a passage. Go. Find Clara. Make a life for yourselves in Britain. Pass yourself off as a widow. Get rid of the stigma that you don't deserve.'

Winnie had never said those words before, though her actions had spoken them in volumes.

'I've never blamed you, I hope you know that, Julia? In my mind, I have often ranted at my Tim. Oh, don't look surprised. Being dead doesn't make him into an angel. And doing what he did to you was against all he'd been taught, and he knew it was wrong. Oh yes, I have been there, that moment when your body betrays you and you cannot do any more than give into its yearnings, but Tim shouldn't have ventured to get you to that state. I'm very disappointed in him. And yet, I wouldn't have been without the result. His darling daughter.'

The silence that fell held the sadness of them both. Julia crossed the room and put her arm around Winnie. 'You've

23

been like a mother to me, Winnie, and the best granny that Clara could have had. I know that cost you a lot.'

'It didn't! Never. I love you both, and don't know what I would have done without you in my life, after I lost . . . Oh, my dear, don't cry. I am cried out. All I want now is to do this last thing for you, and make up for how I have failed you.'

'You never failed me. Why do you say that?'

'I could have taken you into my home. I have room for you here, and yet, I let you both live in that room with that awful woman dictating to you and working your fingers to the bone.'

'You knew?'

'Yes, I knew. I fret over it all the time, but I never made that final decision. I . . . I . . . '

'Oh, Winnie, please, don't. I wouldn't have come. As it was, you stood a lot, but you at least kept your head held high and retained the respect—'

'Respect! That's it. That is why I never made the move. How stupid and callous is that? Forgive me, Julia. Please forgive me, and please, please let me do this last thing to put everything right. I can die happy then. Though I will have something to say to my Tim when I meet up with him again.'

Winnie smiled as she said this and it lightened the moment. It wasn't a shock to Julia that Winnie had been afraid of losing the respect of the islanders, and was glad that she hadn't given into her natural instincts and asked her and Clara to live with her.

Ruffling her hair with her free hand, she held on to Winnie's hand with her other one, and knelt down in front of her. 'You did the right thing, Winnie. You lost so much. Why should you have lost your standing too? And don't be cross with Tim.

He was always very respectful of me. It was just the moment. Being alone on Le Portelet, and only a month to our marriage. It was the one and only time, and we both regretted it, and suffered shame because of it. And although it was difficult, we never did it again. We vowed not to until our wedding night.'

'Oh, Julia, my poor girl. So, you have suffered all the abuse over the years over what was probably a quick fumble?'

Julia laughed at this from the older woman, but didn't answer her.

'Well, my dear. Will you do as I wish?'

The thought of being with Clara was too much of a pull on Julia. Yes, her heart wanted her to stay and take care of Winnie, but when Winnie died, what then? The Germans would be here. The newspaper was full of that being a reality. What would life be like under their regime? Would she ever be able to escape from here? Would she ever see Clara again?

Her head nodded with the impact these questions had on her emotions.

'Good. That's settled. Pass me my bag. I withdrew the money from my bank this morning. Take it. Go home and pack, and be on the next boat that leaves this doomed island.'

Standing, Julia fetched the bag from where it hung on the back of the chair opposite. She waited while Winnie unclasped it, and withdrew an envelope.

'There, my dear, keep it safe.'

'Thank you, Winnie. I would never have the chance to leave without this. And Winnie, would you mind if I slept here tonight, and until I can get a boat? I can't bear to go back to Rose Cottage again, not now Clara isn't there to be looked after. My life there has been hell.'

'Yes, of course you can, my dear, and I would be glad to have you.'

'Oh, Winnie, how will I ever repay . . . I mean, I . . . I will never forget you, Winnie.'

Winnie smiled but didn't speak.

'I'll go and fetch all that I need. I won't be long, then I'll cook us a nice supper.' Julia didn't say that it would be their last ever together, but picked up her cardigan and left the house.

CHAPTER THREE

Clara
Destination: Blackpool

A wretched feeling took hold of Clara. The crossing had been choppy, the boat overcrowded, and there had been nowhere to go to take herself away from those who suffered seasickness. Trying to concentrate on anything rather than the vomit running around her feet, her loneliness had engulfed her as her thoughts had stayed with her mother, and she wondered how she and her granny were going to cope when the Germans came.

Would they be safe? Would Mummy have that awful thing done to her that she'd heard Judy Partridge talking of seeing her sister and her boyfriend do?

Looking around her deepened her trepidation. This hall, somewhere in London, where they'd been bussed to from the port where they'd docked, looked dilapidated. Paint peeled from the walls and a damp patch formed what looked like a map of Guernsey on the wall facing Clara. She looked away from it, not able to cope with the pain that jolted her heart on seeing it.

She'd hardly slept. The sleeping bag provided hadn't cushioned the hard wooden floor, and yet she didn't feel tired. She was too anxious to feel anything other than the deep misery that engulfed her. And now, having taken her turn to wash in the little sink in the toilet block outside, and eaten very little of the meagre breakfast offered – a slice of toasted bread and dripping – she stood still, watching proceedings and wondering what was next.

Official-looking women, wearing uniforms with WVRS badges sewn on them, were going around the crowd of children and sticking labels on them, then directing them to stand in a designated group.

'Right, let's see.' A stout woman with a kindly face peeled a sticker from a sheet on her clipboard and stuck it firmly on Clara's chest. 'Blackpool is where you're going, young lady. Go and join that group over there.'

Clara felt her spirits lifting a little at this. She'd heard about Blackpool, and the illuminations, and the streets of amusements. A small part of her let in a sliver of excitement. She was going to Blackpool!

The journey took for ever. Clara was on a crowded bus that gradually emptied as children were dropped off in towns and villages along the route.

'You're that girl with no dad, aren't yer?'

The girl sitting next to her hadn't spoken before, and what she said now made Clara's heart drop. Ignoring her, she stared out of the window, as she'd been doing for most of the journey, taking in the sights of England, amazed at the distance between places. To her, this country was vast.

'Oi, I spoke to yer. Ain't yer got a tongue in yer head?'

'I don't know you. You're not even from our island, so how come you know things about me?'

'I was stood with someone from where you come from, and she pointed you out. I'm from London. East End. And I ain't got no dad either, and is why I sat by yer. I thought we'd get on, but you've been sat there with your 'ead turned away from me the 'ole journey.'

Clara didn't know what to make of this. She'd never met anyone else without a father before. 'You mean, your mother wasn't married, either?'

'Yeah. I'm a bastard! Like you.'

This shocked Clara, she'd never thought of herself as one of those. Well, not with that swear word attached.

'Me mum's a right one with the blokes. She's in 'er element now with soldiers everywhere, I'm glad to get out of it. But you'd know all about that.'

'I don't! My mother isn't like that. My dad died before they could wed.'

'Lawd, that's a bit of bad luck, innit? Me name's Shelley. What's yours?'

'Clara. Are you going to Blackpool too?' Something in Clara wanted her to be. It felt good to know someone in the same position as herself. And Shelley was honest and straightforward, though she had a funny way of talking.

'Yeah, I'm looking forward to it. We should be there soon.'
Despite the sadness inside her, Clara felt glad of this.

'Look, over there – over that field, that's Blackpool Tower!'
This announcement from the driver was said as if he were as
excited as Clara. Clara followed the direction he'd indicated,
and couldn't believe what she saw. Spiralling up to the sky was
the beautiful outline of a tower, so like the pictures she'd seen
of the Eifel Tower in Paris.

Shelley nudged her and with an excitement in her voice
said, 'I'm going to the top of that, just as soon as I can. I read
that you can, yer know.'

'I'd like to do that.'

'They say that you can see for miles, all the way to the Lake
District, and Morecambe. Be summink, that would, mate.'

Clara couldn't answer Shelley. Her head was full of what
she was seeing and imagining, and she'd been surprised by
Shelley calling her mate. She looked at Shelley properly for
the first time. She had a pretty face, but one with a hardened
look, as if she was used to warding off anyone who crossed
her. A bit younger than herself, Clara thought. And shorter
too, as her legs dangled, whereas her own touched the floor,
but then, she was tall for her age.

Shelley's sandy-coloured hair, cut very short, was a mound
of curls, and she had freckles on her nose. Her eyelashes were
very fair and long, longer than any that Clara had ever seen,
and when she looked back at Clara, Clara saw that her eyes
were hazel, and flashed with temper.

'What yer looking at?'

Clara's cheeks reddened. She hadn't meant to stare; she just
wanted to weigh Shelley up a bit. She looked away.

After a few moments' silence, Shelley asked, "'Ow old are yer, Clara?'

'Thirteen – nearly fourteen.'

'I am too. I wouldn't have been on this bus if it 'ad been six months down the line, I'd 'ave been found a job. I 'ad the choice to stay, but, like I said, I wanted to get away. And I ain't bothered if I don't go back, either.'

Clara was glad that Shelley no longer seemed annoyed at her, but couldn't understand her not wanting to go back. Given the chance, she'd go back right now. She thought of her mother, but those thoughts brought tears to her eyes and blurred her vision. She blinked them away, and pretended to yawn to give a reason for them.

They were driving through a built-up area now, on a wide road. They passed a windmill on the left, surrounded by a green.

'We're in Blackpool, now, mate. I wonder where we'll land up?'

Houses flashed by, big and posh. Nothing of what she saw told Clara that this was the Blackpool she'd been longing to see.

A few minutes later, the bus stopped outside a Salvation Army hall.

The woman who'd sat on the front seat clutching a clip-board stood up. 'Now, all of you are to get out here. You will be sorted out by the local WVRS. Good luck everyone, and please try to settle. You will do that easier if you are on your best behaviour and well mannered. So much nicer to welcome a stranger to one's home who is compliant. Come along, chop, chop.'

With this, Clara found herself standing on the pavement. To her left there were several shops, to her right, a row of houses, and in front of her the church building looked imposing, with its domed roof.

They were ushered inside where a thin, mean-faced woman wearing a hairnet and small round glasses shouted, 'Which one's for me? I don't want any middling little brat, I want someone as'll be useful to me. If I've to keep them, then they need to do a bit in me shop to pay me back.'

'Miss Brandon! Please!' said another clipboard woman. They were all beginning to look the same to Clara. 'You are frighten ing them more than they are already. Now, let me see. You said you didn't want a lad. Well, that leaves a couple of girls . . .'

Clara closed her eyes and prayed not to be picked.

'Clara Portman?'

Her 'yes' came out as a whimper.

'Well, you look as though you are an intelligent girl, and able to work. What about her, Miss Brandon?'

'She'll do. Come with me, girl. Me shop's in Hornby Road and I've been away from it long enough.' With a humph, Miss Brandon made a parting remark. 'Mind, if she don't turn out to be what I'm looking for, I'll be back. Agreeing to this was a means of getting the staff I needed. I don't want, or need, a child to take care of.'

Clara cringed inside, but stood tall. She'd had many a lesson in how to treat those who talked about her as if she were nothing, and she'd found that not letting it show how hurt and afraid you were was usually the best tactic. If the bullies weren't making a mark, they had no incentive to carry on, her mum would say.

She caught Shelley's eye. The wink Shelley gave her helped a little. She wondered where Shelley would land up and if she'd seek her out. She hoped she would. Spending time with her would make life a bit better.

'We will be checking up on all of the children, Miss Brandon. We expect them to be treated well, and to be helped to settle. We are not an employment agency.'

Miss Brandon softened at this. 'Aye, well, I'll be treating her right. I just wanted you and her to knaw as I'll be expecting a little help from her. She's a big strong lass, and I have a weak heart, so in return for her keep she can help me out.'

'Very well.'

With this, Miss Brandon turned and walked out of the room. Clara had a feeling in her that this exchange could only make things worse, as no bully liked to be brought down and there were always repercussions.

Outside, Miss Brandon set a brisk pace for someone with a weak heart. Clara wondered about her, and why she was a miss. She wasn't a bad-looking woman, or at least she wouldn't be if she stopped scowling, and had her hair done in a softer style instead of pulled back tightly off her face in a bun. And she had a good figure, too, but her clothes were dowdy. Too long for a start, as if she was stuck back in her younger days and hadn't kept up with fashion. Her plain navy frock was covered in a full, flowery pinafore that went over her head and tied around her in a crossover fashion. Thick stockings covered the small amount of leg that could be seen, and her feet were clad in heavy-looking brown court shoes. Not good at guessing ages, Clara thought Miss Brandon looked about the same age as her teacher back home, who had just celebrated her forty-third birthday. She seemed tetchy, too. Clara's granny had said something about the change of life making women moody, but she didn't tell her what that was and Clara had instinctively known not to ask.

Somehow thinking of this made Clara feel even lonelier. Here in Blackpool she knew no one, and no one knew her. Everyone knew you on the island, and everything about you. That was annoying at times, but it somehow made you feel secure, too.

They hadn't got far when she heard Shelley shouting her name.

'What now?' Miss Brandon's 'tut' and impatient sigh showed her annoyance. 'What's that lass calling you for. Do you knaw her?'

'I travelled with her on the bus, that's all.'

'Oh, there's that busybody, Mrs Flinch, with her. It seems they want us to return. Well, I'm not going back – you run to them and see what they want. Hurry, I'll walk on, and if I'm not in sight when you return then turn right at the crossroads, that's Hornby Road. Me shop's a grocery store about halfway down on the left.'

When she came up to Mrs Flinch, Shelley wasn't with her. Clara felt disappointed.

'I'm sorry, Clara, with that woman playing up how she did, I forgot to give you these. There's a change of clothing for you. I hope it all fits. Now, do your best with Miss Brandon. She's like she is as she lost her fiancé in the last war. Instead of getting on with life, like we all had to, she turned into a bitter woman – an attitude that has kept her a spinster despite having suitable men who would have taken her on. She's not used to looking after children, or having anyone in her house, so you have to keep out of her way as much as you can, and do everything that you can to please her. We've very few places left where we can put all the evacuees allocated to us, so there's nowhere else for you.'

Clara nodded, then asked, 'Do you know where Shelley is going to be staying, miss?'

'No, not yet. Why, are you two friends?'

'Well, we met on the bus and chatted. I'd like to be her friend.'

'Not something we encourage, dear. Those taking you in don't like it – they think you will compare notes on them, and don't like to feel that they will have another evacuee hanging around their house. Now, off you go. I see Miss Brandon hasn't waited for you. Will you find your way?'

'Yes, thank you.'

'Good, well, you seem to be a quiet and polite girl, so I think you will be all right. I'll try to check on you, but there is so much to be done, and we have to concentrate on those younger than you who had to come without parents. They are our main concern.'

Again, Clara nodded. A feeling of abandonment came over her, and tears that were too strong to hold back any longer streamed down her face as she set off towards her new home. Not that she would ever look on it as home – just a place to stay until she could return to her mum.

'You took your time, lass. And there's been enough of that wasted. Put down whatever it is you're carrying and get started on weighing those spuds out. Those in that sack there. You knaw what a spud looks like, don't you? You should, they come from where you've washed up from. Jersey reds, they are.'

'I'm from Guernsey.'

'All the same to me. Any road, there's a pile of order books there on the counter. Each one has a name on it, and there's a brown paper bag over there and they have corresponding names written on them. Go through the books to today's date, and when you see spuds are ordered, weigh out how many on them scales, and put them in the bottom of the right bag. Now, hurry yourself, as I'm already behind, and folk will be calling to pick up their grocery orders.'

All of this shocked Clara. She'd thought she'd at least have been taken to her room and shown where the lav was. She was dying for a pee.

As she worked, Miss Brandon carried on talking. It took a while to pick up all she was saying, as her way of speaking left Clara wondering at times what she meant. At last she brought up the subject that was most on Clara's mind.

'The lav's out the back, but don't go sneaking out there every chance you get. At night, you'll use a piddle pot, and you'll be the one to empty it, an' all.'

'Can I be excused to visit the lav now, please?'

'What! You've only just got here. Didn't you go up at the hall, then?'

'Yes, but—'

'Well, you can hold it a while longer, I have to get these orders done. Hurry up with those spuds, nowt else can go in t'bags until they're in the bottom.'

Feeling that she would burst if she didn't go soon, Clara tried to concentrate on anything but the lav out back, which she presumed meant it was in the backyard, wherever that was. At last, she finished the task.

'Right. You need to wash your hands now that's done, then you can start on the flour. So get yourself to the lav, then you can wash your hands under the yard tap. There's a bar of soap on the windowsill and a towel hangs on a hook next to it.'

Now that at last she could relieve herself, an urgency took Clara that she struggled to control as she went towards the back of the shop. A trickle of warm wetness found its way down her leg as she stumbled around sacks that seemed to be dumped everywhere on her route. Embarrassment stung her cheeks. Making it out into the yard before the deluge came, Clara stood still in fear, unable to control her bladder.

'You dirty little tyke, you! You filthy rat.'

A trembling set up in her body that Clara couldn't control. The urine on her legs tingled as the wind whipped around her. She wished the earth would swallow her up and take her from this wretched woman and her nasty voice.

'Get yourself cleaned up. No, not in here. You stay out there. You can strip off and wash under the tap. I'll chuck your bags out to you. What in God's name have I been landed with?'

Although the sun shone down on her naked body, the wind that gushed along the back alley and under the gate made Clara shiver and chilled her to the bone. The water felt like ice and stung more than her urine had. Shame filled every part of her.

In the bag given to her, she found a white blouse and grey skirt. Both fitted her, though the skirt was a bit short. A green hand-knitted cardigan lay in the bottom of the bag, as did three pairs of navy knickers. With these on, Clara began to feel warmer.

After rinsing her wet clothes she pegged them on the line that ran between hooks on opposite walls. These walls were around ten feet high, so she couldn't see over them. She knew the one on her left shielded the yard from the road as this was a corner shop, and she assumed that on her right would be the yard of the bed and breakfast house she'd seen next door. The gate would lead to a back alley, and that was it. Her world, enclosed.

Looking up, Clara could see two windows of the flat above the shop overlooking the yard. Although this was a two-storey building, the B&B next door was three storeys and she could see many windows facing her way. All were curtained with heavy nets.

The feeling took Clara that any number of eyes could be looking down on her. Her embarrassment increased with this thought. Putting her head down, she hurried towards the door that led into the storeroom of the shop. It opened just as she reached it.

'Here, you can swill me yard down with this. I've mopped the dirty trail that you left. If you do that regular, you can sling your hook, as useful or not, I'm not housing someone who thinks it all right to soil herself.'

The door banged shut before Clara could defend herself. Feeling wretched and with her head bent away from anyone who might be watching, she threw the disinfected water over the yard and began to sweep it away towards a drain near to the gate. As it formed a trail and disappeared, Clara wanted to open the gate and run through it and keep on running until she dropped in a heap, but instead she upturned the bucket, leaned the brush against the wall and lifted the latch to the door that would take her back inside.

She didn't speak to Miss Brandon, as she remembered that her mum had always told her, 'Least said, soonest mended.'

Oh, Mum, Mum! A sob caught in her throat, but she swallowed it down and listened to the next task, which was to see which customer needed flour and to weigh it out as she had done with the potatoes.

It was while she was doing this that a loud bell sounded and made her jump.

'Is my order ready, Mavis?'

'Naw, it's not. What d'you expect, I've had to take on this brat here, and have been at the Sally Army all morning while them do-gooders flapped around. They don't knaw their arse from their head, that lot.'

'Oh, where's she from, then?'

'Jersey.'

Clara wanted to scream out that she was from Guernsey, and she wasn't a brat, but thought better of it.

'She looks as though she'll be a good hand to you, and that's sommat. I'm lucky, I haven't got any rooms so they couldn't force one on to me. I fetched me mam up from Manchester. I'd rather have her moaning at me every day than take in a waif and stray from a foreign country.'

Clara kept up a steady pace, weighing the flour. Every scoop puffed a cloud towards her, and an even bigger one when she emptied the scoop into the small brown paper bags ready to transfer into the larger ones. Her face felt clogged with it, and her eyelashes thick with it, but still it was better than handling the muddied potatoes, a job that had made her back ache.

'Can't you concentrate on me order before all them as haven't come for theirs, yet? I'm in a hurry, and I can't come back on account of me neighbour has her eye out for me mam and she's going out in a bit.'

Miss Brandon reluctantly agreed and set about cutting a slice of ham from a huge joint, which she put on a circular saw and turned a handle to operate. 'You'll get nowt without your coupons, mind. Have you got them?'

'Aye. Bloody war. I'm right out of sugar, an' all. And me mam likes her tea sweetened.'

'I've saccharin in if you want some.'

All of this was a surprise to Clara. She hadn't known that everything was restricted, but she soon found out when given her next task of weighing out sugar. Very little went into each bag, and yet some must have big families judging by the quantities of potatoes they'd bought.

By the time the shop closed, Clara was exhausted and hungry.

'You needn't think as I'm going to set to and feed you, it's enough for me to look after meself. So, I've a routine set out for you. I've set an alarm clock by your bed for six o'clock. You're to get up when it goes off, and as soon as you're dressed, come down here and prepare the veg for the evening meal. Everything's in the pantry over there. On the cold slab you'll find meat and a stock that I make at weekends by boiling a load of bones. Fry off the meat and onions, then add the veg and stock and then leave it on the side of the grate to simmer.

And you're to remember to pop back in here from time to time to give it a stir so that it don't burn. When you've done that you can make yourself a bowl of porridge, but don't you dare touch the sugar or the honey. The extra that I will get for you will come in handy, as I'm partial to a cake or two. Once that's all done, you can come into the shop and start work by nine o'clock. For tonight we'll have some chips. Here's a tanner. The chip shop's at the end of the road. Get threepence worth of chips and a piece of fish for me. Tell Lena as runs the shop that it's for me, she knaws what I like. Now go on, hurry yourself.'

The chips were delicious, though Clara could have eaten twice as many as Miss Brandon had allowed her.

Sitting on the bed of the cluttered, stuffy room she'd been shown to, she looked around. Her 'bedroom' was no more than a junk and store room, with very little space to move around. In the corner near to the door was a stand with a bowl and a jug of water. Next to this was a bar of carbolic soap that gave off a smell Clara hated. From the window she looked down at the backyard. Her earlier mishap came back to her and reddened her cheeks.

When she lay on the bed the mattress didn't give at all. It was as though she was lying on a slabbed pavement. Her view now was of the ceiling and the white distemper that had once covered it but was now flaking off. The walls, painted a drab mustard colour, showed signs of damp, and the floorboards were bare of lino. What was in the numerous boxes and sacks stacked around her she could not guess at, but the musty smell that came from them had her wrinkling her nose.

Her mind went to her tiny room back in Guernsey, the bed she shared with her mother, and their one chair and how they took turns to sit on the arm. And to the view of the harbour at St Peter Port. Without any bidding, tears once more streamed down her face. Curling up into a ball, she sobbed with despair at how her life had changed. How long would it last? Would she ever get home again? And with this thought came the knowledge that she would rather face the horrid thing the Germans would do to her than be here away from her mum and her granny. *Oh, Mum. Why? Why did you send me away?*

CHAPTER FOUR

Julia
A Decision That Tore at Her Heart

'Get back, whore!'

'No, I have as much right to leave the island as any of you.' Ignoring Frankie Myers, who had always been a nuisance to her from the time they were kids together, Julia shouted above the crowd. 'I have money, I can pay for a ticket. Let me through.'

Jeers from those people stood on the other side of the Port jarred her. 'Cowards, yellow-bellies. Why don't you stay and help us to protect our island, eh? Bloody cowards.'

Feeling hurt, Julia wanted to shout back that she was going to get her daughter, her baby. It also occurred to her to yell at them, 'You've always hounded me, wanting me off the island, now you won't let me go,' but she kept her attention on the activity of the ticket distributers and prayed they would give her a passage.

'Right, there's one more place, but it's at a premium. Twenty-five quid! Which one of you has got that amount to save your yellow bellies?'

'You can have my car, it's up on the dock. Here's the keys, take it.' This shout came from a man standing with his wife, who looked tired and defeated.

'I told you, I only have one place.'

'Just take me, then. I've got the documents to my car here.'

This shocked Julia. She'd thought he was trying to get his wife on, but now she realised he was willing to abandon her.

'I can have your car anyways, you won't be back for it. No, just cash. I'll only take cash.'

Julia saw her chance. 'I have cash. I'll take the last place.'

A few laughed out loud at this, and one said, 'Who did you sleep with to get that amount, whore?'

Julia bit her tongue.

'I don't care how she got it, she seems to be the only one who has. Come on, miss. Give me your money and I'll give you the ticket.'

On board, Julia had the urge to retch, but swallowed hard. The stench of vomit and urine was overwhelming. She knew the boat had done a few trips in the last three to four days, and the sea had been anything but calm. Around her, most of the folk crowded together held a handkerchief over their mouths and noses. Someone in the group in front of her was throwing up. The noise of that almost undid Julia, but she managed to keep from doing the same, her years of training and hospital work helping her.

Looking around, she could find nowhere to sit, and only just managed to place her case on the deck to sit on as the boat took off from the quayside. Bodies swayed towards her, and one woman nearly fell on her, but for Julia putting her hand up to stop her.

'I'm sorry, I—'

'Rhoda!'

Rhoda looked away.

Julia, though used to this, still felt the pain of hurt at the action of her once best friend. 'Rhoda, can't we be friends after all these years? I imagine that you are the same as me, regretting letting your daughter go?'

Rhoda stared down at her, but still didn't speak.

'I won't shame you over in England, Rhoda, no one will know us, or know about me. We were good friends, Rhoda, and now we need each other.'

Rhoda's face softened, but still her body's stance was unyielding.

With a deep sigh, Julia looked away. As much as she would have loved to make friends once more, she wasn't going to beg Rhoda.

Feeling sick to her stomach and with cramped legs, Julia had never felt as glad of anything as she did when those standing reported that they could see the coastline of England. Her ordeal was nearly at an end. At least, the first stages of it. What was in store for her when she landed on English soil she couldn't imagine, but she knew that the first thing she would

45

do was to find out where her Clara had been taken and seek her out.

A joy filled her at this as surely it would be a simple matter of locating where the children from Guernsey had been taken to, and where they had been sent. Those in charge of the children must have kept records of all the placements.

Once she had Clara, she would find a place for them in a small village and integrate into the local way of life. And yes, she would say that she was a widow, and had been evacuated with her daughter. How wonderful never to carry the stigma of an unmarried mother again!

On the dock at Southampton, the WRVS had set up a stall. Posters proclaimed that help and advice was being offered.

Weary to the bones, Julia made her way over to them. A queue had formed. Her fellow islanders jostled her to the back.

'Are you all right, dear?'

The kind voice had Julia's bottom lip quivering as if she was once more a child.

'We're before her!'

'I don't think so. We are here to help all and I saw you shove this lady out of the way.'

'It's no more than she deserves!'

The kind woman, middle-aged and with her hair caught up in a knotted scarf, was visibly shocked by this and looked inquisitively at Julia.

'I'm not a criminal,' explained Julia. 'I – I . . . my fiancé was killed before we could be wed. I had his child after his death.'

'Oh? And for that, you, a supposed gentleman, think you can treat her in this manner? Shocking! Come with me, dear.

46

I'll get you registered as arriving here, and then we'll see about a hot drink and find out how we can best help you.'

The mug of cocoa tasted better than any Julia had ever had as she tentatively sipped it, afraid of scalding her tongue. The steam from it hazed her vision for a moment, but she didn't care. She didn't want to see the scowls and looks of disdain coming her way.

'Now, that's you registered, so, how can we help you? Have you any money, a place to stay, relatives who will take you?'

'Yes, I have money, and I do have a relative. My daughter, she was brought here a couple of days ago on a boat with a lot of other children – an evacuee, but I don't know where she was sent to. I need to find her, then we can make a home together here.'

'Umm, that might be difficult, as I understand it. The children from Guernsey . . . that's where you're from, isn't it?'

Julia nodded.

'Well, they were bussed out of here and taken to various places. The older ones went to London to join evacuees from there and then to be bussed to different parts of the country. It was chaos to be truthful, and keeping tabs on who was going where was near impossible. It was done more by age initially, how old is your daughter?'

With the scant information the woman was able to provide, a dread settled on Julia. She sat on her case, finishing her cocoa. Her head spun the possibilities she'd been given.

'Have you found anything out, Julia?'

Rhoda surprised Julia with the friendly tone she used to ask this. 'Not much, I'm afraid. You?'

'Nothing. By the time I got to the head of the queue, the woman I spoke to just said that she knew nothing of the children as she wasn't on duty that night.'

'From what I know, I think we should go to London, as that is where the kids of twelve to thirteen were initially sent. I was told to seek out the WRVS headquarters, and the Salvation Army. It seems that most of the organisation has been done by them.'

'Christ! London's a hell of a place. Where will we start?'

'We? You're willing to go along with me, then?'

Julia looked around her. The few passengers that were left on the dock weren't showing much interest in them.

'Would you mind if I did? I . . . I haven't been much of a friend, but well, it wasn't easy to be. Roger's mother made it very clear that I wouldn't be welcome at their house if I remained friendly with you. She didn't want her family tarnished with the same brush as you were tarnished with.'

'Was I tarnished? I didn't do anything different to what you did with Roger. Only Roger was more experienced than Tim. You were at it with Roger for a good while before you wed, you know you were, you used to tell me. But, me and Tim, well, we held back, except for the once. Just the once, and for that I have suffered ever since.'

'Oh, I'm sorry. I should have—'

'No. You should have done what you did. Making a happy marriage and keeping friends with Roger's mother was more important than keeping friends with me. But I wish you had told me. I could have lived with that. I have had years of hurt at your rejection of me.'

Rhoda hung her head. A part of Julia didn't want to let her off the hook, but Rhoda was suffering – even more than she was herself, if that was possible. Roger was in the navy and had been drafted with the first wave of servicemen. Julia had heard that he was somewhere out in the Atlantic, and his ship was providing cover for freight ships coming from America. There were reports every day of ships being hit and some being sunk. She looked into Rhoda's eyes, read her pain. She identified with it, and knew that to get through all of this they would need each other.

It was time to forget the past. Putting her cocoa on the floor, Julia stood and opened her arms to Rhoda. 'Let's put it all behind us, eh? We can if we try.'

Once more Rhoda looked around, then sighed. 'Oh, bugger them all.'

It felt good to be held by Rhoda. Some of the hurt of the past years melted away as they clung together. Rhoda's tears wet Julia's neck, and hers dampened Rhoda's lovely chestnut hair, but they didn't care. Their tears were a mixture of happiness and fear, but also the relief of knowing that the fear would be lessened with having each other and rekindling their friendship.

CHAPTER FIVE

Clara
Half-Day Closing

'Get a move on today, its half-day closing. I want the shop spick and span. Move everything in the stockroom, and sweep behind it, we don't want rats, and spillage causes them to come for pickings. I'll serve in the shop. That way, I might for once get a decent few hours off, as it usually falls to me to do everything.'

Dragging the sacks of flour, sugar and potatoes strained Clara's already aching back, but the thought of a few hours off lifted her spirits. She would ask if she'd be allowed to go out for a walk, and if she was due any wages so that she could buy a few things. The thought of these possibilities spurred her on. She couldn't wait to leave the confines of the shop, but daren't hope too much that Miss Brandon would let her.

As she moved the sack of flour back into position, she wondered how Miss Brandon could live so frugally amongst all this produce. She wondered if she could take what she needed, but then Clara had heard her discussing her allocation being cut, so maybe she was only allowed to stock what the government thought was required for her customers. Those ration books would be the reason: they had to be sent into a government department every week, so someone was keeping an eye on the shop's activities. Not that they knew everything. Clara had seen a man deliver a sack of sugar really late on her second night, and he hadn't left an invoice for it.

And Miss Brandon had her favourites. When Clara had helped her put the orders up the day before, a bit more of certain items went into certain bags, and weren't put down on the receipt. The cash for these items had gone into Miss Brandon's apron pocket and not into the till.

As Clara worked, the sound of the bell was constant. Anyone would think the shop was closing for a week instead of an afternoon. Most of the customers ran B&Bs and most had soldiers billeted with them, so had plenty of rations they could buy. The war didn't seem to be touching Blackpool.

'Well, that's it for the day. Have you finished with the sweeping and mopping, lass?'

'Yes, Miss Brandon. I – I was . . . '

'What? Spit it out. I haven't all day to stand here, I want to get me legs up.'

Clara took a deep breath. 'May I go for a walk, please? I won't get lost.'

'Very well, but be back in time to cook me tea. I've a nice chop, and you can have the rest of that spam in gravy.'

51

'I'll be back, I promise. Thank you, and well . . . Miss Brandon, do I have some wages to come, please? I—'

'Wages! Are you out of your mind, lass? What do you think I feed you and house you for? Your food and your bed are your wages. Now, out of me sight, I've had enough of you.'

'B – but there's things I need.'

'You need nowt. You might want stuff, but that ain't need. You have a roof over your head, a bed to lie in, and you're fed. That's all you need.'

Hurrying out before Miss Brandon changed her mind and stopped her going, Clara stood on the pavement, not sure which way to head. She knew she'd come from the right, and that had been all built up, so guessed that if she turned left she might be heading in the direction of the sea and all the amusements. Setting off, she told herself to be careful to notice each turning she made and look out for pointers to remember, so she could find her way back, and she was to remember to look out for a postbox.

Her face reddened at this, as she thought how she'd stolen from Miss Brandon's desk – paper, an envelope and two stamps as she wasn't sure if one would be enough. But somehow she'd known that if she'd asked she'd have been refused, and she *had* to contact her mum.

In the letter, she'd given the address of the shop and told of how unhappy she was in the hope that her mum would help her. Come for her, even.

She hadn't gone far when she came across a pillar box. Kissing the envelope, she pushed it into what looked like an open mouth, and prayed out loud: 'Please, hurry to my mother. Please bring her to me.'

Walking on briskly, to stop herself from breaking down, Clara spotted Blackpool Tower reaching majestically for the sky. Her heart lifted and her step quickened to the sound of the seagulls swirling around, squawking their heads off. For a moment it all felt and smelt like home. But, she couldn't mistake her surroundings for home. Everything seemed a lot more modern than the quaintness of the island.

Here, every building had three storeys, and had the proud appearance only a guest house can have. Pots of flowers adorned each entrance, and having two sets of doors, the outer doors were open. Mats proclaimed WELCOME and signs in windows, which were flanked by pretty net curtains, declared NO VACANCIES. Other signs hung from poles, and squeaked as the gentle breeze blew them back and forth. These told of the facilities offered – late keys available, home from home accommodation. Others told guests, 'Bring your own food, and we cook it to perfection.' This, Clara knew, was due to rationing as she'd overheard discussions on the ways that landladies were overcoming the problems of the shortages.

As she came to the seafront, the sights and smells caught her up in a whirl of excitement. Any thoughts of a war being fought, children being sent from their homes and men being desperately rescued from beaches didn't seem to have any place here, despite the many men in uniform being a reminder. The air was full of laughter and the sound of voices calling out as traders touted their wares. And mingled with the tang of the salty sea, the smell of fish and chips and sweet, hot doughnuts wafted over her.

53

Clara's stomach rumbled at this last. Miss Brandon hadn't bothered to offer her anything to eat, and the porridge she'd had that morning had long been forgotten.

'Penny a go, lass, come and try your luck. Everyone a winner. Throw the ball into the bowl and you win a lovely prize. Look at what I have. There's a nice yoyo, a teddy to snuggle up to, or you could win a new rolling pin for your ma, complete with a pink bow to make it look pretty. What d'ycr say, eh? Go on, have a go. Like I say, only a penny a throw.'

'I haven't got a penny to me name, mister, nor could I give the rolling pin to my mum as I'm not with her.'

'You one of them evacuees, then, lass?'

Clara nodded.

'Well then, have a go on me. Here you go.'

As Clara took the ping-pong ball from him, she felt a happiness seep into her that she never thought to feel again.

'Well, that smile's worth a penny of anyone's money. Take your time, lass. Throw it up in a curve, then it's likely to bounce off any it doesn't go in, and land in one of the others. Your prize depends on the colour of the bowl. Good luck.'

Clara's heart pounded. Her troubles melted away as an excitement and longing to win gripped her.

The clink of the ball as it bounced from one rim to the other held her in suspense until, at last, it dropped into a golden-coloured bowl. Clapping her hands and jumping for joy, a squeal of 'yes' escaped from her lips.

'Eeh, well done, lass, you've won the teddy.'

'Aw, thanks, mister, thanks ever so much.'

The small, brown furry teddy, with one eye higher than the other, felt good in her arms. And though it was a daft thought, the feeling came to her that it loved her, as she snuggled it to her. Tears prickled her eyes, misting her view of the man as she tried to smile her gratitude.

'You've made me day, lass. I had a lass of me own, only . . . Aye well, that's another tale. She's in heaven now, dancing with the angels. Come and see me again, won't you? I'd like to knaw as you're all right. Me name's Arnold. What's yours?'

'I'm Clara, I'm from Guernsey.' Clara found Arnold so easy to talk to that before she knew it she'd told him of her mum and granny and how she was missing them, and even about the island and its folk. But not that her mum wasn't married. That was too shameful to share, and she didn't want Arnold to look down on her.

As she left his stall, Clara noticed the sign that said, ONE WIN − YOYO, TWO WINS − DRESSED ROLLING PIN, THREE WINS − TEDDY BEAR. Her heart warmed at how kind Arnold was. It was as if he'd seen a need in her to have something of her own, and nothing could be better than the teddy, even if she did feel a little silly carrying it now she'd come down from the excitement of winning it.

As she walked along, she couldn't believe the number of folk who smiled at her and greeted her. It was as if Blackpool made everyone happy and forget that they had troubles. It was doing that to her as she passed stall after stall and was called out to sample the sticky rock, or knock a coconut off its stand to win it and small hoops were shoved at her. 'Hook a prize for a half-penny, three goes for a penny.'

And all to a background of music that blared out from an organ grinder. To Clara it was magical.

It was as she came to the tower, that she heard a voice calling her. 'Clara, Clara!'

If she thought she was feeling happy, nothing prepared her for the surge of joy she felt as she turned and saw Shelley running towards her.

'Blimey, Clara, you take some tracking down. I've been looking for that woman's shop every spare minute, and when I find it, it's closed. I knocked and knocked, until some old crow came out of the 'ouse next door and told me you'd gone out in the direction of the sea. And that I'd better make meself scarce, or I'd know it if Miss Brandon came out to me.'

'Oh Shelley, it's good to see you. Where are you staying?'

'I'm with this old couple. A bit strait-laced, but kindly. Their son died in the last lot and they missed out on 'aving any grandchildren. That's why they put themselves forward to take a kid in. I think they'd 'ave liked a younger one, but I don't think as they would 'ave coped. Anyway, I reckon as I dropped lucky there. What about you? What's the old bag like as took you, then?'

As she told Shelley what her life was like with Miss Brandon, Clara noticed Shelley giving a few strange looks towards the teddy bear, and a feeling of being silly for having it came over her. Shelley was older than her years, and Clara doubted she'd be seen dead carrying a teddy through the streets.

'So, you ain't been to no school yet, then?'

'No. There's been no mention, but then at my age, many would be leaving if they had a job, and though I'm not paid, I suppose you could say that I had a job.'

'Lucky you. The kids around 'ere all talk funny and seem a

bit behind to where we was in London. They ain't even learning fractions yet!'

Clara couldn't believe this, as she'd passed that stage some time ago. And though she'd heard tell that the north of England was behind the south, and much poorer, she hadn't seen it that way. Not in Blackpool she hadn't. The streets thronged with folk, and all seemed to have money to burn, given how she'd seen them having a go on everything, and how the cafés she'd passed had been full.

'What are you doing out and about now, Shelley, do they have half days at your school?'

'No, I did a bunk, didn't I? It's boring going over what you already know.'

At this, Clara looked around her. She had a feeling come over her that everyone would know, and that a policeman or school inspector would jump out at them any minute.

'Don't look so worried, I can get away with it. If I'm challenged, I'll just burst into tears and say that I'm missing me mum.'

Clara giggled at this. Shelley was filled with confidence and nothing seemed to worry her.

'Shall we get some chips? I missed out on me school dinner, such as it is. These northerners seem to live on scrag-end cooked in a stew – hot pot, they call it. Of course it's hot, it's been in the bleedin' oven! Though I 'ave to admit, it tastes delicious.'

Clara laughed out loud at this, and it felt good. Her problems melted away. Except she had to tell Shelley that she couldn't buy any chips, which made shame trickle through her.

'Don't worry on that score, I've more than enough. I've still got me dinner money as Mrs Preston gave me on Monday. I told the teacher that Mrs Preston is forgetful and keeps sending me without it.'

This didn't sit well with Clara. It was dishonest and a breaking of the trust the old lady had put in Shelley, but then, hadn't she done the same with stealing the paper, stamps and envelope? It was the situation they had been put in that was to blame, though from what Shelley had told her on the bus, Clara had gathered that she'd always had to fend for herself. This had probably meant that more often than not she'd been less than honest.

Her conscience calmed when they crossed the road and found a bench to sit on, and Shelley unwrapped the newspaper holding the chips. Golden brown, and dripping with vinegar and with a good sprinkling of salt, they tempted her beyond endurance as the aroma coming from them made them irresistible.

Neither of them spoke as they juggled the crisp but fluffy and very hot chips around their mouths, sucking in air in an attempt to cool them, and wiping their mouths with their hands as fat and vinegar that was released with every bite ran down their chin.

Clara had heard tell of certain places being likened to heaven. To her, at this moment, she felt as if she was in Blackpool heaven, and a feeling took her that she was where she really belonged. This northern seaside town had captured her heart. Her only wish was that her mum and her granny could share it with her.

A seagull brought her down to earth as it dived towards her. Squealing and jumping up, she danced around, shooing it away, swinging her teddy towards it. Nothing was going to make her part with the chip she had in her hand, and certainly not a greedy, scavenging bird.

Shelley's laughter resounded around her, making her giggle as she sidestepped the eager, persistent bird. 'Don't just laugh, help me!'

'I can't, ooh, Clara, give it the chip, there's plenty more.'

It was all she could do, she knew that, and though reluctant, she finally threw the chip. 'Not a good idea. I know those birds, once they think you're a soft touch they won't leave you alone, and they'll squawk and squawk bringing their mum, dad, brothers and sisters, aunts and uncles to the feast. Eek, here they come. Run, Shelley, follow me!'

Clara dashed across the road and into the chip shop, with Shelley just behind her.

'I thought as you were taking a chance, me lasses. Them seagulls are thieving tykes. Sit in here and eat your chips, you're very welcome.'

And that was it, to Clara – the ingredients that made Blackpool special, the welcome of its folk. Well, of most of them. Not the Miss Brandons or some of her neighbours, but these folk who worked on the front they were a happy bunch and made her feel happy. It didn't touch the sad part deep inside her, but with a dose of this every week, she knew she would cope better with the misery back at the shop.

'I've gotta ask, Clara, what yer doing with a bloody teddy bear?'

Shelley seemed oblivious to the swear words she used, but Clara felt her cheeks burning, and it wasn't all down to the reference to her teddy bear. The shocked look of the lady who had served them made her acutely aware of how course Shelley was. And Shelley's attitude to Clara's explanation of how she got the bear made her seem years above Clara's age, even though she was the younger of the two of them.

'I wouldn't be seen dead with it, and it's a bit embarrassing walking with you holding it. Why don't you dump it, or give it to the next kid we see going past?' But then she softened as she seemed to become aware of Clara's humiliation and distress. 'Hey, I didn't mean it, I were only teasing. And I'm jealous as well. It must feel like you've got sommat of your own, sommat to cuddle and love. I've not ever had that.'

'You have it, Shelley. Go on, take it. I don't need it. I was going to dump it anyway.'

Shelley hesitated for a moment. 'Would you carry it till we're in a quieter area, then?'

'Yes, I don't mind.'

'Come on then, we'd better start back as I want to get in at the time I would if I were at school. I don't want to worry Mrs Preston. She don't deserve that.'

'Do we go the same way, then?'

'Yes, I'm on the bottom end of Park Road, near to a church, and me school's around the corner from there.'

Clara knew that Park Road ran through Hornby Road and felt glad that Shelley wasn't far from her.

On the walk back she learned a lot about Shelley, and all the 'uncles' that visited her mum. Some of it shocked her to the core, as Shelley told her that a few of these uncles wanted from her what her mum gave them, and once her mum had tried to make her do it with one who offered fifty quid to let him.

A deep pity for Shelley ground into Clara as she listened. And somehow, her own sorrow at missing her mum and granny lessened as she took in the enormity of what Shelley's life had been like. 'What did you do?'

'I bit him. Me mum took the money and shut the door on us, and I fought him off. When he got his thing out, I got down and bit it as hard as I could. He swiped me across me head and sent me sprawling, but he didn't want to do it to me after that. Only thing is, he beat me mum up before he left, taking his money back, and all she had in her purse, too. When she got over the beating, she gave me a pasting till I thought I would die. I hate her, Clara. I hate her with everything that's in me.'

With this, Shelley burst into tears. Sobs wracked her body. Snot ran from her nose. Grabbing her and holding her to her, Clara didn't know what to say. Her own tears threatened, but she fought them back – she had to stay strong for Shelley.

Shelley clung to her as if her legs would give way beneath her, but gradually she became calm and Clara was able to steer her to a low wall. And though she didn't have words that would comfort Shelley, she pushed the teddy into Shelley's arms. Shelley sat rocking backwards and forwards holding the bear to her. Then she put out her hand and Clara took it. They sat in silence. And though Clara couldn't put a name to what passed between them as Shelley looked up and gave her a watery smile, it was as if they both knew they had found a friend for life.

CHAPTER SIX

Julia
A Hopeless Quest

'You have to understand, we had so many of them to deal with, getting them settled took more priority than keeping records at the time, I'm sorry. We should have been more meticulous in our dealings with them, but like I say, there was so many – thousands.'

'Somebody must know, they must. We want our children back. We want them!'

Rhoda's hand in hers helped to steady Julia. She wanted to hit out at the stone-faced woman behind the desk of the council office in Lambeth. But she kept her control. 'Did all the children from the island come here? And if so, why? Why here? Why did you bring the children to London?'

'Those that came without parents, yes. It was easier. There were hundreds here, that we had to dispatch—'

'Dispatch? These were children, not goods and chattels.'

'I'm sorry, you have no idea what it was like, and still is. We cannot let our hearts rule. Hitler is now saying that he will burn London to the ground. Children and their safety is our priority, and if that means they are shipped out that quickly that we cannot keep track of paperwork, well so be it. We gave all children, and those taking them in, strict instructions to write to their parents once they were settled and to give the address they are staying at. That was all we could do.'

'At least tell me the areas you sent them to.'

'I cannot, I don't know. That part was left to the WVRS to organise.'

A sigh of despair came from Rhoda. Julia squeezed her hand. 'At least we have found the area they were brought to, Rhoda, that's something. We're nearly there, love.'

In her heart, Julia didn't believe this. If the council hadn't kept precise records of where each child had been sent, then why would the WRVS?

With this thought her knees gave way. Jarring them back, she clung onto the counter as exhaustion took hold of her. Their search had sent them from pillar to post, and what seemed like every corner of London. Rhoda's money had run out days ago, and already one hundred of the two hundred pounds Winnie had given Julia had gone. Paying travel, accommodation and food for both of them had eaten into it. Everything seemed to cost the earth here in London.

Making a huge effort, Julia thanked the clerk, took hold of Rhoda's hand and turned to leave.

Outside, the rain pelted them. It seemed to Julia that the heavens were crying for her. For she couldn't let herself cry. If she did, she'd be lost.

Finding the church hall that the WRVS were using for all the tasks they were taking on, Julia felt her spirits lift. 'We're nearly home and dry, Rhoda. I can feel it in my bones.'

'Huh, I don't think I will ever be dry again. Does it never stop raining in London?'

Julia laughed, as much from relief as anything, as this showed that Rhoda had regained her spirits, and that would make things easier. Giving in wasn't an option, but trying to keep herself going as well as Rhoda had proved a hard task.

Inside the hall, Julia knew she was in the place that her lovely Clara had been. She could feel it. An excitement gripped her, as it seemed that at last there would be news that would help her.

But on questioning the woman who looked the most approachable, her heart sank. The woman gave the impression of being worldly-wise. She carried on sorting out a jumble of clothes as she said: 'I'm sorry, love, you're not likely to find out where a particular child went to. We had a remit to put them into groups and send them to areas. It was more to do with numbers than names. Maybe you should wait for a letter from your daughter, then you'll know where she is.'

'But we are refugees from Guernsey, we cannot go back and won't be there when the letter arrives. Is there a record of where the children were sent to, what towns?'

'Oh, the Guernsey kids. Gawd blimey, you're asking summink of me there, luv, I can tell you. Pandemonium, it were. They were bussed 'ere for us to deal with as Southampton couldn't cope, nor 'ad they the resources to deal with them all. We weren't in a much better position, as we had a load of London kids to deal with as it were. But we organised it all the best we could. We each 'ad a clipboard with an allocated number that each town could take, so it were pot luck where the children went, but most went north, where it is safer, and a lot to Manchester and Blackpool.'

With these words the last drop of hope left Julia. Somehow she had to accept that she may never find Clara again, or at least until the war ended, then maybe, just maybe, they could both return home and be reunited.

A tear seeped out of the corner of her eye.

'There, now, don't go despairing, luv, you never know what's around the corner. 'Ow about a nice cup of Rosie Lee? That always sorts everything out. Put kettle on, Bessie, these two young women are in need of one of your cuppas.'

Julia understood that what this lady had termed 'Rosie Lee', meant tea. She'd come across a lot of the rhyming slang these last few days and found it, and the people who used it, endearing. There was something comforting about them – solid too, as if they could face everything that was thrown at them.

'If I were you two, I'd get meself busy. It's the only way to deal with what's being thrown at us. Don't give in, that's the way of us East Enders. I'm in the same boat as the pair of you. Me lads are fighting, gawd knows where. Two of them volunteered, they did. Broke me 'eart, but I got stuck in with this lot – though most of them, except me and Bessie, are a posh bunch, who give me and Bessie the brunt of the work as if we were their maids, but I don't care. It's like I say, it's all about keeping busy, keeping your mind off what's going on and thoughts of what might happen. Two strong women like you, could do a lot to 'elp the war effort.'

As she sipped the strong tea, Julia mulled over what the woman had said. The room was a hive of activity and full of laughter and good spirits, yet she doubted if any of the women had been untouched by the war, even though it had mainly been called a phoney war till now.

Most of the women she could see were of the age to have sons old enough to have been called up. What must that feel like? At least she knew that Clara was safe. If she had the extra agony of thinking that she could be shot or blown up at any minute, she'd break, she was sure of it. And yet these women didn't.

'Rhoda, there's something in what that woman said. I mean, about getting ourselves busy. Maybe we should volunteer to help?'

'How would we keep ourselves? I know what you mean. I don't want to give up, but we have to live, and your money won't last long at this rate.'

'I know. It would have to be paid work, but there must be plenty of that. Maybe I could go back into nursing.'

'But I don't want us to be parted, Julia. I couldn't go with you if you did that.'

They sat on two of the wooden chairs that lined the walls. The centre of the hall was a hive of activity with many tables arranged in a square. Twelve women stood inside the square, two at each table. As they sorted the piles of clothes, they folded them and put them into boxes lined up behind them.

The boxes were marked 'boys' jumpers', 'girls' underwear' and so on, covering all the clothing needs of children.

Julia got up and went over to the woman she'd spoken to before. 'I'm sorry to disturb you again, but we've been thinking that you're right, we do need to get ourselves busy. Only we need to do paid work, as we have no means of keeping ourselves. Do you know of any that would help the war effort?'

'Gawd, luv, there's plenty about. There's the Land Army, they work on the farms replacing the men who've gone to war. And the Munitions. There's factories making uniforms, and others making boots. There's the Red Cross, that's if you're a nurse or a doctor. Other volunteers for the Red Cross don't necessarily get paid. What's your name, luv? Mine's Elsie.'

'I'm Julia.'

'Cor, fancy you coming from a small island. I ain't never met anyone who lived over there. Except them poor kids, of course. Lost they were. It were like a foreign country to them, bless them.'

A pain shot through Julia's heart.

'Gawd, 'ark at me, me tongue wags on its own at times. I'm sorry, luv. I shouldn't have said that.'

Julia managed a weak smile. She had to hold on to the fact that Clara was a strong child used to dealing with anything that came her way. She'd had to be, to cope with how the islanders had treated her. But what of Rhoda's child? Janet was a quiet child, shy, and needing of support. How would she fare being away from her mum, and away from all she had ever known? Turning, Julia saw that Rhoda hadn't heard what

Elsie had said. She looked to be in a daze as she sipped her tea. Poor Rhoda, suddenly finding herself without her husband and child.

In that moment, Julia knew that she must be strong for Rhoda. She had to sort out something for them both, and take care of her friend.

Going back to sit with Rhoda, she told her what she'd found out about the type of work available.

Rhoda was quiet for a long time. When she spoke, her body trembled. 'You mean, we should give up looking for our girls? I don't know if I can bear it, Julia. I was in a daze when the rumours started about the invasion. Mine and Roger's mother just took over. Before I knew what had happened, I was saying goodbye to Janet. My heart was torn from me. With Roger being in the navy, I was used to being without him for long stretches, though it is worse now, as he was never in danger before. And I always had Janet. We were a force to be reckoned with against the two grannies. But when news started to come through about ships being sunk, my world fell apart. I didn't object to anything – I just let the grannies take over. Oh, Julia, I need to find Janet. I have to.'

'I know, and no, we won't give up, but we can't keep roaming around like this. I think we should think about doing one of the paid jobs that will help with the war effort, and when we have time off, do what we can to search for our girls.'

'Yes, you're right. But I don't want to get a position down here. I think we should go north and sign up for something there. At least then we will be in the right area. And another thing. Out of those jobs you've mentioned, I'd prefer Land Army. I'm used to working on the land with me mum and dad owning a farm. And besides, I couldn't bear to be shut up in a factory all day.'

'I agree. The north it is then. We'll go to Manchester and sign on at the labour exchange there. That'll be a start.'

With this settled, Julia felt a kind of peace enter her. They had a purpose now. Finding their daughters wasn't going to be easy, but with a plan formed, they could get some order into their lives. 'Right, no time like the present. We'll stay the night in the B&B we've booked into and then tomorrow we'll catch a train to Manchester. You know, it will help just to be in the same area as the girls, because, then, we'll always have the chance of finding them, we'll never give up hope.'

Manchester seemed even more daunting than London had been. The air hung with smoke from factory chimneys and the streets were crowded and grimy.

It seemed to Julia that, but for the kindly cockney lady, all English ladies were of the same unfriendly mould. The woman sitting behind the counter of the labour exchange had a stern face and judgemental manner.

'Your papers are in order, that's one thing. But you can't come in here demanding to be able to stay together – we place all hands where they are most needed.'

Julia held her breath. To be separated from Rhoda now was unthinkable. 'But we both want to join the Land Army. Is that possible?'

'I'm not sure of that. You are displaced persons, and it is difficult to check up on you. You will need references. Anyway. You can make a start by going to the Post Office and registering on the National Service Guide. Then you will need a medical certificate. Have you registered with a doctor?'

'No, we've only just arrived.'

'Well, you will need to do that. But we do have other work available, whereby no such hurdles are put in your way. I think you should go for one of those.'

'No, we want to work on the land, we are used to the open air.'

'Well, good luck with that, but come back here if you're not successful. As it is, I will put you on the call-up register, so that we don't lose track of you both.'

Three weeks later, smoke from the train that pulled into the station swirled around them. Julia caught sight of herself in the window of the station office as some of the mist cleared. She smiled at her image. The Land Army uniform of green jumper, worn over a darker green blouse and with jodhpur-shaped khaki trousers rather suited her, she thought – as they did Rhoda. It felt good too, as folk milling around gave them looks of respect and some even spoke to them, wishing them good luck and saying how proud they were of the young women like them who were taking on war work at home.

She shifted her rucksack a little nearer to herself and thought once more that maybe she'd packed too much into it. Between them she and Rhoda had tried to bring what they could of their personal clothing, but the thick linen dungarees and wellington boots they'd been issued with took up much of the space. Not that they would need much else as they were headed for the tiny village of Chipping, in the Clitheroe Rural District of Lancashire. It wasn't that close to Manchester or Blackpool but they had worked out that Blackpool was twenty-two miles away and they could possibly visit it if they were given a weekend off. Their hope was to find any child there that they knew who might have seen or heard what had happened to Clara and Janet.

Julia was surprised at how quickly things had moved. The time had flown, taken up with medicals and form filling and, finally, a nerve-racking interview in front of a panel of ladies who showed that at least some of the English women in positions of authority had hearts as they agreed to billet Julia and Rhoda together.

'This is our train, Rhoda. We're on our way at last.'

'I feel as though at any minute someone is going to grab us and say that a mistake has been made and we can't go together after all.'

'Me too. So let's jump aboard quickly before it can happen.'

They giggled at this, and as Julia had thought so many times of late, she was glad she and Rhoda were friends once more.

It was as if all previous hurts had never happened, and Rhoda had been her mate down the years. How easier life would have been if that was so, but this wasn't a time for looking back to the past. A whole new future awaited them. An uncertain time but, she told herself, she was to remember what Tim's mum had always said: 'Life is what you make of it. Many obstacles are put in your way, but it is how you deal with them that shows the kind of person you are. And you are a very brave person, Julia, you can do whatever you set out to do.' The thought pulled Julia up for a moment and a tear prickled her eye as she thought of

Winnie. *Oh Winnie, Winnie, I wonder every day how you are. And miss you so much.*

She looked over at Rhoda and took heart from the lovely smile she gave her. *Everything's going to be all right,* she thought. *We have each other. We'll cope. We have to.*

CHAPTER SEVEN

*Clara
Imprisoned*

'I see Germany has invaded the Channel Islands, then?'

Clara's heart sank. She was feeling unwell, with some sort of tummy bug having suddenly attacked her, and had just come back into the shop from her visit to the lav – one trip of many that she'd made this morning – when she caught these words uttered by a small lady who stood in the shop talking to Miss Brandon.

'Eeh, naw. That means I'll be saddled with this miserable tyke for a lot longer than I'd hoped. By, she's getting on me nerves, I can tell you.'

Clara's cheeks burned at this, but she said nothing, and though her heart hurt as she tried to take in the news of her home being invaded, she carried on weighing the dried peas into eight-ounce portions before stacking them on the shelf.

'Don't be so unkind, Mavis.'

Clara looked towards the lady and was struck by how similar to Miss Brandon, and yet, how different she was. Their faces and hair were almost the same, but they differed in the way they dressed. The lady's clothes draped on her, making her seem a bit like a butterfly. And she wore make-up, quite a lot of it, with red lipstick that was smudged at the corner. When she smiled at Clara, it was a kindly smile. Clara wanted to smile back, but the cramping of her stomach stopped her.

'Oh, it's all right for you, Daisy, you don't have to work for your living. Swanning around with them arty-farty types from the theatre, imagining that you're going to be a big star one day. You always had it better than me, even when we were nippers. And then marrying Peter, who was so well set up that he's left you a merry widow. You've no idea.'

'Eeh, Mavis, it isn't like that. Not any more. Me money's near gone, and I'm in that attic room on me own. I came to ask if you'd take me in.'

'Take you in! I'm not a charity. You may be me sister, but I ain't obliged to you.'

Clara, though still reeling from the pain of hearing her beloved island was under German rule, felt sorry for Daisy.

'I know that you're not Mavis, and I would work, I promise you. Besides, we're going to need each other, as Hitler's lot'll be over here next, you mark my words.'

'Well, the thought of that ain't as bad as the thought of putting up with her for much longer, or of having you under me feet, our Daisy. The answer's no. It's not as if I'm a well woman, but I can tell you, the strain of having that one is making me worse.'

'Oh, Mavis, the poor girl is far from home and from her family.' To Clara's surprise, Daisy turned and spoke to her. 'Look, love, if ever you want to, you can come round to mine, to give you and me sister a break. I live in the Blueberry Guest House, at the top end of Hornby Road. I'd like you to come.'

'Well, she ain't going to. What's up with you, our Daisy? She's an evacuee. Not even her own mother appears to have wanted her. Sending her over here on her own, expecting us to look after her. Well, she has to work for everything that she gets and that's that.'

Why Miss Brandon hated her so much Clara didn't know. She'd done her best to please her and had attempted to make friends with her, but it felt like trying to knock down a brick wall with a feather, as nothing she did made a difference to how Miss Brandon thought of her.

Feeling alone and in despair, Clara wished now that she'd carried through with her plan to go to the WVRS on her afternoon off. She'd meant to on the last two occasions and had thought about begging them to remove her from Miss Brandon's care, but each time the lure of escaping to the seafront with Shelley had overridden her need to seek help.

After that first afternoon together, Shelley had been waiting outside the shop the next Wednesday, and the following one, too. Just seeing her had banished all thoughts of doing anything other than having fun together.

Shelley always had money. Though Clara wondered anxiously where the increasing amounts came from, it at least meant they could get chips, and have a go on one of the stalls.

It was good to see Arnold, too, and to have a chat with him. A couple of times, Clara had been on the verge of telling him about her situation, but then she'd not wanted to tar the joy of the afternoon with thoughts of Miss Brandon, or to burden Arnold with her troubles. He enjoyed their company and made them smile, and she didn't want to spoil that.

Her mind went to the time Shelley had enough money to treat them to a ride on the Ferris wheel that stood near to the wonderful Winter Gardens, a building that housed a theatre where top stars like Jimmy Clitheroe and Jewel and Wallace appeared. Oh, how she longed to one day go inside and to see a show. The ride on the wheel had filled her with a mixture of excitement and fear, but she'd loved it, especially when they rose to the top and she could see the whole of Blackpool.

Despite everything, Blackpool was beginning to feel like home to Clara. Her wish now was to be reunited with her mum, but for them to live here and never to return to the island again. Here, her mum could live in peace, as no one would know her situation. The stigma of being an unmarried mother would leave her. Her mum could hold her head up high once more.

But what now? Would her mum ever escape from the Germans? Would they force her to do that thing with them? Would they hurt her? A deeper fear gripped Clara, as she fought against the thought of her mum being in danger, and maybe even under the threat of death! *No . . . No!*

This terrible realisation set her body trembling uncontrollably. A pain, more intense than any she'd experienced since early morning, clenched her stomach muscles. The room spun.

'What's up with her, Mavis? She don't look well at all.'

'A touch of lazy-itis if you ask me. Now off with you, our Daisy, I've got work to do, and I've to keep this one going. With you taking me attention and giving her sympathy, she's playing up more than usual.'

Clara heard a sniffle, as if Daisy had started to cry, and then the bell of the door jingling as it opened and closed. She wanted to get up and run after Daisy, but her legs felt like jelly. And yet she had to move as the urge to run to the lav was strong once more. Stumbling away from the disapproving Miss Brandon, she just made it before her stomach erupted.

'Are you going to be in there all bloody morning? There's work to be done!'

'I'm sorry, Miss Brandon, I'm coming now. But I'm not well. I can't work. I have to keep coming to the lav.'

'You're trying it on, I knaw you by now, lass. Well, you won't beat me. If you need to be out here in the yard, you can set to and scrub it. Get all this moss off the walls and scrub the paving slabs. You'll be near enough to the lav then.'

The sound of the water from the yard tap filling the metal bucket couldn't block out the feelings zinging through Clara. Some were of pity for Daisy, but she couldn't give thought to these as the news she'd heard overwhelmed her. She tried to imagine what it was like on the island. Were there tanks, and soldiers with guns pointing at everyone? Where would the soldiers live? Would they turn folk from their houses? Who had been killed? And were her mum and granny safe?

The agonising questions made her head ache. Scooping her hand, she caught some of the cold water and rinsed her face in an effort to stem the sweat that poured from her. Her desperation took all caution from her. She put her head under the tap and gulped down the cold water not knowing whether it was drinkable or not.

No sooner had she done this than she had to run to the lav again to relieve herself.

Feeling tired and drained, Clara did her best with the moss that had made a carpet of itself to line the brick walls, but she hadn't made much headway when Miss Brandon appeared in the doorway of the stockroom.

'Are you useless at everything? Here, use this scrubbing brush and trowel. How you think you can dislodge the stuff by just using water and a cloth, I don't knaw. It was bad enough them making me take a young-un in, but to be saddled with the likes of you is more than anyone should be asked to do.'

Something in Clara snapped at this. Turning, she shoved Miss Brandon with such force that the woman lost her balance and sat down heavily on the stone step. At the sight of her face blotched with blue patches, and her gasping for breath, fear zinged through Clara. Unsure what to do, she stood and stared down at the hated woman, wanting for all the world to spit at her.

'How dare you! By, you've got some clout, lass. You're nowt but a bloody ungrateful tyke. Right, that does it. You're going. I ain't putting up with the likes of you no more. Help me up.'

Shame at her action washed over Clara as she extended her hand. But far from being too weak to get up, Miss Brandon was on her feet in a flash and lashing out at Clara. Bruising thumps landed on her arms and shoulders. Crying out in agony, Clara leaned forward for protection, but gasped as a heavy blow to her back winded her, leaving her unable to defend herself.

'I'll teach you, madam.' With this, Miss Brandon grabbed the yard broom, lifted it and brought it crashing down on Clara's head. Clara sank into oblivion, welcoming the black cloud that took her into its midst.

When she came to, Clara's head pounded as if a drummer was inside it beating out a frenzy of music. Her shoulders burned. She tried to move but couldn't, and her mouth wouldn't open when she attempted to call out.

Cold, clammy sweat trickled down her forehead, and stung her eyes as the realisation came to her that her arms were bound behind her back and her mouth taped with what she could only assume was the sticking plaster that had been used to secure a cracked window in the storeroom and left on a shelf nearby.

A draught brushed her skin, giving her hope that there was an opening somewhere through which she could escape. But when she opened her eyes a dizzy feeling took her. After a moment this passed and she could see that above her there was a broken window. In the light that filtered through this, Clara took in her surroundings. She was in the shed that stood at the back of the yard, to the left of the gate.

With the fear of her situation deepening, her stomach churned and heaved, but there was nothing but bile to bring up. The vile-tasting liquid burned her throat and set up a spasm of coughing. Unable to spit it out, some of it came down her nose. She couldn't breathe! Frantically blowing through her nose cleared it. But her eyes had filled with tears which tumbled after each other in a torrent.

Terror filled her as she writhed, pulling against her bonds with all the strength she could muster, only to find that there was no escape for her. This deepened her desperation. *I'm going to die! Help me!*

There was a moment when her limbs no longer obeyed her, and the fight went from her as her strength ebbed and she knew, with blessed relief, that she was descending into the nothingness that had claimed her before.

How long it was before Miss Brandon came out to her, Clara didn't know, but as she tried to fight through what seemed like a tangle of lace curtains blocking her mind, she became aware that the noise that had woken her was the rattle of the door. She lifted her head, expecting the door to open, but there was no sound now.

A shadow crossing the small light from the window took Clara's attention. She looked up into the evil glare of Miss Brandon. A shudder rippled through her body.

'Don't think you're coming out of there, missy. You're an animal and from now on you're going to be treated like one. I've told everyone that's been into the shop that you're ill in bed, and they can think that for a few days. Because you're going to stay where you are till I'm ready to let you out. That'll teach you. What kind of a person are you to push an old lady over, eh? I should fetch the police to you. But I've decided that keeping you in here is more of a punishment than they would eek out to you.'

Into the short silence that followed came the sound of hammering. To Clara's intense horror the shed became darker. *No, no, please, don't cover the window!*

But as she thought this she found herself in complete darkness, momentarily relieved as the cardboard put over the window was moved to one side and she saw the ugly madness that was Miss Brandon peer through at her. Despair gripped her.

To the rhythm of the last nails being hammered into the cardboard, Clara's mind yelled, *No, no. Please God, no!*

Her plea went unheard. Darkness descended, leaving her cold, alone and afraid. *Mum . . . Mum. Oh, Mum, come for me. Please come for me!*

CHAPTER EIGHT

Julia
An Instant Attraction

'Reet, me lasses, we're off up to top field to start the haymaking. Pick up your billycans and your snap. Mrs Pickering will bring us some hot tea later.'

Rhoda's glance showed that she was really excited about this prospect, but from what Julia could remember of seeing the farmers at this kind of work, she wondered if she was up to it.

'It's a bit backbreaking at first, but you'll soon get used to it, Julia. I love it. I love the smell of the freshly cut hay, and jumping out of the way of the field mice we disturb, and eating my sandwiches in the fresh air. Come on, there's nothing like haymaking to make you feel well and alive!'

'Ha! If you say so, Rhoda. I just hope I'm up to lifting a pitchfork of hay, I've never done it before.'

Julia rubbed her aching back. Two days in to working as a Land Girl, she already had sore muscles and a bruise on her leg. Lady Jane, as the most stroppy of the milking cows was called, had kicked out at her yesterday evening. She hadn't wanted her udders pulled in the first place and had mooed her objection and shifted around. But she'd waited until Julia had an almost full bucket – her first – before kicking out and upturning it and catching Julia on the shin.

The pain had been bad, but the embarrassment worse as the experienced dairymaid, Polly, a tall, skinny girl, had burst out laughing, making Julia feel like a fool.

Polly lived in the farm cottage. It was a tied cottage which she had, until a few months earlier, shared with her husband, the hired hand, but he'd gone off to war. She gave Julia the impression that she knew everything there was to know about farming, and thought little of inexperienced girls coming to work on the land. She was kinder to Rhoda, after hearing of her background in farming, but didn't give much quarter to Julia.

Polly was the same age as Julia and Rhoda but, as Mrs Pickering had confided to them, Polly didn't have any children. Having lost two in late pregnancies, she'd suffered damage that had left her unable to have any more. This had been told to them in a way that suggested they were to make allowances for Polly, and so Julia had apologised and asked for help. Polly had liked that, and admitted that she'd tested Julia on the diva-like Lady Jane, and had thought she'd coped well.

A little hope had entered Julia at this. Maybe Polly wasn't so bad and they could end up becoming friends. She hoped so.

Julia and Rhoda had arrived at the farm three days ago and had been given lodgings in the barn, even though the house was huge and would have accommodated them. Not that Julia was complaining as the space made for them was cosy. It was in the loft of the barn and was accessed by climbing a ladder and entering through a hatch, which could be closed and latched, giving them privacy.

Mrs Pickering had seen to it that everything they needed was provided. Two comfy beds, a dressing table and a rail to hang clothes over, and a thoughtful addition of a feather-cushioned sofa, which gave them somewhere to sit and relax. There was a stove in one corner which provided warmth and was just big enough to stand a kettle on. Above this was a shelf with mugs, cocoa and even a caddy of tea! Milk was in abundance, and easily supplied from the fridge in the corner of the dairy. Across the yard was a lav, and outside this a tap where they could collect a bucket of water for all their needs.

'You can heat water on the stove for washing yourselves,' Mrs Pickering had told them. 'I've put a screen up in there for you to stand your pot behind and to have a wash in private, then once a week, you can come into the house for a bath. And you can use the scullery to wash your clothes, though avoid Mondays and Thursdays as that's when Kath comes up from the village and does all the washing we make, as well as the farm and dairy clothes.'

After each day's work Julia had felt like taking a bath to ease her aching limbs, but had managed a strip wash which had refreshed her. Thankfully she'd slept like a log, and though she'd woken with stiff limbs, she'd felt ready for what the day would bring.

Her thoughts were constantly visiting the agony of not knowing where Clara was, and wondering how Winnie was, but the work drained her and left no energy for any emotional release.

'Up you get, lassies. Old Rosie here can take us up to the field.' Farmer Pickering broke into her thoughts as he bid them to climb into the horse-drawn cart before patting the huge shire horse and telling it: 'Reet, me lass. You've not got much of a burden, so make haste. We've to get on with it today, as that cloud over the hills is set to visit us later.'

Julia climbed aboard and sat down on the wooden bench that lined the sides of the box-shaped cart. Next to her lay three pitchforks, the sight of which told of the hard day's labour ahead. Trying not to think about whether she would cope, she looked over to where Farmer Pickering had pointed, and thought for the hundredth time since arriving here what a beautiful setting they were in.

To the north of them stood the Trough of Bowland, and in the distance the Bowland forest – an area of stunning beauty. The weak sun lit the tops of the mountains, but vied with the clouds that had broken away from the brewing stormy ones and playfully drifted and danced, teasing the sun's rays and making a roaming pattern of light and shade over the crags and caves. Dotted amongst the dark green of the swaying heather and the lighter green of the grass, the hill-sheep ambled effortlessly along the steep slopes in search of a tastier patch of grass than their last. Julia felt a peace enter her as she gazed on it all, and a feeling came to her that all would come right.

She glanced over at Rhoda, who was chatting away with Farmer Pickering about her father's farm. 'We grow a lot of potatoes. Not all Channel Island spuds come from Jersey, you know. We can rival them any day. And we grow wheat and barley, too.'

'Oh, ye'll knaw all about haymaking then?'

'Yes, I help every year. I love it.'

'And what about ye, Julia? I understand ye've never farmed afore? Well, don't worry, it'll soon become second nature to ye.'

Julia smiled unsurely. 'I'll do my best.'

'Aye, well that's all a body can ask of ye.'

If Julia had been asked to draw a typical farmer, her picture would have been the image of Farmer Pickering with his ruddy complexion and smiley eyes. She'd have penned his hair exactly as it was, too – curls framing a bald patch. Even his clothes were what you would picture a farmer in – a check shirt and baggy trousers, which ballooned as they disappeared into big rolled-topped wellingtons. His manner was pleasant and accepting. He hadn't once complained about their being women and not up to the job, but had been grateful to see them, and had every faith that they would be able to replace his farmhand and the young men he employed at busy times through the Farmers Guild, who'd all gone to war.

By midday, Julia didn't know which part of her ached the most. Digging her pitchfork into yet another heap of cut hay, she wondered how on earth she was going to lift it and add it to the ever increasing height of the haystack they were building. Somehow she managed it, but was glad to hear Farmer Pickering telling her to take over the driving of the horse as it pulled the mower.

'I reckon as you can steer the horse in a straight line. It'll give you a respite from the lifting.'

Never had Julia felt more relieved as she did when she sat on the metal saddle-type seat. Geeing the horse along, she was filled with admiration for Rhoda, who was still lifting and throwing the hay as if she'd only just begun to do it.

It was while they were taking a break and eating the doorstop sandwiches, filled with delicious cheese, that they saw Mrs Pickering hurrying across to them. Julia hoped she'd brought the promised hot tea, but she didn't seem to be carrying anything. Her husband got up and went to greet her.

'Now, then, me lass, what's to do?'

'Oh, Dave, I had to send for Gareth. I've had no time to make tea for you all. Cowslip has gone into labour. But it weren't normal, Dave. Without warning she suddenly haemorrhaged. I was making her comfortable, when blood shot everywhere. Any road, Gareth needs some help. Polly's not in, she must have gone down to the Women's Institute meeting. They have a special committee to arrange the garden party, and I can't help Cowslip with this shoulder of mine.'

'All right, Minnie. You can drive the horse and mower, Julia can go down to help Gareth. On your way, lass. Go to the cowshed, where you did the milking. You'll find the vet in the bay at the bottom. No doubt the cries of Cowslip will guide you.'

By the time Julia reached the shed, the sound of poor Cowslip bellowing her pain made her forget her own aches. The vet had his back to her. He was on his knees and she could hear him muttering endearments. 'All right, old girl, we'll soon have you calved. Good girl.'

'I've been sent to help you, but I haven't a clue what to do, though I was a nurse, I never dealt with births. My name's Julia, I'm one of the Land Girls.'

Gareth didn't look at her, or introduce himself. 'Well, at least you won't faint at the sight of blood. Come around here. This side. That's right.'

Julia could see that he had his arm right inside Cowslip. Her heart went out to the animal. The pain in her flared eyes tore at Julia's heart.

'I'm attaching a rope to the calf's foot. When I say, I want you to get hold of it and heave for all you are worth.'

Julia took the bloodied rope and wound some of it around her wrist. How tough this was going to be, she had no idea, but somehow, she determined, she would help Cowslip all she could.

'Right, heave!'

With her foot against the wall, Julia pulled the rope, keeping it taut by taking the slack and winding it around her elbow and arm. Sweat ran down her face. Her breath came in short pants as she willed the calf to come out.

When it did, it came with such a force that she fell backwards. The jarring of her back winded her. Unable to move, she lay gasping for breath, listening, praying the calf and Cowslip would be all right.

'Come on, little one. Come on.'

Turning her head, Julia saw that the vet was rubbing the lifeless calf vigorously and understood that this was to stimulate life into it. She looked over towards Cowslip and saw that she too was lifeless. Spurred on to do something, she rolled over and managed to rise. 'What can I do to help? I . . . is Cowslip . . . is she dead?'

'No, but she will be if not seen to. Take over here. Keep rubbing the calf. I need to stem Cowslip's bleeding.'

Where Julia found the strength she did not know. It was as if someone had taken her over as she rubbed the little calf. 'Come on, baby. Come on, breathe, breathe!'

The calf moved. Joy filled Julia.

'Well done, that's right, keep going.'

As the calf tried to rise, Julia thought that nothing had ever come close to the feeling she was experiencing now. It was as if this was her own child being brought back from the brink of death. This thought knocked some of her joy as Clara came to her mind and her heart felt the pain of longing once more.

Putting these thoughts aside, as they threatened to overwhelm her, Julia turned to see how Gareth was doing with Cowslip. To her dismay, the cow was still, and Gareth, squat on his haunches, held his head in his hands. His despair touched Julia deeply.

'You did all you could. No one could have done more. At least you saved the calf. Look, it's on its feet!'

Nothing prepared her for what happened to her as Gareth looked up and she saw him properly for the first time. His grey eyes, misted over with tears, showed his distress as he stared at her. His dark hair, wet with sweat, clung to his scalp in tight curls. His handsome face, splashed and smeared with blood, had a sadness about it that she wanted to love better. She wanted to say some soothing, reassuring words, but she couldn't speak, nor could she look away. His eyes were like a magnet to her.

All the loneliness of the years since Tim had died melted away and she knew that in Gareth she had found her soulmate.

Pulling herself up, at such a preposterous thought, Julia felt her cheeks redden. She looked away, then immediately wanted to look back and recapture the tangible feeling that had passed between them, but she dared not. She heard him rise, felt him close to her. Stealing herself to look up at him, she watched his mouth curl into a smile.

'Nice to meet you, by the way. Julia, you said? Pretty name.'

'Thank you. I like yours, too. I've never met a Gareth before.'

The silence that fell was weighted with her feelings and those she knew Gareth was experiencing. She didn't move when his hand came towards her. He plucked a piece of straw from her hair. The act made her realise what a mess she must look, as he did, too, but somehow it didn't matter. Nothing mattered. Only the moment they were in – the meeting of their souls.

The calf rubbing up against her broke the spell. She giggled, but then felt an overwhelming urge to cry. 'Poor little mite. Orphaned at birth. What will happen to it?'

'It's a male. Minnie Pickering will nurse it, feed it milk from a bottle and bring it along. They will decide whether to let it remain a bull, or have it castrated and rear it for market and eventually become Sunday dinner for a few families.'

'Oh, no!'

'Ha, now don't go all soft on me. It's the natural way of things. Poor Minnie and Dave have lost a valuable part of their livestock in losing Cowslip, so they will need to recoup some of that by rearing her calf to give them the maximum return. I feel terrible about it.'

'You're not responsible.'

'I know, but I sometimes wonder if my clients think I am on occasions like this. Anyway, I don't know about you, but I could do with a cup of tea.'

'And a wash. You look a mess!'

At this Gareth laughed out loud. 'Well, if I wash under the tap over there, will you make me a cuppa?'

Julia laughed with him. 'Not until I've washed, too.'

They were sitting on a bale of straw drinking their tea, when Julia's new-found world fell about her.

'Well, I suppose I'd better go up to the top field and break the news to Dave and Minnie, and then make tracks. I mustn't be late home for dinner. That would put me even further in the constant doghouse that I am in with my darling wife.'

'Oh! You're married! I – I mean . . . I – I . . . '

Gareth's head bowed as if in shame. Julia thought it right that he should feel guilt - not that he'd said or done anything improper, but he must have felt what she had. He should have told her sooner. He'd made a fool of her.

'Julia, I've only just met you, but well, at this moment, I'm wishing that I wasn't married. Oh, it's something I have wished a thousand times before, but always, I've just got on with things, but having met you . . . I . . . I . . . No. Forgive me. I shouldn't have spoken like that.'

With this Gareth rose and without looking back marched away from her in the direction of the top field.

Every part of Julia trembled. The weakness that she'd felt whilst working the field, overcame her and the tears she'd denied herself she now allowed to trickle down her face as a bereft feeling took her. It was as if she'd been given something beautiful only to have it snatched away. The feeling was akin to the one she'd had when Clara had left. *Oh, Clara, my beautiful daughter, I miss you.*

With this thought, the stark truth hit her. She was soiled goods. And even if he was free, Gareth wouldn't want her. No one had ever wanted her. Not for herself. Plenty had thought her a loose woman and made passes at her. But love her? No.

Rising, she gathered the mugs and was about to take them to the kitchen when she heard her name. Looking round, she saw Gareth standing by the end of the cowshed. As he walked towards her, his hand brushed through his now dry hair, lifting the curls. The sun caught the golden lights which the dampness had suppressed and she realised that his hair wasn't as dark as she had first thought, but was more of a chestnut colour. Silhouetted against the sun, he looked beautiful. Julia caught her breath.

'Julia, I – I . . . '

He stared at her for a long moment. 'Yes, Gareth?'

'Nothing. I'd better get going. I'll see you around. Hope you settle in.'

With this, he turned from her and strolled like a man on a mission towards his car.

Disappointment settled in Julia. She couldn't take in what had happened. Overriding her feeling of missing out on something was a deep sense of loss. Why Gareth walking away from her should give her this feeling she didn't know; she only knew that in the short time they had been together something had passed between them that would be very difficult to deny or to ever forget.

CHAPTER NINE

Clara
A Devastating Loss

'Clara, Clara!' The sound of Shelley's voice penetrated the darkness. Clara wanted to cry out, but couldn't. Curled up in a ball, her limbs felt too stiff to stretch out. A rattling noise made her realise that Shelley was in the back alley shaking the gate.

Making an extreme effort, Clara straightened her limbs. The crusted sacks beneath her released the smell of urine and excrement. She wrinkled her nose. Shame filled her, but her need to attract Shelley's attention overrode this. The fog that encroached on her brain gradually cleared. *It must be Wednesday! I've been here two days! Shelley must think I'm in my bedroom.*

In her desperation to attract Shelley's attention Clara kicked out and banged her feet on the shed wall. *Please hear me, Shelley, please!*

'Clara, Clara, where are you?'

With the noise Clara managed to make, Shelley went quiet for a moment, then shouted again. Though painful to do it, Clara kicked again. Silence fell. Clara wanted to kick and kick, but knew if she was to make Shelley understand it was her, her kicks had to be in answer to her name.

Next time, Shelley called, 'Clara, is that you banging, where are you?'

Clara kicked again, as hard as she could. Pain jarred her legs, but she didn't care. *Oh, Shelley, please find me. Please.*

'Are you trapped somewhere, Clara?'

Clara kicked out once at this, hoping that Shelley would take that as a yes.

'Shall I climb over the gate?'

Again, Clara kicked out.

A scrambling noise followed. 'Bloody hell, me skirt's caught on a bastard nail and ripped it!'

Clara wanted to laugh, such was her relief at hearing Shelley. Kicking out once more, her heart soared at Shelley's words. 'Are you in the blooming shed?'

Another kick, and Clara heard the cardboard being ripped from the window. The draught this let in filled her with joy as she squinted against the light, unable to open her eyes to the glare. The joy was replaced by prayers as she begged God to let Shelley see her and be able to get to her.

'Gawd, Clara! What's happened? Where's Miss Brandon? Blimey, you're tied up! Hold on, girl, I'm here now, you're all right, Clara. I'm coming in.'

Clara held her breath as Shelley rattled the door, but it didn't give. Now she had grown accustomed to the light and could open her eyes she saw Shelley appear at the window again. 'I'll go and fetch Miss Brandon and—' Clara's frantic kicking stopped Shelley in mid-sentence. 'What? What you trying to tell me, Clara? Has Miss Brandon done this to yer?'

Exhausted from all her efforts, Clara managed to kick once. 'Gawd blimey!'

After this there was silence. Then Clara saw Shelley put her hand through the gap in the broken window and take hold of the jagged glass. Once more she held her breath as Shelley rattled the glass, loosening it bit by bit. At last it gave way, allowing Shelley to lift it free. Taking the piece out that was left was an easier task.

Clara's heart soared with hope as Shelley's head popped through the open space removing the glass had made.

'Cor blimey, it stinks like shit!'

As weak as she was, Clara felt her dignity ebb from her and drag her lower than she'd ever felt. A tear that found the path of the many she'd shed ran down her cheek.

'Don't worry about it, Clara. I'm going to climb through. I'll 'ave to fetch that chair from the alley that that old man sits on. 'E ain't out there today.'

What it would take for Shelley to climb over the gate and back again with the chair in her hands, Clara couldn't imagine. She just prayed that she would manage it. Hearing the chair clatter to the ground had her cringing in fear that Miss Brandon would hear. But then, she'd probably be in her bed by now and, having swallowed whatever the liquid was she always took, it was doubtful she would hear anything. Often she'd fallen asleep on the sofa after taking it and, unable to wake her, Clara would leave her there, only to find her still there the next morning.

A hoarse animal-like sound came from Clara as Shelley ripped the plaster from her mouth. The pain made her think that some of her skin had come off with it.

'Sorry, luv, but it's the best way. Peeling it slowly hurts more. Now, let's get your hands untied. Why has that bitch done this to yer? She should be strung up.'

A loud sniff told Clara that Shelley was crying. She tried to say something but couldn't – her mouth wouldn't work.

The pain of the plaster coming off didn't match that of Shelley releasing her arms. The moan that came from her had Shelley taking her and holding her. Deep, painful sobs wracked Clara's body. But some comfort seeped into her at the soothing words of Shelley as she massaged her arms, and the life gradually came back into them, easing the pain.

'That evil witch, I'll do for 'er one of these days!'

Clara could only nod her head, causing more tears to drop from her brimming eyes.

'Come on, Clara. Let's get you out of 'ere and washed down, eh? Yer stink like the bog back 'ome, and that's a stench to match I can tell yer.'

Standing wasn't a problem, the kicking had brought the life back into Clara's legs, but weak from hunger she stumbled when she tried to walk.

''Old on to me, luv. We'll get you to the tap, then yer can 'ave a drink and I can wash yer down.'

During all this, Clara knew moments when she wished she'd died as Shelley removed her soiled clothing and used what she'd ripped from the towel that hung by the tap to clean her bottom half. It seemed that nothing fazed Shelley, and Clara wondered again about how harsh her life had been with her mum.

This thought was confirmed as Shelley told her, 'Don't worry about all this, luv, I've done it a few times for me mum when she'd drunk a skinful and emptied her bowels, or had a beating and been bedridden for days.' Shelley was quiet for a moment after this, then, in a more wistful way, said: 'Despite everything though, doing this for you ain't making me glad that I ain't with me mum. But then, blood's thicker than water, they say.'

Clara thought Shelley was going to cry again, but instead she joked away the feeling that had taken her. 'Ha! 'Ark at me coming over all sentimental. Them times were the only times that me mum were kind to me, and that were 'cause she bleedin' needed summink!'

Clara managed a smile, but inside she felt the pity of this. And as she had done many times over the last couple of days, she thought of her own mum, and her kindness, and the love that she had surrounded Clara with, and she wanted to wail out against the injustice of the separation from her, which she found hard to bear, and of the hardship of lovely Shelley's life.

'Now, mate, can yer 'old on to the wall a mo longer while I fetch that chair for yer? Then, I can climb over the gate and get me satchel. I've me school skirt and blouse in there, and me PE knickers. The skirt'll be too short for yer, but—'

'N – no need.' The words rasped Clara's throat. 'Th – there's a key. It's under the mat. Y – you can get to my room.'

'But what about the bleedin' witch? I don't want to come across that bugger, she might kill me. Or worse, call the cops.'

Clara felt a giggle rising in her at this, but suppressed it as she was afraid of it. Afraid that she'd giggle till she cried, and then cry until she screamed, such was the pent-up emotion inside her. 'It – it'll be all right. She'll be asleep. My bedroom's at the back. T – turn left at the top of the stairs.'

Shelley seemed to take an age to come back. Clara found it hard to keep her limbs still with the exposure of her body, and the shock of what had happened to her.

When she did return, Shelley spoke sternly to Clara, 'Now don't be getting ill. You've got to stay strong. Dig deep, that's what we East Enders do. Nothing gets us down. It's the only way'

'But what are we going t – to do?'

'I ain't going for no bloody cops, that's for sure. They'll do nothing but stir up more trouble for yer. We don't want them sniffing around. Besides, I've punished the old witch meself. I've been into her bedroom. She was snoring like a pig. I got all her clothes and ripped them to shreds, and then I found this tin. I reckon it's got enough cash in it to sort you out, luv.'

'Oh, Shelley. No. You shouldn't have. Th – that gives her a reason t – to call the p – police. She can say that I stole from her then ran away.'

'I didn't think of that. I just wanted to punish her. Sorry, mate.'

While Shelley dressed her, Clara tried hard to think of a solution to Shelley's actions. She knew that Shelley had only done it for her, and that it was the way she'd learned to deal with things while growing up with her mum. Living off her wits had matured Shelley beyond her years, but not in the same way as Clara. In many ways Clara was older and wiser in her mind than Shelley was.

Clara knew that she could do nothing about the destroyed garments, but she had to persuade Shelley that they needed to put the stolen money back, and intact. As she thought this, she realised that she would have to be the one to put the cash back, because she couldn't trust Shelley to do it.

Shelley's reaction to this was as Clara expected. 'Don't be bloody daft! What're yer going to do for money? 'Ow yer going to eat? Where yer going to sleep? This cash will get yer all of that, and on to a train to Manchester, where yer can get work. Yer look old enough to work, though you've no shape to yer. Not that that's a problem. Yer can buy a bra and stuff it out, yer'd look sixteen easy, and get set on in one of them munitions factories.'

'I know, that seems an easy solution, but it's not a good one. Look, I know you meant well, but you've made it more difficult for me. I could have gone to the WRVS and told them what had happened, but now ... Oh, I just don't know. But I do know that if I take the money, things will be worse for me. Miss Brandon might not dare report me missing for fear of what might happen to her if I am caught and tell the tale of what she did to me, but with her money gone, she will have a way of getting out of it all by siting me as a thief that she had to control.'

They were both quiet for a moment. Clara felt a mixture of emotions – anger at Shelley for making things worse, and relief at being free, which she knew she owed to Shelley. Mixed with these, she bore a deep fear for her future.

Getting up from the chair, made her wobble for a moment, but she steadied herself. 'Give me the cash tin, Shelley.'

'Let me take a bundle out for yer first, mate. You'll need it and she owes yer.'

'No. Please, Shelley. I'll manage.'

'Well, I think yer off yer 'ead.'

Taking the box, Clara made for the open door. Inside a feeling of terror came over her, but she ignored it and made for the stairs. They creaked at her step.

When she reached Miss Brandon's bedroom, her heart pounded. The door swung open. The sound of Miss Brandon's snores reverberated around Clara, reassuring her and propelling her forward. Standing in the bedroom, she looked over at the hateful woman, and felt glad for the first time at the scene around her feet. Shelley had really done a good job – the clothes were in tatters.

Creeping forward, Clara realised that she didn't know where the cash tin had come from. Several drawers were open as well as the wardrobe door. Thinking it wouldn't matter anyway, as the fact that no money had gone was the important thing, she lay the tin down on the dressing table and scurried out of the room.

'Huh! Who – who's there!'

Fear clenched Clara's stomach, but gave wings to her feet. Jumping forward she managed to get through the door and close it. How she got down the stairs she didn't know but once in the yard she shouted to Shelley: 'Come on, she woke up. Hurry.'

'Oh gawd. Can yer manage to climb the gate, Clara?'

'No. I'll have to fetch the key. Hold on.'

All weakness gone, Clara ran into the stockroom. She stood a moment and listened. Nothing. *Please, please let Miss Brandon have gone back to sleep!*

Snatching the key to the gate from the shelf where it was kept, she hurried outside. 'Come on, Shelley, be quick.'

'I'll grab the chair and put it back for the old man, I won't be a mo. You start on your way and I'll catch up.'

Clara felt as though she had been given strength she didn't know she had as she hurried down the back alley, avoiding the dog mess, the overspill from the dustbins, the old rusting bike and the tattered armchair that littered the way.

Shelley caught up with her as she turned onto the road. They hurried on in silence. It wasn't until they reached the seafront that the strength left Clara. 'I have to sit somewhere. My legs won't go any further.'

'I ain't surprised, mate. 'Ere, you sit on that wall. I'll go and get us some chips. You ain't eaten for days.'

Clara sat on a small wall surrounding one of the large seafront guest houses. She gazed across the road at the sea. Calm as a millpond was the saying she'd heard the locals use when it looked like this. The gentle breeze rippled the water but didn't whip up any waves. It all looked so lovely.

Crowds milled about, some ambling from one side of the road to the other, some with a purpose. All looked and sounded happy. Even the rows of young men clad in white T-shirts and navy shorts, being drilled up and down the beach and shouted at by an army sergeant in full uniform, were having a bit of banter with each other. The only thing spoiling the view and the atmosphere was the sight of the coils of barbed wire on the sandy beach, put there to deter invaders.

They and the soldiers reminded Clara that there was a war on.

'They look daft, don't they?' Shelley nodded towards the soldiers. 'But it's 'eartbreaking to think of them soon going off to war, innit?'

'It is. They don't look much older than us.'

'No, a couple of years or more. Still, no use us worrying. 'Ere's yer chips, luv.'

Though the chips smelt lovely, Clara found that she couldn't eat many of them. She felt better for what she did eat, and for the rest she'd had, but it wasn't long before a deep worry hit her. *What now? Oh God, what now?*

Shelley had been quiet while they ate, but she didn't seem to have much of an appetite either. As she screwed up the remains of her chips in their newspaper wrapping, she voiced what Clara had been thinking. 'I'm worried about you, Clara. I ain't got any ideas as to what yer can do. I can't take yer back with me, my pair of old ducks would have a fit. If I were in London, I'd know what to do in a shot.'

In that moment, an idea came to Clara. 'I could hitch a lift to Manchester.'

'Which way would you go, then?'

'I'd ask somebody.'

'What about Arnold?'

'No, I can't bother him. It wouldn't be right to. I'll start walking. I know that the sea is west, and that Manchester is south east of here.' Turning, Clara pointed, 'So it must be that way.'

'Clever boots. 'Ow do yer know that?'

'I don't know. My teacher always said that I have a headful of useless facts, and nothing more.'

'Well, she's wrong, 'cause that one's very useful to yer . . . I'll tell yer what. I'll come with yer. Yer'll never survive on yer own, and I ain't happy with them old codgers. They're good to me, but they get on me nerves with their fussing.'

'Would you? Oh, Shelley, I'd love you to. We can survive together, you with your wits and me with my brains.'

'Cheeky sod!'

They both laughed at this. And with the laughter, some hope entered Clara. Everything felt so much easier with Shelley to accompany her. And she made her mind up to accept whatever Shelley did to help them as she was already regretting not having brought Miss Brandon's money with her. Like Shelley said, she'd earned it.

'I won't be a mo, Clara. I'll nip these chips over the road and feed them to the seagulls. You wait here, luv. And, Clara, it may sound soppy, but I'll always be by your side. You're the best mate I've ever 'ad.'

Clara smiled up at Shelley. She couldn't speak, her heart was too full.

She watched Shelley deftly walk in and out of the traffic, the horses, pulling drays, and the crowds of folk. When she reached the curb, Shelley turned and looked back at her. Clara raised her hand and waved. Shelley waved back, before continuing on her way. It was then that Clara noticed the tram. She rose to her feet. 'Shelley, watch out! *Shelley!*'

But Shelley was gone, and the air was filled with screeching brakes, screaming women and the pounding of feet as the crowd surged towards where Shelley had been.

CHAPTER TEN

Clara
Taken In

'What are you doing here at this time of night, then?'

Clara cringed away from the torch that shone in her face. Her body shivered.

'You're cold. Here, what's your name?'

Clara couldn't see the man who was bending over her, but she could smell his beery breath. 'Leave me alone.'

'Now that's sommat I can't do. Leave a lass of your age out here in the dark and on your own. Where're you from? And why're you out here at this time of night, eh?'

'I've nowhere to go.'

'Hotch up and tell me all about it. I'm Wally. And as you can see by me uniform, I'm in Blackpool training to go to war, so what about you?'

Clara sidled along the bench. Her limbs protested at her doing so. She didn't know how long she'd sat there, not moving, staring out to sea, until it disappeared into a sheet of black night and left her with the sound of it lapping the beach, with only a twinkle of moonlight visible on its surface. All around her was dark as the blackout curtains had been drawn. But she hadn't felt afraid. Just numb.

The bench dipped as Wally sat beside her. 'Now, tell me how you come to be here.'

'I ran away from the wicked woman who was meant to take care of me. Sh – she locked me in the shed . . . Shelley, my friend . . . she helped me, then a tram . . . ' She could go no further, as sobs wracked her body.

Wally's arm came around her. 'Well, that's a tale and a half. I heard about a lass being mown down by a tram earlier. Bad job. So she were your mate? I'm sorry to hear that. And you've run away from the woman who is meant to be looking after you. So where's your mum and dad, then?'

Through her sobs, Clara told her story. Something in her told her that she could trust Wally. He was a soldier. And they were honourable, weren't they?

'Well, now, don't you worry, no more. I don't think you should go back to that old bag. Nor to no WRVS. They're a load of do-gooders, who don't do any good if you ask me. Look, me old man's got a guest house. There's a few women in there, they'll take care of you. And there's one of your own age, an' all. Her name's Lindsey. She ran away from a convent orphanage where they were treating her bad, but she's all right now, with the women in the house. As long as you know to keep what you see under your hat and to do as you're told, you'll be happy and well cared for.'

Clara didn't like the sound of this, but as the moon went behind a cloud and complete darkness descended, she knew she was too afraid to stay where she was.

'Come on, then. Let's get going, eh?'

The walk from the bench in South Shore to the guest house wasn't long. Soon Wally was saying: 'Here we are, then. Cookson Street. It's just along here.'

The house was in darkness, and looked intimidating to Clara. She wanted to turn and run, but exhaustion engulfed her, and the promise of the warmth the house offered and the meal Wally had said would be served to her overrode any fear she felt.

The door was opened by a woman of the like Clara had never seen before. The light from the hall framed what Clara could see was a buxom figure. She had bright red hair that stuck out at all angles like curled wire. Her clothes were bright, yellows and reds, and her face plastered with make-up. 'I've a young lass for you, Dolly.'

When they moved into the hall, Clara saw that the woman was even stranger than she'd first thought. She wasn't a woman at all, but a man dressed as one. Black stubble shadowed her chin and upper lip.

'Well, who have we here, Wally? Eeh, I don't knaw how you do it. You go for a stroll and bring back a gem, but this one looks too young this time. She's got no shape to her, despite her being tall. Here, love, you started your monthly yet? How old are you?'

The deep voice confirmed that Dolly was a man. This left Clara feeling confused and embarrassed, and the questions asked had never been asked of her before.

'Let her get in first, Dolly. You're scaring the life out of her. Where's Lindsey? I thought she could help her to settle.'

'She's having her first encounter, poor lass. She's with that Adamou from Manchester. He took one look at her and wanted her. He's important to your dad's plans, so he said we were to let him have what he wanted.'

'Christ! Not the Cypriot? What's me dad thinking? Any road, take care of this young lass, will you? I'm AWOL, so I'd better get going and try to sneak back into barracks without being seen. I'll see you tomorrow, Clara. You'll be all right with Dolly.'

Clara didn't think she'd be all right ever again, but she was too tired to protest. It had been one of the longest days of her life, and one of the saddest she'd ever known.

'Come through. Right, the set up here is that you see all, and say nowt. Got it?'

Clara nodded.

The room she was taken to was like no other room she'd ever been in. Everything in it seemed to be green. Green velvet chairs, green curtains, even the lighting had a green hue to it.

'Sit down, lass. Have you eaten?'

Clara could only shake her head.

'Reet, hold on.' With this Dolly went to the door, opened it and yelled: 'Flo, bring some ham and pickles, and hurry up! Oh, and a glass of that lemonade, an' all.' She turned back to Clara. 'Now, lass, tell me about yourself. What're you doing out in Blackpool at this time of night? Where's your parents?'

Dolly's smile widened as she listened to Clara. 'So, this old bag, do you reckon as she'll be looking for you?'

'No. She will be too scared of what I say if I'm found. She'll be afraid that I'll go to the WRVS, which is where I'll go in the morning, if you just let me stay tonight.'

'I shouldn't go there, lovey. They'll just put you with another lot that don't want you. You stay here, I have a job for you. You can be a runner. You just fit the bill. You'd easily pass off as a lad.'

'What's a runner?'

'You'll run errands and pick up bets from the local pubs. Lindsey'll show you the ropes, she's been doing it till now, but she's developed into a beauty and is wanted by the men that come here looking for a good time. She's serving her apprenticeship at this very moment.' Dolly laughed out loud at her own joke, but then became serious. 'Not that I'd wish anyone, let alone our lovely Lindsey, to have to lie with Nick the Hick, as we call him, on account of him seeming to have constant hiccups. But it has to be done, everyone has to earn their keep around here. None of us cross the boss. Did Wally tell you about his dad?'

It seemed to Clara that everything rhymed. But that didn't make it funny. Her heart thudded. 'No, he just said that he ran this guest house and that he would let me stay, and find me a job.'

'Oh, he'll do that all right. He runs everything in Blackpool. His name's Mickey. No one does owt without his say so. He owns most of everything, and what he doesn't own, he gets protection money from. Nowt he does is legal, so it's important you keep your mouth shut about owt you see and hear. Understand?'

Clara nodded. 'I – I don't reckon as I'll stay, thanks. I – I – '

'Oh, you'll stay all right, lass. Now, you've been here and knaw about us, there's naw turning back. So, you can get that out of your head. You can share the attic room with Lindsey, she'll show you the ropes. Ah, here's your supper. Tuck in. You'll feel better after that.'

Although afraid, and with the feeling that she'd lost her appetite, Clara hadn't seen such food for a long time, at least, not put in front of her with the invitation to have as much of it as she wanted. Her hunger came back at the sight of the delicious ham and thick slices of bread. But she couldn't do it justice. A few bites and her stomach felt full and bloated. 'I'm sorry, I haven't eaten for a few days.'

'Aye, you said. That old bag wants shooting. Well, you're all right now, just as long as you do as you're told and keep your head down. Ah, here's Lindsey now. Eeh, Lindsey, lass, were it that bad?'

A sobbing girl came through the door. But even though her crying had swollen her eyes and reddened her face, Clara thought her very pretty. Her fair hair tumbled to her neck in a mass of waves and curls. Her huge eyes, though bloodshot, were pale blue, and were framed by long black lashes. She went straight to Dolly and fell at her knees.

'I'm sorry, Lindsey, lass,' Dolly stroked Lindsey's hair, but then said the strangest words, which made Clara blush as she had an inkling what they meant. 'You knaw the way of it. Eeh, I could kill Nick the Hick, but I'd better go and see if he's all right, and that he pays full whack for having had you. Sit with Clara a mo. She's new and she's going to take your old job over.'

As if a child of much younger years than Clara, Lindsey did as she was bid and switched her body from leaning on Dolly to leaning on Clara. Her sobs wrenched at Clara's heart, and without thinking, she stroked Lindsey's hair just as Dolly had and heard herself making soothing noises.

'I'm sorry for what's happened to you, Lindsey. Was it bad?'

'It were. He's a brute. He hurt me, but he didn't care.' Suddenly Lindsey looked up into Clara's face. 'Don't stay here, Clara. Get out now, while Dolly's busy. It'll be for the best, no matter where you land up, it'll be better than here. Go!'

The door opened at that moment. 'What's that you're saying, Lindsey? I know you've had a bad time of it, but you ain't turning against us, are you? You'll be all right in a couple of days, and you'll earn some good money now that you are available to the men. Mickey himself has a fancy for you, an' all. If he takes to you, your bread will be thickly buttered. Now, go on up. Clara can help you to wash, and you can get to knaw one another, but don't be putting her off, if you knaw what's good for you.'

Dolly seemed to have many personalities. Clara had thought her strange at first, and then kindly, then had felt fear when Dolly told her she wouldn't be allowed to leave here, and now, after being understanding with Lindsey a few minutes ago, she was having a go at her, condoning what had gone on, and preparing Lindsey for more of the same. It crossed Clara's mind that Dolly was the type who could be a nasty piece of work if you got on the wrong side of her.

Feeling sick to her stomach with fear, Clara followed Lindsey up the stairs. The landing had many doors leading from it, and from behind one or two came moaning noises, and the sounds of beds creaking.

Lindsey opened one of the doors, which led into a bathroom. Clara turned on the taps to fill the bath. Steam filled the room, making her feel hot and bothered. Lindsey hadn't spoken since they'd come up the stairs, but when she began to undress, she groaned with pain, and Clara was shocked to see how bruised her body was. 'I'll help you, Lindsey.'

Once Lindsey was in the bath, her silent weeping tore at Clara. 'I'm sorry for you, Lindsey. And I'm scared.'

'Don't be. I should have got away a long time ago, but it's been easy up to now. You'll be all right. The men won't want you as you have a lad's figure. Wash me back for me, then will you run up to the attic room and get me nightie? It's through that door, turn left, then up the narrow steps.'

Clara felt glad to do anything at all for Lindsey, and ran all the way to the attic bedroom, surprised at how her strength had come back now that she had someone to look after.

Once in bed together, deciding that Clara should share Lindsey's bed for tonight as neither had the strength to search out linen for the second bed in the room, Lindsey talked and talked. She told of how she'd been brought up in a convent in Manchester, of the cruelty of the nuns and of how she'd run away to Blackpool and found herself taken in by Dolly. 'What about you? How did you land up here?'

After telling her story for the third time that day, Clara's pain cut into her. 'I don't know what happened to Shelley after that. I ran and ran, and found myself sitting on a bench, quite away from where it happened, but I know now that she was killed as Wally told me he'd heard a young girl had been killed by a tram. It must have been Shelley, she stepped straight into the tram's path. I – I'm going t – to miss her.'

'She sounds as though she was a good friend. I'm sorry, about what happened. But we can be friends if you like. It'll be good to have someone of me own age, I'm fourteen.'

'I'm that, too. Just turned, on fifteenth August.'

'Well, we'll look out for one another. Being a runner ain't too bad, you just have to be a bit careful that you don't attract the attention of the cops, and that the money you collect is allus spot on, as well as the bet, and whose it is. I'll make sure that you get it right.'

'Thanks, Lindsey.'

'Now, I need to sleep. See you in the morning, eh?'

As the room became quiet, Clara's mind filled with all that had happened to her, and her body trembled, but then she thought of having found Lindsey and none of it seemed so bad. Lindsey had coped. Yes, she'd been broken a bit by what had happened to her, but she was strong again now, and Clara knew that she had to be like Lindsey.

Her last thoughts before falling asleep were of her mum. And, as she had a million times since hearing the news of the invasion, she wondered what was happening on her island, and to her mum. A tear ran down her cheek, but with her newfound maturity, she knew that weeping wasn't the answer. She brushed it away. *I have to stay strong. If I'm to cope with how things have turned out for me, I have to.*

CHAPTER ELEVEN

Julia
The Fundraising Event

'Funny, having a fundraising event to raise funds to have a garden party to raise funds for the war effort, don't you think?'

'Julia, you're not answering my question. What do you think you are doing? Gareth is married!'

'I know. I told you, remember?'

'Well, then, you should stop it now. You shouldn't have gone out with him the other evening as it is, but now you're thinking of going again! What will Farmer Pickering think?'

'He won't think anything, if you do as I ask. Please, Rhoda. We could go to this whist drive together, only you go in, and I don't. You know how to play, I know that you attended such things back home. I don't, I was never invited.'

'Oh, Julia, we said we wouldn't speak of that time again. I feel terrible about it.'

'I know. I'm sorry. But please do this for me. I have to be with Gareth. I know it's wrong, but we didn't do anything we shouldn't. We just talked. He's very unhappy. He has asked for a divorce, but his wife threatens to kill herself if he does that to her.'

'Why can't he make her happy then? He must have loved her in the beginning.'

'I don't know. From what he says, he did think himself in love with her, but she is a very difficult person. She wanted children, but can't have any. She says it's his fault. She plots her cycle and demands he makes love to her at the right time.'

'Well, that should please him. It would my Roger, I – I mean, well, you know.'

'You're blushing, Rhoda!'

'Oh, shut up. All right, I'll do it, but I don't like it. You're living up to what everyone says about . . . Oh, I'm sorry, I didn't mean that. Oh, Julia, forgive me.'

'It's all right. I know what was said about me. I'm not and never have been the kind of woman they called me. Those men who said they'd been with me hadn't. They tried, but I didn't let them, but they had to boast, didn't they? And they had willing ears to boast to. But Gareth's different. Something passed between us the moment we looked at each other. I just wish that he wasn't married.'

'He is giving you the "my wife doesn't understand me" routine and you are falling for it. Be careful, that's all I am saying. Now get ready, or I won't make the first cut.'

Julia's heart jumped for joy. She didn't like the clandestine nature of her meetings with Gareth, but she had to respect his wishes to keep their meetings a secret.

When she reached the edge of the village and saw Gareth's car parked just up the road, a surge of happiness zinged through Julia. So much so that she broke into a run and was out of breath by the time she sat in the passenger seat.

'Hello, you made it! And you look beautiful.'

'Thank you. I – I, yes, didn't you expect me to come?'

'I hoped.'

Julia felt a shyness come over her at this. A small part of her held a fear, as tonight it was her turn to talk. Gareth had chatted on for all of the last time they were together, only asking her at the end to tell him about herself. She had used the excuse that it was late and that she would tell him the next time they met.

As Gareth reversed the car and turned in the opposite direction to the village, he didn't speak and a silence fell between them. Julia thought of all he'd told her. She was unsettled in her mind since Rhoda had challenged her actions in meeting Gareth.

She'd learned that he had lost his parents in a road accident and that through this he'd met Vanda, as she was the solicitor for the man whose car had rammed that of his parents. Vanda had kindly agreed to see Gareth after the case and explain exactly what had happened in more detail than the court had. They had got on well and had married after a six-month courtship. This had been five years ago. Even during the courting days, Gareth had had doubts, but filled with grief over his parents, he snatched at what happiness Vanda did offer him.

'She was incredibly sexy. Still is, when she wants to be. And that's her in a nutshell really. What she wants to happen, happens. She pulls out all the stops to make it so. Even our love life happens to order – Vanda's orders. There's no spontaneity about it. And no love. Not any more.' It was then that he'd gone on to tell her about their lack of children. And the plan that was supposed to change that, which had been going on for three years now with no success.

Julia thought of Clara, and how different life would have been for her if she hadn't caught for a baby so easily, but then pulled herself up as she would never wish not to have Clara. Her arms ached to hold her every minute of the day.

'This is the place.'

The car slowed. Julia looked up to see they were outside a pub. The Railway Inn's board swayed in the wind. It showed a picture of a steam engine.

'Fancy a drink?'

'Aren't you known in there? We don't seem to have come far.'

'I thought I would bring one out to the car. If that's all right with you? You seem very tense tonight. You haven't spoken a word.'

'Yes, that will be nice. A gin and tonic, please. Sorry, I've been a bit distracted. I – I know that I have to tell you my story, and I'm afraid you won't want to see me once you know.'

'Oh dear, is it that bad? Are you a runaway murderess? Or, maybe a kidnapper of men! Or a witch who will turn me to stone!'

Julia laughed. 'No, none of those.'

'Good. I'll get our drinks and then you can tell all.'

After Julia had sipped a third of her drink, and they had discussed village small talk and how she was settling in, Gareth turned to her. The bench seat gave him ample room to lift one of his legs and to sit with his knee rested on the seat so that he was facing her. 'Now, what is your dark secret then?'

There was no easy way. 'I'm unmarried, and yet I have a child.'

In the silence that followed, Julia's heart became as heavy as a brick. Gareth kept his eyes on hers. At last he spoke. 'Tell me about it. How did it happen, when did it happen and where is your child?'

In the telling, Julia felt some relief. Gareth didn't speak, but his expression was one of pity for her. And this showed in his words when she'd finished her tale.

'Oh, Julia, that's one of the saddest tales I've heard. My God, those islanders are a bigoted lot.' He slid closer to her. 'Can I hold you, Julia?'

She couldn't object. Standing her glass on the dashboard, she went into his arms. Doing so, she knew it was where she belonged.

His body felt solid. He smelt of aftershave – a woody, nice smell. The warmth of him enveloped her, and she could hear his heartbeat. When his hand stroked her hair, she was undone. Lifting her head she accepted his descending lips onto her own. Opening her mouth to his probing, she melted under the impact of his tongue in her mouth, of feeling its pressure on her own, and the thrill of him gently withdrawing it, and placing it back in again. An involuntary moan escaped her as Gareth quickened the pace of this movement and brought his hand to cup her breast. All of it was as if for the very first time for her. She'd never experienced anything like this with Tim.

When the kiss came to an end, Gareth's face stayed close to hers. She could hear his desire in his breathing, and see it in the depths of his smouldering eyes. 'Julia, I love you.'

The words thrilled her. Her body filled with happiness. 'I love you, too, Gareth.'

With this, she was once more in a deep kiss with him. Her breasts thrilled to the touch of his caress. She wanted him; she wanted him desperately.

The sound of a car horn made them jump apart. Glaring lights had Julia screwing up her eyes.

Gareth swivelled round. His neck straining, he looked towards the turning headlights. As the glare left the car, Gareth's deep sigh settled Julia's nerves a little.

'It was Tom. He'd be playing the fool. He's my best pal. He has a farm up in the hills, and knows my situation. I told him just now when I fetched the drinks that I had you in the car. He's pleased for me. He'd be just wanting to make me jump. He'll be laughing his head off now.'

For Julia, the moment was spoiled. To be part of a joke between these two friends somehow sullied what had just happened. She slid back to her own side of the bench seat.

'Take me home, please, Gareth. And, I'm not sure that I want to see you again. Not like this.'

'What! Julia, no. I love you. I want to see you. I'm so sorry about that. I can see how it looks, but it wasn't like that, I promise. Tom is known as a big joker, he—'

'If you love me, then divorce your wife, and come to me. I can't do it this way. I thought I could, but I can't.'

'I have no grounds for divorce, and no matter how many grounds I give to Vanda, she wouldn't let me free. She's vindictive.'

'How do I know that? How do I know that you're not just looking for an affair to relieve the tedium of the regime of your love life? I don't know you, Gareth. I've been a fool. Please take me home.'

Without another word, Gareth picked up the two glasses and offered hers to her, but she shook her head, and he opened the car door and emptied the contents on to the car park as he got out. Julia watched him walk across the dimly lit gravel, and her heart ached. She loved him, more than she'd ever loved anyone, but she had to walk away from him. She had to.

'Julia? Julia, are you all right? You're crying. What happened?'

'I've been a fool, Rhoda. I – I should have listened to you.'

To go into her friend's arms was a small comfort, but nothing could lift the misery that Julia felt.

'Tell me about it? Did Gareth try it on with you?'

'It's not that. I was willing, I wanted to, but then . . .'

After telling Rhoda everything, Julia felt even more ashamed. It all sounded so dirty.

'Well, I met the said Vanda tonight, and I can tell you, she's a force to be reckoned with. So, Gareth isn't lying. There was a sort of meeting before the whist drive. Well, I say a meeting. It was more Vanda telling everyone what was going to happen, and when one woman objected to something, my word, she made short shrift of her. The woman actually left the village hall. Another one went to go after her, and Vanda raised her voice to her. "Sit down at once, Jean, if you don't want to be

120

expelled from the fundraising committee as well as Ivy." Jean sat down. Well! I was flabbergasted. How can one woman hold so much power over so many others? No one raised any objection after that, and Vanda just continued to read out what was going to be, who was going to run which stall, and to each she gave a list of what was expected of them. She ended by saying: "Please ladies, do exactly as is on your lists. I do not want to bawl anyone out on the day, or dismiss their stalls from the event!" Then she sat down. You could hear a pin drop until she declared the whist drive open and the first cuts to be made.'

By the time Rhoda finished, Julia wanted to laugh out loud at the relief. Somehow she'd imagined that everything Gareth had said was a lie, but now she realised he was telling the truth.

'I know I wouldn't want to cross her, Julia. As I listened, I understood what life must be like for Gareth. I can imagine her giving him a list at the beginning of each month telling him exactly when he is to perform with her in bed, and at what time, and how long he is to take, not to mention how he is to do it, and God help him if he digresses from that.'

'Oh, Rhoda, stop it. Poor Gareth.'

'No, don't poor Gareth him. Is he a man or a mouse? If he puts up with it, then it is his own fault. Don't you be his salve, Julia, because that is all you will ever be, and if he cannot stand up to Vanda now, then he never will, and you will end up the eternal mistress. And what if she finds out? My God, I wouldn't like to think what she would do. Keep well away, Julia. Keep to the resolve you made when you made Gareth bring you home tonight.'

Julia knew that Rhoda was talking sense, but she so wanted Gareth, and loved him, as she'd never loved before, and she didn't think she could keep to such a resolve. No matter what happened as a result.

On the day of the garden party, Julia set out with Rhoda. Mrs Pickering had let them off dairy duties. 'It's Saturday afternoon and the village is having a fun day. We don't get many of those, so run along, girls, and enjoy yourselves.'

As they went out of the gate, Rhoda said, 'Silly, I know, but I feel really excited.'

'Me too, Rhoda, like I've been let off from school.'

'Ha, those were the days, do you remember? Fishing at the brook with our jam jars, and eating our butties with our muddy hands. Then paddling. Oh, the freedom. It's hard to imagine what is happening on our island now.'

They fell silent. No news was coming out of Guernsey, so they could only wonder at the regime their neighbours were living under.

'Let's stop a while. I don't feel like going on now.'

They stepped off the side of the road, and into the gateway of a field where cows were grazing – a peaceful scene that they were so used to back home. They were within a quarter of a mile of the village now, and from their high vantage point, they could see the layout: the lovely church with its immaculate churchyard surrounding it; the village green, a hive of activity and colour as the garden party was beginning to get under way; the mills, seven in all, belching out smoke from their vast chimneys, a sight that was at odds with the rest of the landscape.

When they reached the village, crowds milled around. There was a lot of activity around the pub car park, where a cattle market was taking place.

The scene before them gave Julia the feeling of a peaceful summer's Saturday afternoon that the war couldn't touch. The Phoney War, folk were calling it, and yet they were mobilising themselves as the folk of this parish were today, to be ready for the worst. Today, funds would be raised to send to the war effort, and to cover the cost of getting all the iron and steel scrap they had amassed down the hills to the towns where it would be transported to the munitions factories. Julia wondered at it all.

The plight of her own island and the islanders was never far from her mind.

'Let's head for the pub first, Rhoda, I could do with a drink.'

'Uh uh, hoping to catch sight of Gareth, are we?'

'No. I said that's over.'

But her heart betrayed her when she caught sight of Gareth's chestnut hair in the sunlight. He was bending over a cow and stroking its hind quarters. He looked up at that moment and caught Julia's eye. His gaze held hers.

'Gareth, Gareth, oh, there you are. You are meant to be judging the cows, not looking at the local scenery.'

Gareth reddened and turned his attention back to the cow.

'I presume that's Vanda?' Julia asked Rhoda.

'Yes. And Gareth obeying her command.'

'Oh, lord, she's coming over.'

'Hello, girls. Been let off for the afternoon? Jolly good. Come along, this is no place for women, even if you are farm-hands. Follow me, I'll take you around the stalls.'

Rhoda's glance made Julia smile, but inside she was left feeling cold at the implication of Vanda's words. She seemed to put a lot of meaning into them which had been directed at Julia. She couldn't know, could she?

Looking back at Gareth, Julia once more caught his eye.

'My husband seems to be of great interest to you, Miss . . . ?'

'Julia. No, of course not. I – I was just wanting to say hello as we delivered a calf together up at the farm.'

'You did what? What is Farmer Pickering thinking of letting you girls do work of that nature? I will be having a word with him, and if he persists in giving you such work, I shall report him.'

'Oh, we have to do all manner of farm work, nothing is barred. He was within his rights putting me to help Gareth.'

'Mr Maling to you. My husband is a respected member of the community. He is not Gareth to anyone but his friends.'

With this, Vanda marched off. Julia and Rhoda followed her as if her word was law, such was the effect that she had on them.

When at last she left them to their own devices Julia was glad of it. 'Wow, no wonder Gareth does as he is told.'

'Doesn't that put you off him, Julia? It would me. He's nothing but a lap dog.'

'I can't imagine anyone being anything else with that woman. You didn't object to her bossing us around, did you?'

Rhoda didn't answer this, but changed the subject. 'Oh, look, tombola, I love that. Let's go and have a go, shall we?'

After three failed tickets, they wandered away from the stalls to the tea tent. 'Let's sit a while. I suddenly feel very sad, wondering what my Janet is doing today. I hope she is having some good times. When do you think we can go looking for them, Julia?'

'Maybe we could get a weekend off and try then. Though I'm not sure how we'd get to Blackpool.'

'We could ask around. There must be a train. Perhaps from Clitheroe. We could get a lift to there.'

'And what then? What if we do find them? We're committed to staying here for the duration now, they're not going to let us off.'

'I know, but at least we will know they are safe and can arrange to visit them.'

'That would be wonderful.'

Julia looked around her. Happy families seemed to be the theme of the day, as folk milled around in groups, laughing and having a go on all the stalls. Julia knew, though, that they too were mostly missing someone from their ranks, as there were very few young men around.

'Julia, Julia.'

At the sound of her name, Julia turned. Gareth stood in the shadows of the tent. She looked around her. No sign of the dreaded Vanda. 'I won't be a mo, Rhoda.'

'Are you mad?'

'Keep an eye out for me. Please, Rhoda.'

'Oh, Julia, Julia . . .'

As she went up to Gareth, Julia's heart lurched.

'Julia, I must see you, I must. I can't stop thinking about you. I will do something about leaving Vanda, I promise, but just agree to see me again. Let's meet and make plans. I love you, Julia.'

Without thinking, she asked, 'When?'

'Can you get away tomorrow night?'

'I'll try.'

'Oh, Julia, please, please make it. I'll wait for you in the same place as last time. Vanda will be at church, so we won't have long. She always attends Sunday evening service as she sings in the choir.'

Taking her arm, he gently pulled her with him behind the tent. 'Oh, Julia, my Julia.'

As his lips found hers, she was lost. There would be no fighting this love. She and Gareth were meant to be together.

CHAPTER TWELVE

Clara
Life as a Runner

'Who's this, then?'

'This is Clara, Ruby. She'll be doing my job and picking up the bets.'

They were at the back entrance to the Fallen Leaves pub on Manchester Road. Ruby, a middle-aged fat woman, had a scowl on her face that had Clara shaking in her shoes.

'Righto. What're you going to be doing, then, Lindsey, sitting on your arse?

'I've been put on the game.'

'Oh, I feel sorry for you, lass. But life is what it is. If you tangle with such as Mickey, then you live by his rules. You take note, miss what's-your-name. As no doubt, you'll end up the same.'

'I'm Clara. And, yes, I'll be careful.'

'Careful? You'll have no say in it, once these flower.' To Clara's acute embarrassment, Ruby tweaked her breasts, then put her head back and let out a cackle of laughter.

'Stop it, Ruby. It ain't funny. I hate it, and if it weren't for Clara, I don't knaw what I'd do.'

'Aye, it's a pity, and it's good to have a friend who'll look out for you. Reet, here's me bets, there ain't many, on account of there only being old men around these days, except for the servicemen, but I have to be careful who I approach. If Mickey complains, tell him I'm working on the airmen and'll have more for him next time.'

'He won't be happy, Ruby.'

Ruby tutted. 'Well, he'll have to do the other thing, won't he, I can't get blood out of a stone.'

As they turned away, a lad called out to them. 'How y'doing, Lindsey? Who's this, then?'

'Hello, Tinker. This is me new friend. I'm handing over me job to her. Her name's Clara.'

Tinker nodded at Clara. A tall, gangly lad with a freckled face and a shock of ginger hair, he smiled at Clara. She smiled back. 'Hello.'

After Lindsey had told him her tale, he hung his head. 'That ain't reet, Lindsey, that Mickey shouldn't be putting you on the game, you're too young.'

'It's how it is. Any road, what are you doing up this end? I thought you'd be working today?' Lindsey turned to Clara. 'Tinker works on the fairground, the Pleasure Beach. Have you seen it yet? The rides are great, especially the big-dipper.'

'Yes, I've seen it, but I haven't been on anything.'

'I'll give you a free ride if you like. Any time, just come down and I'll sort it.'

This sounded wonderful to Clara. She thought of her and Shelley riding the big wheel, and her heart felt heavy. *Oh, Shelley, Shelley.*

'What's that look for? You look like you lost a bob and found a penny.'

'She gets like that on account of her mate being killed the other day, by the tram.'

'Oh, reet. That were a bad business. Folk forget. They cross the road and think that's it. They forget that there's still the trams coming along. Sorry to hear that. Any road, I'm to get going, or I'll be late for work. I'll see you around, Lindsey.'

Clara marvelled at how accepting Lindsey's friends were of her fate, as if it was a natural thing. Yes, they expressed their sympathy for her, but no one told her not to do it, or offered her a solution – a way out of doing it. Not for the first time, she wondered at the power this Mickey had over folk. She'd yet to meet him, and dreaded doing so.

When she finally did meet Mickey, on their return to the guest house, Clara was surprised to find that she couldn't hate him as she wanted to. He had a way with him that put you at your ease.

'Is it yerself, then Lindsey, and who's this you have with you?'

'This is me mate, Clara. She came into the house a few days ago, your Wally brought her in. She's learning to do me job as runner.'

'Oh, is that right? Well, welcome, Clara. Have you every-thing you be needing?'

Clara could only nod; her tongue felt tied in knots. She hadn't been sure what she'd been expecting, but it hadn't been a nice-looking Irishman, with twinkly eyes and curly black hair. She guessed he was around her mum's age, maybe a bit older. He was smartly dressed in the whitest shirt she'd ever seen and black trousers. He had his thumbs behind his braces, and snapped them against his chest. 'So, it is that I hear you were very pleasing to Nick the Hick, Lindsey. You're a good girl, so you are. I hope he wasn't too rough with you?'

Lindsey put her head down. 'He hurt me, Mickey. I don't want to go with him again.'

Clara held her breath.

'So I heard. Well, you must have fought, when I told you you were to be pliant. Now that's not pleasing to me, Lindsey. Isn't it that I give you a free home? A place to lay your head, and to keep your belly full? Is it too much to ask that you do me bidding, then?'

'Naw, Mickey. I'm sorry. I just didn't knaw how to go on.'

'Well, I presume that you do now. There's a soldier in bedroom four waiting to be pleasured. Get yourself up there and make him a happy man. He's paid well, so he has.'

Clara gasped.

'It isn't for you to be looking so scared, Clara. You won't have anyone fancy you for a while, by the looks of you. Now, hand me that satchel you're carrying, and let's see what the bets are today.'

Clara handed the bag over, and watched Lindsey climb the stairs. Just before Lindsey went into the room, she looked back at Clara. Clara wanted to shout out as she saw the tears running down Lindsey's face, but she kept quiet, afraid of what Mickey would do.

'Right, I have another errand for you. You're to go to Dolly and she'll put you in the picture. Don't be dawdling now.'

Glad to get out of Mickey's presence, Clara went into the sitting room. Dolly was there with two women, both over made up and wearing revealing clothing. 'This is Sandy, and this here is Trudy. This, ladies, is our new runner, Clara.'

'Where's Lindsey?'

This was from the one called Trudy.

'Mickey's put her to work. She's with a bloke at the mo.'

'The rotten sod. Lindsey's only a bairn.'

'A bairn with tits and that makes her old enough. Now, don't let Mickey hear you talk like—'

The door had opened. The women had all frozen to the spot.

'So, I'm a rotten sod, is it? . . . *Is it?*'

Mickey crossed the room in a flash. The punch he threw landed Trudy on her back. Blood spurted from her nose. 'Well, isn't it that Jason is about to pay us a visit. Maybe he can show you who the rotten sod is, Trudy.'

'Naw. I'm sorry. I were just feeling sorry for the lass, that's all, Mickey. I'm sorry.'

'We'll see how sorry you are when Jason's done with you. I said I'd find him a playmate this time, as he's delivered the goods I wanted, so clean yourself up and be ready to give him a good time.'

Clara cowered in the corner. Fear shook her body. Mickey looked over at her – his scowl had her holding her breath – but then he turned away and went out of the room.

131

'Bloody hell, Trudy, what were you thinking?'

The sobbing Trudy looked up at Dolly. 'Not Jason. Dolly, don't make me.'

'You daft lass. I can't change Mickey's orders. It took all me persuasive powers to have him stop that bloke coming here, and now with one stroke, you've undone that. Well, I'm sorry for you, lass, but you brought it down on yourself.' Picking up her handbag, Dolly rummaged in it. 'Here, Clara. Take this and make yourself scarce. Go and have a go on some of the stalls, or sommat. And don't come back for at least an hour. Just afore you do, go to this address and hand this note over. Wait a while and then bring back to me what they give you.'

Taking the coins and the note, Clara sidled past Trudy. She wanted for all the world to fling herself at the young woman and hold her, as she saw the fear in her, but she went past and out of the door.

Once outside, she ran for all she was worth towards the seafront, hesitating when she neared Arnold's stall, wanting to go to him, but afraid to do so. He would want to know about Shelley, and he'd want to do the right thing by her, maybe, even call the police, and that would mean being sent back to the evil Miss Brandon. No, she didn't want that. As bad as things were at the guest house, she preferred being there to being with the hateful Miss Brandon.

After wandering aimlessly about, not interested in playing any of the stalls, Clara made her way to the address she'd been given. The door opened to her knock. A hand came through. A voice said, *give me what you have*. Clara handed the note over.

The door closed. She waited. When it opened again, a little man, no bigger than a boy of seven or eight, stood there. He handed her a rolled-up piece of cloth. 'Don't drop it. And hand it straight to Dolly when you get back.'

Back at the house, the atmosphere was subdued. Dolly took the roll, told Clara she'd done well, then told her to go to her room and to stay there, and that Flo would bring her food later. 'Don't even put your head out from around the door. Now, go on, but be up in the morning as there's more errands for you. You're to collect some money for Mickey tomorrow, lass.'

Clara sat on her bed, her thoughts running away with her. She thought of her mum, and her granny and of Shelley, and tried to make sense of her own situation. No one treated her badly, and yet she was in a constant state of fear.

Noises drifted up to Clara as she sat staring at the wall – a scream that made her blood go cold, and the opening and shutting of doors. She put her hands over her ears, lay down, pulled her knees up under her chin and allowed the tears to run down her nose and trickle off the end of it.

She didn't know how long she'd lain like this, listening to the strange goings-on in the house, when the bedroom door opened and Lindsey crept in.

Sitting upright, Clara hardly dared ask if Lindsey was all right, but she didn't have to. When Lindsey lit the lamp, she could see she was.

'Hey, you made me jump, I thought you were asleep!'

'I tried, but all the noises kept me awake.'

'I knaw. Did you go to the dwarf's house?'

'Yes.'

'Well, you would have brought back hashish. They'll all be stoned any minute now.'

'And Trudy? Is she all right?'

'She'll have had a beating, poor lass. They told me what happened. That Jason is a cruel bugger. He cuts up rough with the girls. But she'll be all right now, she'll be smoking the weed with the rest of them and feeling on top of the world. They'll party all night.'

'Are you all right, Lindsey?'

'Yes, I'm relieved if owt. He were all right, that soldier. He was gentle and loving. I liked what he did. If it was like that all the time, I wouldn't mind this game. Money for pleasure.'

Clara wasn't so sure about this, but she said nothing.

'Come on, lass. While they are off their heads, we can sneak out and have some fun. That soldier gave me some extra money for meself. And if we go to the fun fair, Tinker'll give us a few free rides. I can buy us a hot dog. Come on, get your coat, but be quiet about it.'

In the excitement of the fairground, which proudly proclaimed itself to be the 'Pleasure Beach', Clara forgot her fear. Neither could she imagine that there was a war on, as they rode the big dipper, screaming every time it descended a steep incline, and worked away at the swing boats until they were soaring high.

Without even knowing it was happening, Clara found herself laughing her head off, for the first time in a long time, especially when they went into a tent and were confronted by the laughing policeman. Her sides ached with laughing along with the wobbly figure.

'Oh, Lindsey! I've never had so much fun.'

'I knaw. Come on, let's go and get a hot dog.'

As they neared the caravan that had steam coming from its windows, Clara was assailed with the delicious smell of sizzling sausages and fried onions.

Biting through the soft bread and into the hot sausage, which released a cascade of flavours like no other she'd ever tasted, the thought came to her that she could put up with all of the bad things that happened in the house if she could escape like this every now and again.

As Clara finished her hot dog, Lindsey linked arms with her. 'I'm glad that you came to the house, Clara. Me and you can be good mates, and look out for one another.'

Clara had the feeling that she had Shelley back. Yes, Lindsey was different, but in her ways she was like Shelley. Fun-loving, and a daredevil, ready to take a chance, just to have some lighter moments in her life.

Clara squeezed Lindsey's arm. 'We will. I'll always look out for you, Lindsey. You're a good friend.'

And at that moment, Clara knew that this would always be so. She missed Shelley more than she could say, but she had Lindsey, and no matter how bad things got in life, they would be there for each other.

'Let's go back now, before we're missed.'

With this from Lindsey, Clara realised for the first time that maybe they were doing something they shouldn't. 'Will we get into trouble, Lindsey?'

'We will if we're caught. Mickey doesn't like anyone doing owt that he hasn't given permission for. He likes to control us all.'

The fear that Clara had forgotten seeped back into her as they neared the guest house and she sensed the tension in Lindsey.

They turned into Cookson Street to find the guest house ablaze with light. On the doorstep stood Mickey, smoke coming from his pipe, his hat worn at a jaunty angle, and with a beer bottle in his hand.

'So, the wanderers return. And where is it that you've been, then?'

'We only popped out for some air, Mickey. Everyone was busy, so we nipped out, we haven't been gone long.'

Clara could feel Lindsey's body shaking. Her own fear deepened.

'Long enough it is, that I had to turn a customer away. And I don't like doing that.'

'I – I thought after the soldier, I . . . '

'Well, isn't it that you're not the one to be paid to do the thinking around here? Get here, you little tyke, you.'

Lindsey stepped forward, only to be knocked back again by a vicious blow. Clara went to run, but Mickey caught hold of her hair and yanked her back. A thump landed on her back, taking her breath away. 'So it is that you've not been here five minutes and you're away doing as you please. Well, that's not the way of things. You move when I say that you move, you breathe when I am for giving you my permission to do so.'

Clara leaned against the wall, gasping for breath. She could do nothing as she watched Mickey cross over to where Lindsey lay and land a vicious kick in her side. She called out in protest, but this brought Mickey reeling round and stepping towards her. She cowed against the wall. A blow knocked her head backwards. 'Now, get yourselves to your room, I'm for wanting no more of you going off, do you hear?'

Somehow, Clara managed to stand without leaning on the wall. She made her way over to Lindsey and helped her up. Together they staggered into the house and up the stairs. Once in their room, they sat down on their beds. Neither of them spoke, but Clara knew that this was their future. That they really did have to look out for one another, as they were in the clutches of a monster.

In that moment, most of her childhood left her, but the part of her that wanted her mum when anything bad happened stayed with her, and she lay back and cried and wailed for her, until Lindsey hushed her.

'We have to be strong, Clara. We have to be strong together.'

Clara thought of her island home and all she'd taken there, and she knew she could be strong, but she just didn't know how much would be asked of her. She never thought she'd be beaten, as that Miss Brandon had beaten her, nor to be imprisoned, and then to be in the clutches of someone like Mickey and beaten again.

When she'd been sent to the mainland, she'd thought she would be met with kindness, and taken care of until the war ended. What would her mum think if she knew the truth? *Oh Mum, Mum . . .*

CHAPTER THIRTEEN

Clara, Julia and Vanda
Knowing True Love – Knowing Betrayal

Julia sat on the milking stool milking Lady Jane and felt glad that the cow was behaving herself for once and seemed to have got used to Julia's touch, as this left Julia time to enjoy her thoughts.

She was still reeling from the couple of hours she'd spent with Gareth over a week ago and her stomach muscles tensed as she thought of how they had almost made love. But something had stopped her, just as he was about to take her. She hadn't wanted to say no, but a fear in her had stayed Gareth. His reaction had been fraught with frustration, but he'd understood. Kissing her, he'd tried again, placing his hand on her thigh and gently squeezing, but she'd asked him to give her time.

Her body had thrilled at his touch, and begged of her to give into him, but a fear had held her back. Now, as she sat and relived those feelings, she couldn't understand herself. Gareth had said he would be careful, that he would withdraw in time so that she didn't become pregnant, but though she trusted him, something prevented her from allowing him to go that far.

The thought of his marriage, the feeling that he might be using her – whatever it was, going the whole way hadn't sat easy with her, but she regretted that now. Her thoughts gave her a tingle that ran from her stomach to between her legs, making her clutch her muscles tightly.

'You're doing all right with her, well done you. It took me a lot longer to get her to let me milk her.'

Julia jumped, but managed to keep her voice straight. 'Thanks, Polly.'

Usually cold towards her, Polly hardly passed the time of day, so it was nice to hear her use a friendly tone.

'I don't knaw if you knaw or not, but we hold a barn dance now and again. You and Rhoda should come, its great fun. There aren't many men to dance with, a few old farmers, but they're quite nifty on their feet. Oh, and Gareth sometimes comes along, if Vanda does.'

At the mention of Gareth's name Julia's heart skipped.

'You knaw Gareth, don't you? I saw you talking to him at the garden party. I'd be careful if I were you. Vanda can be a vixen if crossed.'

Julia felt her colour rise. 'Oh, I don't know him, only in as much as I helped him to bring that calf into the world a few weeks back, and we say hello. Vanda has no need to worry.'

How she said this so calmly, Julia didn't know, but she was surprised as Polly leaned closer to her. 'Just be careful, that's all I'm saying.'

Then, as she straightened, she shocked Julia to the core. 'Any road, it won't be a problem, him having an eye for you, as he's had his conscription papers.'

'Oh no! I – I mean, I . . . ' her heart dropped like a stone. Gareth going to war!

'Seems old Barry Taylor, our previous vet, is having to come out of retirement and look after the animals for us. The War Office take no prisoners. Some professions are exempt, but not vets it seems. Oh well, perhaps Vanda will be a nicer person once she understands what the rest of us are going through. She can be a bitch, that one.'

Julia's hands shook as she lifted the yoke and placed the two buckets of milk on each end of it. Carrying it around her neck, she took it to the large churns that stood by the gate for collection and emptied the milk into one of them. This done, she stood a moment, trying to steady herself. The thought of Gareth going away was unbearable to her.

'Are you all right, Julia? You've stood there an age staring into space. What's that Polly been saying? I saw her talking to you.'

It was Rhoda. She lowered her yolk and emptied the milk she carried, as Julia had. Trying to keep her voice steady, Julia told her what Polly had said.

'Perhaps it's as well, love. I mean, well, nothing can come of this attraction that you have for each other. Nothing but trouble that is. Look, let's go ahead with our plans to go to Blackpool, eh? We'll talk to Farmer Pickering later today about getting the time off. The haymaking is all done and it's not quite time to pick the potatoes yet, there's always a lull on the farm around now, so it'll be the best time.'

Even the thought of this trip didn't lift Julia, and yet it was the thing she wanted to do most in all the world. Going to Blackpool held the hope of finding her Clara. She would concentrate on that thought, and pray that it happened, as she had no right to her other thoughts – of how she would miss Gareth, and fear for him, and . . . *Oh God, I can't bear it, I can't . . .*

'Look, let's go down to the pub tonight and discuss our plans. It'll be fun, especially if we have a chance to talk to Farmer Pickering and get his consent today.'

'I – I can't, Rhoda. I'm meeting Gareth. It's the WI meeting tonight and Vanda will be there. I was thinking of calling it off, but now . . . Well, I have to see Gareth. I need to hear it from him, and, well . . . I need to be with him as often as I can before he leaves. Oh, Rhoda, I can't believe it. How do you bear it?'

Rhoda sighed. 'It's not easy. Sometimes it's unbearable, being away from my husband and daughter, but there's nothing I can do, and moping won't help, so I just get on with it.'

Julia's heart went out to Rhoda, and she felt guilty. She'd somehow become complacent about her friend's situation, thinking they were in the same boat, but they weren't. Rhoda had far more to contend with and Julia knew that she was about to find out just how much, once Gareth had left to go to war. And yet, she didn't have the right to feel this way. She wasn't Gareth's wife.

'The worst thing is not knowing if Roger even knows where I am, or if he has received my letters. Oh, don't let's talk about it. Come on. Mrs Pickering will be serving breakfast any minute, and we've still the dairy to wash down.'

'At least Polly has taken the cows back to the meadow. Look, I can see them all filing out in an orderly manner.'

'Yes. They know exactly what to do and when. That is except for their mess. They drop cowpats whenever and wherever. Race you back. And bagsy I yield the hose today, while you brush. I've done that for the last two days.'

'I think the first one back should get to hose down. Ready, steady . . . You cheat! Rhoda, you set off too soon!' But Julia's protests dissolved into a fit of giggles as Rhoda surged ahead laughing her head off.

The moment lightened, and Julia felt able to cope once more. She had tonight to look forward to. And she knew there would be no saying no this time. Tonight she would let Gareth make her his. She would join her soul to his, in the only way that they could. Because, no matter that Gareth belonged to another, he was hers in his soul, and she was going to have every part of him to place into her memory of him.

Vanda stared at the back of the woman who'd just spoken. A cough from her companion had the woman reeling round to face Vanda. Her face dropped into an expression that asked to be allowed to die. 'I – I . . . I'm sorry, Vanda, I didn't see you there. I – I . . . '

Vanda couldn't speak. Had she heard right? Did Glenis Hardman just say that Julia, the land girl, would miss Gareth more than *she* would?

'Perhaps you had better explain yourself. You were talking about my husband and one of those girls on Pickering's farm,

142

I believe.' Though this came out in a measured way that spoke of her disbelief and held her dignity, Vanda could feel herself crumbling inside. Not just with the humiliation, but with fear. Her Gareth wouldn't betray her, would he?

'I – I have nothing to say, it was just a joke. I – I . . . excuse me, I have to go.'

Vanda placed herself in Glenis's way. 'I don't think so. You were talking about my husband, and I have a right to know what you were saying.'

The women in the hall fell silent. The Women's Institute meeting had suddenly become much more interesting to them.

Glenis did as any trapped animal would – she went on the attack. 'Well, it's none of my business, I'm sure, but Gareth was seen kissing one of those girls from the farm. The pretty, dark-haired one.' At the sight of Vanda crumbling, Glenis softened. 'I don't think it is true, Vanda, you know what the gossipers of the village are like. He probably spoke to her for a little longer than they thought was proper, that's all.'

'Yes. That will be it, Vanda.' Vanda turned towards Lucy Maynard, who had been in conversation with Glenis. 'I heard Gareth telling my husband that one of the girls up at Pickering's had really shown some mettle, in helping him to calf that cow they lost. They were probably just talking about that.'

But Vanda's mind screamed at her, that the first version – the kissing – her Gareth . . . betraying her, was the true one.

Putting down the cake she'd picked up just before she heard the snippet of conversation that had shattered her world,

Vanda turned to face the room. A sea of faces swam before her – scornful faces, with expressions that delighted at her downfall. She had to get out of here!

Stumbling towards the door, she grabbed the handle but it wouldn't turn. Panic gripped her. They were locked in! 'Where's the key! Who's got the bloody key?'

'Vanda, it isn't locked, dear. There, it sticks sometimes, remember?'

'Don't patronise me, Phyllis Granger! Get out of my way.'

Once through the door, Vanda took a gulp of fresh air, then crumpled against the wall. Behind the doors, she heard a peel of laughter, and Glenis's high voice saying, 'Ha! She had that one coming to her.' And then all the room erupted in laughter.

Humiliated beyond endurance, Vanda pulled herself up straight. *Why didn't I see this coming?* she wondered. *We're happy, aren't we? We have orderly lives, everything runs smoothly. Gareth's life is how a vet's should be – trouble free, no worries. His house is run well, he has the time to devote to his practice that he needs. We know where we are with each other's emotions. When we are expected to perform, when we can sleep without being disturbed. It's how it should be. And when we do perform its magic, isn't it? All a couple could wish for, except . . . But babies will come. They will. They have to!*

Pulling herself up straight, she walked away from the hall with her head held high, conscious of dozens of eyes watching her through the windows. Well, she'd show them. She'd go home and confront Gareth, and then, once he had put her mind at rest, they would go out together. They'd go

144

to the pub, along the road from the church hall, where all the women made for once the meeting was over, and she'd make a show of just how close she and Gareth were.

Julia thought she would die with the feelings that were trembling through her as Gareth lifted his head from the deep kiss they had been in. 'Are you sure, my darling? Oh, Julia, I so want to make you mine, but only if you want to.'

'I do.'

A deep sigh came from Gareth as his lips met hers once more. They had driven just a few miles and parked in a gateway in a secluded area.

The kiss was gentle at first, but then deepened into a frenzy of tongues meeting and caressing, and hands finding places that thrilled. Somehow, clothes were discarded, without each consciously undressing.

The feel of Gareth's naked body against her own gave Julia a moment's doubt – a moment when she became aware of their surroundings, as the wind whipped the trees lining the gateway into a frenzy, and branches tapped the car window. But then as the sensuous feel of the leather seat of the car caressed her back, she lost herself in the ecstasy of the moment. Gareth was really going to make her his own.

All doubt left her as he entered her. She was lost. Lost to the exquisite feeling coursing through her, to Gareth's touch, to his movements inside her, and to his sighs that built to a moan that reverberated through her.

The moment held her fulfilment. Nothing could compare to what she was experiencing as Gareth's lips kissed every part he could reach, taking her nipples one by one into his mouth and gently sucking them. 'Oh, Gareth, Gareth, my love, hold me, hold me!'

The cry heralded a feeling that Julia could hardly bear, as wave after wave built to a crescendo inside her. Gareth's name tumbled from her. Her love for him flowed through her, as she urged him to hold still, to allow the pulsating of her inner self, that she could not control.

Trying to hold on to the feeling, but not able to, Julia clamped her legs around Gareth, rendering him unable to move. She felt his deep groan, his body shuddering and pulsating with hers, and then becoming still.

Realisation hit her as she came down from the feelings. She'd prevented him from pulling out of her!

They lay quietly, still joined, gasping for breath and reeling from what had just happened to them.

Gareth moved first. Kissing her face, his words were of love, and of thanks for all she'd given him. And she was enraptured. The worry of it left her. It was meant to be. She was Gareth's and nothing could take that from them.

Holding his face in her hands, she told him, 'I love you, Gareth, and I belong to you.'

'Oh, Julia, my Julia. I love you too. I love you with all that I am.'

His body moved, not to leave her, but to grind deeply into her once more. The feelings that had burned her, feelings that she'd never imagined possible, rekindled and answered his demands as she thrust herself towards him and accepted him pounding her with everything that he was, as if for the first time.

Gasps of pleasure came from her as in a fever of renewed passion they sought and found the heart of each other once more.

This time the release was total, and hollered from her, as if she was an animal, as she writhed beneath her Gareth, taking all he had to give, and giving all that she was to her man.

Neither of them was aware of the car's interior lighting up, as they clung onto the last remnants of the feelings that gripped them, and cried out their undying love, their desire, taking their love to its ultimate consummation.

By the time it was over, the car was in darkness again.

They lay still across the bench seat, reluctant to uncouple, kissing away the tears that seeped from their eyes. They whispered their love, lamenting having to part, until Gareth moved gently from inside her and held her to him.

'I've never experienced anything like that, Julia. Thank you. Thank you for accepting all of me.'

'Oh, Gareth, I could do no other. I love you. Oh, why does it have to be so complicated? I want to be your wife, to have your children, to live a normal life.'

'Don't cry, darling. I can't bear it. Not you crying with anguish, I can't. Your tears of love that joined mine were something I've never known, and melted my heart, but to hear you so distressed, that's unbearable. We will be together. I promise.'

'How? You have to go away in a couple of weeks. You have no time to file for a divorce. But even if you had, you said that Vanda won't let you go. Oh, it's impossible!'

'Don't despair. There will be a way. Will you write to me? I can't bear to be away from you and not hear from you.'

'Yes. I'll write. But you must find a way that we can be together, Gareth. Even if we live in sin. You have to leave Vanda now. You have to tell her tonight.'

Gareth lifted himself to a sitting position, and manoeuvred himself to begin to dress. Finding her clothes, he gathered them and handed them to her. 'I'll sort out something, I promise. I'll talk to Vanda tonight. It's not going to be easy, but she will have to accept it.'

'Promise. Promise me, Gareth. I – I mean, there could be consequences of what we just did. I can't face that alone. Not again. I love you, I gave myself to you. You have to take care of me now.'

'I will. I give you my solemn promise. But, let's hope that nothing comes of what we just did. Nothing except the cementing of our love. I can't think of you having to live with that stigma again, as I can do nothing in the immediate future about setting up home together. I have to report in two weeks. My destiny isn't in my own hands.'

A sinking feeling took Julia. Gareth was right. There was nothing he could do about his situation, or hers, if her worse fears were realised.

Leaving Vanda and setting up home with her wasn't an option open to him. Well, leaving Vanda was, but them being together, no.

'Couldn't you announce your intention to leave Vanda? And make our love public?'

'I don't know, darling, it seems terribly cruel to do it just like that as I am about to leave. Let's think about it. And let's hope that our getting carried away doesn't have consequences. I mean . . . I'm sorry, Julia. So sorry. I'm torn in two now. We should have taken care. I'm going to be worried sick about you. Oh, my darling, I love you, and yet, it all seems so hopeless. This bloody war!'

They clung together. At a time when Julia knew that she should feel safe, she didn't – a deep fear lay in her as if a lead weight had been tied to her heart.

CHAPTER FOURTEEN

Clara and Lindsey
The Ebbing of Life

Clara woke to the sound of Lindsey heaving her heart out into their piddle pot. She scrambled out of bed and went to Lindsey to hold her. 'Oh, Lindsey, I thought you've looked peaky lately, what's wrong with you?'

'I've me belly up, that's what. Eeh, Clara, what am I to do? Mickey won't let me stay and have a babby here. Where will I go? I can't go back to no convent. I can't.'

Clara didn't know what to say. How can someone as young as Lindsey fall for a baby?

'Maybe it's not that, Lindsey, maybe you've caught a bug.'

'I've not seen me monthly for two months now, Clara. You knaw what that means as well as I do.'

'Is that how you know that you're pregnant?'

'Aye, it is. And now that you've started yours, you'll have to watch out. Your breasts are developing at last, but that's nowt to be proud of as it will lead you down the same path as me.'

A shiver went through Clara that wasn't all down to the freezing cold. There was no cheer in this attic bedroom at the best of times, but since winter had begun to bite, it held no comfort at all.

'Don't worry. You've a way to go yet. You're still like a boy in your figure. But me. Oh God, what's going to happen to me, Clara?'

As Lindsey said this, she once more leaned over the pot and heaved. The yellow bile she brought up smelt bad and had Clara heaving with her.

'Eeh, Clara, give over. I need the pot. Turn away, or have a sip of water or sommat.'

When the bout passed, they sat together on Lindsey's bed holding hands.

'Lindsey, we'll have to tell Dolly. She'll know what to do.'

'Aye, she'll send me to an abortionist, that'll be her answer. But I'm scared, Clara. The last girl who went there never came back. We buried her in a pauper's grave.'

Clara couldn't speak. This was something she had no knowledge of. When she did find her voice and ask what an abortionist was, she felt sick to her core. 'You mean, they take the baby from you? From your stomach?'

'Yes. Well, it ain't exactly a babby, just the beginnings of one.'

For Clara this was all too much. It was not something she could even imagine. She put her arm around Lindsey and held her close. The thought of losing her was too hard to bear.

151

She thought of the lovely Shelley, saw her face as she turned and waved, and a tear plopped onto her cheek. Shelley would have known what to do. But Clara felt helpless. She could see no alternative to offer Lindsey. They could run away, but how would they look after a baby?

'Look, don't worry. I've left this long enough. I'm to go to Dolly. It's me only way. Maybe I'll be all right after the abortion, some must be. Maybe that girl just got unlucky. I mean, if every girl died after what she does, that woman wouldn't do it, would she?'

They dressed in silence and then held hands as they sought Dolly out together.

'Eeh, lass, I've been meaning to get one of them caps for you. I thought you a mite young to get caught. Naive of me. Or, rather, bloody stupid! I put off till tomorrow what I should've done today. Mickey'll kill me. You'll have to go to Mrs Rindle. There's nowt else for it. You'll be all right. You're a strong lass. That Patsy was a poor thing as it was. Nowt'll happen to you. Here, take this tenner and get yourself round to hers. Do you knaw where she lives?'

'Aye, I went with Patsy. Can Clara come with me?'

'I don't see why not. There's no horseracing today, so no bets to pick up. Mind, there's some deliveries later, but you'll be back for them, so that'll be fine.'

Deliveries were a mystery to Clara. She had to ride a bike with an attached basket. The basket would be full of small brown bags, all covered over with newspapers to make her look as if she was a newspaper boy. The packages had to be dropped off at various addresses, and money collected for each one. Always she was cautioned that if she saw a policeman she was to pop a few rolled newspapers through a few doors until she was out of their sight.

The unsavoury characters who took delivery of the parcels scared her, but she knew she had the protection of Mickey. And though they moaned about the amount of money they were to give her, they all paid up.

Her curiosity got the better of her this time. As she walked along Cookson Street with Lindsey she asked her, 'What's in them parcels that I have to deliver, Lindsey?'

'I never asked, but I guessed at contraband. Black market stuff, or drugs. The sort that put you on cloud nine, like hashish. I did have a parcel split once, and that had white powder in it, so I thought it might be cocaine, but I don't knaw for sure.'

Clara wondered at this world she found herself in. It was a million miles away from her island life.

They knocked on the door of a house in a back street – Clara hadn't noted its name. All of the houses had a small garden in the front and looked as though they had known better days – as if they had once housed moneyed folk but had fallen from grace. They had bay windows and steps to their doors. The one they were stood in front had a shiny brass knocker, which reverberated in a hollow way as if the house it summoned was empty.

They waited. Then they heard the sound of shuffling feet, and of bolts being drawn back. When the door eventually opened, an old bent-over woman appeared.

'Yes? Who is it?' Her eyes squinted against the light.

She looked as though she belonged in the last century. Her long, grey frock swept the floor as she beckoned them in and they followed her along the dark hall. On her head she wore a bonnet of the kind that Clara had only ever seen in pictures. Her wiry grey hair stuck out from the bonnet in unruly curls that framed a face that was the most wrinkled one Clara had ever seen.

As the woman opened the second door of the hallway, she asked, 'How far gone are you?'

'I – I missed two of me periods.'

'Humph! You should have come afore now. You girls allus leave it late, then expect miracles. Well, I ain't got none. I can have a go, but I ain't saying as it'll be successful. Get your clothes off, I'll be back in a mo.'

The room was quite bright, which surprised Clara. There was a large window that looked out over a backyard. There was little furniture in the room. A set of shelves along one wall contained rows of brown medicine jars, and other jars made of pottery. These were sandy-coloured and had labels on them.

Seeing Clara's curiosity, Lindsey leant towards her and whispered, 'She's a medicine woman, a sort of healer, as well as seeing to unwanted pregnancies. They say that she has healing powers and that her potions can cure owt from headaches to gout.'

As Lindsey spoke, she undressed. At the back of the room there was a bed, like the ones that doctors had in their surgeries, a kind of stretcher on wheels. This was covered with a white sheet. Everything looked clean and clinical which reassured Clara, giving her confidence that the woman knew what she was doing.

As she came back into the room, the old woman gestured with her head to Lindsey. 'Reet. Get yoursen up on that trolley. There's a stool there to step on.' She was carrying a tray laid with instruments, which she put down on a table next to the trolley before disappearing again.

'Oh, Lindsey, are you going to be all right? I'm scared.'

A tear ran down Lindsey's face. Her eyes held a terror. Her naked body shivered. Clara took her hand. It felt cold yet clammy in hers. Her own fear had her heart racing. Sweat beads formed and trickled down her face.

When the door opened again, the woman backed in with a bowl of hot water in her hands, and some orange, rubber pipes over her arm.

'D'yer want t'stay, lass? You can go into me other room if you like. It's a waiting room, and you can sit and look at some magazines or comics while I get on with things here.'

Lindsey's grip tightened on Clara's hand as if she was silently begging Clara not to leave her.

'No, I'll stay with my friend, thank you.'

Everything in her wanted to turn and run but she took a deep breath and tried to muster up some courage to support Lindsey. Turning towards Lindsey so as not to see what was going on, Clara looked into her friend's terrified face and gave her a weak, everything-will-be-all-right, kind of smile. Then something in Lindsey's vulnerability gave Clara strength, and she widened the smile and gave Lindsey's hand a reassuring squeeze as the woman said, 'Reet, open your legs and bend your knees, lass. That's it, as wide as you can.'

Lindsey clung on even harder to Clara's hand, making her almost cry out as her nails dug into her skin. But it was the blood-curdling scream that came from Lindsey that almost undid Clara. She flung herself across her friend and hung onto her, trying to make soothing noises through the tears that rained down her cheeks.

The colour drained from Lindsey. Froth appeared at her mouth and incoherent words came from her blue lips.

Clara sobbed: 'Lindsey, Lindsey, don't. Oh, Lindsey, be strong. Be strong.'

'There. That's the last of it. I've just to wash her out.'

Clara looked towards the woman and was shocked to see her covered in blood. Even her face was splashed with it. She steeled herself to look towards Lindsey's open legs. A dish lay between them, its contents resembled a piece of liver, but all in bits. And so much blood, the sheet under Lindsey ran red with it.

She watched as the woman placed the end of one of the rubber hoses in the hot water in the bowl, sucked it, and then placed that end, now running with water, inside Lindsey.

Lindsey moaned. Clara knew fear as she looked at Lindsey's grey-tinged pallor. 'Is she going to be all right?'

'Aye, she'll take an hour or so to recover, but she'll be fine. There's a bit of bleeding, but nowt to worry over. I'll bring some fresh water and you can wash her down, and dress her. She'll need to rest for an hour afore she can leave. The body makes up the lost blood in naw time, so don't you be worrying.'

As she washed the shivering Lindsey down, a feeling took Clara that she was no longer a child, that she'd been dragged into adulthood before she was ready, that all she had known was gone for ever. She wanted to mourn that, to kick and scream against it, to be allowed to go back – back to what now seemed like carefree days. She knew that a thousand times over she'd rather face the unfriendly folk of the island than be where she was now, witnessing the horrible procedure of a child being taken from the womb of her friend.

Shifting her position so that she could wash Lindsey between her legs, Clara was gripped by fear as Lindsey suddenly began to shake uncontrollably. Her tongue protruded from her mouth and her eyes stared out of her head as her body jerked in movements that had her almost falling off the trolley.

Clara screamed out her anguish. 'Help! Help!'

The door was flung open and the woman appeared. She looked now as if she hadn't done anything to Lindsey as she was clad in a long white frock under a grey apron which she'd passed over her head and tied at each side. There was not a spot of blood in sight, and she looked for all the world like the innocent old lady.

'She's fitting. That'll be the shock.' As she said this, the old woman picked up a roll of cloth and threw it towards Clara. 'Ram that into her mouth. Make sure it's placed on her tongue to stop her from swallowing it, then help me hold her.'

Trying to get the roll into Lindsey's mouth wasn't easy as her teeth were clamped together, but once this was done another fear gripped Clara as the old woman shouted: 'Oh, no! Oh my God, she's haemorrhaging. Quick. Help me to elevate her legs.'

Clara stared in horror as blood spurted from Lindsey, but she managed to do as she was bid, and soon they had blocks under the bottom half of the trolley, making it look as though Lindsey would slide off the other end.

Prayers tumbled from Clara: *Please, God, don't take Lindsey, Please, please!*

'It's slowing a bit. Here, get me purse from over there. Now, get that tenner out that the girl gave me. In the front part of the purse, you'll find an address. Run like the wind, girl, and tell the old doc to get here quick.'

The house was easy to find. After all her deliveries and collections, Clara knew Blackpool really well. Once she had established that she was in Chesterfield Road, she knew that Whalley Road was off the Gynn.

A man, even older than the abortionist, answered the door. After Clara had explained what was happening, he grunted.

'Huh, old Ada been at her butchering again, has she? One of these days, that old witch will swing from a rope.'

'Please hurry, sir.'

'My hurrying days are over, lass. I can only do what I can do, and that ain't always what folk want of me.'

'But me friend might die!'

'I shouldn't wonder at it. That old witch should be stopped, but we've all got so many skeletons in the cupboard that we can't do a lot to stop her. Let me get me coat. You run along to the Gynn and get a cab for me. That'll be the quickest way that I can get there. Did she send some money with you?'

Clara handed over the tenner, before running back to the Gynn Island.

The old woman met them at the door. 'She's badly, Ted. You'll need all your skill to save her. And it was a simple procedure, too. Everything went well at first.'

'These things never go well, Ada. You shouldn't be doing them. Let them take their chances. They did that that gets them in the family way, so they should face the consequences, better that than losing their life. I don't knaw if we can cover up many more of them – the coroner was more than suspicious last time.'

'I knaw, you're reet. And it's not as if I end up making owt, as I allus give it to you, but I feel sorry for the lasses, it ain't their fault they land on me doorstep. This one's with Mickey, so do all you can, he were reet upset over the last one.'

'Bloody hell, Ada! You'll have us both killed in our beds one of these days. Let me take a look at her.'

As Ada led the doctor through, she turned to Clara. 'Not you, lass. You get back to Mickey's. No doubt you've sommat he'll need you to be doing. But listen up. If he puts you on the game, you make sure you've got some protection in place. Don't do owt without it, d'yer hear me?'

Clara wanted to protest, but she knew that if she was absent from Mickey's when he needed the deliveries done then she'd be in for a lot of trouble. She didn't want that, she wanted to be able to come back here and stay with Lindsey. If she got all done that she was meant to, then Dolly might arrange that for her. She'd want someone keeping an eye on Lindsey and looking out for her.

'Can I just say goodbye to Lindsey, please? She may wonder where I am. I'll be quick.'

'Aye, she looks unconscious, but she'll hear you. Be quick.'

Seeing Lindsey lying motionless like a lifeless doll, her skin a grey colour, made Clara gasp with pain and fear. 'Lindsey, its Clara. You're going to be all right. The doctor's here. Fight,

Lindsey. Don't die. Please, Lindsey, please don't die. I've to go, but I'll be back, then I won't leave you until you're better.' With this she bent and kissed Lindsey's cold cheek.

As she left the house a feeling came over Clara that she would never see Lindsey again. Her heart felt as though it would break.

CHAPTER FIFTEEN

Julia and Vanda
Revenge Has No Fury

Saying goodbye to Gareth had been a wrench. He'd been gone for three weeks now. With no word from him, Julia was beginning to doubt him. And to add to her worry, her period was six days late. Her shame prevented her from telling Rhoda this. How was it that she'd lost herself so deeply in Gareth's love-making that she'd taken such a risk without even thinking about it? And not once, but twice! *Dear God, please let my period start. Please. I promise you that I'll never do anything as bad as going with a married man again, I promise, but please, please don't let me be pregnant!*

But even as she pleaded, she knew it was too late. Her anguish creased her, her fear almost drowned her. *What am I to do? What can I do?*

'Julia, there's someone to see you.'

Julia looked up from scattering feed for the chickens. She'd had to break the ice from the trough that the chickens got their water from, leaving her fingers so cold that she could hardly grasp the handfuls of grain to give them. Tipping the small sack upside down she scattered the rest of the contents and moved towards the door of the hen coop.

Rhoda's voice had held an anxious tone.

When Julia stepped outside the coop she knew why. Vanda stood outside the house, her arms folded, her look one of anger and defiance.

Oh, Lord, she knows! But how? And why now? With Gareth gone, and it all happening weeks ago, how could Vanda find out?

As she came up to Vanda and went to greet her, Vanda's face changed. An ugly expression crossed it. 'Have you heard from my husband?'

'No. I – I, why should I?'

'Don't come little Miss Innocent with me, missy!'

Mrs Pickering, who had stood by the door of the farmhouse, stepped forward. 'I think you had both better come inside. Julia? Vanda? Please, I don't knaw what this is all about, but it's better you talk it through inside. I can make you both a cup of tea.'

'I don't want to drink tea with my husband's mistress, thank you very much.'

'What? Julia, is this true, lass?'

Julia's face coloured. She felt out of her depth and couldn't think what to say. The word mistress had thrown her. It sounded so dirty, but then, she was dirty, wasn't she?

Rhoda had audibly caught her breath. Julia looked over to her, hoping she would be able to help her out, but the look of shock on her face told that she wasn't able to. No one could, Julia realised. She was in this alone.

Taking all her courage in her hands, she held her head high. 'Gareth and I are in love, yes.'

'What? He isn't free to be "in love"! He's my husband! How dare you come here, and disrupt our lives. And in love, you call it. A dirty tryst in the back of his car, in a gateway. Is that what you call being "in love?" You're disgusting. *Disgusting!*'

Mrs Pickering stepped forward. 'Now, Vanda. I know you're upset, but are you sure about this? I mean—'

'Sure? They were seen! Glenda Boslin's husband saw them. He turned his car in the very gateway and saw them both. Naked! And, doing it! He saw it was Gareth's car, and then saw this one lift her head in full view of his headlights. He took a while to tell me, but Glenda made him in the end.'

'Julia?'

Julia looked into Mrs Pickering's shocked face. A memory of the car lighting up came to her, but at the time she hadn't registered it. *Oh God*. She wished she could be anywhere but here with the accusing faces of Mrs Pickering, and Rhoda, and the hate-filled one of Vanda staring at her. 'We're in love. Gareth loves me. I – I'm sorry, but I, well, I think you know that your marriage is over. Gareth is going to get a divorce. We're going to marry.'

'Divorce! Are you out of your head? Gareth loves me. He cried when he left. He . . . he . . . ' Vanda looked around her from one to the other of them. Spit ran from the side of her slack mouth. 'She's lying!' Turning to Mrs Pickering, her body seemed to slump. 'Help me. Make her go away. Please help me.'

The plea was childlike. Julia was filled with a great shame and a feeling of everyone hating her.

Mrs Pickering moved forward, just as Polly came around the corner. 'Polly. Help me with Vanda. She's had a nasty shock.'

'Oh? What's happened? Oh! Is this to do with you, Julia? I warned you.'

'You knew?'

'Not for sure, Mrs Pickering, but there was talk. I told Julia to be careful, and not to do anything she would regret. It seems she didn't heed my warning, if this is about her and Gareth?'

'It is. Help me get Vanda inside to a chair.'

Vanda's sobs wracked her body. They creased her face into an ugly expression. Snot ran from her nose and spittle from her mouth as huge gasps and moans came from her.

Julia stood motionless, not sure what to do as she watched Mrs Pickering and Polly take Vanda inside the house.

Once the door had closed on them, Rhoda moved to her side. 'Oh, Julia, what now? I didn't know it had gone this far.'

A tear seeped out of the corner of Julia's eyes. 'It's worse than you think. I'm late.'

'No! God, Julia!'

'Please don't abandon me, Rhoda. I was driven by love. I love Gareth. And he loves me. He does.'

'I'm at a loss as to what to say.'

'What can you say? What can anyone say?'

'You'll have to tell Mrs Pickering. It will be up to her what she does. If she reports you, then it will be up to the government, the Department of Agriculture and Fisheries. If they dismiss you, you'll be on your own. Oh, I don't know. It's a mess, Julia. I thought that you and Gareth were going to be discreet, and sensible! Why? Why risk a baby?'

A despair entered Julia as she felt a distance opening up between herself and Rhoda. A distance that she'd endured before, and didn't want to endure again. 'Will you stand by me, Rhoda?'

The question hung between them. Julia couldn't read Rhoda's expression, but then a movement gave her hope as Rhoda stepped forward and opened her arms. Going into them, Julia's emotions gave way and sobs wracked her body.

'Poor, Julia.' The stroking of her hair soothed her. 'We'll get round this somehow. Will Gareth stand by you?'

'Yes, he promised. Oh, I just wish he would write so that I knew where he was. Once I tell him, I know that he will leave Vanda and support me. He said he would.'

'Let's hope he keeps his promise. In the meantime, you will have to hope that Mrs Pickering allows you to stay on, as I just don't know where you could go.'

The door from the kitchen opened at that moment. 'Look at them! They're in this together! Well, you won't get away with it, you hussies. I'm telling you now, you won't take my husband from me.'

With this, Vanda turned and ran towards the yard gate. Polly went to go after her, but Mrs Pickering stopped her. 'Let her go, Polly, her need is to be at home. Lass has to think through her marriage and what she is going to do. Julia, will you come inside with me a moment, please? Polly, you and Rhoda get on with your chores. We'll be all behind at this rate.'

★   ★   ★

Julia felt as if she was standing in front of her old school-mistress as Mrs Pickering took a chair from under the table and sat on it without inviting Julia to do the same. 'Julia, I am ashamed, and very disappointed in you. What have you to say?'

'I – I'm sorry, Mrs Pickering. Please let me stay. I know that Gareth will sort everything out when he comes home after his training. He promised me that we would be together.'

'It's true, then? Everything that Vanda suspects? You've actually started relations with Gareth, knawing as he were married?'

Julia hung her head. She wanted to scream out that Gareth was as much to blame. That it wasn't all her, but instead she just said, 'We are in love.'

'In love! Gareth is married. He's supposed to be in love with his wife. Poor Vanda is distraught. This is a wicked thing that you've both done to her, and just as her husband has to leave her to go to war. Don't you knaw that men are gullible, lass? Don't you knaw that if we women invite them, they come running? You should have had more care for others' feelings. Not just Vanda's, but meself and Mr Pickering. We've given you a home! And this is how you repay us, by having a sordid affair with our vet!'

Julia cringed. She had nothing more to say. She'd been tried, judged and found guilty. Just as she always had been.

'Well, I'll have to talk over your position with Mr Pickering, but I for one want you to leave here. The Ministry'll have to place you elsewhere. It's cruel to expect Vanda to carry on living in the same village as yourself. Everyone'll knaw what you've done to her. And with her being a very proud lady, she'll fall heavily. I don't think that she deserves that. She's innocent in all of this. Now, go and get on with the daily chores. I'll speak to you again later, with me and Mr Pickering's decision.'

Julia left the house without a word. Outside she found Rhoda herding the cattle inside. They were only let out for a few hours in the morning, but had to be housed inside where it was warmer and they could be fed and watered. Joining Rhoda, who was shouting 'cup, cup' at the top of her voice, she shrugged to Rhoda's enquiring gesture.

'I'll know later, but I don't think they are going to let me stay.'

Rhoda expressed her sorrow. She didn't want to carry on here without Julia, but she would have no choice.

Vanda reached home. Her heart was full of the need for revenge, and for that revenge to mean the end of those conspiring girls on Pickering's farm. No logic entered her overwrought mind as she thought of ways to rid herself of them both.

I'll kill them both! It's the only way! But how?

No common sense entered her at her appalling thoughts as she stomped from room to room of her house. Stopping in her husband's dressing room, she opened his wardrobe door. Her anger erupted as she looked at his clothes. Dragging them down off their hangers, she screamed at them: 'You betrayed me! You betrayed me!'

With a strength she didn't know she possessed, she tore at his shirts, feeling satisfied as the material gave and ripping sounds filled the room.

With them strewn around her, she caught her breath. Gareth's suits swayed on the rail in front of her. Running to the kitchen she took a knife from the drawer. Back in the dressing room, she stabbed at the suits. 'I hate you! I hate you!' Falling to her knees, she clung to a pair of Gareth's trousers. 'I love you. Oh, Gareth, I love you. Why? Why? How could you do this to me?'

Curling up into a ball, Vanda whimpered. 'We were happy, weren't we? We had everything in our lives sorted. Orderly, the way you liked it. We were good together. When it was the nights for our love making, we were sexy with each other. We played the game. We gave each other feelings that took us to a wonderful place. A place where we swore, and spoke dirty. A place where we found pleasure in everything we did with each other. How could you betray that?'

A picture of Julia came into her mind. And she knew that while that girl was around, all that Gareth was would be compromised. 'Girls like her are evil. *Evil!* They tempt men away from their wives. But why, my Gareth . . . why?'

Vanda wouldn't let her mind stray to the truth of it – that Gareth was in any way unhappy. She could only see Julia as the temptress and knew that if she wasn't here when Gareth returned then everything would go back to normal.

Crawling on her hands and knees, she made it to her own bed. The bed that Gareth visited her in when it was their night for love. Exhaustion took her as she lay on top of the covers. As her eyes closed, she thought of every possibility of how to rid herself of the evil bitches. One way that came to her had her smiling as the picture she conjured up of their burning flesh gave her intense pleasure. *Yes, that's it! And no more than they deserve. And I have the means – the cans of spare petrol in the garage!*

Vets, like doctors, had special permission to hoard a couple of cans to make sure they had enough if they were called out to an emergency. *Well, my plans are an emergency. I need that petrol to destroy those bitches!*

It wasn't until the flames roaring from the barn where Julia and Rhoda slept licked the sky that a realisation of the horror of what she'd done came to Vanda. Running to her car, she drove like a mad person back to her house.

Waking to strange sounds, Julia coughed. Her throat burned. She tried to see across the barn to where Rhoda slept, but a wall of flames met her. '*Rhoda! Rhoda!*'

Getting out of bed, she went towards the flames, but the heat beat her back. *Oh God . . . God!*

Voices called their names. Screams, hysterical screams, came to her. Smoke swirled around her, whipping up a heat that scorched her lungs and clawed at her skin. She had to get out! Crawling on all fours to the hatch that led to the ladder, Julia managed to pull the bolt free. Lifting the latch, a belch of smoke engulfed her, choking her.

'Help me! Help me!'

'Julia. Climb down. Quickly! The hay down here's alight, it'll all go up. Hurry, hurry. Where's Rhoda?'

Julia couldn't answer the anguished voice of Farmer Pickering. Her strength was ebbing from her; her mind wouldn't think straight.

A hand grabbed her ankle. 'Come on. Place your foot on the rung. Rhoda! *Rhoda!* Can you hear me, lass? Come this way towards my voice if you can!'

But there was no answering call.

'There. One step at a time. That's it. Get her outside, Polly. I'll go in and see if I can find Rhoda.'

Julia's whole body shivered with shock as she sat at the table in Farmer Pickering's kitchen. Mrs Pickering sat opposite her, not talking, her face showing her shock.

The clanging of bells made them both jump. The door opened and they looked towards it. In the light of the fire, Julia saw a fire engine and men scurrying about outside.

A policeman walked in through the door with Polly and Farmer Pickering behind him. Farmer Pickering's face was blackened, his body clad in soot-ridden, torn pyjamas. Polly's hair was tied in pipe cleaners, her nightie smutted and ripped.

'We – we didn't . . . There's no sight of Rhoda.' Polly slumped down at the table. 'Oh, Mrs Pickering, that poor girl, that poor girl.'

A sob came from Mrs Pickering, but she didn't move. She just stared at the policeman. Farmer Pickering went to her side.

Julia couldn't take in what Polly was saying. Rhoda? Was she saying that Rhoda was gone? She couldn't be, could she? *Oh God, no . . . no!*

Questions came at her, but Julia could only nod or shake her head as the policeman made notes.

'Now, you're saying you heard nowt till the shouting of Mr Pickering? I need you to confirm this verbally, lass.'

Julia swallowed, 'Yes . . . Oh, I don't know. Something woke me. Noises, then shouts and screams.'

'I did, Officer, I heard sommat.' Polly's face was whiter than it had been, her expression showing that something had just dawned on her. 'I – I heard a car. It's what woke me, it was going like the clappers. Its lights shone in me bedroom window, and as it rounded the bend, it skidded. I looked out . . . I think as it were Vanda Maling's car.'

'Naw!' Mrs Pickering looked from Polly to Julia.

A deep shudder in the pit of her stomach had Julia wanting to retch as she read the accusation in the look. *Oh, God! No! No!*

'Vanda Maling? Why? I mean, surely not. Unless, someone stole her car. I mean, well, I can't imagine owt else.'

'Officer.' Farmer Pickering's voice was grave. His eyes found Julia's, but his look wasn't of condemnation, as his wife's had been, but of pity. 'There's sommat as you should knaw.'

Vanda heard the vehicle. She hadn't stopped shaking since she'd got back home. Moving to the window, she peered out. *The police! Oh, God! They know . . . How? Help me, help me.*

Her mind screamed at her what would happen if the Land Girls were dead, as surely they must be. *I'll hang! Oh God, no! And the shame of a trial . . . No! Oh, why did I do it? Why?* At that moment, she knew what she must do.

Rushing over to the bureau where Gareth kept his keys, she grabbed the bunch she needed, and crossed the kitchen to the door that led to Gareth's surgery. Once inside, she locked the door again. *By the time they get in here, it will be all over. You'll be sorry then, Gareth, you bastard!*

171

With this thought all feeling left her. No fear or remorse entered her – she was an empty shell. Rummaging through the drawers of medications, she found a box of the lethal injections that were used when an animal couldn't be saved. Ripping open one of the pods, Vanda filled a phial with the liquid. She felt nothing as she stuck the needle into her thigh. Within seconds, she was lying on the floor. Her mind gave her Gareth, swirling around her. His smile that she loved warmed her as the life ebbed from her.

CHAPTER SIXTEEN

Clara and Lindsey
Feeling the Wrath of Mickey

'So it is that you've not been well, Lindsey? And why is that, then?'

Clara was shocked that Mickey seemed to be in the dark about what had happened, but as she looked at Dolly's terrified face, she realised that Dolly had kept the truth from him. And she'd most likely found a way of putting the blame onto Lindsey.

When Lindsey didn't answer, Mickey's face became a mask of anger. 'Well, you can get your arse off that sofa, as Nick the Hick is coming around later, and he wants you ready for him.'

Without thinking, Clara blurted out: 'She can't, Mickey, she's had an abortion, and she nearly died. She's still not well.'

'An abortion, is it? And how did such a state of affairs come about?' His gaze went to Dolly.

'I have too much to do around here, Mickey. I can't be seeing that the girls do as they're told, I can only give them the cap and tell them to wear it. If they don't, then what can I do?'

'So, you were for having sex with the punters with no protection. And what did you think would happen, you stupid cow?'

'She wasn't given it, Mickey.'

As soon as the words were out, Clara saw Dolly's face change. She shrank away from the anger Dolly directed at her and the screeching of her voice: 'Get out, you, you bitch! How dare you lie? What d'yer knaw about it any road? Eh? Nowt. You posh, think-yourself-better-than-us little runt! I reckon if you knaw so much that you should take Lindsey's place. You've flowered well over these last few weeks.'

Mickey looked from Clara to Dolly, then back at Clara. His eyes travelled from her feet to her breasts. 'I think you might be right, Dolly. Can you fix her up? Make her look a bit older. Give her a bit of glamour. That should do it?'

'Naw. I'll do it. I'll go with him.' Lindsey stood up, but her body swayed. Stick thin, she still looked as though death had trampled her. A vicious shove from Mickey sent her reeling backwards. She landed heavily on the sofa.

Her cry gave Clara wings. Hurtling herself at Mickey, she flailed at him with her fists. 'Leave her alone, you bully. You could kill her!'

A pain seared her head as Mickey grabbed her hair. 'Gerroff, you little tyke, you.'

The slap he gave her stung Clara's cheek. Losing her balance her body slammed into the sideboard.

'She's getting to be trouble. It'll do her good to have a session with Nick the Hick. I'll get her ready, Mickey.'

'I'm not finished here yet. I'm not convinced that you did right by Lindsey, Dolly. I reckon as you're getting a bit complacent with the whole set-up.' Mickey had grabbed the front of Dolly's frock. His left fist swung back, and then forward with such a force that when it landed, Clara heard the sickening sound of Dolly's jaw cracking.

Out cold, Dolly lay prostrate on the floor. Mickey lifted his foot and landed a vicious kick in Dolly's ribs. 'I've had enough, Dolly. Is it that you are hearing me, you freak? You man in woman's clothing? Get yourself up. And get this one ready. Nick has to have one of them, and with this one being a virgin, I reckon he'll let it go that he can't have Lindsey this time.'

Clara felt a terror enter her. Her mind wouldn't give her the truth that she was to have that awful thing done to her that had made Lindsey pregnant. *No, God! No. Don't let it happen.*

Mickey left and slammed the door behind him.

Lindsey's voice penetrated Clara's fear and offered hope, 'Help me up, Clara. Come on, we've got to get out of here. We have to escape before Dolly recovers.'

At a moan from Dolly, Clara hesitated in going to Lindsey. Dolly's plea had her unsure of what to do.

'Don't leave me. Help me up. If you go, he'll kill me . . . Lindsey, Clara, please don't go!'

'Naw. Clara, we have to go. Come to me. Give me your hand. We're getting away from here before it's too late for you. Let Dolly stew. It's naw more than she deserves.'

Clara looked from Dolly to Lindsey, and in that moment she knew they had to get away. Where they would go, she had no idea, but they would find somewhere. Surely someone out there would help them. Arnold? Yes. She didn't want to involve Arnold, but he would help them, or at least he would know what to do.

Stepping over Dolly, and kicking away the hand that tried to grasp her leg, Clara made it to Lindsey.

'I'll scream. If he hears me, you'll be done for, you scumbags.'

'Dolly, if you never do owt else for anyone in your whole life, let us go. We've never done owt to you. Just give us time to get away. Do sommat decent for once.'

Dolly looked up at them, her expression one of hate. Her mouth opened, but Lindsey was too quick for her. Where she found the strength to throw herself over Dolly, Clara didn't know, but Dolly couldn't move, and Lindsey held her hand over her mouth so that she couldn't shout out either. Dolly's muffled cries showed her pain.

'Quick, get to the kitchen, Clara. Find a cloth of some sort that we can stuff into her mouth. Dolly's eyes opened wide, her expression begging them not to do this, but though Clara felt afraid and sorry for Dolly, she knew that Lindsey was right. They had no choice.

Once outside, they ran as fast as both of their injured bodies would let them. Holding hands, they made it to the corner, then stood out of sight and peeped back at the house. Nothing stirred.

'Come on, Clara. We can make it to the tram, down Talbot Road. I've a couple of pennies in me pocket.'

Shivering from the cold, they alighted from the tram in South Shore. Clara could see Arnold at his stall. 'I know that man over there. Shall we ask for his help?'

'I don't knaw. D'yer think as he'll want to call the police?'

'He might, but would that be a bad thing?'

'Aye, it would. It could go two ways. They could send us to a care home, or, if we get the lot that's in Mickey's pay, then we could land right back where we came from, and facing the wrath of Mickey.'

This terrified Clara. She didn't want either of those. But who did she know that might help them?

'Let's go and find Tinker. He allus has an answer for any problem. He'll be at work now.'

As they walked towards the Pleasure Beach they passed Arnold's stall, but he was busy with customers and didn't notice Clara. She wanted for all the world to go to him. He must have wondered what had happened to her. He may not even have known about poor Shelley, or at least not that she was the girl who had been killed. She made up her mind that as soon as they were safe and settled, she would visit him and let him know what had been happening.

Tinker could only suggest that he sneaked them into his bedroom at his lodgings. 'We all stay in the same lodgings, paid for by the family as owns the rides. It's part of our pay. It's a good lodging. And the bloke as runs it won't bat an eyelid at me bringing you back there. Look, I'll be finished soon. Go into the café and keep warm, tell them that you're waiting for Tinker. They won't mind.'

As they sat on a bench in the café, an old couple came in. They sat at the table near Clara and Lindsey and the man spoke to them. 'By, you two look cold. Where's your coats and scarves? It'll fair freeze your lugs off out there.'

'We ain't got no coats, mister.'

The man looked at them more closely. 'You look as though you bumped into a wall. Has somebody had a go at you?'

Clara felt afraid at this. The man was kindly and may have wanted to do something about helping them, but his helping them might land them in more trouble if he thought to call the police.

Lindsey was quick off the mark, though. 'We got into trouble with a gang as stole our money. But we're all right. Our mate's coming to take us home in a while. The cops can't do owt as the lads were long gone, so they were happy that we have someone to take us home.'

The old man stared from one to the other of them. Clara could see that he didn't believe them, but his wife saved the day. 'You poor things. Well, let us buy you a nice hot drink. What would you like?'

'Naw. That's all right, ta, missus.'

'I insist. Bert, get the girls a drink. Get them a mug of cocoa each, that'll warm them up.'

The cocoa tasted delicious. Its warmth undid a little of the knot in Clara's chest. In doing so it let in the full extent of their situation: no money, no real place to go, no clothes. It all seemed hopeless. Things had been bad at Miss Brandon's, but they had been a lot worse since she'd escaped from there. But she couldn't go back there, could she? And what about Lindsey? No, they had to find something together. Jobs and somewhere to live. *It's impossible. How can we do all of that? And*

Mickey won't give up on us, he'll be looking for us. Probably at this very moment! With this thought, she turned and looked out of the window. The street outside was in darkness. The darkness seemed to envelop her. Her body trembled. Lindsey's hand found hers. She looked back into Lindsey's huge, sunken eyes and a worry set up into her as she noted the tinge of grey to Lindsey's pasty face which showed how ill she still was. Feeling protective of her, Clara willed herself to find the strength she needed to care for Lindsey. She had to help her to get well again.

The door opened, letting in a draught, and Clara looked towards it. Shock held her rigid. The last person she expected to see had walked into the café. But from the greeting the woman behind the counter gave her, it seemed that Miss Brandon's sister was a regular customer here.

'Hello, Daisy, love. You finished for the day, then?'

'Hello, Betsy. Aye, I've brought Tiggy out for a walk, she hates being cooped up in that shop all day. She loves the seafront. I've tied her up outside for a mo, while I have a warm.'

'You look tired, love. Running that shop's not a good idea for you. You're the artistic kind. Have you been to the theatre lately?'

'Naw. I've naw time. I miss it. And I miss me pals. But they're all coming to see me on Sunday. As for the shop, what choice do I have? Our Mavis left it me as long as I kept it open and running. I'm not allowed to sell it for ten years. But me money was running out, so at least it gives me an income.'

The couple who'd bought them cocoa got up then. 'Afore you get into a long conversation, Betsy, we'll pay our bill and get on our way.' The woman turned to Clara and nodded her head. 'Hope everything turns out for you lasses.'

With that they went through the door before Clara could give them her thanks. Betsy had taken their money without acknowledging them, and carried on talking to Daisy as if nothing had happened.

'Your Mavis was a mean old cuss, and aye, I knaw that's speaking ill of the dead, but I spoke ill of that one when she were alive, so it ain't nowt different. Here – here's your mug of tea, lass. Get it down you.'

'Ta, Betsy. You've had a few in then, for such a cold night?' As Daisy said this she looked towards them. 'Clara! Clara, where have you been, lass? Eeh, it is you, isn't it? By, what's happened to you, lass?'

Lindsey's hand tightened around her own, her fear conveying itself with the gesture. 'It's all right. Daisy is lovely, she won't cause us trouble.'

Daisy brought her tea over and sat on the bench next to them. 'Eeh, look at you, you look like someone has bashed you. And who's this?'

'I'm all right. I – I, we were attacked. This is my friend, Lindsey.'

'Dear, dear. Where did you go to? Me sister – she's gone now, by the way, she said as you ran away, but I could never understand why she wouldn't report it.'

'I did run away, Daisy, but only because she locked me in the shed. Me friend, Shelley . . . sh – she got killed by a tram . . . '

'Oh, that poor lass as was an evacuee from London?'

'Yes. She helped me escape, but then she went across the road and was knocked down. I've been with Lindsey here, since. We've been working for a bad man who treated us rough.' Lindsey nudged her. 'It's all right, Lindsey, don't worry.'

'But, everyone knaws, Mickey. You have to be careful.'

'Who's Mickey? Is that the man you've been working for and who did this to you?'

'Yes. I – I lied about the attack, Daisy. Mickey is a bad man and he did this to us. We can't go back to him, and Lindsey has nowhere to go, she's an orphan.'

Betsy leaned over her counter and called over, 'I knaw who she's talking about. He's a rough diamond, that Mickey. He's an Irish fella who runs all the criminal activity around here.'

'Well, I've never heard of him, Betsy.'

'Naw, and you don't want to. You don't want to cross him either, so don't be letting your soft heart tempt you to take these girls in, because if they belong to him and he finds out, there'll be hell come down on you.'

'I can't just leave them. Clara here is an evacuee from the island of Guernsey. She was billeted with our Mavis, but Mavis treated her cruelly. I feel responsible for her. I'm not afraid of no Mickeys of this world.'

'You should be, Daisy, but I can see where you're coming from. Lass should have some help. Why not take her back to the WVRS? Them lot's responsible for her, surely?'

'Naw, I'm taking her in and that's that. And her mate. They'll be safe with me.'

'On your head be it. Though it's unlikely as Mickey'll come looking in a small grocery shop. He's allus got bigger fish to fry. It's just if someone sees them as knaws they've been working for him.'

'Well, you lasses will knaw to avoid them, won't you?'

181

Lindsey again squeezed Clara's hand. But Clara couldn't see anything wrong with going with Daisy. To her, it seemed that it could be the saving of them.

'We'll make sure no one sees us, I promise, Daisy.'

'Well, that settles it. You can come home with me. I need your help in the shop, Clara, and you can have your old room back, but it won't be like last time.'

'Ta, Daisy. But what happened to Miss Brandon?'

'Heart attack. Not long after you left. The shop's mine now, not that I want it, but it keeps me head above water. Well, when you're ready, we should get going.'

'We need to wait for our friend. Tinker works on the fairground, and he was going to take us to his boarding house.'

As she said this Tinker walked in. Clara could see that there was something wrong the moment she looked at him.

'You'll never guess, but I've been laid off! With the war and everything, they're closing the fairground down for the winter . . . who's this?'

'This is Daisy.' Clara told Tinker about them going with Daisy, and how she knew her.

'Looks like you've landed on your feet. Now, it's my turn to go begging. I've a week to get out of me digs.'

'Well, I could fit the three of you in, with a squeeze, I suppose.'

'Bloody hell, Daisy!' Betsy was aghast. 'You're not a home for waifs and strays. Though, I knaw Tinker. He's a good lad, and he'll be useful to you.'

'How old are you, Tinker? Are they likely to be taking you any day now for conscription?'

'I'm sixteen.'

'So, you've a bit of time afore they come calling for you. Eeh, I only came out for a walk, and now I've landed meself with the three of you. I hope none of you will give me trouble.'

'We won't, Daisy. And thank you. I promise I'll work hard for you. I know the ropes, and once Lindsey's well I can teach her. Tinker can do all the heavy lifting and the deliveries. Have you still got the bike?'

'I have, but Tinker will have to clean it up. It was left in the yard and has gone a bit rusty. But let's get on our way. It's late, and I haven't had me supper yet. There's plenty for you both. Will you be all right, Tinker?'

'Aye, I've got me pay. I'll have a slice of Betsy's steak and kidney pudding and some tatties afore I go back to me digs. I can come to yours tomorrow and start on that bike, but I'll not move in until I have to leave me digs. Where's your shop, then?'

Clara told him where the shop was. It felt strange to her to be going back to it, but she was relieved, too. She was sure they'd all be all right with Daisy. She couldn't get over the coincidence of her walking into the café where they had been waiting for Tinker. *Thank you, God, for answering my prayers. Maybe you could make everything right now. Make Lindsey better, and end the war, so that I can go home to my mum.*

She knew this was a futile prayer, at least about the war ending soon – the news was full of London being flattened by air raids. She thought of Shelley's mum and wondered if she was safe. Poor Shelley. How she missed her. But she wondered how they would have fared. Where would they have ended up that day? Thinking back to it now, Clara felt a cold feeling settle inside her. That had been the day she'd been taken in by Wally.

Outside the café, she looked both ways, as did Lindsey. There was no one around – just Daisy's little dog, wagging his tail and twisting his lead into knots as he tried to get free and go to his mistress.

Would they ever feel safe again? Clara didn't know, but for the time being they were safe. Surely, no one who used the shop would know Mickey? With this thought, she made her mind up that she would make sure Daisy had a tale to tell of where she'd been. She had to make Daisy aware of how careful she must be.

Getting back to the shop wasn't a good experience for Clara. Memories of the cruelty meted out to her revisited her, and she expected Miss Brandon to pop up from every nook and cranny. She put a brave face on it, though, and helped poor, scared Lindsey settle in.

The stew Daisy offered them was delicious, and Clara was glad to see that Lindsey ate some, too.

Daisy talked non-stop about her friends from the theatre, and it all sounded so exciting. 'That's it! I will get you both jobs in the theatre! Tinker will be enough help here, for me. They are crying out for seamstresses. Jeannie will teach you. The pay isn't good, but the love and friendship more than make up for that. And you will be safe. The theatre crowd are a community on their own. They will love you both and protect you. I just knaw it! We'll talk to them about it on Sunday. Naw, better than that, we'll go to see them tomorrow. It's half-day closing, remember?'

How could Clara forget? Wednesday. The only day that good things used to happen. And now it sounded as though they would again, as the thought of working in the theatre excited her beyond words.

CHAPTER SEVENTEEN

Julia
A Hope for a Better Future

It had been two weeks since the fire.

The cold church was full, and yet there was not one friendly gesture towards Julia from any of those attending the funeral.

She sat on the front row, between Farmer and Mrs Pickering, staring at the coffin that lay on wooden supports just in front of the alter. Polly sat on the further side of Mrs Pickering. She hadn't spoken to Julia for the whole two weeks since the tragedy had happened.

Christmas had come and gone, with no festivities, and a cloud had hung over the household as they waited for today.

'It's the shock, dear. She'll be all right,' Mrs Pickering had said, when Julia had commented on Polly's attitude. But then she'd gone on to say: 'Anyway, we'll have to talk about your position here. I don't think that it can change from when I said that you will have to leave. The village is up in arms about what happened. Their sympathy isn't with you, and life could be very uncomfortable for you and for me and Farmer Pickering.'

Julia had agreed, without having an inkling of where she would go. She still didn't, but she knew that a decision would have to be made now that Rhoda was being laid to rest.

It was difficult to imagine Rhoda gone. And, Vanda, too. Both had seemed so alive. Guilt entered Julia for the umpteenth time since the fire. All of this was her fault. But for her affair, both women would still be alive.

The sound of the heavy church door opening stopped the vicar's reciting of some words he'd dug up for the occasion, none of which fitted Rhoda or her life. A gasp rippled around the congregation. Julia turned her head. A feeling stung her as she saw Gareth walk up the aisle towards her. His eyes bored into her.

'Excuse me.'

Mrs Pickering looked up at him. 'This isn't a good idea, Gareth. You only buried your wife two days ago!'

'Please let me in, I need to support Julia through this.'

With a humph, Mrs Pickering moved along and made room for Gareth. Julia's heart soared. She couldn't believe this was happening. She knew that Gareth was home from his training camp on compassionate leave and that Vanda's funeral had taken place, but she'd had no contact from him, and had been broken-hearted to think of him not getting in touch. The service continued, but mostly it went over Julia's head.

187

Gareth's nearness was all she could think about. When his hand found hers, she thought that she would burst.

But her happiness was shattered when the service ended, and a voice from the back shouted: 'Disgraceful! You should be ashamed of yourselves.'

The vicar raised his hands in a pacifying gesture. 'Please, everyone, let us keep calm. We are here to put the soul of our sister Rhoda to rest. Please show her the respect that she deserves. Remember that we are a substitute for her family, who are far away and may even not be aware of her passing.'

'You should tell that to those two, vicar. How can you condone their behaviour?'

'I'm not doing so, and I am as disgusted as you are, but I must keep my attention on the dear departed.' Turning to Gareth, he said: 'Perhaps you would both leave before the cortège? I really do think that would be for the best.'

Gareth rose and helped Julia up. They walked out of the church. People on both sides of the aisle tutted their disdain, and Julia couldn't blame them.

Once outside, Gareth pulled her to him. 'My darling. I'm so sorry.'

'You shouldn't have come, Gareth. Not like this. Those folk were right.'

'I know, but I couldn't keep away. I did until it was time for Vanda's funeral, and then thought that I would just leave and write to you. I was about to go. I was nearly boarding the train, when I seemed to come to my senses, and my only thought was to be with you, no matter what anyone thought or said. You needed someone to help you, and I wanted it to be me.'

The organ music suddenly became louder as the church doors were opened. 'Let's get away from here, Gareth. Hurry, they're coming out.'

With this, Gareth took hold of her hand and hurried away from the church with her in tow. 'We'll go to the station and go away for a couple of days. I've over a week before I have to be back in barracks.'

'No, Gareth. We can't. I cannot just walk out. Mrs Pickering wants me out, but not like this. Besides, I am in war service and that is binding. I'll join the procession to the graveside and say my goodbyes to Rhoda, and I'll meet you tomorrow. I'll go back to the house and pack my things and say my goodbyes.'

'But, I thought you would go back to them. Where will you stay? I was only thinking of a couple of nights together. I have to report back for training then.'

'I don't know where I'll go, but I will find somewhere. I can't stay here, and I do have to get leave from the agricultural department running the Land Army. Now go, and come to pick me up tomorrow. Have you still got your car?'

'Yes. It's locked in the garage. I was going to leave it there. Can you get a lift to the station for ten in the morning?'

'I'm sure Farmer Pickering will sort something out for me. Now, I must go.'

'Julia, I love you. I love you beyond words. Everything will be all right, I promise.'

With this, Gareth left her. Julia waited for the procession to come up to her. Once it did she re-joined Mrs Pickering. Her reception was cold, but she wasn't rejected.

Though Polly had a go at her, of course. 'How can you behave in that manner, Julia? You have shamed Mrs Pickering.'

'I didn't arrange it, Polly. I just handled it the best way that I could. I'm sorry, Mrs Pickering. I'll be gone tomorrow, I promise.'

'Well, that's for the best. We can't go on like this.'

They had reached the dug-out grave. To Julia, it was a cold, lonely place, on the edge of the churchyard, but she'd been told that all the empty spaces between where they were going to lay Rhoda and the other graves were taken. The village folk had reserved their family plots. Though one grave, freshly covered over, was away from all the others. *Vanda. So, there you lie in ground that isn't consecrated as befits a murderess, but is because of you taking your own life. Well, I'm glad that you did. I'm glad that you're dead. I couldn't walk this earth if I thought that you walked it too.*

The wind howled around her as these thoughts assailed her, giving her the impression that Vanda was answering her.

A flurry of snow settled around them. Julia pulled her coat a little tighter around herself. She couldn't move away when the others did, and stood looking into the open grave long after they had all left. *Oh, Rhoda. I'm so sorry. I'll miss you. But I promise you that as soon as I can, I will look for our daughters. And I'll always look out for your Janet.*

A cough behind her brought her back to the moment. 'I'm sorry, miss, but we have to complete the burial now.'

'Yes, of course.' Moving away, Julia's heart weighed heavy in her chest. For poor Rhoda to be buried here amongst strangers and never to return home didn't bear thinking about. *And how am I to face her family if ever I do return to the island?*

★　　★　　★

190

Farmer Pickering gave Julia a lift to the station without quibbling. Mrs Pickering handed her a small bag as she was about to leave.

'I don't knaw where you'll land up, Julia, but I suspect that you are meeting up with Gareth?'

Julia nodded. 'I'm sorry. I – I know you think that I shouldn't but we do love each other.'

'Aye, well, be careful. Men like Gareth fall in and out of love with women quite often. Don't become a Vanda. Here, I've packed you some sandwiches.'

'That's kind of you, thank you. May I write to let you know how I am from time to time?' Despite everything, Julia had a heavy heart at leaving this kindly couple – none of what had happened was their fault after all. And she didn't blame Mrs Pickering for the actions that she'd taken.

'Maybe best to leave it here, lass.'

Mr Pickering intervening lessened Julia's hurt. 'Well, I don't agree. I'd like to knaw how lass fairs, and how Gareth does too. I heard a lot of tales amongst the farming community about how his life was with Vanda, and none of us would have swapped with him.'

Mrs Pickering sighed. 'Well, all right, then. A letter now and then would be nice, as I will wonder about you. But please heed what I say, and take care. Don't be gullible.'

With this, Mrs Pickering surprised Julia by leaning forward and kissing her cheek. 'If Farmer Pickering and I had daughters, they would be yours and Rhoda's age. I'll take care of Rhoda's resting place. Now, off you go.'

Tears misted Julia's eyes. Not even the fact that she was going to Gareth lightened her heart. She'd come to this farm with Rhoda, and now she was leaving without her. And, it hurt to think that Rhoda's family didn't even know what had happened to her. Though Roger would know soon, as the woman who had visited from the Department of Agriculture had said that she would see that he was informed.

Her heart went out to him. She knew that he'd not be able to share his grief with his parents and sister as he wouldn't be allowed to visit the island. And what would he make of how Rhoda died? With this thought Julia released a deep, sad sigh as she wondered if Roger would put the blame on her.

She hoped with all she was that he wouldn't. Roger had always been a fair-minded man, and had often spoken to her if he'd had the chance to without his parents finding out. He'd once told her how sorry he was about what had happened to her, and that if he was at home more he'd have tackled folk's attitude.

She wasn't sure that he would have, but it had been nice to hear it.

At the station, Gareth sat on a bench, his look one of rejection. He didn't raise his head as she approached; he seemed lost in thought.

'Gareth?'

'Oh, Julia, I hardly dared hope that you would come.'

Julia gasped as he stood. His airman's uniform suited him so well, and he'd been running his hands through what hair the air force had left on the top of his head, giving it a rakish look. His appearance was a stark reminder that Gareth was in the forces and they wouldn't have long together. His kiss was a light peck on the cheek, even though there was no one around.

'Are you all right, Gareth?'

'Will we ever be all right again, after what has happened? I feel so responsible, so guilty.'

'I know, I do too, but we couldn't have known that our love would cause all that it did.'

'I should have known. I knew what Vanda was capable of and that her mental health was poor. I wanted her to get help a long time ago, but she could never admit to having flaws.'

'Hindsight is always a telling thing. Even though you had concerns, it is as I say, you couldn't have known. We have to try to get over it all. It's the only way. Tell me. Where are we going?'

'I have one more week before I have to report. I'm stationed at Biggin Hill, learning to be a pilot. But it is uncomfortable as there are many raids on the airbase by the Germans, and worst of all, I will soon be posted to Canada for the completion of my training. I want you near to me until then, and for you to be there when I get back. So, I thought we would find somewhere for you in Maidstone, which isn't too far away. Then, at least when I am off duty, I can see you.'

'How long will you be away?'

'Eight weeks. After that I will be taking part in air raids and in missions aimed at the defence of our country. Our boys are doing a great job intercepting and fighting off the Germans, though it is never enough. You will see the awful destruction in London when we arrive, as we have to change stations there to get a train back out to Maidstone.

They were sitting on the train in a carriage to themselves when Julia finally plucked up the courage to tell her news.

'Gareth. I have something to tell you. I – I'm having your child.'

'What! Oh God! Really? Oh, Julia, Julia.'

She was in his arms. All worries left her as he held her and kissed her, snuggling into her neck, wetting her with his tears. 'We'll be married, Julia. I was going to ask you, but was going to wait for a year to go by. But now I will apply for a special licence. Will you marry me?'

'Yes, yes. Oh, Gareth, yes.'

A happiness like none she had ever felt entered Julia. Gareth really and truly wanted her. He really loved her, she wasn't just his affair. *How did I ever think that I was?* But then, having faith in anyone loving her had been difficult.

As she came out of the passionate kiss that had followed her acceptance of him, Gareth asked, 'Are you happy, my darling, really happy? Can you live with what happened?'

'It will take time, but yes. I miss Rhoda so much and my heart breaks for her family, and like you I feel the guilt of why she died, but I can reason that out. My main source of sorrow is being parted from my daughter. I feel terrible about having another child when my first born is out there somewhere, living a life without me. It will seem that I replaced her. Oh, Gareth, I hate this war. How am I going to bear being parted from you, and being even further from where I believe my Clara is?'

'We will find her, I promise. Have you written to the Blackpool Council? They may have her registered as living there now, and even attending a school.'

'No, I never thought of that. I'm not even sure she is in Blackpool. She could have been taken to Manchester, but yes,

I will write to both. Like you say, they would register the children on the census, it's the law. At least it is in Guernsey and our laws came from the mainland. Oh, Gareth, that's the first small hope that I have had since looking for her.'

London was a shocking sight, and brought the reality of war home to Julia. Until now it had been something that was happening, and which had torn her from Clara, but to see the destruction for herself, and to feel the heart of this proud city bleeding its pain, ground into her what it really meant.

The streets were littered with debris. Air-raid wardens and firemen battled to clear heaps of burning rubble, ambulances roared past them, leaving Julia imagining the carnage rent on those being ferried to hospital. And among it all, children played. Their playground was a smouldering inferno, yet their laughter rang out as the fireman teased them, turning a hose on a group that were causing an annoyance.

As they passed one group of wardens, they stood up straight and saluted Gareth. 'Evening, sir. I would get your young lady away from here as soon as you can. It's another clear evening, and we're expecting the Germans any moment.'

'Is there anything we can do to help?'

'No, sir, you have your job and we have ours. Just stop as many of them as you can when you're up there engaging them. That'll be all the help we need from you.'

As he finished speaking the siren wailed, deafening Julia.

'Hurry, darling. We'll make for the Underground. I doubt we'll get a train out of here until much later.'

The sky above them darkened as the drone of aircraft filled the air. People around them began to run. Wardens hurried folk along, herding them into shelters. Grabbing Julia's hand, Gareth broke into a run, pulling her along with such force that she thought she would fall. Her shoes hindered her. Why hadn't she dressed in a more practical way, instead of donning heels?

'Kick your shoes off, Julia. We have to run!'

A whistling noise heralded the first wave of bombs. Explosions sounded all around them. Dust, stones and pieces of glass flew through the air. Terror gripped Julia, but she did as Gareth said and ran in stockinged feet.

As they entered Kings Cross station and turned towards the Underground, a force hit Julia, sending her flying. Winded, she lay on the pavement, a weight holding her down. Smoke and dust blurred her sight. 'Gareth, Gareth, help me! Help me!'

'I'm here, Julia. Stay still, darling, I'm coming.'

Gareth shifted whatever it was that had her pinned down. Then his arms encircled her, helping her to rise. 'Can you stand, darling?'

She found that she could. As her vision cleared, she saw the body of an elderly man lying on the floor next to where she had been. Unable to speak, she looked up, her eyes a question.

'Yes, it was the man who hit you. There's nothing that can be done for him.'

Julia looked down at the man again, and saw that half of his head had gone, as had one of his arms. As an automatic reaction, she went to brush herself down. Her hand spread the sticky blood that covered the front of her. 'Oh God!'

'Keep yourself together, darling, we have to make it to the Underground.'

Around, them, people ran in panic, pushing and shoving, screaming with fear.

'*Stop!*' Gareth's commanding voice had the effect of calming the situation. 'Everyone, form an orderly line. One here behind me, and the other behind my fiancé. That's right. Now, we will all get to safety. Hurry, but don't panic, and don't jostle for position.'

Once they were all sitting down on the Underground platforms, one man stood up. 'Three cheers for the officer – hip, hip!'

The 'hoorays' that followed this prompting were deafening.

''Ere, luv, you can 'ave the first cap of tea. I take me 'at off to yer.'

The lady who had said this wore a WRVS badge. She handed a steaming cup to Gareth, and then one to Julia. 'We owe a debt to you, luv. And no doubt will owe a bigger one afore this lot's over. Sup up.'

Someone started to play a mouth organ, and someone else began to sing. Before long, the atmosphere was as if there was a party in progress, as some of the men pulled bottles of beer out of coat pockets, and another man handed cigarettes around.

Julia felt her body coming to a calm place. She looked into Gareth's face and read his concern for her.

'I'm fine. I'm not hurt. Well, except for my feet. My stockings are torn to shreds, and my feet feel as though I've run over hot coals.'

Gareth's arm came around her. He pulled her close. 'This isn't how I saw us spending our first night together, but for all that, I'm glad to be here. These folk give you another way of looking at life. They teach you that in numbers we can be strong. That we can shore up the weak, and that we'll never be beaten.'

Julia snuggled into his shoulder. *No, we'll never be beaten. We may be a bit battered at times, but while we have each other, we will never be beaten. We'll win through. We will find Clara, our child will be born safely, and we'll live a normal life together. A happy family life.*

PART TWO

1941

LIFE AND WAR TAKE OVER

CHAPTER EIGHTEEN

Clara
Finding Herself

Christmas had been the best that it could have been; only the sadness at not being with her mum marred it for Clara.

She, Lindsey and Tinker were settled in with Daisy. The weeks had been a hive of activity as Daisy needed the help of all three of them at times, yet Clara and Lindsey were also pulled into the hectic life of the theatre as the company put on its annual pantomime.

Working with the wonderful colours of the costumes was like heaven to Clara. And to see Lindsey getting stronger and taking to the life of a seamstress as if she had been doing it all her life made life seem 'grand as owt', as the Blackpool folk called everything that was good.

'Now, come along, gals, get stuck in, we need those pixie costumes in good repair for tonight's show.'

Jeannie danced between them. Curls of smoke swirled around her from the cigarette balanced in the end of her long cigarette holder. Jeannie never walked, or hurried, but always glided, her arms expressing whatever she was saying. Her wig, as Clara was sure it was, balanced precariously to one side of her head, and with her make-up plastered on her face the impression she gave was of a real-life panto dame. And yet she wasn't an actress, but the head seamstress, whose talents could turn an old piece of rag into a wonderful costume as if by magic.

Clara wanted to be like her. Well, not look like her, but possess her talent.

'Oh, and I have news. What do you think of this?' Jeannie held up a sparkling waistcoat. The back of it was lilac and the sequins adorning its front picked up all the colours of the room.

'It's grand, Jeannie. But who is it for?'

'Ah. That is my news, Lindsey. We have a young pianist joining us. Yes, I did say, young. He has come from a circus that has had to close down. He's French. Now, I knaw what you are thinking – why isn't he in the services? Well, he is blind. Yes, poor lad. But, he is the most amazing pianist I have ever heard in my life. You will meet him later. His name is Anton.'

Clara felt an excitement zing through her. Jeannie always had that effect on her, but for some reason the thought of this young man joining the company had sparked her imagination.

'Now. These are the trousers that he will wear with the waistcoat. They need finishing off. Lindsey, you can do that.

And this is his shirt. The cuffs need completing, Clara. Ooh, you gals are such an asset to me.'

With this, Jeannie swanned out of the room. Clara giggled. Jeannie tried hard to perfect her accent so as to sound posh, but ended up speaking a mixture of American and broad Lancashire, which always made Clara laugh.

Life was good. Everything was looking up for her, Lindsey and Tinker. Only recently, she had found out more about Tinker. His real name was Gordon, but he was known for his wheeling and dealing which was how he had earned his nickname. She'd also found out that he was born into a gypsy family, and that his ma had sold him to a pedlar when he was eight. This pedlar had trailed him around the country, using him as a slave, until one day, Tinker woke up to find the man dead, and so he'd run away and ended up in Blackpool.

It seemed to Clara that most who end up in Blackpool had a story to tell.

Within an hour, Jeannie was back. 'Well, have you finished?'

'Yes. Lofty is ironing them.'

'Good. Well, hello, Lofty. You are doing a good job, I hope? This young man is very special.'

Lofty stood tall on his stool as he ironed the clothes. A dwarf, he only came as high as the ironing table when he stood on the floor.

An adorable man, Lofty always had them in fits of giggling with his antics. Clara loved him. He was also an actor, but there were few parts for him. He earned his money by ironing the costumes, and he was excellent at it. 'For sure, being one of the little people, I do a good job, a magical job with everything I touch, Jeannie. Now aren't you for knowing that?'

Everyone laughed. But Clara found herself blushing. She'd heard that there was a thing between Jeannie and Lofty, but didn't like to think about it. Jeannie gave truth to the rumour now as she blushed and giggled like a young girl.

Clara put her head down and concentrated on the elaborate scarf she was sewing tassels onto, having finished the cuffs of the shirt for the mysterious pianist.

As she did so, she thought of what colourful people these theatricals were, and how she loved them all. Soon the cast would be in for rehearsals, and if she finished the last of her work she could go into the stalls and watch.

Lindsey didn't understand Clara's fascination with it all, and always wanted to get out into the air and have fun along the seafront, but Clara was afraid of bumping into someone who knew them. After all, both of them had been runners and that meant they had come into contact with a lot of folk. So far she'd persuaded Lindsey to only go out at night.

As if reading her thoughts, Lindsey asked her what she was going to do for the afternoon. 'Don't say you're going to watch the rehearsals again, Clara, you must knaw everyone's lines off by heart. Let's do sommat different with our two hours off, eh?'

'Please don't ask me to walk the prom, Lindsey. I'm scared.'

'Well, how about we catch a tram to Fleetwood? Naw one knaws us there.'

'Aye, and being Tuesday you could catch the market and spend some of your money. You must be loaded with how you've worked. All work and naw play . . . '

'Awe, you tell her, Lofty. She won't listen to me.'

'Well, she has a point, Lindsey. We all knaw what Mickey's like, and he'll be seething that you two got away, knowing what you knaw. You can't take any chances. Though, I'd say you'd be safe in Fleetwood.'

'We've got to get there, though. And that means going down to the front to catch the tram! Any one of a number of folk could see us.'

'You're right there, Clara, but I have a suggestion that will get around that.' Everyone looked at Lofty as he spoke. 'I suggest that you don't go today. Let's work on it. Get your thinking cap on, Jeannie. We need to disguise these two so they can go out and have some fun.'

'Eeh, that's a grand idea, Lofty, love. I'll do that. I can get make-up involved – they love changing anyone's appearance. Get yourselves ready, gals, you're going to become two different people.'

Clara laughed. 'Don't be too elaborate, Jeannie. We want to look normal, not like two freaks, but unrecognisable.'

'As if I would! You're talking to the gal who turned a thin blond boy into the artful dodger, and a rounded, but extremely handsome actor into Fagin. Both were unrecognisable. And I was nominated for best costume award.'

'That was in her younger days in London,' Lofty explained. 'But she hasn't lost her skill, and is called upon to make many a transformation that would win her that award if they bothered to look north of the border for talent.'

What Lofty wasn't saying was that Jeannie's drinking had lost her her top job in the London theatres. This was common knowledge, but was never spoken of. Daisy had told Clara and Lindsey. She'd kept them amused on many an evening with her tales of all the members of the company, even telling of the affair between Lofty and Jeannie, and laughing about how everyone speculated on how they managed to make love. This had made Lindsey giggle, but Clara wanted to escape the room.

'It would be grand if you could disguise us, Jeannie. We'd be safe then, to come and go. I feel like a prisoner.'

'Leave it with me, Lindsey, but don't take any chances till I've sorted it.'

'So, you'll come into rehearsals with me then, Lindsey?' asked Clara.

'It's the only alternative. We can't go home in the light. We allus have to wait until dark. But then, I can allus fall asleep.'

This is what Lindsey usually did. She just didn't have the interest in the goings-on of the theatre that Clara had, though she did enjoy the background work.

The orchestra struck up, playing the music to the slapstick of Lofty, dressed as an elf, and Shorty, a tall gangly man, dressed as a sunflower. Their antics had Clara laughing her head off. With not a word spoken, their act was hilarious and made all the more so by the whistles and timely hooters coming from the orchestra.

After this the stage director, Panda, as he was known as, because he had the darkest circles around his eyes, shouted for silence, before making an elaborate announcement. 'Tonight, at this point, we will have an interval before the main scene. The curtain will close, and I will need volunteers to take the drinks and popcorn around, as I want that completing before the second act. While that is taking place, we will introduce our new pianist. *Anton!*'

With this, there was a scurry of scenes being moved and a grand piano was pushed onto centre stage. When all fell quiet, Clara could hear the tap, tap of a stick on the floor. She held her breath. This then was the new pianist.

When he came from behind the curtain, Panda counted his steps. 'Now, turn to your right, and bow.'

As Anton faced her, Clara drew in her breath. He was beautiful. His dark hair shone under the stage lighting. His face was the handsomest she'd ever seen, and his skin looked golden. She wanted to clap her hands together, but instead she sat quietly, waiting.

'Now. Turn to your left, and then left again. One step forward. Touch the piano. Slide your hands along. Can you feel the stool behind you? Right. That is how you will enter the stage tonight, Anton. And, play!'

What happened in the next few minutes was magical to Clara. The piano seemed to talk to her, as the most beautiful music came from Anton's fingertips. Something inside her wanted to sing out, if only she knew the words, or even what the music was called. Not that it mattered that she didn't, as the magical strains entered her and lifted her to a place where she'd never been – a place of dreams. When it came to an end, her face was wet with tears and her heart cried out for her mother. The longing that had waned a little with her happiness had been brought back by the supreme beauty of the music, putting her in touch with her inner self. She wanted to wail and sob her sorrow and her longing to see her mum.

'Hey, Clara.' Beside her, Lindsey stretched the sleep from her limbs. 'What's to do?'

Clara let out a little laugh. 'I'm all right. It was the music, didn't you hear it? Oh, Lindsey, it was amazing. Look, that's Anton who we have been sewing for. He is the most wonderful pianist.'

'Mmm, and handsome too. Things are looking up around here, Clara.'

Clara didn't want Lindsey to talk like that about Anton. He was special – he wasn't just another good-looking lad for Lindsey to drool over. But she didn't say anything. She rose and went towards Panda.

'Where're you going? Clara!'

'Panda is looking for volunteers to sell the popcorn and drinks in the interval. I'm going to offer my services.'

'But you've to work in the background. We have to help to dress the acts and make any last minute repairs as always. You can't do both.'

'I'll speak to Jeannie. I'll only be out here for ten minutes. I want to hear Anton playing again.'

'My, you've got it bad. Well, it's up to you, I suppose. Any road, it's about time you took an interest in the male species. I'll tell Jeannie that I'll cover for you. She'll be fine with it.'

'Ta, Lindsey. But I'm not taking an interest in Anton, only his music.' But as she said this, Clara knew she was fibbing. For the first time ever, something had stirred in her, and she knew that her growing up was complete. It started when Lindsey had her baby taken from her, and it had been a gradual process since then, as more and more, she knew that she was changing into a young woman – in her mind as well as in her body. *Well, now my heart is catching up, as I have given it to a lad. I've given it to Anton.*

CHAPTER NINETEEN

Julia
Alone Again

Julia looked around the small flat that Gareth had rented for her. On the ground floor it had its own small garden, something she was glad of as she could sit out in the summer months when she would be almost ready to give birth sometime around August. In her mind this month was the worst time to have another child. August was her Clara's birthday month. Guilt entered her at this thought, and she hoped with all her heart that when she and Clara were reunited, Clara didn't think she'd sought to replace her.

Her hand went to her stomach, and to the small bulge forming. It still felt very bruised from the incident in London but, so far, nothing had happened to suggest that her baby was harmed in anyway. She remembered from her nursing days sitting with the midwives, and marvelling at the resilience of the foetus. They often told tales of women who had been involved in accidents, or had been beaten by their men, and yet their babies clung to life in the womb. This thought reassured her, but still she sent up a prayer: *Please keep my baby safe.*

The week had flown by. They had achieved so much before Gareth had to report back for duty – finding the flat, which they had done on their second day in Maidstone, then trawling around second-hand shops to furnish it. She loved the dark oak furniture they had found   the sideboard with its brass handles, and table and chairs to match. Then there was the sofa, a deep maroon that had a couple of worn patches on the arms. These she'd been able to cover with antimacassars, and had matching ones for the back of the sofa and for the arms of the two fireside chairs.

Next they had purchased the bed, and tonight was to be their first night sleeping in it, as till now they had stayed at a guest house. They'd taken separate rooms as their identity cards showed them not to be married. It had been agony knowing that Gareth was just along the corridor. But in the middle of the second night there'd been a tap on the door, and that had been the pattern of each night since.

Remembering Gareth's love-making sent a shiver of anticipation through Julia of the same happening tonight, but with much more abandon as they would be in their own bedroom, and no one knew they weren't married.

Her heart fluttered as she thought of the special licence they had, valid for three days' time. Then she would be Mrs Gareth Maling. Oh, it was going to be so wonderful. She even had a new costume that Gareth had treated her to. It was perfect for the wedding. Pale blue, with a pencil-slim skirt. Oh, how she had longed to wear a pencil-slim skirt. And the jacket was so prettily cut into her waist, and then flared out over the hips. There wasn't a collar or lapels, but instead the neckline was accentuated by a pattern, stitched in black bias that extended to the waist, where a black, shiny, slim belt finished the design. It was beautiful, and the best outfit that Julia had ever possessed. Under the jacket, she would wear a small black, camisole blouse and Gareth had bought her a string of pearls and a veiled hat in matching blue. A pair of short white cotton gloves and high-heeled white satin shoes, and a small clutch bag, also in white satin, finished off her outfit. These she'd bought herself from the last of the money she had left over from what Winnie had given her.

'Winnie's contribution,' she'd told Gareth. 'As I know that, wherever she is, Winnie will be smiling down at me on the wedding day she always longed for me to have.'

'Oh, and will she approve of your choice of husband, my dear?'

'Yes, she will. In many ways you are like her own husband was. Steady, dependable, adorable, funny, charming . . . '

'Hey, steady on. You make me sound a cross between an old fuddy-duddy and a rake!'

They'd collapsed in laughter then, and it had been a good moment, as they hadn't laughed together before. Gareth had commented on this.

'You know, we haven't had the lightest of starts, have we? A clandestine affair, then all that happened as a result. We've been clothed in guilt. But, I think it is time we put all that behind us and celebrated our love for each other. And we should do that with laughter, and friendship, and by being passionate lovers.'

This had led to a kiss, and then a rush back to the guest house, where they'd been greeted by the knowing look of the landlady. They'd both thought she would take them to task, but she knew by then that they were planning their wedding and that was only a few days in the future, so chose to turn a blind eye. Not that they had felt relaxed with this, and had still made love as quietly as they could. But, no matter that they had to be careful, the experience had been wonderful.

With nothing more to do but to wait for Gareth, Julia decided to try on her wedding outfit. She hadn't had all the items together until yesterday, and hadn't wanted to have a dress rehearsal in front of Gareth. She had to keep some surprises for the day!

Standing in front of the long mirror of their wardrobe, Julia gasped at the sight of herself. Twirling around, she was reminded of the day she'd tried on her first wedding outfit. *Oh, Tim. I hope you will be happy for me. I know that I haven't behaved properly and that much sadness has been caused by my love for Gareth. But we do love each other so much. And I will never forget you. You will always be my first love, Gareth understands that.*

As she thought this she looked heavenwards, hoping that was where Tim was. A box on top of the wardrobe caught her eye. She'd seen Gareth bring it into the guest house after he'd popped out to do what he called 'personal shopping'.

Her curiosity got the better of her. Getting the dressing-table stool Julia stood on it and reached for the box. Feeling guilty, but unable to resist, she placed it on the bed and lifted the lid. A note lay on top of the tissue paper inside: 'You found me! This is to keep you warm on the day, my darling. But, whenever you wear it, it will be my arms that are around you.'

Smiling at Gareth's guessing that she'd find it and open it, she unwrapped the tissue paper. 'Oh, how lovely!'

Pulling out the beautiful, golden fox-fur jacket, Julia wrapped it around her shoulders, then snuggled her arms into the sleeves. It looked stunning. Holding the front together around her, she knew a moment of bliss. Gareth's arms were around her!

Touched by this loving and romantic gesture, Julia sat on the end of the bed. With her little chat with Tim's spirit still in her mind, she thought about what she and Gareth were doing. Were they right to wed so soon? But then, in the end, what choice did they have? Gareth would soon be going to Canada and their future was so uncertain. They had discussed this, but they hadn't dwelled on it, as on top of everything that had happened it was too painful to do so. But from a practical point of view, they had agreed that they wanted their baby born in wedlock. And Gareth had said that he needed to put Julia down as his wife so that she could receive a wife's allowance from the air force while he was away. He had already set up a fund for her to draw from, explaining that the wheels of the services sometimes turned slowly in administrative matters, and her allowance may not start for a couple of months. They hadn't discussed his house in Chipping. And Julia hadn't wanted to broach the subject, so for now that was left as it was.

All these thoughts made Julia sigh. There was so much for them to face still, and on top of that, for her, there would always would be a missing piece to her happiness. If only she had contact with Clara. But, even in that, she had some hope. Now that she had an address, she would do as Gareth had suggested and write to Blackpool Council. Surely, they would have her registered? And if they didn't, she would try Manchester Council. *Someone must know where you are, my darling.*

Before she could get too down with these thoughts, Julia changed back into her day frock, carefully put her wedding clothes away, and went back through to the living room.

Straightening the table cloth for the hundredth time as she passed it, she willed the clock to strike the next hour and then the next. She so wanted it to be evening and for Gareth to walk through the door. She had a casserole slowly cooking in the oven, and had bread proving, ready to bake to go with it. The aroma from both made the flat a proper home – the first Julia had known for many years. Hers and Gareth's home.

When at last the time came for Gareth to walk up the path, her heart fluttered, leaving her feeling breathless. She couldn't help herself – she stood by the window and looked out for him coming.

But, it wasn't Gareth who walked up the path, it was another airman.

Holding her breath, Julia opened the door. His face was unreadable. Fear clutched Julia's heart. Her voice wouldn't work. She could only stare at the officer and wait for him to speak.

'Ma'am, I'm Captain Barry Everett, a colleague of your fiancé.' He bowed in a very formal way. Julia waited. 'I'm afraid that orders were changed, and Captain Gareth Maling has already been flown out. He had no time to leave base to come and say his goodbyes, nor to make any arrangements. He asked me to deliver this note to you. I'm very sorry, ma'am.'

Julia took the envelope. Still she couldn't speak. She nodded at Barry and closed the door, hoping he understood that she wasn't being unfriendly, but was in a state of shock.

The letterbox opened, and Barry shouted through. 'Please let me know if there is anything I can do to help you. Gareth is a good friend, and I know he will want me to see that you are all right.'

Walking into her living room, where just a few moments ago, happy anticipation had been her companion, Julia sat down on the sofa. Her mind wouldn't accept what she'd heard. *Gareth, gone? He can't have. No! What about our wedding? Oh God. How long before he is back?*

Ripping open the envelope, she stared at the few words written.

My darling,

I am shocked to the core at the turn of events, and can say nothing about why I have to go, or even where to. I know that you will understand this. But what are we to do? I have no time to make any different arrangements for you financially than we already have in place, and won't be allowed to set up the payment to you from my salary that we had spoken of as you are not yet my wife. I am so sorry, but I hope that you will manage.

Oh, my darling, I feel as though I am leaving you and our unborn child destitute, but I have no choice in the matter.

My heart is breaking, and my arms ache to hold you one more time before I leave. You will be in my thoughts every minute of every day, my darling.

I promise, I will write as soon as I am allowed, so don't despair, my dearest. I love you like I have never loved another soul. You are my soul — the other half of me. Gareth x

Inside, Julia wanted to wail her distress, and scream against the injustice of it all. But she sat motionless, staring into the embers of the fire.

She couldn't take in what had happened, or its implications. None of the practical things Gareth spoke about had any impact on her. All she could realise was, that her Gareth had gone. There would be no wedding. Her child would have no legal daddy. *Another bastard! A horrible word, but that is what my second child will be, just like my first. My darling Clara. Why? Why? What did I ever do to deserve this? What did my children do? Oh, Gareth, my love, my love.*

Without her bidding, tears flowed down her face, a river of tears that offered no relief. They didn't ease her pain, or show her a way forward, they just tore her heart in two.

CHAPTER TWENTY

Clara
A Love is Born – A Fear Embedded

It would soon be Easter. The news talked about by Daisy, and Jeannie, was of doom and gloom, as bombs were still raining down on the poor folk of London. And Plymouth and Wales had both had a pasting. Many had died, and wonderful build-ings, especially in London, had been destroyed.

Clara remembered the feeling of fear that all Blackpool had felt when, back in September, their own North Station had been a target and twelve residents had lost their lives. What it must have been like to have that happen night after night she couldn't imagine.

But still, despite everyone's fears of more raids due to the Vickers factory being here, Blackpool was largely unscathed and continued to enjoy a happy and prosperous atmosphere.

Folk still flocked in to have a few days' respite from the war and what it was doing to their everyday lives.

Clara finished repairing the cuff of a costume that had become worn and put these thoughts out of her mind. Like everyone, she'd found the best way to deal with the fear of what might happen was not to think about it for long. Instead she gave her mind to how the excitement was growing in the Grand Theatre. Once Easter came, the summer season acts would arrive and rehearsals for their show would begin. The pantomime season was over, and the production for this in-between stage was a comedy play. Every house was packed to the rafters, mostly with airmen, but also with those coming for a short winter break.

Tidying away her work, Clara couldn't wait to get out. Today, with no matinee to play for, Anton was joining her and Lindsey for a trip to the seafront.

She and Lindsey had made a few visits now, and her confidence was growing. They both looked so different – older than their years. Lindsey always had, but now Clara knew that she did too. She'd be fifteen in August, but she looked seventeen – and felt it too. Life had made her grow up faster than she should have.

She loved her new look. Her hair was now auburn, although she had to regularly rinse it with henna to keep its colour. It seemed to make her natural curls much more abundant and tighter, which suited her. Her bust had developed, but Jeannie had suggested she pad them to give her a good shape. And she wore make-up, which added to the illusion that she was older. Her clothes, too, had changed. Now, she wore adult fashions – pretty frocks topped with a cardigan, and her favourite outfit, a white twinset and flared navy skirt. Her confidence grew as she looked into the long mirror on the wall. *I have a job recognising myself – no one else will ever guess who I am.*

The big test was the day that she and Lindsey had gone to Arnold's stall. They'd had two goes at trying to win a prize before Clara hinted at who she was. Arnold had looked at her in a funny way, adjusted his glasses and given her an intense stare.

'Clara? What's happened to you? I looked for you for months after I read about Shelley. That was a terrible shock. I've thought about you often. Where have you been?'

She'd told him that it was a long story, that one day she would tell him all about it, but for now, if ever anyone asked after her, he was to say he hadn't seen her.

Arnold hadn't queried this, which she wondered at. But one thing Clara had learned was that the folk of Blackpool seemed to know more than they let on, and all reacted differently than you would expect to any situation. Sometimes she wondered if they were some sort of secret society.

'What are you daydreaming about, Clara? I've been watching you and your head's been bobbing from side to side. You look like you're having a conversation with yourself.'

'Ha, I suppose I am. Are you ready, Lindsey? We need to get going. Get your coat on and let's paint the town, as they say.'

At that moment, Anton came into the room. He hardly used his stick at the theatre now as he knew his way around. He had a way of lifting his head, as if listening to something they couldn't hear. 'Clara?'

'Yes, I'm here, Anton.'

'Tell me what you are wearing today.'

She loved how he always wanted to know about her. 'I have my twinset on, and my flared skirt, but it's very cold so we'll need our coats. I'll get yours down for you.'

Helping Anton on with his coat and tying his scarf gave Clara a warm feeling that she couldn't understand. It was a feeling that had visited her often when around him. It made her want to put her arms around him and protect him. *He's like the brother I never had*. But this thought didn't explain how she felt, so she ignored it and reached for her own coat.

When they got outside, they all shivered against the biting March wind.

'Eeh, this is too much for me.' Lindsey pulled her coat around her. 'I'm not for no seafront on a day like today, it'll be worse down there. I'm going back to Daisy's.'

Clara looked at Anton. 'What do you think, Anton?'

'I would like to go. I was looking forward to it, and you said that we can go into the amusement arcades if it's cold. I'm also wanting to try the fish and chips you said is delicious.'

'We'll see you later, then, Lindsey, love. Tell Daisy that I'm having my tea out, but will bring Anton round for one of her cakes.'

Linking arms with Anton made her feel warmer. Lindsey was right – the wind could cut you in two. It was good to get him out, as his schedule didn't give him much time. As he worked late he slept late in the mornings. His digs were just around the corner, and after his landlady had walked him round to the theatre the first couple of times, he'd managed that journey on his own. He didn't leave the theatre until midnight, what with his practice, playing at the matinee, eating with the rest of the crew and then playing again in the evening, and it was only now, during this lull between seasons, that he had more time off.

They walked in silence huddled together, battling their way against what felt like a great force holding them back. Anton laughed, making Clara giggle. But then his arm came around her and, as she snuggled into him and put her own arm around his waist, she had the feeling that this was where she belonged. It was akin to being in her mum's arms, only different – better even.

His confidence amazed her as he walked as if he could see all the obstacles around him, and she knew that he completely trusted her to guide him. Looking up at him, she wondered that such beautiful eyes couldn't see. They were the palest blue, and wide open.

Once they turned the corner onto the prom, the going was easier, as the wind wasn't as forceful as when they were walking towards it. Spray from the sea tingled her face.

'Is it raining, Clara?'

'No, the sea is angry, the waves are coming over the sea wall and spitting at us.'

'It's shouting at us, too. What does it look like?'

'Grey, and churning. But when it crashes into the wall, it has a white border, like a fur wrap, but then that wrap bursts into a million fragments that look beautiful. It is ever changing. Sometimes, when it is calm, it is like a sheet of pale blue glass and at others it gently laps the sand, and then draws back as if caressing the shore.'

'You have a beautiful way with words, Clara, you make me see what you see. Will you describe what the prom is like, and tell me what is that music that I can hear? It sounds like an organ?'

'The music is from a Wurlitzer. There is a man feeding it with cards that have a pattern of holes.'

'Oh yes, I have heard of them, they are magical.'

'The man is wearing a yellow suit with large black dots all over it. He has a podgy, smiley face and every now and then he takes off his bowler hat and offers it to the crowd gathered round him for them to drop pennies into. When he does this, the folk laugh because what looks like curly hair around his ears and forehead comes off with his hat and he is as bald as a badger.'

'Ha ha, that's a good way of amusing the crowd and getting them in the mood to give him their money.'

'Oh, that talent is rife among all those along the front. I'll take you to meet Arnold, he's a really nice man.' She told him about Arnold and his kindness. 'I've often wondered what happened to the teddy. Shelley never mentioned it again.'

'I'm sorry about what happened to her. Don't be sad, Clara. She is in a better place, and it was her destiny. We all have our own path to travel. Shelley trod hers, and now she is happy, I'm sure of it.'

The words, or something similar had been said to her many times, but the way Anton said them gave comfort.

'Carry on telling me what you can see.' His hold on her tightened a little. The gesture told her he understood how she felt. His wanting to know more was to distract her.

'Well, you know there are a lot of people about as they are jostling us. They aren't taking heed of the wind, or the cold. They are excited, as folk always are, no matter how many times they walk this way. Most are in uniform. Airmen and soldiers. But there are a lot of mothers and grandparents with children too. All are colourless, they are wearing winter grey, and khaki and navy blue. But there is an array of colour coming from the stalls. And it's all moving, as the strings of lights are swaying, and the blinds covering the stalls are flapping. There's bright oranges, blues and yellows, lots of stripes, and just a hundred yards from us is a candy-pink and white stall, that sells candyfloss, and sticks of Blackpool rock.'

'Yes, I can smell it, and those fish and chips mingling with it. And everyone seems to be shouting at once.'

'That's the stall holders, trying to attract punters to have a go. There's a coconut shy. The canvas covering the walls is bright orange. The man running it has a bright orange shirt on, with colourful braces. He has sayings pinned all round. One says, "Money talks, mine always says goodbye."'

Anton laughed.

'Another says, "This is the best place to show how you can use your balls."'

Anton was quiet for a moment, and then his head went back and his laughter was the loudest she'd ever heard from him. She didn't understand why — she'd never found that saying funny, and had just thought it referred to knocking the coconuts off their perch with the wooden balls.

'Oh, Clara, Clara, *mon amour*, I never expected you to read anything like that out to me! And the funniest thing is that I suspect that you have no idea what the innuendo is behind it.' Anton bent double. His laughter made her laugh, but she really was clueless as to why it was so funny, or what she was supposed to have an idea about.

Anton put his lips next to her ear and whispered the explanation. Clara had the feeling that her whole body blushed.

She was surprised that he should say such a thing to her, but then, Jeannie was always laughing at something he'd said to her, and often said, 'Oh, to be French and not have any inhibitions.'

The moment held an intimacy. Something happened to her that she couldn't explain, or understand, but she wanted to hold on to the feeling. No. More than that, she wanted to hold on to Anton. To have him as close to her as was possible, and to be held by him. Not in the chummy way he had his arm around her now, but held close to his body.

Anton fell silent. His face was turned towards hers, his eyes looked into hers, and it was difficult to believe they couldn't see her as he spoke her name. 'Clara, my Clara. *Mon amour.*'

'Hey, you. Why aren't you in uniform? Conchie, are you?' Clara jumped. Anton's body jerked as the soldier pushed him. 'We'd all like to stay at home with our girlfriends, conchie, but that would be cowardice, wouldn't it? Our country needs us, or don't you care about the freedom of your fellow man, eh?'

Clara leapt forward as the soldier pulled back his arm, his hand forming a fist. 'Don't! He's blind!'

The soldier's face dropped into a gape. His arm lowered. His stare was intent as he looked into Anton's face. 'I'm sorry, mate. I didn't realise.'

'Shame on you! You're nowt clever. You're only in uniform 'cause you have to be. Conscripted – made to join up, when lads like mine volunteered the moment war broke out.'

Clara looked round and into the face of Ruby, the landlady of the Fallen Leaves pub. Her involuntary gasp had Ruby looking more closely at her. Then she smiled, and with

224

meaning, said, 'Eeh, I thought for a mo that you were some-one else, lass. My mistake.' Her wink had Clara smiling back at her.

'But as for you, lad, I'd get on your way, and think on afore you start accusing others.'

The soldier apologised again, touched his cap and walked away. Ruby looked into Clara's eyes, then winked again. 'Well, nice to have met you both. I've to get on me road as well. I've a pub to run. And you, young man, should carry sommat as tells of your disability, that way you won't get into bother, as it's not easy to see your affliction. Let this be a warning to you both, as neither of you look what you appear to be, and folk could get you into a lot of trouble.'

With this, Ruby was gone, but Clara was left with every limb of her body shaking uncontrollably. Ruby had known who she was, and had been trying to convey that if others who knew her saw her, they would recognise her too. How had she imagined they wouldn't?

'Let's go to Daisy's now, Anton.'

'*Mais non*! What about my fish and chips? I'm not afraid. I understand how the soldier feels. I am frustrated at not being in my own country and fighting with my fellow countrymen, but it is that I have to accept how my life is, and to get on with it as best that I can.'

She wanted to tell him that she was in danger, too, but he knew nothing about her former life, just as she knew nothing of his. They had accepted each other on face value. Life was like that in the theatre. You were just you, and if you fitted in then you were one of them. Nobody pried into your past. Not even Daisy, who liked a gossip, would tell anyone

225

anything she knew about any of the troupe if it would do them harm.

'Tinker will fetch fish and chips for us all. And we will come down together again, but with your stick.'

Inside, Clara wondered if this would be so. Seeing Ruby had unnerved her. Ruby had seemed to be on her side. But what if she'd been play-acting so as not to raise Clara's suspicions that she'd let Mickey know she was in the town? Ruby had never struck her as a person she could trust.

'*Mon amour*, there is something else wrong, I can feel it.'

'N – no, only that I am cold. Please, Anton, let us go.'

'*Mais oui*, we will go, do not worry, but I feel your distress. You can tell me what is the reason for it, or no, it is up to you, *ma* Clara, but I have this urge to know all there is to know about you.'

'And I you, Anton. We will talk, I promise.'

'You can trust me, *mon amour*, as I am part of you and you are part of me.'

With this he opened his arms and Clara snuggled into his body. She wanted to stay there for ever. She knew that, yes, she was a part of Anton and always wanted to be.

CHAPTER TWENTY-ONE

Julia
Falling

Julia tried to ignore the rapping on her door. She knew it was the landlord. She had no money to give him and feared being evicted.

'I know you are in there. Do I have to fetch the police?'

Getting up off the sofa wasn't easy with her bulk. Opening the door let the June sunshine flood into the hall. 'I – I'm sorry, Mr Westfield. I haven't got the rent.'

'Then I want you out of here. Right now. Pack a few things and get out. The furniture will pay me back what you owe me.'

'But I have nowhere to go, and my baby is due in two months!'

'Take yourself to that convent on the outskirts of the town. They take in unmarried mothers. Disgusting, it is. I don't like having the likes of you in my property. If I'd have known that the pair of you weren't married, I'd have not let you move in till after you wed. I got the shock of me life when the agent told me you had different names. Oh, I know, he said that you and that airman had intended to marry within days of you being here, but that didn't happen. Have you heard from your fiancé yet?'

'Only the once, and nothing since. But I know when he can he will contact.'

'Where is he then?'

'I don't know, and you should know better than to ask. As you say, we aren't married, so no one will give me any information. I only had his friend as a contact, but he has been reported as missing. He never came back from a bombing mission.'

'Like a lot of them. So, you don't know if your man's dead or alive? Ain't you got no family that you can go to?'

'No.'

'Well, I'm sorry for you, but I ain't no charity. But, I'll do one thing for you. I'll pay your fare to St Joseph's convent. Now, get your things together, and I'll go and get a cab.'

Fear gripped Julia as she closed the door and leaned heavily on it. A convent! Didn't they take your baby from you? This wasn't the first time she'd heard about St Joseph's. Her hands went to her belly. *I can't bear that, I can't. Oh God, help me!*

The past months had been an agony of uncertainty and heartbreak. Gareth's first letter after a few weeks spoke of him undertaking special training. He said he wouldn't be able to contact her often, but that he loved her and had put something in place to support her. Since then, there hadn't been a word, and though she'd hoped with all her heart that there would be a communication from Gareth's solicitor, nothing had come. If only she knew who the solicitor was, at least then she could make contact and ask for help.

Gareth hadn't yet moved his personal things from his quarter in the barracks to here, so she had nothing that she could search through. And a visit to the bank that held the funds for her had been met with a cold stare from the bank manager, who had made her feel like a criminal. 'Captain Maling's left the one fund for you, madam. That has nearly depleted. He left no further instructions in your favour.'

A few weeks after Gareth's first letter, Julia had decided she would have to contact Gareth's friend to see if he had news. She'd been turned away at the base, and then had seen his name listed as missing in action in the local paper.

Despair had filled Julia. Her own money had gone, and Gareth's only ran to one further week's rent. She hadn't known where to seek help, other than the parish relief, but they turned her down. 'I'm sorry, you aren't registered here. How long have you lived here?' Julia had answered the questions of the woman, who was taking particulars of those seeking help. When it came to the question of where her husband was, she'd had to explain that she wasn't married. Thankfully the woman hadn't been unkind. 'Well, my dear, the best thing you can do is to present yourself to St Joseph's convent. They take in unmarried mothers. Unless you have family to turn to, then that is your only solution. I'm sorry.'

In the meantime, she'd been told to go to the Salvation Army church, and there she had been given food. Without that she would have starved. She hated going there in the evening and sitting with all the others who, for one reason or another, were in need – most because they drank too much, some because they had disabilities and couldn't fend for themselves. It wasn't because she felt above these people, but because she wanted to be helping them, instead of being one of them. *Oh, Gareth, Gareth, where are you? Why don't you contact?*

But with a sinking heart, she realised that it truly was too late. The dreams this flat had held for her lay in tatters and there was nothing she could do but to go to the convent for fallen women.

As she stood outside the grey walls of St Josephs, tears streamed down Julia's face. A nun with a smiling face opened a hatch that was part of the heavy wooden door. 'Yes? What can we do for you?'

'I – I need refuge, please. I'm pregnant, and . . . well, I'm not married.'

'All right, dear. Stay there while I fetch someone.'

The nun who opened the door didn't have a smiley face, but a very stern one. 'Well, what's your story?'

'I – I have nowhere to go. My landlord evicted me. I'm due to have my baby in a few weeks.'

'Hum, I can see that. And I can see that you're no spring chicken, either. A sorry state of affairs. Women of your age should know better. Come with me.'

Julia knew in her heart that the woman was right. Yes, she should have known better. Hadn't she been through this before? Hadn't she put one child through enough? *Oh, why,*

why didn't I stick to my resolve, and make Gareth leave and divorce Vanda, and marry me before I lay with him? But she knew why. Not in a million years could she ever have resisted him. Her love for him was too strong.

The hall they entered smelled of polish and her feet squeaked on the shining linoleum. The berating from the nun continued as they walked: 'And you can dry those tears, it's too late for tears. I'll get you booked in, and then you will bath, ready to be examined by our midwife. If she thinks you need further medical treatment she will send for a doctor.'

The nun told Julia to call her Sister Bernard. 'Now. Sit down. Name?'

As Julia gave her details, they sounded sordid. 'No, this isn't my first child.'

'Oh, one of those, are you? Well, we'll soon get rid of this one for you, too. There's women crying out for babies – married women who can't have them naturally, and will love your unwanted child.'

'It isn't unwanted, and I don't want to give it up.'

'Oh, and what pray do you intend to do with it then? If you can't even look after yourself while its still in your womb, how are you going to look after the two of you?'

'My fiancé will come back from war. We will be married.'

'Does he know that you are pregnant?'

'Yes, but—'

'There are no buts, Julia. Why isn't he supporting you? War, or no war, he could do so. I'm sorry, but it looks to me as if he has seen his chance to escape his responsibilities. I don't think you will see hide or hair of him. Now, you are from Guernsey, so I presume any family you have is there?'

'No, my parents . . . they are dead.' She dared not say that her parents were in Germany. That was something she was afraid of anyone finding out in case they thought she was a risk to security. 'My child was evacuated. I have lost touch with her as no records were kept of where she was sent to.'

'So, you brought your first child up?'

'Yes.'

'And now you are in the same position again!' This was said on a deep sigh.

Julia blushed. She couldn't blame the sister for how she was judging her.

'Well, we won't allow you to take your new baby from here. You have no way of taking care of it. We would be failing in our duty to an infant. The child will be found a good home.'

'No, please, I couldn't bear it. Can you find someone to take care of my baby until I get on my feet? I can get a job and a home, and then—'

'We don't have such a facility. Get used to the idea, Julia. And for heaven's sake, stop those tears!' With this, Sister Bernard stood up. 'Right. I will show you the bathroom. When you have bathed, put the robe on that I will give you, and come out of the second door of the bathroom. You will be in the clinic then, and we will go through the necessary medical checks.'

As she lay in the hot bath, Julia allowed her whole body to weep. She felt so helpless. Caressing her belly, her thoughts were despairing. *My darling, how will I live without you? What will your daddy say when he comes home? Will he blame me? Will he hate me?*

She tried desperately to think of a solution, but none would come. Her thoughts went from escaping as soon as her child was born, to maybe trying to find help from somewhere beforehand, but for now she knew that she had to surrender to the regime here, and to try to make the best of her situation.

Despite having had no medical care through her pregnancy, everything was found to be in order. The midwife had introduced herself as Sister Grace. A woman of about Julia's age, she was efficient, but not unkind, and not judgemental, either.

Now Julia found herself in a long dining room, as lunch was about to be served. She and all the pregnant girls, who were all much younger than her, were dressed in the same grey frocks. Buttoned from the hem to the neckline, it was more of a smock, but comfortable to wear. Over this they all had a white pinafore, and all had their hair tied into a scarf, which had been put on the back of their head and pulled forward and tied above their forehead. None of them wore make-up, and all had thick grey stockings on and dark brown shoes that were more like a man's.

Some of the girls only looked around twelve or thirteen. Julia hoped they were older. She couldn't bear the thought of children of that age being put into this position. Orders were shouted by a nun who stood at the top of the dining room, her arms folded, her look cold and full of loathing.

A girl came up to Julia. 'You have to get your own cutlery, and a mat. Follow me, I'll show you what to do.'

The girl was one of the younger-looking ones, but she seemed to have an old head on her shoulders.

'Thanks. My name's Julia.'

'I'm Cissy, short for Cecilia.'

'Oh, I like Cecilia.'

'I don't, and I don't want to be called it. Only one person used me proper name, and he did this to me. He were me teacher.'

Julia didn't know what to say. She wanted to take the girl into her arms. There was nothing attractive about Cissy, and pregnancy hadn't helped as it had given her a blotchy skin, a symptom Julia had seen before. Her hair was a lank, mousy colour and hung from each side of her scarf. Her long nose and buck teeth gave her the appearance of a mouse. Julia's heart went out to her. She imagined Cissy hadn't attracted much attention in her life, and that maybe the teacher she spoke of gave her that, as he lured her to have sex with him. 'I'm sorry, Cissy. Teachers should care for you, not do this to you.'

'He told me he did care, then he denied ever touching me. He said that I was covering up for a lad in school. A snotty-nosed lad who everyone picked on. He said that he had caught us doing it. Everyone believed him.'

Julia put out her hand and stroked the girl's hair. Cissy smiled up at her. Julia's heart lurched, and her feeling for her Clara was, for the first time, one of fear. What if someone like that teacher had Clara? *Oh, Clara, Clara.*

'They don't take kindly to tears in here.'

'Oh, I hadn't realised I was crying. I seem to do that a lot lately. It's as if my body leaks tears without me knowing it.'

'I wouldn't think you'd be scared, not being older like you are.'

'I'm not scared, just sad. Very sad. Anyway, let's get our things, we don't want to get into trouble.'

Once they had laid the table they were all given duties. Julia's was to slice the loaves of bread. She concentrated hard on the task, and tried to get her emotions in check. None of the young girls around her were crying, and all looked at her as if she was some sort of alien being. A loneliness engulfed her. There wasn't one woman of her own age to relate to. She felt like a freak.

After lunch, those as advanced in their pregnancies as Julia was were sent to the dormitory to rest. Julia was shown to a room with six beds in it. On the end of her bed was a pile of duplicate clothing to what she had on, as well as a pile of underwear, a towel and a bar of soap. Instructions were given to her as to where she should wash and where to put her dirty clothes. She was to change every three days. The thought of wearing her knickers that long repulsed her and she was glad to see a radiator by her bed. She would wash the gusset of her knickers every night and dry them on the radiator. This convent was well in advance of many homes, Julia thought, as it had inside bathrooms and flush toilets.

To her surprise, Julia slept as soon as she lay her exhausted body down, and it was a shock to be woken by a loud bell. Opening her eyes she saw another nun standing in the doorway of the dormitory. 'Up you get. Come on, all of you. Swill your faces, and get to your duties. You. New girl. Make your way to the kitchen.'

Julia wondered at the sour nature of the nuns. She had thought of nuns as being gentle creatures, holy beings full of kindness. Apart from the smiley face that had looked at her through the hatch, none of the nuns she'd met had so far had fitted that image. They were frightening, stern and not kind at all.

In the kitchen the smell that hit her made her feel sick. The air was stale with old cooking smells and had a wet-mop stench to it.

'So, you're the new intake, then. Tut, we don't get many as old as you, in here. Well, as I understand it, you have two months to go to your time. You will work as hard as everyone else until you are within a month of giving birth and only then will you ease up. My name's Sister Francis. And you will do exactly as I tell you to do. You can start by peeling that lot, and hurry about it, I want them on the stove in ten minutes.'

Julia looked at the three buckets of potatoes and gasped. It seemed an impossible task.

'Get on with it, you won't get them done by staring at them.'

By the time Julia had the last one peeled, her right hand had a blister in the palm and her head spun. Today had changed her life so drastically that she was still in shock. The room began to spin. From somewhere in the distance, she heard Sister Francis say, 'Catch her, William!'

She didn't feel herself being caught, only falling. Falling for real, when these last days she'd felt only her inner spirit falling and deserting her. For a moment, she didn't want to be caught. She wanted the blessed peace that seemed to be offered to her by the black hole that had opened up in her mind. And so she let go and tumbled. Deeper and deeper she fell, swirling around in a nothingness, until a voice called to her – Gareth's voice. *Hold on, Julia, my darling, I'm coming.*

It was then that she hit the bottom of the black hole with a thud and opened her eyes, only to close them again and drift into the peace that had settled in her. *Let me go, let me go, I can't face the future, I can't.* With this Julia felt a peace engulf her.

CHAPTER TWENTY-TWO

Clara and Anton
A Journey of Discovery

The summer show was in full swing and Clara loved it. She'd sat in the theatre many an afternoon listening to Anton playing during the matinee. Over the last couple of months their love for each other had grown but, apart from the short time that followed the matinee before he had to get ready for the evening show, they had spent little time together, and not much of that had been alone. The afternoon they'd had seemed such a long way away, and neither had broached the subject of their pasts again.

Today, they had both been given some unexpected time off. The matinee was cancelled due to a death in the family of one of the supporting acts. Another act had been booked, but couldn't make it until the evening show.

Anton wanted to visit the seafront and to do the things that he had been denied on their last visit. Clara was nervous about it, but she had a plan. She had borrowed some sunglasses from Jeannie. They had what looked like small wings on them, just like those worn by Greta Garbo. She felt sure they made her unrecognisable as the gangly girl she had been when she worked for Mickey. Besides, months had gone by now, and Mickey must have realised that neither she nor Lindsey were going to talk to the police about him and his gang. They both knew they should for the sake of the poor girls who might have been in Mickey's clutches now, but they were too afraid to.

'Clara?'

'Yes, I'm here.' She stood in the foyer waiting. Looking up, she marvelled at Anton coming down the stairs with all the confidence of a sighted person, but was glad to see that he carried his stick. Her heart raced at the sight of him, but she found herself saying something as ordinary as, 'It's raining, but I have an umbrella.'

'It would on my only day off.'

It seemed to Clara that there was a strain between them. Was Anton remembering that they'd promised so many times that they would talk the next time that they were alone together? She knew that she was, and that she didn't want to tell him everything as she had promised she would.

As soon as they were outside, Anton's arm came around her. They snuggled under the umbrella together. This was the closest she'd been to him since their last trip out and for a moment she forgot the worry of him asking her questions, and allowed the lovely feeling inside to fill her with joy. 'Oh,

Anton, it's so good to be out together. Shall we eat first? I'm starving.'

'Yes. Fish and chips. I haven't had any since the last ones that we had at Daisy's. The crew have often fetched some in, but I declined as I wanted my next time to be with you, with the smell of the salty sea, and the sound of the Wurlitzer around us.'

'Oh dear, the rain's coming faster now, so I don't think you're going to get your wish. I think we'll have to enjoy those smells and sounds on the way to the café, but eat our chips inside.'

'Ah, but I don't mind the rain.'

'Well, I do. It will make my hair dye run.'

'You dye your hair? *Mais non!* I didn't know that. Is it still not the dark brown that you described to me?'

Clara wished she could take the words back. 'No, it is auburn.'

'*Mais pourquoi?* It is lovely in its natural state, I am sure. And all this while, I have framed the features that I explored with my hands with dark brown, glossy hair. I had a picture of you in my head. I don't want to change that.'

'Oh, Anton, it is part of what I was going to tell you.'

'The fear that I feel in you?'

'Yes.'

'Let us get to the café, *mon amour.*'

The inside of the café felt warm. The windows were streaming with condensation and there was a smell of damp clothes in the air, mingled with that of the smoke from the customers who were puffing away on cigarettes. The aroma of fish and chips muted all of this, and whet Clara's appetite.

Even though they were sitting inside, the fish and chips were served wrapped in newspaper, which she loved. All other smells faded as the special aroma was released as she unwrapped her portion.

Unwrapping Anton's, she guided his hand to them, then giggled as he burnt his fingers.

'Ha, they've just come out of the fryer, not like those we had at Daisy's that Tinker fetched, so take care.'

Anton cautiously picked up a chip, blew on it, and then bit into it. Clara waited for his reaction, knowing that he had enjoyed them last time, but remembering that the French were fussy over their food.

'Mmm, that's divine. I didn't say before, but we French do something similar with our potatoes – *pommes de terre frites*. But they are much thinner than this. I like that they have the vinegar on them.'

'*Je parle français.*'

'Oh?'

'*Oui, je suis de Guernsey.*'

Anton looked at her with his unseeing eyes wide open, giving him an expression of surprise. '*Mais non!* Why didn't I know this before? Tell me about your childhood and how it is that you are here.'

Anton marvelled at her story. She stopped short of telling him the last part, as she didn't want him afraid for her, and just told him that she was unhappy with Daisy's sister and had run away.

'Daisy is altogether different, it is difficult to think of them as being sisters. She has helped me to forget what my life was like living in the shop before she took over. I love her like I love my granny.'

At this, and without warning, Clara had to wipe away a tear. Anton's hand clasped hers. 'One day you will be reunited with your *mère et grandmère*. This is something that I know. But what of your *père*? Is he still on the island too?'

'N – no, he died, before I was born – a boating accident.' Again, she didn't tell the whole truth of it, and yet it wasn't a lie.

'*Mon amour*, it is that I sense a deep pain that you cannot touch. I am your friend, Clara. I so wish that I could see you, but I feel attuned to you. As if I have access to your soul. I feel that there are many things on your mind. Secrets, you are afraid to tell. Never be afraid. None of us are perfect, we all have, how you say, *Le squelette est dans le placard*.'

'Skeletons in the cupboard. So, what are your skeletons?'

'I am the son of a murderer and rapist . . .'

'Oh, Anton! I don't know what to say. I can't bear to think of you having a broken heart when none of what you have said was your fault.'

'No, I have always been brought up to know that I was wanted by *ma mère*, but what breaks my heart is to know what happened to her and how much she endured.'

'Was your mother the one who was raped, or did your father rape another woman?'

'Yes, it was *ma mère*. Sh – she was eventually murdered. She had me as a result of the rape, and then the rapist, who had got away with it by saying that she was willing, came back. While trying to rape her again, he murdered her, as he could not get the better of her other than by beating her. She fought so hard against him. He was executed. *Grandmère* brought me up, she was a linguist and taught me to speak English. She was an accomplished pianist, and she taught me to play the piano. I came to England recently, but have always been around people from many continents in the circus world and the theatre and so I used my English often. I – I was born blind. It is not known why as no one in my family has ever been blind, but of course, we do not know about the family of the man who did those horrible things.'

Clara noticed how Anton never once acknowledged this monster he spoke about as his father. She clung onto his hand, not knowing what to say, and yet wanting to say so much. She could feel him trembling.

'So, *mon amour*, whatever your secret is, it cannot be worse than what I have shared with you.'

Telling him of her own birth came easy then, and for the first time she saw the beauty of it, and not the shame. 'My mum and dad were very much in love, and I have been told so much about him and what a good man he was. His mother, my granny, stood by us, and always loved me.'

'Oh, *mon amour*, it is that those bigoted people have made you feel less of a person, when you were born of love. Clara, I know that we are only young, but I am falling in love with you. I want to be with you for ever.'

Clara didn't know what was happening to her, but the surge of feelings she had for Anton made her feel as though she was floating out of her body and into his. His hand burned hers. His unseeing eyes, though expressionless, seemed to her to express his love for her. 'I feel the same, Anton. I love you.'

243

His arm came around her, but before she could snuggle into him a voice brought them back to reality. 'Now then, you two, I don't allow canoodling in me café. It ain't polite and embarrasses me and me customers. Besides, you've sat there long enough, I ain't a warming place, and others are waiting for tables.'

Clara became aware of how full the café was. Her face reddened. A soldier laughed. 'Awe, leave them alone, Doris. Can't you see they're in love?'

'That might well be, but I ain't providing naw love nest. Come on, the pair of you, on your way.'

As they passed the soldiers, they all cheered them. Doris smiled. 'You're allus welcome, but treat me place reet, eh?'

'I – I'm sorry, Doris. We were only talking.'

'Hey, don't I knaw you? You used to come in here a lot. You and another girl. A cockney. By that were only last year. What's happened to you, lass? You look years older. And where's your friend?'

Shocked at being recognised once more, a fear zinged through Clara, knocking her confidence. She explained what had happened to Shelley.

'Aw, poor lass. Well, owt like that would make you grow up fast, and if I remember reet, you're an evacuee, an' all, so that'd make anyone leave their childhood early. You've had to toughen up to face the world, lass, I can see that. Well, like I say, you're allus welcome, and can stay as long as you like when I'm not busy, but you're to remember, I don't have no canoodling.'

'We apologise, we forget ourselves. Thank you, madam, for the lovely fish and chips. And we will come again. *Bon soir.*'

'Eeh, you're French.'

Another soldier chipped in. 'Ooh la-la.' He swaggered his hips.

Everyone laughed, and Clara couldn't help but join them. This relaxed Anton and he too smiled.

'I feel sorry for you, mate, not being able to see your girl-friend. She's a beauty.'

'I know. I can see with my hands.'

A roar of laughter followed this and Anton became flustered. '*Mais non*, I – I did not mean . . .'

'We know, fella. Good luck to the pair of you. Looks to me as you've had your share of troubles.'

Clara thanked him.

Outside, the rain had calmed but for Clara the afternoon was spoiled. A trace of the warmth of Anton's love was still with her, but overriding that was the fear of how she was so easily recognised. She donned the glasses that she'd taken off inside the café, but still she felt vulnerable. Even though earlier she'd tried to convince herself that Mickey would have forgotten her by now, she knew that no one crossed him and got away with it. A shudder shook her body.

'You are cold?'

'No, I'm just a bit damp, and it unnerves me when I am recognised. I'm sorry, Anton, to do this to you again, but can we go to Daisy's? We still have four hours before we have to be back at the theatre. I'll tell you why on the way.'

'*Ma pauvre*. Clara, I'm shocked at what you told me. *Mon amour*, you must be so afraid. And poor Lindsey. She has been

245

through so much. It seems we are all waifs and strays, as the English say.'

'Yes, that is just what we are. And so is Tinker. I sometimes feel that everyone in Blackpool is hiding from something, or trying to forget their past.'

'Tinker too? I liked Tinker and it is that Lindsey talks a lot about him. I think she is a little in love with him, no?'

'Oh, I hadn't thought about that, but yes, come to think of it, I think she must be, and he with her. Funny that she has never spoken of it though, only of them being very, very good friends. But then, so are she and I, but any excuse she gets she goes back to Daisy's to be with Tinker, and they often go out for walks together in the evenings. They say that it is to walk the dog, but . . .' Clara wondered at her own naivety. But then, why wouldn't Lindsey say anything? Maybe they just hadn't realised it themselves?

As they made their way to Daisy's Clara fell into chatting with Anton in French. The more she used the language, the more it came back to her. Somehow, this link deepened the bond between them, and she knew that, even though she was still only young, she loved him, and wanted to be with him for the rest of her life.

Some of her fear subsided as they left the seafront, but deep inside she was unnerved, and prayed that Mickey never found her and – especially – Lindsey. Lindsey had been much more involved with Mickey's dealings, and knew so much about him and his gang. He wouldn't let her off lightly.

By the time they reached Daisy's she felt a lot more settled, and decided not to voice her fears just yet to Lindsey, though she knew that she would have to tell her how once again she had so easily been recognised, and to warn her to take care.

The atmosphere in the little back room of the shop was jolly. They found Daisy, Lindsey and Tinker playing a card game, where the loser had to act out a scene given them by the others. Daisy was in the middle of being Juliet, and was giving it her all, as she fluttered her eyes at a blushing Tinker.

Clara and Anton joined in the fun and the next couple of hours, before they had to return to the theatre, were the happiest Clara had known. Anton couldn't play, but was tasked with giving out the forfeits. He gave Clara the forfeit of singing a song that had been used in the pantomime, adapted from Walt Disney's *Pinocchio* – 'When You Wish Upon a Star'. It was a popular song and was heard on the radio all the time. Clara loved it, and knew all the words.

'Anton, we have a piano, you must accompany her.'

'Take me to it, Daisy.'

With Anton's music filling the room, Clara's confidence soared and she let the song surge through her.

When it came to an end, there was a silence, then as one, the four stood and clapped and cheered her.

A joy filled her. It was as if they were a huge audience giving her a standing ovation.

'*Mon amour, c'était magnifique!*'

'Whatever *he* said with bells on, lass. By, Clara, I didn't knaw as you had such a beautiful voice!' With this, Lindsey came to her and hugged her.

Over Lindsey's shoulder Clara saw Daisy wiping a tear from her eye. But it wasn't a sad tear – her face was smiling. Tinker looked at her as if he didn't know her. But then, Anton said, 'Come to me, *cherie.*'

Leaving Lindsey's arms she crossed the room into Anton's open ones. '*Ma belle chérie talentueuse.*'

She looked up into his face and thrilled at the admiration she saw there. And she knew that she wanted to be what he had called her – his beautiful, talented, darling – for ever.

CHAPTER TWENTY-THREE

Julia
Despair

Julia recovered within a couple of days. She'd been allowed to rest for a day, but checks by Sister Grace showed that all was well with her.

'It's always a shock having to come in here. I'm always advocating that extra care should be given to help women to settle in, but I'm never listened to.'

It seemed that Sister Grace, at least, was what she purported to be – a woman with a vocation, a compassionate and holy woman. But Julia hadn't found these qualities in any of the others she had come into contact with.

Now back in the kitchen, Julia had decided that she would do her best to please, and to help the younger girls whom she realised must be so much more terrified than she was. Finishing the chore of peeling the buckets full of potatoes, she leaned back, wondering what was to happen to them. A wiry-looking man, who had filled two large saucepans with water, came over to her and, without a word, lifted the peeled potatoes and emptied them into the pans.

'That's William. 'E's deaf and dumb. 'E's been 'ere all his life. Born 'ere he was. But they couldn't get anyone to take him, not even an orphanage, so they reared him themselves. 'E knows more than 'e cottons on to, though, as his actions can surprise you at times.' The girl who'd spoken looked in her early twenties. She had a nice face, with dimples when she smiled, and short blond hair.

'I'm Billie, short for Belinda. I would 'ave met you a couple of days ago, but they carried you off before I got the chance. You're to make apple pies, a dozen of them, and I'm to help yer. I 'ope you can make pastry? I'll peel the apples, as I'm too 'eavy-'anded for pastry. I've only got a month to go, so I'm mostly on light duties. I give a 'and where it's needed. What's someone of your age doing in this predicament, then?'

'I'm not that old! I'm thirty-six. I've had a rough time of it lately.' There was something about Billie that Julia liked, and so she told her story to her. Unburdening herself to someone who listened and wasn't judgemental, she felt a lightening of the load on her shoulders.

'I'm sorry for yer, Julia. Are yer sure this Gareth means to do right by yer?'

Julia attacked the rubbing in of the fat into the flour – she'd never dealt with such quantities and found it heavy going. 'Yes. I couldn't be more sure of anything as I am of his love for me. I don't understand what is happening, or where he is,

250

but if he could contact me, he would have. I can only think that the work he has been sent to do is top secret and so important that he has no choice, and isn't in a position to do anything about my situation.'

'Well, you 'old on to that, love. You're going to need sommat to 'ang on to in 'ere.'

'What happened to you, Billie?'

'I was raped by me bleedin' uncle. Dirty old git. 'E's been after me for years. I told me mum, but she didn't believe me. Then I had to babysit me cousins one night. He'd got 'is call up, and him and me aunt got drunk. 'E walked me 'ome, and got me in the alleyway. I fought 'im, but he were too strong for me. I can't wait to rid meself of his bastard.'

Julia felt sick to her stomach. For all she'd been through, she'd never experienced something like this. 'I'm sorry, Billie. What are you going to do afterwards?'

'Go 'ome, and try to pick me life up. I 'ad a boyfriend, but 'e wouldn't stand by me. 'E didn't even tell me when 'e was called up. Anyway, I'll get sorted. I'll go into war work. Munitions or summink. That pays a lot of money, and you can soon get on yer feet. What about you?'

'I don't know. I've only been without hope for a couple of days. I've done nothing but cry since my landlord evicted me. I was forced to come here as I had no money and nowhere to go. I wish I hadn't, as I don't want to lose my baby. Do you know of any way that I could keep it?'

'Keep it! Are you mad? Well, there ain't no way that I know of. I mean, you just said that you had no 'ome and no money. Gawd, you'd 'ave more than a job on yer 'ands trying to keep you and a baby going. I'm sorry for yer, but yer going to 'ave to get used to the idea that they will take yer baby off you. I can't wait to get shot of mine. And I 'ope me uncle cops it for a bullet, but that 'e has a very slow and painful death, because all I want to do is dance on his grave.'

Even though what Billie said filled Julia with despair, she had to smile at her. It was a watery smile, and she had to wipe her runny nose, but she felt better for the lighter moment.

'That's the way, luv. Do as we Londoners do, "Pack up your troubles in your old kit bag and smile, smile, smile . . ."'

'What are you girls doing? Who is that singing? Shut up and get on, those pies need getting into the oven, and now! Then get on with making the custard.'

Sister Francis scurried by looking hot and sweaty. Behind her, William astonished Julia by marching, as if he was a soldier.

'See, I told yer. 'E ain't no more deaf than I am. Dumb perhaps, but he must have heard me singing and knew that it was a marching song in the Great War.'

'No. He would have picked up on the vibration. A lot of deaf people can detect noise, especially music. And living in his own world, if he is clever, he could perhaps read, and that's how he knows more than you think.'

'Yes, 'e can read. One of the nuns, the one who answers the door, taught him. No one knows 'ow, but she spends hours with him. She's Sister Anne. She's not quite right in her 'ead. But she's lovely with it, and has the patience of a saint. Well, she is a saint really. She's kind and thoughtful. Anyway, 'ow do you know that about deaf folk?'

'I was a trained nurse at your age. We dealt with many things as we are only a small island, and we had a few deaf children that we looked after, and were trained to work with.'

'Well then, yer've got your career sorted. They're crying out for nurses, mate. Get rid of that thing, then go to the Red Cross. They'll take yer on.'

'My baby isn't a *thing*, Billie, and neither is yours, no matter how it was conceived. It is a child, and I cannot think of getting rid of mine.'

Billie's head dropped. 'Look, luv, yer better off thinking of it as I do . . . as I've *made* meself think of it. It's the only way, 'cause we're going to 'ave it taken away from us, whether we want it or not.'

Billie picked up the apples she'd peeled and sliced, and filled the tins that Julia had lined with pastry. She kept her head down, but Julia heard her sniff, and realised with shock that Billie was in just as much pain as herself at the prospect of losing her child. Shame came over her. She shouldn't have spoken like that.

'I'm sorry, Billie, that was insensitive of me. I – I believed your bravado. I see now that what you say isn't what you feel in your heart, and that you are just trying to prepare yourself. I – I won't mention it again. But I will pray for us both.'

Recovered, Billie snapped, 'There ain't no prayers that will 'elp, I've tried that route.' With this, she marched off calling out to Sister Francis, asking if she was needed for anything else as her legs were hurting her.

Julia was mortified. In Billie, who was the nearest to her age of all the girls she'd seen so far, she'd thought she had found a friend, and now she'd managed to alienate her.

By the time Julia got into her bed that night, she ached all over, more so than she had ever done on the farm, but sleep eluded her as she frantically went through the possibilities of how she could keep her child. Polly came into her thoughts. *Would she foster my child until I can take care of it myself?* But no, that didn't seem a possibility. Even if Polly might want to agree, she had her job on the farm, and she wouldn't want to face the wrath of the villagers. What of Mrs Pickering? Would she help? She never seemed over-bothered by what those in the village thought.

But trying to give herself hope proved fruitless. In her heart she knew that even getting to the village was beyond her, as she hadn't a penny to her name. Tears threatened, but she swallowed hard and controlled them. She'd cried enough to fill a river, and still hadn't found any release from her pain. She had to be strong. She had to think everything through logically.

Her head hurt when she closed her eyes. Moments later a sudden scream shot them open and had her sitting up. The dormitory was dimly lit, but she saw that the girl two beds away was in a bent position. Calling over to her she asked, 'Are you all right? Did you have a bad dream?'

'No. A pain woke me, and I think I've wet the bed.'

Another voice shouted, 'Yer'll be for it if yer have, Mildred.'

Mildred sobbed. One or two of the other girls moaned about the commotion. Julia got out of bed and went to Mildred. As she got to her the girl cried out in pain again. Her fingers dug into the hand Julia had offered her. 'Are you due, Mildred?'

'No. I've another three months to go.'

'Can't you shut 'er up? We're trying to sleep 'ere.'

'No. I'm sorry, but I'm going to have to put the light on to see what's happening. Mildred is in trouble.'

As Julia put the light on, the mood changed. Questions came from two of the girls. 'What's wrong with 'er?'

'She's not 'aving the baby, is she? It's too soon.'

Julia didn't answer, but hurried back to Mildred and pulled the covers back. Trying not to show her concern at the pool of blood she saw there, she calmly but urgently bid one of the girls to fetch help. 'Now, lie down, Mildred.' Turning to the others, she commanded, 'Quick, as many of you as can, bring me your pillows, we have to elevate her feet.'

'Gawd, what's 'appening?'

'Stay calm, Mildred. You're losing blood, I'm going to try to stop that. Don't worry.'

By the time Sister Grace appeared, the blood flow had lessened. 'Well done . . . Sorry, what was your name?'

'Julia. I'm a trained nurse.'

'I'm a terror with names. And this is Mildred? Right, get your dressing gown and come with me, Julia, I may need your help. I'll send for the doctor, but from experience I know that he can take his time getting here.'

The sister moved the chocks from the bed's wheels and pushed it towards the doors, calling out to one of the girls, 'Prop the doors open, Sally.'

By the time this was done, Julia had caught up with Sister Grace. She marvelled at the calmness exuding from the midwife, who even took a moment to switch off the light and call out, 'Get back to sleep all of you, Mildred will be all right.'

With this, Julia's own training kicked in, and she found herself ready to take orders from her superior. Something

255

inside stirred. *This is what I am meant to do. I have wasted so many years. But then, rules and convention were against me.*

Julia marvelled at the equipment that Sister Grace had to hand in the theatre-type room they entered. As she lifted the telephone, she told Julia to don a gown and scrub up. A feeling surged through Julia's veins that she hadn't felt since her nursing days – a pride in herself. For couldn't she make a difference to someone's life? Or even help to save it? And Sister Grace was showing that she had the faith in her to do that.

What happened afterwards all came naturally to Julia as she attended to Sister Grace's every instruction with professionalism. She marvelled at the sister's skill and knowledge as she stemmed the flow of blood. Mildred was sedated throughout, with Julia checking her vital signs and administering the chloroform as needed.

'Well done, Julia, excellent work. You say you were trained. Have you been working as a nurse?'

They were sitting in the sister's office sipping tea, waiting for the doctor to arrive.

Julia found herself feeling so comfortable and safe that she told Sister Grace all that had happened to her.

'My, that is a sorry tale. Poor you. Yes, you made some silly decisions as regards allowing both of your fiancés to have their way with you before marriage, and I am very disapproving of you going with a man while he was still married, but you could not know what tragedy that would lead to. I don't think you should blame yourself for that. It seems to me it happened because of this Vanda's mental instability, though it

256

was triggered by her husband's actions. He should carry the guilt, not you.'

As Sister Grace rose and went to check on Mildred, Julia thought about what she had said and knew that there was truth in it. Gareth hadn't been free to ask her out, but then, she could have said no. Sighing, she realised that she could analyse it all for ever and not arrive at any conclusion other than that a series of wrongdoings on the part of all parties, except poor Rhoda, had brought about what had happened. And that she must accept her part, and forgive herself. It was all that she could do.

Re-entering the room, Sister Grace said, 'She's fine. Though I think she has lost her baby, poor thing.'

'She was going to lose it anyway, Sister. Maybe this way is kinder than knowing you have a child out there but not knowing where it is. I know what that feels like and am broken-hearted that it is going to happen to me again.'

'I understand. Oh, I know that I can never know what it feels like, but I do understand and sympathise.'

'Is there no way? Isn't there anywhere that helps a mother to keep her child? I'm desperate to keep mine, Sister.'

'Such a facility is sadly lacking. I have broached the subject with Reverend Mother before, as I see the pain of girls over and over when I deliver their babies and can't even let them see them. But none of my fellow sisters understand. They think it a just punishment for the sin the girl has committed, and our duty to see that the child does not suffer because of that sin.'

Julia felt defeated. Tiredness once more seeped into her. Sister Grace must have seen this. 'Get yourself a nice bath,

257

then get back to bed, Julia. Keep praying. And I will join my prayers to yours. God is good. If it is in his plan for your child to stay with you, then that will happen.'

Julia wondered at the logic of this. How could God have any other plan for a child than to let it stay with its mother? And yet, He seemed to have many plans that didn't make sense.

Everything changed for Julia after that, as she was assigned to help Sister Grace. She loved the work and stayed in the surgery for many hours longer than she needed to.

The day they brought Billie in in labour, Julia had mixed emotions. This was her first birth. Julia's stomach churned as she knew she would have to face the emotion of seeing Billie part with her child. She hoped that the bravado Billie had shown would stand her in good stead.

Panting with pain, Billie smiled at Julia. 'I'd 'eard you were 'elping Sister Grace. A bit near your time, ain't yer?'

'I don't do any heavy work, Billie, and I can rest when I need to. I'm loving it so far, though, you're my first birth. My job till now has been monitoring. I must have missed you each time you came in. Are you all right with me being here?'

'All right? I reckon as it's the best thing as could 'appen for me. You understand 'ow it is, and that will 'elp.'

Keeping a professionalism she didn't feel, Julia smiled and began the checks that Sister Grace had taught her. In any other circumstances, she thought she would enjoy midwifery, but at this moment she wished she was anywhere but here.

Billie's baby made hard work of coming into the world. Julia's part was mostly to keep Billie calm, encourage her on and to mop her brow. Nothing prepared her for the scream Billie let out as her child slipped from her.

Froth gathered around her mouth as she begged: 'Give it to me. *Give me, me baby now!*'

'Billie, you know that I can't. Julia, help the afterbirth to come, I have to go.' Taking the baby to a side table, Sister Grace wrapped it in a blanket and disappeared out of the door.

'Stop her, Julia. *Please* stop her. *Julia, for pity's sake stop her . . . Me baby, me baby . . .*'

'Shush, Billie. Shush.' All professionalism left Julia as sobs wracked her body and she held Billie in her arms.

'No! No, Julia, I – I want me baby. I want me baby . . .'

Julia rocked Billie backwards and forwards. 'Hush, Billie. I – I am so sorry. Hush, my dear.'

Billie became quiet, but her body still shook with sobs as she clung to Julia.

'Help me, Julia. Make me strong.'

'You will be, love. You will get stronger. I promise. But, I don't know how you will come to terms with what happened. I – I just don't know.'

The two women clung together, their heartbreak bonding them. After a few moments, Julia realised that she must tend to Billie. The afterbirth hadn't yet come away. Making a huge effort, she untangled herself and began to massage Billie's abdomen. 'I'll need you to bear down, Billie. We need to get the placenta – the afterbirth away.'

Billie mechanically did as she was told, and the red mass that had given her baby life slipped from her. Julia, too, went into automatic mode, and shut down her emotions. Wrapping the afterbirth, she took it through to the incinerator and, without thinking about it, she fed the afterbirth into it.

When she went back to Billie, she found her quiet and very still. 'I'm going to clean you up now, Billie, then I'll get you a cup of tea.'

When Billie was washed and in a clean gown, she surprised Julia by asking her to look out of the window. 'See if there's a car out there, Julia.'

Julia pulled the curtain back and looked outside. She was shocked to see the windows of the dormitories opposite had a young girl staring from each one. Looking down she saw a car in the drive. 'Yes, there is a car, Billie.'

'Help me off this bed, Julia.'

Julia guessed what was going to happen, but knew that when it was her own baby she would want to watch it right up until it disappeared, just as she had when Clara left her.

They stood together, their arms around each other, staring down. After a few moments, one of the nuns came out from the convent door below, carrying a bundle. A woman followed her out. When they got to the car, a man opened the door. An old man. The nun handed the bundle to the woman.

Billie's head came down onto Julia's shoulder. Julia put her arm around her. When Billie whispered, 'Goodbye, my child, Mummy loves you', the tears trickled down Julia's face. *I won't be able to bear it. I won't.*

Billie clung to her, but she didn't cry. It seemed that she had shut her emotions down. Julia helped her to the basket chair and wheeled her through to the recovery ward.

'Stay with me till I'm asleep, Julia.'

'I will.'

Stroking Billie's hair, Julia tried to convey all the comfort she could. Billie soon fell into a deep sleep. Julia rose and headed for the bathroom. She couldn't face Sister Grace again tonight.

CHAPTER TWENTY-FOUR

Clara
A Fear Realised

'Lindsey? Lindsey, where are you? We have to go.' There was no answer to Clara's call.

'This isn't like Lindsey. Was she in bed when you got up?'

'I don't know, Daisy. I rushed outside to the lav, and then had my wash down here, as I like to leave her free to get ready in the bedroom. By the time I'm washed she's usually down. I'll pop up and make sure she's all right.'

Opening the door to their bedroom, Clara gasped! Lindsey's bed was empty. *Oh God, why didn't I notice that before?*

'Tinker, Tinker!' Tinker appeared at his bedroom door. 'Tinker, have you seen Lindsey?'

'What? No! Why, has she gone somewhere?'

Fear clutched Clara's stomach.

Tinker flew past her and, as if not believing her, checked the bedroom himself. Daisy flapped at the bottom of the stairs. 'Oh, where is she?'

Clara's mind would only give her one conclusion. 'Mickey!'

'Ech, naw. Don't say that, lass. Perhaps she went out for a walk early, or she's gone into work ahead of you.'

'But why should she? She's never done that before.'

'Are you saying, then, that Mickey's men came in the night and took her from her bed?'

'N – no, but then, I didn't see her come to bed. I was asleep before you and she came in. Did she come in, Tinker?'

Tinker hung his head. 'We – we had a row. I stormed off.'

'Tinker, no!'

'Eeh, lad, you shouldn't have left her. You knaw as she's in danger.'

'I'm going to Mickey's,' Clara grabbed her coat from the hook behind the door and made as if to go out, but Tinker stopped her.

'You can't do that, lass, it's too dangerous. I'll go to the police.'

'No, Tinker. For one, we don't know which ones to trust, and if we get the wrong ones they'll inform Mickey! And two, if Mickey has a visit from the police he'll order Lindsey's murder for sure. She's a witness to his activities.'

'But, Clara, lass, if you go, they'll have you, an' all. They're not going to let you walk in there and demand Lindsey's release. We've to think about this. Find a way that we can get into that guest house without being seen, find Lindsey and get her out of there. You go to work and leave this to me. I'll sort it, I promise. I have friends. Some of them could break

263

into the Tower of London and steal the Crown jewels and not be caught. They'll help me.'

'Aw, lass, I agree with Tinker, his way seems the only way. D'yer want me to phone work and say as you're not coming in?'

'No, thanks, Daisy. I'll have to go. I don't know how I'm going to concentrate, but Jeannie laid out several costumes last night that have to be ready for tonight. Only minor repairs, so I will manage them, but I'm so scared for Lindsey. If there's any news, please get it to me.'

Swallowing hard so as not to cry, Clara gave Daisy a quick hug and went out into the backyard to retrieve her bike.

Her mind was in a turmoil of fear and her heart beat wildly. She wasn't going to work – she'd told the lie just to get out of the house. Something didn't ring true. Why would Tinker leave Lindsey alone? No boyfriend would do that, even if they had fallen out. At least, not a decent boy. But what to do? Could she appeal to Dolly? This didn't give her hope after the way she and Lindsey had left her lying on the floor and hadn't helped her. What about Arnold? She'd always had the feeling that Arnold was more knowing than he let on. Why didn't he question her when she asked him never to tell anyone he'd seen her? Yes, she'd go to Arnold. But first she'd go to work and explain to Jeannie and leave a message for Anton for when he came in later.

Arnold greeted Clara with a knowing nod. He looked around as if afraid of being seen with her. 'Come to the back of me stall, lass. I'll just close me flaps, it's early yet for punters, any road.'

He opened a door at the side, let her in and then locked it. She found herself in a kitchen area. From here she couldn't see the front of the stall, though there was a small window high up. She imagined Arnold used this to keep his eye on things while he brewed himself a cup of tea.

'I knaw why you're here. But you're in danger, lass. Mickey has your friend, and he's put the word out that he wants you an' all. He wants to make an example of you both. He don't like it that you got away from him, nobody does that. It was like insulting him.'

'How do you know him, Arnold?'

'Lass, everyone knaws him. He runs the show in Blackpool. How do you think the rock makers can carry on making rock, and the fish and chip fryers can carry on frying their fish? They need sugar and oil and all manner of stuff that's on ration, they get that through Mickey. And then there's us. None of us stallholders can operate unless we pay protection money to Mickey. If we don't then we'd soon be out of business.'

Clara was shocked. 'But what can I do? I'm scared, Arnold. I'm scared for Lindsey and I'm scared for myself. What do you think will happen to us?'

'I don't like to say. But he won't kill you. Killing two young girls would whip up bad feeling towards him, one that would give the police a chance to get to him as not even his notorious friends in the gang world would stand by him on that one. If you were older, maybe he'd get away with it, but you're not yet sixteen. That would look bad and get the sympathy of folk against him.'

Clara's body trembled. *Not kill us, but beat us and . . .* She wouldn't let her mind visit the possibilities of what else would happen to them.

'As for what you can do, well there's nowt you can do for your mate, but for yourself, get out of Blackpool. Get your theatrical friends to help you, they have a network of their fellow kind all over the country. Go now, Clara, and hurry, lass.'

'I can't, Arnold. I can't abandon Lindsey.' A tear ran down her face. Her bowels felt as though they would empty themselves as her stomach churned with terror.

'Well, there's a little hope on that score, lass. Sit down afore you fall down.' Arnold indicated a chair. 'Now, what I'm going to tell you, you mustn't breathe a word of. If you do, I'm a dead man. But there's a gang from London, the Hill's gang, looking to take over Blackpool. They're on their way. There's going to be hell – gang warfare. So Mickey is going to be otherwise engaged than looking for you. Now, that's scheduled for tomorrow, so we have to hope that Mickey is just keeping your mate prisoner until he picks you up, as he would think like that. He's sadistic, he would want you both to see what is happening to the other. But this is his downfall, as he will lose his chance. This gang that are coming won't leave until they have control. They are powerful and will beat Mickey's lot hands down . . . '

'I – I'm going to be sick!'

Arnold moved faster than she'd ever seen him move. He grabbed a bucket that smelt of urine – a stench that had her retching uncontrollably. Arnold rubbed her back the whole time. 'All of this is too much for you, lass. You should have come to me when you ran away from that shop.' Moving away from her, he fetched her a glass of water. 'Drink this now, you've nowt more to bring up.'

He took the bucket and emptied it down the sink and swilled

it. In her imagination she could see him having to do this when he'd used the bucket to relieve himself, but then there were no other facilities for him, and it was no different to the lavs that had to be emptied. Trying not to dwell on that, her mind turned to how Arnold had known that she had run away from Mickey's, and she remembered the day when she and Lindsey had visited him and he'd asked her where she'd been. Had he known then that she had been in Mickey's clutches? He must have done, as he hadn't queried her when she asked him not to tell anyone he'd seen her. A fear of a different kind entered her – that of doubt. Could she trust Arnold?

'Don't look at me like that, lass. I'm on your side. I'm the only one who can save you, as I'm a sort of traitor to both the London gang and Mickey. But neither of them realises that I want rid of the lot of them. Oh, there'll allus be one gang or another taking charge here, but I knaw things. I knaw of a half-decent bloke from Ireland who's ready to step in. He's a gentleman. He's the one I'm really working for.'

All of this sounded so unreal that Clara felt that she could believe it. No one, except perhaps a film maker, could invent such a thing. Besides, she'd been daft to doubt Arnold – he'd always been her friend.

'You will help, Lindsey, won't you, Arnold?'

'I will, I promise, but it's going to take me about a week to get everything in place. I want you safe in that time, so do as I say, and get your theatrical friends to get you away. Leave the rest to me.'

Somehow Clara felt reassured by this. She stood up on shaky legs, turned to Arnold and flung her arms around him. 'Thanks, Arnold.' His arms came around her.

'Stay safe, lass, stay safe.'

Clara had the feeling that this is how a father would be, and at that moment she knew that she loved Arnold as if he was her father, and knew above everything that he would keep his word and Lindsey would be freed.

When she came out of his arms, she saw a tear trickle down his cheek. For a short moment, she became the adult as she patted his cheek. She could see the pain of his loss and wondered what had happened to his daughter.

As Clara steered her bike into Church Street, a van screeched to a halt just in front of her. Her heart stopped. She was forced to mount the pavement, and tried desperately to turn around, but a hand grabbed her. Terror locked her throat, preventing her from crying out. She heard a man tell passers-by: 'She's been out all night, her mam's sick with worry. Bloody young-uns, eh?'

Clara looked at the staring faces and shook her head.

'Get in the car. You should be ashamed of yourself.'

'Grab her bike, Doug, and shove it in the back. And you get in with it.'

The man who'd spoken shoved Clara into the front seat and shut the door. Clara could only stare. She had the sensation of being strangled by her panic. As the van set off, two hands came around her from the back. She couldn't move. 'Just try owt, and I'll knock you out.'

She wanted to struggle, and kick out and scream, but her body had stopped obeying her. She could hardly breathe.

When the van turned into Cookson Street, Clara knew her world was going to end. Excruciating pain ripped at her scalp as she was yanked out of the van by her hair and roughly manhandled into the door. Dolly met her. With her arms folded and a smile creasing her face, she said, 'Welcome back, lass.' Then her voice changed. 'Take her down the cellar and tie her up with the other one. And, lads, all your Christmases have come at once. I'm going to get the others to watch, and you can do just as you please with them both, but make it good. Make it so that no other prossie or anyone who works for Mickey ever dares do what these two did. But don't kill them, and only do what the doc can put right. Oh, and settle a score for me, an' all. These little tykes left me when I needed their help.' Her eyes rested back on Clara. Clara shrank away from the evil she saw in their depth. 'I don't forget easy, lass. And you're about to find that out.'

In her mind, Clara begged of God to help her and Lindsey.

Hardly able to keep her footing, she was shoved down the dark stairs. Trying to grab hold of something – anything – she tumbled down, bruising her legs and back. As the door closed behind her, a complete darkness enveloped her.

'Clara . . . oh, Clara.'

'Lindsey! Where are you? I can't see. I – I, oh, Lindsey. I'm scared.' Sobs wracked her body, uncontrollable sobs that hurt her head and sent snot running freely down her nose.

'I can see you, Clara. Your eyes will get used to the dark. There's a small light coming through that pavement-level window. I can't move as they've tied me. Oh, Clara . . . T – Tinker did this!'

Lindsey's sobs gave some control to Clara as her need was to comfort her friend and to be strong for her. As the room became lighter, she looked towards where the sounds were

269

coming from. Getting up, she used the hem of her frock to wipe her face. 'Don't, don't cry, Lindsey.' Crawling over to Lindsey, she took her in her arms. Together, they rocked backwards and forwards.

After a moment, Lindsey asked, 'How did they get you?'

'I went to Arnold. He's going to help us Lindsey, I just hope that he's in time. Y — you said Tinker did this?'

'Aye. Me best friend, the lad I fell in love with. He — he betrayed me, Clara. He asked me to go for a walk with him. He said as he had sommat for me, but he wanted us to be alone when he gave it to me. We — we walked towards the prom, and th — this van pulled up beside us. The way it skidded to a stop, I knew, and I went to run, but Tinker held me. He looked at me and said: "I'm sorry, lass. But you're me ticket out of here. I ain't going to no war. Mickey's going to give me money and get me to Southern Ireland."

'I screamed at him, but he helped the men get me in the back of the van. They gave him a package, and then said he'd get his travelling orders and tickets shortly, but he needed to deliver you first.'

Clara couldn't take it all in. 'Oh, Lindsey, not Tinker, no, not Tinker! Oh God. He must have followed me! He'll know that I went to Arnold!'

A sense of hopelessness engulfed Clara. Her fear was such that she couldn't comprehend what would happen. She thought about what Dolly had said: 'Do what you want with them . . .'

She clung on tighter to Lindsey.

'Clara, see if you can untie me hands. These binds are killing me.'

Getting behind Lindsey, Clara found that she couldn't see, only feel the ties. 'Can you turn towards the wall so I can get light on to your hands, Lindsey?'

It didn't take long to undo the knot. As soon as she had, Lindsey grabbed her. They hugged one another without speaking, bound by a deep fear, but more so by a deep love. Some courage came to Clara. Whatever happened to them, she'd be strong for Lindsey.

CHAPTER TWENTY-FIVE

Julia
Hope Swells Julia's Heart

Julia woke the next morning feeling drained. Getting out of bed, she dressed quickly, and whilst the others were getting ready, slipped out and went to the maternity ward. Billie was sitting up.

'How are you, Billie?'

Billie put out her hand. Her face was deathly pale, her eyes sunken into blackened sockets. Taking her hand, Julia sat on the end of Billie's bed. She couldn't speak; the sadness in Billie touched her heart.

'Julia. I – I have a plan. I . . . '

'Don't try to talk, love. You need rest.'

'No, I must tell you. You have to find a way.'

Julia moved closer. The urgency in Billie's voice told her that this was important to her.

'I – I will look after you and your child.'

'What? How?' Hope soared through Julia.

'I've got Sister Grace to send a note to me mum. Me mum didn't want this for me, but she couldn't take the shame. Me mum's not short of a bob or two, and she told me that if I went away and had me baby took away, she'd 'elp me get on me feet when it was all over. She'd tell folk that I were away doing war work. Anyway, she don't want me to come back to the house yet, as that'll set tongues wagging as to why I've been released from whatever she's told them that I'm doing. So she'll set me up wherever I want. So, if I get sorted, then you can come and live with me. If these 'ere think that you have somewhere to go and can take care of your baby, then they will let you keep it. We need to get Sister Grace on our side. She ain't got a lot of say in what goes on, but in this she could swing it for us. It has to 'appen quickly, though. You've only got a few more weeks left. I have to get out and get set up, then if they want to come and inspect they can.'

'Oh, Billie, I don't know what to say. "Thank you" just doesn't seem to be enough. Do you really think that they will go for it?'

'Aye, I do. I overheard a conversation. Sister Bernard was saying that more and more babies were having to go to the orphanage, as there just weren't the couples to take them. With men being away, most women were coping on their own, or 'aving to go out to work. And she said that the nearby orphanages were stretched to their limits and they may have to send kids up north. I think my baby was taken to an orphanage. A young couple would have come if it had been adopted. That were a middle-aged woman and an old man. If

273

we can find out where, then that's where I want to set up home. As maybe, if we get a good thing going, they'll let me 'ave me baby back.'

'Oh, Billie, that would be wonderful. My daughter is up north somewhere. I would go up there in a shot. I'll do all I can to find out where your baby went to. I have Sister Grace's confidence now.'

'We have to set this up before I am judged as fit enough to be posted to war work. I just 'ope as me mum comes soon.'

'Oh, so do I, Billie. You've given me hope.' Julia bent down and brushed Billie's hair back with her hand. 'I'll try to find out if your child was a boy or a girl, too. But Billie, I can't be seen to be too close to you, not for a couple of days, until I have the information. So I'll just be professional around you, but don't worry. I will be beavering away in the background.'

With this Julia left Billie. Her heart was racing with joy. *Please, please, God, let us pull this off.* She smiled. *Maybe this was in your plan for me and Billie. Well, if it is, then we are going to need your help to make it happen, so be with us. Please, God, be with us.*

'Oh, there you are, Julia.'

'Good morning, Sister. I – I'm sorry that I left before you came back. I . . . well, I was badly affected by what happened.'

'I can imagine. Are you all right now?'

'Yes. Well, not altogether. But I'm coping. I want to work, or I'll have too much time to think about things. I've checked on Billie. Physically, she's fine, but she is emotional.'

'That's to be expected, Julia. Never think that it comes easy to me to do what must be done. It doesn't. But if I let my heart rule, I'd have to give up my calling. At least I know that women like you are well cared for, and I can do what I can to make that a little better for you. I cannot change the way of things. I try. Little by little I chip away at this and that, and I pray, but God can work slowly sometimes, we just have to be patient.'

'You really think that God has a plan for each one of us, Sister?'

'I do. And for each of the babies that I deliver. I have to believe that. I know that the majority cannot look after a child. Parents are too ashamed to help them, too. And how would they fare living on their own with a baby? They wouldn't. The child would suffer, so I have to trust in God to send the best solution for the child, and the mother, in the long run. I know they will always suffer, but they can rebuild their lives and find happiness.'

'But what about those of us who, with a little help, could look after our child?'

'God is helping me with that, too. Together we will get that halfway home for unmarried and widowed mothers. But it won't be yet, so until then, we have to work with what we have.'

'Sister, can I ask you something? I've heard a rumour that a lot of babies are going to orphanages. Is that true?'

'Of course it is. It has always been so. It's nothing new. It's just happening more frequently now due to the world being at war.'

'So, if my child went to an orphanage, and I got on my feet, could I ever apply to have it back with me?'

'I don't see why not. It may be a lengthy process involving courts, but yes. It could happen.' Sister Grace paused. 'Julia, are you asking me to see that that happens for you?'

275

Julia lowered her head.

'Please don't. Look, the only thing I could do, is let you know how you can find out, but you must do so in a way that I don't know that you have, as I can never lie in court. During your recovery days, take a look at the records. They're kept in that drawer over there, all the details of every child born here. All on index cards and in alphabetical order according to the mother's surname. It's not locked, as until now no one but me and the doctor use these rooms. I can't tell you how much of a relief it has been to have your help. So much so that I have asked Reverend Mother to apply to our mother house for a trainee nun to be my assistant. They are in favour, so I am very happy.'

'Thank you, Sister. I promise, I will never let you down. Working here with you has renewed my calling, and though it is tearing me apart to know that my fate is the same as the girls, I will help you. I can handle that in the same way as you do, the way we were taught to as nurses.'

'Yes, we were. Now, have you had breakfast? You mustn't miss your meals, no matter how down you feel. That's another thing we were taught. We have to keep our energy up. Run along and eat, then you can come back and help me with my clinic. Today I check up on as many of the girls as I can. With your help, that could be all of them.'

Julia couldn't believe how well that had gone. She now knew how to access all the information Billie would need. She just had to find out Billie's surname.

Reaching the dining room, she had to run the gauntlet of Sister Francis's disapproval. 'Getting above yourself, aren't you, madam? Nurse or no nurse, you should be here at meal time like the rest of them. There's only porridge left now.'

A bowl of stodge was pushed towards Julia. 'Thank you, Sister Francis.'

A 'humph' accompanied Julia as she walked away and sat down. The girls around her questioned her on Billie's progress. Julia wished she could alleviate their fears, and for the first time, really understood what Sister Grace went through. None of them realised what a saint Sister Grace was, or how much she cared about them, working away in the background to improve things for girls of the future. Julia longed to tell them, but that would break Sister Grace's confidence, and she didn't deserve that. So she just reassured them that Billie was fine, and that yes, she would try to tell them when Billie was leaving so that they could wave to her. Her thoughts went to Mildred. That poor girl had left without goodbyes. Even Julia hadn't seen her go.

She and Billie had two weeks – the time a new mother was confined to bed – to find out where Billie's baby went and to hope that Billie's mum came up with what they needed. And then Billie would only have a couple of weeks to find a place, and for them to make the application because, if Julia went her full time, and now she would be praying to be late, they needed time for Billie to get settled and to convince the nuns that they could make this work.

Back in the surgery, after breakfast, Julia asked if she should check on Billie.

'Yes. I'm worried about her blood pressure. It has been erratic with every monitor. So will you take that duty, Julia? I have the use of William for an hour later. He helps me to get set up, he unfolds and moves examination tables to where I want them, and gets the scales in place, that sort of thing. It leaves me free to get the surgical instruments ready. You can help with the sterilisation of these later and whilst you do, I can talk you through the checklist of procedure that we follow when giving an ante-natal examination in readiness for the clinic this afternoon. Oh, Julia, I can't tell you what a help you are. And, Julia . . . well, I will help you all that I can. I promise.'

Sister Grace gave Julia a lovely smile. For a moment, Julia wanted to hug her, and to tell her of the plan she and Billie had hatched. She hated deceiving this wonderful woman, but if she did tell her, Sister Grace's sense of honesty and duty might mean she had to thwart what they were doing. No. Julia would have to wait until Billie was ready and everything was set. Then she would ask for Sister Grace's help. But she would never let her know that they were settled where they were because she'd broken her confidence and checked through her records for Billie.

'Are you asleep, Billie? I have to do your blood pressure.'

Billie opened her eyes.

'You look a lot better, love. That's a good sign.'

Billie smiled, and as she had before, she reached out for Julia's hand. Julia squeezed it, then let go and patted it.

'Let me get this cuff on you, then the machine can cover what we say, just in case – walls have ears, you know.'

Billie giggled. The change in her was immense. Hope was the best healer of all.

As she pumped the blood pressure monitor, Julia told Billie what she had discovered so far. 'So, just as soon as I can, I will take a look, but I need your surname.'

'Blaider.' Billie spelt it out for her. 'Me dad has an 'aulage

278

firm: Blaider Construction Materials. Only 'e's as tight as a duck's arse, but me mum has 'er ways of getting what she wants and she's got a good stash. Self-made they are. They both worked for a building firm, me mum in the office and me dad in the yard, and they saved every penny. Me and me sisters went without and were always told that we would benefit in the end. Well, after what me mum's brother did to me, I'm due to benefit now. And if she don't play bleedin' ball, then I'll threaten to shout from the rooftops where I've been and who put me there. I'll go to the bleedin' papers if I 'ave to. Me dad's someone of note, so the papers would think on it as worth printing something detrimental about him. I think we're 'ome and dry, Julia.' Again, the lovely smile.

'We will be. And we won't rest until we have your child with us, I promise.' Releasing the blood pressure monitor, Julia noted the reading was a little high. 'You have to keep calm, Billie. Don't go over things that will get you worked up and anxious. If this doesn't settle down, you could be sent into hospital. We have to be together to make things work.'

'I will, luv. It's when I think of me bleedin' parents that I blow steam from me ears.'

Julia laughed.

'Julia, as I see it, we can both get part-time jobs. That way, you will 'ave time with your kid and time to look for your other one. And when we've got the money, we'll go for a weekend to Blackpool. We're sure to find your girl.'

Julia squeezed Billie's hand. 'That sounds like a good plan, though I want to go back into nursing, and there aren't many part-timers in that profession. So we'll see, eh? Rest now. I'll be back in an hour to check you again, and I want your blood pressure back to normal.'

It was evening before Julia got the chance to look through the records. She had helped with the clinic, and then rested for most of the afternoon once it was finished. All the girls, including herself – Sister Grace had examined her before clinic started – had been found to be healthy, though one was so near to confinement, and the head very low, that they had debated keeping her in the labour ward. In the end, Sister Grace had said that the best thing for her was to carry on with her duties and let nature take its course. 'Rest all afternoon, Julia. Then if I do need you later, I won't feel so guilty. But hopefully, hers will be a simple delivery, of the kind I've managed alone for many years, and I won't need you.'

'Well, as these things happen in the night more often than not, why don't I come and take over from you after my dinner, until about eight? There's only Billie to monitor, and you could get a rest in case you are needed in the night.'

'That would be very kind. Yes. I'll do that. Now, off with you.'

Later, once Sister Grace had left to go to her room, Julia stood by the window waiting for her to cross the courtyard. The evening sun still had a lot of warmth in it, and its rays took the chill of deceit out of Julia's bones. *What I am doing isn't wrong! It isn't! Without the information the plan we have cannot work. This is a two-way thing. Billie must have the hope of getting her child back, and I need to keep my child. It's the only way.* Julia winced as she realised she'd been holding her hands in such tight fists that her nails had dug into the palm of her hand.

At last she saw Sister Grace in the courtyard below. She watched her walk across in her purposeful way, her nun's veil and long robe blowing in the breeze. All the nuns here wore black and white, and all had their faces tightly enclosed in their caps, which gave them puffed-out cheeks and rabbit-like expressions. Julia smiled at this, and as she saw Sister Grace enter the building opposite, she hurried over to the desk containing the drawer of files.

It didn't take long to find the 'Bs', or Billie's fresh-looking card. But she was struck by the number of cards. All these poor girls, made pregnant and abandoned here, having to give their babies up. It broke her heart.

Looking at the card, her heart beat faster. 'Yes!'

Mother – Belinda Blaider, unmarried. Delivered of a son. Baby Blaider, named and christened George by Father Patrick, before dispatched to WRVS war haven for babies in Blackburn, Lancashire. No orphanage place found. Information of progress will be supplied six monthly, or on any change of circumstances.

Quickly closing the drawer, Julia rushed into Billie.
'Billie, Billie, I have news.'
Billie cried silent tears while Julia begged her to be strong.
'All sorts of illnesses can attack you in these first few days of your confinement, Billie. Your body defences are low. And even though it is a natural process, childbirth is a shock to your system. So you are vulnerable to infection. Please, please be strong.'
Billie dried her eyes. 'I will be. I will. What's 'appening to me, I won't let 'appen to you, Julia, I promise. It's just knowing

281

that I 'ave a son. A boy . . . George. I like that name. It's our king's name, and he's a lovely man.'

'He is. And his lovely wife, Elizabeth. There's more pictures in Sister Grace's newspaper of them in the East End. You know, they could have left these shores, or at least sent their girls, the princesses away, but no. They decided to stay with us and go through what we are going through.'

'Warms yer 'eart, don't it? Though I'd like to bet that their bleedin' sugar bowls are full. There's only so much that they'll share with us.'

Julia laughed at this. 'You're wicked, Billie. Come on, let me do your checks.'

'Julia, this is going to sound bleedin' daft, but I want yer to know as I love you. I've never met anyone like yer, and I'd give me life for yer.'

Julia blushed, but she knew that she felt the same. 'And I love you, too. You have shown me more love in the short time that I have known you than anyone else has in my life. Anyone, who isn't connected to me by blood, that is. Though some of them, my own parents for instance, never showed me much. Winnie, who was to be my mother-in-law, showed me love, but it wasn't like yours. She couldn't open her home up to me when I most needed her to. That all changed, and I couldn't blame her, not under the circumstances. And I have known the greatest love from my daughter, and from Gareth. Oh, Billie, do you ever think that life will get back to normal again, and we will be reunited with our children?'

'It won't be for bleedin' trying, if we don't. We'll make it 'appen. We'll work towards it, Julia. Together.'

'We will, love. Now, I have to insist on being the nurse and you, as my patient, have to do as I tell you. Rest, my dear friend. Rest and get strong.'

With this, Julia kissed Billie's cheek and left her. She'd never met anyone like Billie in her life. But she was so glad that she had now. And she knew that as they got to know each other more, and became dependent on each other, that their love and friendship would deepen and that it would last them a lifetime.

Sitting at the desk in the surgery, Julia thought about Gareth. A longing entered her that was tainted with guilt. For Sister Grace had made her see the immorality they had shown – Gareth more than her, as he'd had a wife. And she knew that when they were reunited, they needed to start again. They needed to put right the wrongs, somehow, and build their love on more solid ground. She went to the window and looked up to the sky. *Wherever you are, my love, keep safe. Come back to me and to our child.* Her mind went to Clara. As it did, she shuddered unexpectedly. A weird feeling passed through her. *Clara, Clara, what's happening to you, my darling daughter?* She shook herself mentally, and walked away from the window. *I'm being silly. I'm sure that my Clara is safe. If only I knew where!*

CHAPTER TWENTY-SIX

Clara
A Terrifying Ordeal

'I've wet meself, Clara.'

Clara didn't know what to say, so she squeezed Lindsey a little closer. They had been down the cellar together for what seemed like hours. Clara wanted to pee badly, but hung on, squeezing her legs tightly. Every noise coming from upstairs had them cringing in fear.

'What time is it, Clara?'

'I think it must be getting on for noon. I was with Arnold by nine-thirty, and two hours at least have gone by.'

'Did they say owt to you?'

'Yes, I – I don't know if I should tell you.'

'Eeh, was it that bad?'

'Dolly said that th – the two men who brought me in

could do what they wanted to us. That she would get all the others to watch, to show them what happens if they cross Mickey.'

'Oh, Clara. That were probably Gilly and Dougie. They're notorious for being sadistic.'

'I don't want to be hurt, Lindsey . . . I – I'm scared.'

'What you have to do is to keep thinking that it will come to an end. And if the others are watching, they might intervene. I've seen it. Mickey were beating a woman once, and the others all screamed and screamed until he stopped. He threw the woman onto the floor and left in disgust. He was like nowt had happened when he came back that night. The woman still works here.'

They fell into a silence for a few minutes. Lindsey broke it. 'What did you say about Arnold helping us?'

'I went to him because I didn't know where to go, or what to do. He knew everything, Lindsey, where I'd been, and how I was working for Mickey and how we escaped and that the word was out to get us back in. But he knew a whole lot more.' Something stopped Clara from giving Lindsey details. Arnold had told her not to tell a soul and that meant Lindsey, too. 'Just to say, that what he knows could help us, but I don't know how, only that I believed him when he said his contacts would make a move, and then we would be safe.'

'Who'd have thought it? Arnold? I thought that he was just a stallholder.'

'I don't think anyone is what they seem in Blackpool, especially those working the stalls. Arnold opened my eyes to a few things this morning.'

Talking about a rescue had lulled them both into feeling a bit better, and they chatted on, with no tears and no talk of being afraid. But that changed when the clinking of the lock echoed around them. They jumped closer and both began to wail pitifully.

Clara felt a trickle of wet warmth run between her legs.

'It bloody stinks down here.' A torch flashed on them. 'Get up!' A hand pinched Clara's arm. At the same time she heard a whimper of pain from Lindsey. Whenever Lindsey cried it gave Clara strength. 'Let go, you bully!'

'Ha, a tyke with some fire in her belly. Well, we'll soon knock that out of you.' His swipe sent Clara's head rocking on her shoulders. For a moment her eyes seemed full of flashing lights.

'Leave her alone, she ain't done nowt. It were me, I made her run away with me!'

'Phew, you stink more than she does, you filthy tykes.'

The men dragged them to their feet and up the stairs. Each stone step dug into Clara's ribs. They were thrown face down onto the floor in the hall. Clara blinked. As her eyes became used to the light she could see feet around her. She heard a gasp, and then another.

'You lot can shut up, an' all. And take heed, what these girls get is what will happen to you if you do what they did, so don't even think about it.'

Looking up, she saw the men who had captured her. One was big with no neck, a bald head and beady eyes. She assumed this was Gilly as she remembered hearing Doug's name and how he had a shock of blond hair and pale skin. His eyes were evil-looking as he stared down at her. There seemed a moment when everyone stood like statues, then as if one, Gilly and Dougie pounced. Dougie grabbed her.

The carpet runner along the hall burned her thigh as he dragged her body along. Her pleas of 'No, no, I'm sorry' weren't heeded. Murmurs of fear came from the women who followed them. One even shouted at Dolly to stop what was happening, but then squealed as she took a blow. From the glimpses Clara got of them, she only recognised a couple of them. All worked as prostitutes in the house.

The room they were taken into was one Clara hadn't seen before. There was a huge bed with straps hanging from the bedstead, and on the wall hung whips and contraptions in leather and metal. Clara couldn't make out what they were. Dropping her on the floor Dougie came round to the front of her. Clara kicked out at him.

'Oh, no you don't.' Dougie caught her legs and held her so that she could only twist and turn, but soon exhaustion took her.

'One of you, come round here.' Gilly's rough voice growled at the cowering women, now standing outside the door.

None of the women moved. 'Dolly, get it organised, for fuck's sake!'

Dolly reacted to this from Gilly, demanding of someone called June, and another, called Sherry, to move into the room and do what Dougie ordered them to.

Through a throat that had been scoured with crying, Clara tried to beg. 'Don't ... *please* don't.'

'Get her stinking knickers off. Then hold her legs.'

Once the women had her legs, Dougie rubbed her wet knickers in her face. 'There, you dirty tyke.'

Clara heaved.

She looked towards where she thought Lindsey was, but couldn't see her. As if on a bobbin, her head bounced from side to side. '*Lindsey!* Where's Lindsey?'

A groan from behind her had her body wriggling round to look. Lindsey's was enclosed in a contraption that looked like a straitjacket, a strap was held in place across her mouth. 'Lindsey, oh, Lindsey.'

A whip cracked. Clara twisted back round. Above her Dougie held a whip, ready to crack it down across her body. Her pleas went unheard. The whip came down and the slicing pain made her catch her breath so deeply that she didn't think she would ever release it. A scream forced itself from her mouth. Her eyes misted over; the agonising pain seared her.

A vicious kick turned her body. She could see Lindsey once more. '*Lindsey . . .*' Lindsey's eyes bulged from her head with the agony she couldn't release as Gilly hit her body with a knotted length of rope. '*No!* Stop him. Someone stop him!'

The words grated from Clara and her mouth filled with saliva – frothy, nasty-tasting saliva. She wriggled and looked at those watching. Some wept. Some held their hands over their mouths.

Growling like an animal, Clara urged them to stop this happening. Swear words tumbled from her, but the sound of the cracking of the whip had her clamping her teeth on her lip in agonising terror. The searing pain ripped at her heart. Blood mingled with the spittle in her mouth. A sound came from her like none she'd ever made before.

'Right, I think you're ready now, you little snake. You. Help me get her onto the bed. It's time this virgin was broken in.'

Dolly came forward. Clara couldn't protest. Her body burned with indescribable pain. She couldn't fight him putting the straps around her arms, or resist the jerking of her body into a position where she couldn't move and her legs were open.

A scream from one of the women and the gasps of the others had her opening her eyes. Dougie had a knife and was going towards her open legs. The screaming went in a wave from one to the other of the women. One appeared next to Dougie and pulled at his shirt. 'Naw. Naw. You evil bastard. Naw!'

Dougie's arm shot out and sent her flying. Others surged forward. But all stopped when a massive bang resounded around the room, followed by another and another. Dougie looked at Gilly. Gilly stood with his hand in the air, blood running down his arm. The women and girls scattered, their screams drowned by men shouting, explosions booming and loud bangs as if doors were being kicked. Clara couldn't decipher it all – her brain wouldn't process what was happening. She lay limply on the bed, her body crying in pain and shivering uncontrollably.

'*Get down! Down!*'

Dougie rolled off the bed onto the floor at this yelled command. Gilly flung himself down. A masked man barged in, followed by another. Clara saw that each held a gun and a truncheon, but as she registered this, she heard two sickening thuds and long moans as if the air had left the bodies of Dougie and Gilly for ever. And she hoped that it was so.

'God above, will you look at the state of these young girls. Holy Mary, is it monsters that this gang are?'

For a moment, Clara wondered if it was Mickey, but the accent was slightly different, and she remembered Arnold saying there was an Irishman wanting to take Blackpool over. It was all too much for her to think about, and though relieved to have been saved from what Dougie was going to do to her, she couldn't take it all in. The room was a haze. Her fear for Lindsey overwhelmed her.

'Will some of you ladies get yourselves in here and see to these young girls. Not you. Isn't it that you're a strange one, and my guess is that you're for being a ranking member of the gang, so it is.'

Dolly's whimpering voice came back at him, 'Yes, but willing to serve you, Paddy.'

'Well, tell me where it is that Mickey is hiding, and how is it he isn't here?'

These voices faded and a kindly feminine voice came to her. 'Poor lass. Eeh, I've heard of saved by the bell. He was going to cut your virginity with a knife, the bastard. Well, it's all over now, lass.'

'H – how's Lindsey?'

'She'll be all right, lass. We're going to clean you up and get you both to hospital, but neither of you are to say what happened to you. We don't want the cops all over this place. And you don't want to make this new lot mad. Make sommat up, like you had an accident, or sommat. You crossed the road in front of the horses and they reared on you both, sommat like that. Right?'

Clara nodded.

'Good girl, you'll be fine. Just put it behind you. Mickey's done for, so you're free now.'

Clara let her body go slack. The moans of agony coming from Lindsey as they undid her tore at Clara. She heard one moan form her name.

'Lindsey, Lindsey, I'm here. I – I'm all right. We're safe now.' She couldn't manage to say any more, but prayed fervently that Lindsey would be all right. Into the prayers came the words the woman had spoken. They rolled around her head, taking all the space and blotting everything else from her mind. *It's over. We're free. Free!*

She couldn't cry any more. She couldn't protest about the pain when someone lifted her and wrapped her in a blanket and carried her out of that building that she hoped never to enter again.

'Lindsey?'

'She's with you, lass. She'll sit next to you in the car. You'll soon be cared for. Now, remember, both of you, get your stories straight. Not a word about how it really happened, what you've seen, or owt about this place.'

Clara nodded. She didn't care anything about Cookson Street, and would never enter it again as long as she lived. But strangely, as bad as this had been, she didn't want to leave Blackpool.

Blackpool held some bad folk – Miss Brandon, and Mickey and his gang. And yes, she'd learned that a lot of the folk running stalls were less than honest when it came to their dealings, but it also held lovely folk, who cared about you. The theatre group, Daisy, Lindsey, Arnold and her lovely Anton. These were what made Blackpool magical and the place she wanted to be for as long as she lived.

Her mind went to her mum. Over a year without seeing her, or hearing from her. Would she ever again know that love and protection her mum had given her? How many more months would go by, or years even, before they could be together? Or would they never see each other again? '*No!*'

Lindsey's hand came out and touched hers.

Strangely, they weren't asked any questions about what happened by the policeman that the hospital had called in. He just asked the nurse for time alone with them, and asked them their names and ages, and scribbled on a pad.

'So, you both were involved in an accident, then? Horses weren't it? Eeh, you should be careful crossing the road. Them animals are soon spooked.' He scribbled some more. After a while, he said, 'Well, we won't need you for any further enquiries, just do as you've been told, and I'll report back to my chief, then that will be the end of it.'

Clara wanted to spit at him. He'd obviously been briefed before he'd come to interview them. When he'd gone, she turned her head to look at Lindsey, who lay in the bed next to hers. 'Why do they allow something like this to go on?'

'I think it's because it's better to let the gangs sort themselves out and restore peace. The cops are no match for them.' Lindsey went on to tell her the same thing that Arnold had told her – how the gangs of Blackpool kept everything running.

'Dolly once told me that without them Blackpool would close. They supply all that is needed to keep it up and running. Dolly said even the government knaws of their dealings, and turns a blind eye. And that's what we're to do, Clara. Just be thankful that it's all over. That cop will report back to whoever the top man of the new gang is that we didn't grass, and he'll be happy with that. He's got naw interest invested in us. We're free, lass. We just need to get better, and forget all about it.'

Clara knew that was going to be difficult to do. But she also knew that Lindsey was right. Trying to make things right was beyond them, and would only lead to much worse things happening. They had a chance now to live freely and to get on with their lives.

'Lindsey, I miss me mum.' This came out on a sob. 'I miss the life we had. I want to know how she is, and what is happening to the folk on the island.'

'I reckon as we could find that out for you. I mean, we may not be able to find out about your mam, but we could find out what is happening on Guernsey. There will be news reports. Though it might not be what you want to hear.'

'I know. I've been afraid to ask and have blocked it out. I felt that I couldn't cope with knowing. But now I could cope with anything. And I know that I need to know about my own folk.'

'Aye, I can understand that. I have longed to knaw about mine. I must have some, somewhere. Why they didn't take me in, where they are from? Have I a granny and granddad? But I have no way of finding out.'

'We're in the same boat in a way, Lindsey. We're alone in the world. I have two grannies and a granddad and a mum, but I can't be with any of them and I don't know what is happening to them.'

'Don't cry, Clara, lass. Crying makes everything worse. We've to be strong, and to look out for one another. Aye, and we're to be careful who we put our trust in, an' all.'

With this, Clara remembered the deceit of Tinker and she filled up with hate for him. 'Do you think that Tinker will be gone, Lindsey?'

'I don't knaw. With Mickey ousted, who will give him his travel tickets? I mean, you can't just go where you like now. You can't up and leave just because you don't want to go to war. I'd say as Mickey was going to give him a new identity and a valid reason for him being allowed out of the country.'

'Well, I hope he disappears. I never want to see him again, though I'm sorry for what you must be feeling, but I hope he doesn't get out of being sent to war, and that he comes to experience the fear and pain that he's put us through.'

Lindsey was quiet. Clara wanted to take the words back as she tried to imagine what it would be like for her if it had been Anton that had done this to them. She could think of no words to say to comfort her friend.

'You have a visitor, girls. Now. Ten minutes, and ten minutes only. Normal visiting is six till eight.'

'Eeh, me lasses. A policeman came and said you'd had an accident and were both in here. I've been out of me mind since Jeannie sent a message to say that you had left a note, Clara, lass. I knew where you'd gone, but could do nowt. Aw, look at you. By, that Mickey has a lot to answer for.' Daisy mopped her tears.

'Shush, Daisy, someone might hear you. We had an accident, we ran out in the road in front of a farmer and his horses and they reared on us, and that's all. The cops have been, and that is the story. We have to leave it at that.'

'Aye, I understand. But look at you. My darling girls.'

'Daisy . . . has Tinker left?'

'Naw. He said he'll come and see you later. He's looking after the shop.'

Lindsey's audible gasp told Clara that she felt the same way as she did about this news.

'Here, me lasses, I've brought you me iced buns, I knaw as you both like them.'

Clara felt sick at the thought, but smiled at this lovely kindly woman, who in her flowing clothes looked more like a gypsy queen than a shop owner. She wanted to hug her. 'Thanks, Daisy, we'll eat them later.'

'I'll go now. I'll call at the theatre and tell them all there about your accident, as they're all worried.'

She kissed them both and left, leaving the lovely aroma of her flowery perfume behind her.

'Daisy knaws the score, she asked naw questions, and just got on with it. She'll not say owt to them at the theatre. Jeannie and all but Anton will all knaw, or guess, what's gone on, and'll keep quiet about it. Anton, bless him, will believe everything he's told, so can't slip up and let owt out. We're home and dry, Clara, except for Tinker. Sommat has got to happen about him. I can't go on living around him. I want him gone from me life.'

'Well, that'll happen. He's turned seventeen. It won't be long before he gets his call up. We'll just have to put up with him until then, but we don't have to be friendly with him.'

'You're right. There's nowt we can do. But I hate him. I hate that I thought meself in love with him.'

'My mum used to tell me that hate was destructive, to me, as well as those that I hated. And that no matter what folk did to me, I was to forgive them and not retaliate.'

'Name-calling and bullying at school ain't nothing like what Tinker has done, or Dolly, or Mickey and his lot. I'll never forgive them, Clara, never.'

Lindsey was right. What had been done to them both, and the treatment she'd received from Miss Brandon, were unforgiveable. And she knew that she'd never forgive them either. But she did want to forget.

'I'm thinking of leaving Blackpool. I've known nowt but hurt here.'

'Please don't, Lindsey. I want you to stay. And we have known good things, too. It should all get better now. Apart from Tinker, all the bad things are over.'

'I'll think about it. I feel so tired. Eeh, Clara, why us, eh? We both came here as young-uns hoping to find safety, and we've both been through the mill. Why? It all beggars belief.'

Clara hadn't got an answer. Lindsey had been through so much more than she had. She'd never known her mother's love. She'd had a baby taken from her and nearly died, and had suffered at the hands of men who were more like beasts.

'Lindsey, I'll take care of you. I'll see that you're never hurt again. I'll always be by your side. And if ever I find my mum, I'll ask her to be your mum, too. I know she will. I know she will love you like I do.'

A sob came from Lindsey. Clara got out of bed and went to her. Getting into bed with her, she snuggled into her with her arm around her, and Lindsey cried until she fell asleep. Clara held back her tears, and used what energy she had to try to console Lindsey, telling her that they were sisters now, and would always be there for one another.

★   ★   ★

When Daisy came at visiting time, she told them that Tinker had gone. She didn't say any more, and batted away their questions. She left after fifteen minutes, telling them that Jeannie would bring Anton in. 'They've got a replacement for him for the evening performance, lass, so he'll be able to stay till the end of visiting.'

After she had left, Lindsey said: 'I told you she knew what was going on. She's sent him packing. I bet she put two and two together, then with our reaction to him still being at hers, went home and got rid of him.'

The news had cheered them both.

When Anton and Jeannie arrived, Clara felt some of the pieces of her world knitting together again as she assured Anton she was fine. They sat holding hands, chatting away and just loving being together.

'What's this I hear from Anton about you having a corker of a voice, then, Clara, lass?'

Clara blushed at Jeannie's words. She didn't answer but Lindsey did. 'She has. She sounds grand, Jeannie.'

'Well, then, when you're better, we'll see about rehearsing you for a part in our winter show. How would that be?'

Clara was shocked, but the thought warmed her through. She'd never thought of being a performer, but suddenly it was what she most wanted to be. 'That'll be grand, lass. Ta ever so much.'

They all laughed at her mimicking Jeannie and Lindsey's accent. It was a lovely sound. Full of hope for the future. *Yes, with these folk around me, and especially my Anton, life can get better. I can forget all the bad.* A happiness Clara had never expected to feel again flooded through her, and the pain of her injuries lessened. *Nothing can touch us now. Nothing can make me and Lindsey feel scared or unhappy again. If only . . .* Pulling away from thoughts of her mum, Clara tightened her grip on Anton's hand. He knew immediately what had troubled her. 'One day, the war will end. One day, you will be in your mother's arms, *mon amour*, I promise.'

CHAPTER TWENTY-SEVEN

Julia
Starting a New Journey

Julia cradled baby Charlie to her. Christened Gareth Charles, she had adopted his second name as the one she wanted to call him by.

Leaning back on her pillows, she smiled at Sister Grace. 'Thank you for all you have done.'

'You did all the work, Julia.'

'No, I mean in fighting for me to keep him while we wait to see if everything is acceptable with what Billie has sorted.'

'Yes, that is a worry. Reverend Mother won't condone you leaving here with him unless she is satisfied that you can care for him. I am so worried about that, Julia. If you do have to part with him, it is going to be so much more difficult for you than if I had taken him from you as soon as he was born.'

Julia held Charlie to her. *That won't happen. It can't. I have to trust Billie.*

'I must say that it is proving more difficult with you wanting to move up north,' continued Sister Grace. 'I have my suspicions about that, but all I will say is, I hope that everything turns out well for you, and for Billie.'

Julia wanted to say that the reason for going up north was so that she might find Clara, but Sister Grace's knowing look, which held no condemnation, stopped her. If Sister Grace knew what Julia had done to find where Billie's little George had been taken, she'd accepted it, and didn't seem to want to delve into it further.

'So, it is a matter of waiting, now. Reverend Mother has been in touch with the mother house, who will contact our convent in Blackburn. One of the sisters there will be dispatched to the address Billie has given us. And, if she is satisfied that it is a suitable home, and that Billie can support you financially until you are able to work yourself, then we are home and dry.'

'Billie wrote to say that she has a job in the Munitions, and is earning a man's wage – more than enough to cover the rent and food for us all. But I wanted to take up nursing again, Sister.'

'And so you should. But why not wait until little Charlie is older?'

'Because I feel that I will go mad being in the house on my own, wondering where my daughter and fiancé are. When I'm working, I can cope. Besides, nurses are so badly needed, and I too want to help the war effort.'

'Well, I will pray for you. My prayers have got you this far. Let's concentrate on the next hurdle, rather than give God too much to sort out. Remember, there are millions petitioning him, and he can only give so much to each one.'

Julia smiled. Sister Grace's simple faith inspired her.

'Now, time to put Charlie in his cot. His tummy's full. I'll change his nappy, and you get some rest.'

Julia hated parting with Charlie, but she knew from caring for patients that it was as it should be. She must get as much rest as she could. She had to prepare herself.

But her mind wouldn't let her rest. She went from plotting how she would find Clara to longing to know where Gareth was. Her letter to the council hadn't been answered, and she didn't know if Gareth had written or not. Surely, no matter what he was doing, they would allow him to contact his family, even if he had to tell a lie about his involvement in the war and where he was. Just to know that he was safe would be enough.

At this thought, she decided that when she left here she would call at her old landlord's address to see if he had picked up any mail from the flat. A hope surged through her. What if there was a letter from Gareth and a letter from the council? Though would he have kept them this long? Something told her it was possible, as he knew where she was, and that she wouldn't be able to get out to collect anything from him till after her baby was born.

She crossed her fingers, not wanting to ask God to help, as she didn't want to take his attention away from making sure everything went well at Billie's. That was priority. She couldn't lose her son. She couldn't!

★　　★　　★

Three anxious days passed before Sister Grace had news. She came into the post-natal ward clapping her hands. 'Julia, oh, Julia! Everything is all right!'

Her last steps towards Julia were a skip and a jump, and then she bent down and put her arms around her.

'Oh, thank God. Thank God!'

'Thank Him, indeed! The report says that Billie is renting a lovely terraced cottage. It is clean and well furnished. She has a full pantry, coal shed and a wood stack, ready for the colder weather. Her income is plentiful, and there are two bedrooms. It sounds like a little palace. There was a note of concern that one woman should support another, but I told Reverend Mother that you intended on going out to work once your child was old enough and would pay Billie back then. This satisfied her. Billie even paid enough money to the sister who visited for your fare. This has been put into a central fund and Reverend Mother will reimburse you from our own funds. You're on your way, Julia. Well done! I have never seen a mother leave here with her child.'

Julia squeezed Sister Grace. 'Oh, it's wonderful. How can I ever thank you?'

Straightening, Sister Grace looked down at her. 'You can thank me by never letting this happen again. By writing to me and letting me know all of your news. And most of all by being happy. You have found a wonderful friend in Billie. I never had her down as this kind of person. I thought her hard baked and unfeeling. How wrong I was. But then, Julia, you are the kind of person who brings out the best in most people, if they give you a chance to. I will miss you.'

With this Sister Grace wiped a tear from her eye. Julia did the same. Happiness surged through her, but she knew that she loved Sister Grace and would miss her every day.

'I will never forget you and what you have taught me, Sister. And yes, I will write to you. Please keep praying for me. You seem to have a special favour with God. Ask him to reunite me with my Clara and Gareth and to keep them both safe for me.'

'I will. I think it is wicked that you don't know where Clara was billeted. But so many forces were against you both. It will be my priority to badger God into doing something about it.'

They hugged again.

'Well, now. I have to get on. I have another birth imminent. And I want to persuade Reverend Mother to let you move into a room that we have free in the main house. I am concerned for this other girl. If she is brought in here and sees you have been able to keep Charlie, it will break her heart.'

This made Julia realise just how lucky she was. 'Sister, I hope that one day you do get the halfway home you talked about, and that mothers get the chance to keep and care for their babies.'

'So do I, Julia, so do I.'

Julia couldn't give her mind to this sad aspect of life in this convent, she was too full of joy. She leaned over Charlie's cot and took his little hand. 'We're going home, my little son, we're going home.'

As Julia left the convent a great cheer went up. She looked up at the dormitory windows and every one had one or two girls hanging from them waving handkerchiefs. She hadn't realised they knew about her situation, but in such a small environment it was hard to contain news.

Her emotions were mixed. There was joy at leaving with her Charlie, but sadness as she knew none of those waving would be doing the same. She blew them all kisses as she got into the waiting cab. Sister Grace handed Charlie to her, then bent and kissed her. 'Stay in touch, Julia, and find happiness.'

Julia couldn't speak. She could only smile a tearful, grateful smile.

Once out of the gates she asked the driver to take her to her landlord's address before taking her to the station.

'I'm sorry. There was a couple of letters, but I sent them back to where they had come from.'

'Why?' Julia swallowed her dismay.

'Well, it ain't my job to hold on to mail.'

'You knew where I was, you forced me to go there. You could have forwarded them to me!'

'Yes, and you could have paid your rent, young lady.'

It was hopeless arguing with this stubborn money-obsessed man. Now Gareth wouldn't know where she was, and no one at the barracks would tell her where he was. 'Can you remember where they came from?'

'Yes. The War Office.'

This shocked Julia. Were they from Gareth? Did he have to communicate to her through the War Office? Or were they call-up papers for herself? She had heard that all young women were being mobilised. She may never know, but at least she could try to make sure that when Gareth finally came home he had a starting point in finding her.

'Please do one thing for me, and I promise you that I will one day come to you and pay what I owe. Please take my forwarding address and if anyone ever comes asking you about me, give it to them. Please.'

'Very well.'

Julia wrote the address of Billie's cottage down on a piece of paper that the landlord had fetched. 'Thank you. Thank you so much. And you have my word that one day you will get the money I owe you.'

Back in the cab, she picked up the sleeping Charlie from where she had laid him and cradled him to her. Her silent tears wet his shawl. *Did your daddy write to me? Oh, Gareth. Gareth.*

On the train, the idea came to her that if the letters had been from Gareth, then surely she would be allowed to write back to him using the same channel? Hope seared through her. But what should she say? She'd heard that all letters going to and from families were read and censored. This was done to ensure that no information could fall into enemy hands as it was so easy to unwittingly say something that could prove useful. She would have to be very careful. Obviously the War Office knew of her in connection with Gareth – well, if the letters were from him, they did. But what would she be allowed to say? How could she be sure her letters would reach him?

Billie was at the station waiting for her. Their greeting was a flurry of hugs, tears, cooing over Charlie and more tears. 'We did it, Julia, luv. We did it!'

'You did, you clever girl. How can I thank you, Billie? You've saved my life.'

'And I've saved me own, too. I couldn't bear you going through losing a second child, once I knew what it felt like to lose one. I feel as though I've kicked the bleeders in the backside. Won a victory over them, and shown them that we women can look after our kids with a little 'elp.'

Julia laughed. 'Oh, it's good to be here. I can't wait to see the cottage.'

'I've a cab waiting. Give me your bag. You've enough on your plate carrying little Charlie.'

The cottage was lovely. The living room led straight off the road, and had a fire as its focal point. Surrounding that was a three-piece suite in red leather, with deep seats and huge chunky arms. A multi-coloured rug covered the beige lino-leum floor, from the fire to under the suite, and a table and four chairs stood by the window, with a dresser full of crock-ery on the wall opposite the fire. Everything shone as if Billie had been polishing for hours, lovingly preparing a home, this thought brought tears to Julia's eyes. They were of relief and a feeling of being safe and free.

'You haven't seen the half yet. Me old mum's been very generous. I reckon she were glad to get shut of me. Come through and see the kitchen. And we have a scullery at the very back and a backyard that catches the sun.'

Julia couldn't believe it all. The kitchen had a black-leaded stove that was burning away, spitting sparks from a log that sat on the top of its embers.

'I chucked that on before I left. I'll just give it a poke, then I'll put the grate plate over it and bring the kettle to the boil whilst I show you the rest of the cottage.'

'It's lovely, Billie. I love the pair of rocking chairs each side of the grate. It'll be nice to sit there opposite one another on a cold winter's night. She looked around the rest of the kitchen and loved everything, from the pretty rose-coloured curtain around the deep pot sink, which matched those at the window, to the scrubbed table in the centre of the room, and the kitchen cabinet painted in cream.

'And through here, we have the boiler for washing our clothes, and the mangle. Let's go upstairs, eh?'

The stairs led off the kitchen. They were enclosed by a wall each side, but light came from a window on the landing, which was small and from which both bedrooms led. Billie had chosen to give Julia the back bedroom. 'It's nice and light and gets the sun, and you look down on the yard, where I 'ope to get some nice pots of flowers in time. It's also the biggest, so there's plenty of room for Charlie, and for Clara when we find her.'

Julia couldn't speak. The room was a lot larger than she expected, and contained a double bed, a cot and on the back wall a single bed. The candlewick eiderdowns were a pale blue, the bedheads and chest of drawers a deep mahogany. A cream and blue rug lay each side of the bed, and net curtains billowed at the open window. 'There's a cupboard in the corner too, which will be useful to you, luv.'

'Billie, what can I say? It's all a dream, and you're sharing it with me. I can never thank you enough. How I will repay you I have no idea.'

'Yer don't 'ave to. Just 'elp me get me little George back. That'll be all the thanks I need. Now, there's a nosy parker along the block 'ere, she's been asking all sorts, so I told 'er as I were bombed out in London, and so were me cousin. But that your man was away at war, so we decided to come north where we thought we would be safe. So, we need to get you a wedding ring.'

From feeling like crying, Julia went to wanting to laugh out loud. Billie had such a way with her. It was hard to believe that she was ten years younger than her. She had a wise old head, as Winnie would say.

'What's that look for? Aren't yer 'appy with it all?'

'I love it, Billie. It's perfect. I just had a moment when Winnie came to my head – I told you about her, my late fiancé's mother? Well, it just made me feel sad for a moment.'

'Well, we've lots of them things that can do that to us, but like I said to you once before, do as us Londoners do and broaden your shoulders. "Keep smiling through."'

'Ha, do you have a song for every situation?'

'Probably. It's part of it. Yer feel down, or everything's on top of yer, so yer sing.'

With this, Billie danced towards the stairs, singing, 'Keep smiling through, just like you always do . . . '

When she got to 'And you know we'll meet again, some sunny day', she was at the bottom of the stairs, and looked back up at Julia. 'We will, yer know. Me and my George, and you and your Clara and Gareth. We just 'ave to make it happen. Now for a nice cup of Rosie Lee.'

A feeling settled in Julia that she could cope. She had Billie to help her, and she had her little Charlie and this lovely home.

She wouldn't mope around the place. She'd follow Billie's example and keep her spirits up. And yes, she would help Billie to get George home, and work towards getting Clara with her, and she'd write to Gareth through the War Office. She smiled at Billie. 'Mmm, a Rosie Lee would be lovely. We can toast our new home.'

PART THREE

1942–1943

NEW ROLES – NEW LIVES

CHAPTER TWENTY-EIGHT

Clara
A Budding Star – A Deep Loss

Clara had taken to the stage as if born to it. As she stood in the wings waiting for her cue, she had to pinch herself yet again.

In the winter show, she had sung in the interval accompanied by Anton, but now she had a part in the pantomime. It was only a bit part. She sang a beautiful song that Frank Sinatra had made famous the year before, 'Two in Love', whilst Cinderella and Prince Charming shared the final dance of the show.

Her nerves were always on edge as her moment approached, but once the music began, she felt it enter her and she was where she was meant to be. Standing in the lights, leaning on Anton's grand piano, singing her heart out. When the cast took a bow, she joined them and hoped that some of the clapping and cheers were aimed at her.

This chance to show her talent had helped her to heal. Her body had healed quite quickly, but her mind had taken longer. Now it seemed as if none of it had happened, but she worried about Lindsey. For Lindsey had sunk deep into the doldrums. Clara knew that the betrayal by Tinker was the cause and she wasn't sure how to make things better for her friend, but working with Daisy had helped. Lindsey had found that she had a flare for running a shop, and trade had doubled since she had been in charge. Clara still worried, because Lindsey had picked up with some old contacts who were loosely involved with the gang on Cookson Street. She'd said it was necessary to obtain the 'extras' that she couldn't get from the suppliers.

Putting all of this out of her mind, Clara concentrated on her coming performance. On stage, the prince took Cinderella's hand. *This is it*. Opening the curtains, Clara stepped through. The prince was on one knee. The audience were enraptured. A hush had descended. Anton, looking beautiful in his silk suit, took his seat. Clara felt like the princess herself, in her long frock that belled out and had layers of chiffon covering a silk underskirt. The effect was of rainbow colours, with the underskirt pink and each chiffon layer edged in a different shade. Her hair was back to its natural shiny, dark brown and had been fashioned into ringlets to fit the period of the show. For a moment, the lights were on her and Anton as she began to sing, then they moved to the prince and Cinderella, with a dimmer light on her. Her voice soared, as did her heart when Anton smiled at her. The moment was magical.

The audience stood as the scene came to an end with shouts of 'bravo'. The curtain call came after that and, taking her place at the end of the line-up, she walked forward and bowed, just as they all did. When she lifted her head, she looked at the first row and into the smirking grin of Tinker!

Her stomach churned. He was looking straight at her. She gave him a look of disgust as the curtain descended. When the curtain call came for the second time, he'd gone.

Behind the stage Panda and Lofty grabbed her. 'You were amazing, darling.'

'Thank you, Panda.' He kissed her elaborately on each cheek.

Then Lofty took her hand and asked of her, 'Bend down, so that I can kiss our rising star. I'm so proud of you, my darling girl.'

'Oh, Lofty, I'm loving it, thank you so much. I'll see you tomorrow. I need to see Anton now.'

'So, I've got no chance, then? Oh well, I'll go and pester Jeannie.'

Laughing at him, when laughing was the last thing she felt like doing, Clara left him and hurried after Anton. But then she remembered just in time that he didn't know anything about what had gone on, so she couldn't unburden her worry over seeing that Tinker was back.

'What is it, *ma cherie*? You seem frightened.'

'No! Ha, I feel just the opposite. I'm shaking with excitement. I'm so happy. Wasn't it wonderful?'

'*Mon amour*, you are holding something back from me. And have been since the accident. It is that I don't like secrets between us.' He took her hands in his. 'When you are sixteen, I – I want us to, I mean, you know how much I love you, but we only have a few months to wait now, before I can make you my fiancé. There should be nothing that we don't know about each other, you once promised.'

Trying to lighten the moment, she asked him, 'Are you asking me to marry you?'

'No, not yet. It wouldn't be right, but in August, yes.'

'Oh, I love you so much, Anton. And the answer will be yes. It is now, and a few months won't change that. And, I – I'm sorry. I cannot explain, but yes, I did lie to you. What happened to me, it didn't happen how we said; I – I was afraid to tell you, Anton.'

'Are you no longer afraid? Those men that you told me of . . . is that it? Was it them who hurt you and Lindsey? And why did Tinker go so suddenly? Was he involved?'

'Anton, I promise I will tell you the truth. I should have done so at the time, but everyone cautioned against it. You will know why when I tell you. I'll meet you in the foyer in fifteen minutes. We'll go for a walk. I daren't tell you here in case we are overheard.'

Clara had kept her style – there was no going back for her to the young girl she had been. She may have only been fifteen, but inside she felt much older, and so still wore the fashions that she'd adopted when trying to disguise herself. Clothes weren't easy to come by with rationing, but Jeannie had contacts, and many an item came her way that she didn't need for any of the productions. Cast members and backroom staff had the pick of these.

The coat that Clara was wearing had come from this source and she loved it. Mid-brown in colour, it had a belted waist and then flared to her calf – a little longer than worn today, for this coat was ten years old, but otherwise, was still in fashion. But it was the enormous, lighter brown fur collar that she loved. It spread to cover her shoulders, and continued down the lapel to her waist. The cuffs, too, were edged with the same fur. The collar she could pull up around her ears. But she wouldn't need to do that tonight as she had a matching hat that Daisy had crocheted for her. It was a bit like a tea cosy, as Daisy had used the same pattern she'd used to make one of those, but she hadn't left the holes for the spout and the handle, and had crocheted a flower which she had stitched onto the side. The effect was very glamorous and was very much the fashion of the day.

As they walked out arm in arm, Anton remarked on the coat. It had been the cause of their first real kiss. She'd been describing it to him and he'd taken hold of the collar and traced his hand along it until he had reached her face. Cupping her cheeks he'd kissed her lightly at first, but then had become more passionate. But the moment had been spoiled by their inexperience as their teeth had clashed, and this had sent them into a fit of giggles. His kisses since then had been back to the lighter kind of pressing lips together for a few seconds, but still she thrilled at them.

Telling Anton what had happened shocked him so much that he couldn't speak. He clung on to her, encircling her in his arms.

'*Mon amour*, it is that I am glad that you are free, but to have that happen to you, and to Lindsey, too. I can't comprehend that there are such monsters out there. And Tinker! I cannot believe that he was in league with *le diable*.'

As they walked on, she told him, 'He still is, Anton. He showed up at the theatre tonight. I saw him during curtain call. He had a nasty smirk on his face. That's what scared me. Why has he returned? We don't know what made him leave as one minute Daisy was saying he was coming to see us in hospital, and the next he was gone. We suspected that she gave him some money and an ultimatum to leave, as she may have picked up on our fear of him and realised that he had something to do with what had happened to us.'

'Oh, *mon amour*, I am afraid for you. I will pay a cab to take you home, I'm not happy with you walking alone.'

They had reached the promenade. Their breaths looked like curls of smoke in the hazy gas-lit street. Most folk had their heads down and walked briskly. Probably making for home after seeing a show or being up in the Tower Ballroom, or just leaving one of the many bars. The sea wind had a bitter cut to it, though the sea was calm and glittered in the strong moonlight.

But Clara couldn't appreciate the beauty of it all, her mind was with Lindsey. 'I think I will go now, Anton, I need to warn Lindsey of Tinker's return. I'm afraid for her.'

Anton was reluctant, but he hailed one of the cabs standing in a line not far from them. Then he surprised her by saying, 'I will come with you.'

With the unease in her getting stronger, Clara welcomed this.

The house and shop were in darkness when they arrived. This wasn't unusual, but something made the hair on Clara's arms stand up. Why wasn't Tiggy barking her head off as she always did? Clanging the bell didn't bring anyone to them, apart from an irate guest next door, who put his head out of the window and told them to stop making such a racket.

'Something's wrong, I know it is, Anton. What should we do?'

'Go for the police?'

'No, we can't, we don't know the extent of who is involved if there is trouble. I'll have to climb over the back gate and get the key.'

After Clara had let herself and Anton inside, calling out didn't get a response. Lighting all the gas mantles in the stockroom, Clara saw chaos. The place had been ransacked. She told Anton to keep very close to her so that she could guide him through. The kitchen was the same. Clara could hear her heart thudding and feel it banging the inside of her chest.

A noise made her jump. Going through into the hall between the shop and the stairs, Anton suddenly said, 'Shush.' After a moment he explained that he'd heard a muffled sound coming from the living room.

Opening the door and lighting the mantle had Clara gasping. 'No! No, no!'

Lindsey was tied to one of the chairs. She looked unharmed, but on the floor lay Daisy, unmoving and with dried blood all over her face. A huge blood stain covered the carpet beneath her head. Next to her lay the bloodied body of Tiggy.

'What is it? Clara, what's happened?'

'Stay still, Anton, Daisy is on the floor.' She told him about Lindsey. 'I need a knife from the drawer in the kitchen to free her. Don't move in case you trip.'

In seconds she had Lindsey free.

319

'Oh, Clara. It – was him – Tinker! I – I think Daisy is . . .'

Crossing over to Daisy, Clara could feel that she was cold to touch. Trying her pulse as her mum had shown her when they played doctors and nurses, her heart sank. 'She – she's dead!'

'*Naw . . . naw, please, naw, Clara!*'

A strength came to Clara. She took hold of Anton and guided him to a chair, then took Lindsey in her arms. 'What happened, Lindsey? Tell me.'

'W – we were just going to lock the shop. I – I had the key in me hand . . . when a force pushed me back. Tinker barged in. He took the key and locked the door before we could do owt. We both fought him, but he is strong. He pushed Daisy to the floor, then dragged me into here. He had me arms around the chair and me feet shackled in naw time. I was helpless against him. And . . . he – he must have had it all planned, Clara, as he had the cords and tape with him. Any road, Daisy came in then. She had her rolling pin. She hit him on the back, but it didn't seem to hurt him. He – he turned, grabbed it from her and cracked her across the head . . . and then did the same to little Tiggy. Oh, Clara, it was sickening. Daisy hasn't moved since.' Clara held Lindsey while she calmed enough to carry on. 'I was screaming. B – but then Tinker put that tape across me mouth. Then I heard him riffling through everything. He came back in here with Daisy's tin with her savings in it, and he had all her jewellery, an' all. Before he left he said it was all my fault and yours. He said he should have been in Ireland now. But if he had more money, he still could go. Th – then he called me a lot of names, and said that I had ruined his life. He made me think he was a mad man, Clara, he had no care of Daisy.'

'So, you don't think that he was working for anyone?'

'Naw. He was on his own, otherwise he'd have used the threat of someone doing sommat to me if I told. That's what made me think he was mad. He didn't think of owt like that. And his eyes. His eyes were evil looking – staring. He wasn't the Tinker that we knew.'

'Clara.' Feeling her world descending into the horror it had once been, Clara was steadied by Anton's calling her name. 'We must go to the police. You mustn't touch anything. I know you have freed Lindsey, and they would expect that of you, but nothing else must be touched.'

'You're right, Anton. I just had to make sure that Mickey had nothing to do with it.'

'Tinker said that Mickey was dead. I remember now. He was rambling, saying that Mickey was a good fellow, but the new lot had him killed, and with his death all his own chances had gone.'

'We didn't hear of any deaths.'

'Naw, but I think Gilly and Dougie were killed, too. They couldn't have survived that crack to their skull. It would all have been covered up. Any road, don't let's talk about them. They have nowt to do with this. This is Tinker, and Tinker alone, and he's killed our Daisy, our lovely Daisy, and . . . Tiggy. Poor Tiggy, he did his best to defend Daisy.'

Lindsey began to sob again, but Clara held on. She wanted to scream and sob, but she knew she had to act quickly and keep calm.

'So, it's eleven-thirty now. And Tinker didn't leave the theatre till nine forty-five. So he wouldn't have got far, wherever he planned on going.'

'The theatre?'

'I'll tell you later. Get the fire made up, Lindsey. It's freezing in here. Keep yourself warm, but like Anton says, don't move anything. We have to go to the police.'

'Don't leave me, let me come with you. What if he comes back?'

'Lock all the doors. I'll take all the hidden keys from outside. We might get lucky and be able to hail a cab, there's always some cruising around the hotels in this street hoping for some late business.'

Lindsey tried to persuade them, but in the end, though Clara could see she was petrified, they had to leave her. She would be safer locked in the house than they would be walking the streets if Tinker was lurking around still.

'We'll hurry. I promise.' With this Clara and Anton left. Clara couldn't believe how calm she felt and how she could feel nothing. It was as if she was closed down. Anton kept his arm around her but didn't speak. Poor Anton, although he had been born of evil, he'd been protected from it all his life and didn't know how to cope with it other than to be a comfort to her.

Clara looked up at the clear, starry sky and wondered how much more she and Lindsey would be asked to bear. When she thought back to her childhood, it seemed such a long time ago, and as if it had only lasted months. She should still be a child, but there wasn't a trace of one in her.

CHAPTER TWENTY-NINE

Julia
Two Torn Lives Healing

Julia tucked seven-month-old Charlie into his pram and smiled down at him as he gurgled at her. He hated his arms under the covers, and the moment she tucked them in he wriggled them out. He thought it was a game, and real giggles came from him each time he freed them. But she had to win the game, as she needed to take him out to the post office to post yet another letter to Gareth and the March winds that swept down from the hills and across the Pennines surrounding Blackburn gave no quarter. They were bitter.

After her first letter wasn't returned, she determined to write once or twice a week in the hope that they were getting through to Gareth. In them she detailed Charlie's progress, and told of her life together with Billie. Today, she had told him that she was worried about Billie as she had a yellow tinge to her skin. She knew that munitions workers were called the canary girls because the sulphur they worked with interfered with the pigmentation of their skin and hair, but she wondered about the long-term effect it would have on them. She didn't want anything to happen to Billie.

No reply had ever come from Gareth, but Julia had done as she'd promised herself and Billie – she'd got on with life in a cheerful manner. She was the housewife. She kept the cottage spick and span and washed, ironed and cooked for the three of them. It wasn't what she wanted to do, but it was how it was.

Curious neighbours had been quietened with the story that Billie had made up, and had accepted them into the community. And, best of all, Billie had an interview with the committee of the WVRS refuge for orphaned children in a few days from now. Billie could hardly contain her excitement. Julia tried to caution her against disappointment, but had every hope for success as the day before, the promised letter from Sister Grace had arrived.

Julia had kept in touch with Sister Grace, and in a letter to her the previous month had confessed what she'd done. Sister Grace's reply to that had put her mind at rest.

My Dear Julia,

You didn't do wrong as such, nor break my trust. I told you where the information was, and I didn't tell you that you must not go to it and look through it. I have since guessed that you had done.

I am so happy to hear how your life is steadying and Billie's too. I will always be grateful to her for making it

possible for you to keep Charlie. I will do all I can to help
you both.

As always you are in my prayers.

Sister Grace

Julia had written straight back and asked for a letter to help them approach the WRVS. When it had come, it was more than they could have hoped for.

My Dear Julia,

Please find enclosed a separate letter for you to take along to the WRVS. I am pleased to tell you that I have rung them and spoken to Harriet Marple, who is in charge there. I told her about both of you, and how I thought that Billie deserved to have her child back and would make an excellent mother.

I told her that you would be sorting out the care of your children between you and that you are willing to have her visit your home and to examine any evidence that she wants to that shows that you are solvent and run a happy home.

I am praying for you both.

May God bless you and be with you.

Sister Grace

For Billie this had been the surety that she would get her George back, but though Julia couldn't see a reason why not, she just couldn't quite believe it could be that simple.

With Charlie now asleep, meaning that she could tuck him in as she wanted to, she walked to the post office. On the way she thought about her own future. As much as she loved being a full-time mum, she had so much to give to help the war effort, and a compelling urge to nurse.

And what about Billie? Just suppose this exposure to sulphur is killing her? *Oh God, I can't let that happen. She's working in that place to care for me and Charlie. Yes, there is the motive – a very strong one, to have everything right so that she will be given George back, and my commitment to care for him is a big part of that, but what good will that be if her life is sacrificed? We could reverse our roles. I could be the one earning the money, and she could take over what I do.*

Every day the news was of the war escalating. The Japanese had become involved, more U-boat attacks were happening at sea, the army were failing in Burma and the RAF were making more and more raids. The world had gone mad. You couldn't walk down the street without seeing casualties of war, men broken in both body and mind. They tore at her heart strings, making her feel that here she was, a strong young woman with a skill, yet she was doing nothing to help. The papers were constantly reporting on how more nurses were needed. Well, she couldn't go abroad to nurse, but she could work in the local hospital and free up a nurse who could.

Her mind made up, she decided to speak to Billie about it later.

As they entered the gate of the ordinary-looking building in Lancaster that proclaimed itself the Lancaster headquarters of the WVRS, Julia could see that Billie was shaking. She looked better today, having taken time to use her panstick make-up and apply a little rouge, so that you couldn't detect the yellow of her face. She also wore gloves to cover her hands, though Julia had pointed out that she would have to remove these to shake the hand of the interviewer, if offered.

'It ain't right that I should 'ave to beg for these women to return me kid, Julia. I feel as though I'm on trial. I've done all that anyone could ask of me. It's a bleedin' travesty.'

'Billie, try to see it as them protecting your son. Not from you, but from harm in general. They need to be sure that he will go to the best place for him. Them taking care of him isn't a way of punishing you, but a way of ensuring that children born in unconventional circumstances, or orphaned, are taken care of. If you think of this as you getting your own back on the system, you'll come across as aggressive. And, love, please try not to use bad language – these folk can be very prissy.'

'You're right, I know that. What I would do without you, Julia, I just don't know. Are you all right carrying Charlie?'

'Well, he's no lightweight, but I'm fine. We're here now, so let's do this. We'll win George back together, eh?'

The woman who greeted them was clothed in disapproval. Julia's spirits sank. *Please don't let them alienate Billie, as that will bring out the worst of her.* Not that there was much of that side to bring out of Billie, but she did have what she called her Londoner's fighting spirit, and that could create the impression that she was a rough diamond with more of a temper than she had.

The hall they were shown into had a polished floor, and was lined with wooden chairs. 'Wait here.'

Julia smiled at the poker-faced woman and thanked her. Billie had a look of thunder on her face. Not wanting to antagonise her more by taking her to task, Julia thought to lighten the moment. 'It's like waiting in the doctor's surgery. Look, there are even some magazines. I can't believe we are here at last. You're on your way, Billie. We'll soon have George with us.'

Billie smiled her lovely smile and visibly relaxed.

'Oh, Billie, love, with that smile, you'll melt hearts. And you look so lovely, just as you are. They'll not be able to resist you.'

Billie blushed, which enhanced her loveliness. And she did look lovely. She'd splashed out on a new coat and matching hat. Green, with a small dark brown fur collar, the coat flared out from the shoulders and looked lovely on her. The hat was shaped like a bell, and really suited Billie's round face. Underneath her coat she wore a fashionable costume with a pencil-slim skirt and little box jacket that she'd brought with her from her home in London.

Julia squeezed her hand. 'It'll be fine, you'll see. Remember, Sister Grace has paved the way for you, and she'll have a lot of influence.'

This didn't prove quite true when finally they sat in front of three women on the other side of a long table which, apart from the chairs they sat on, was the only furniture in the small room. None of the women smiled. Disdain emanated from their pores, let alone their eyes and body stance.

'Right. Shall we begin? Which one of you is *Miss* Blaider?'

Julia felt Billie stiffen at the emphasis of 'Miss'. She prayed that she would do as she had coached her and keep calm.

'I am, madam.'

The polite answer spoken in a gentle tone reassured Julia, and she could see it had a good effect on the woman asking the question. She let out a sigh of relief.

328

'So, you are here to seek custody of your child, George Blaider?'

'I am, madam. I am in a position to take care of him, and I've loved him since the moment he was born, even though I've never seen or 'eld him . . . but, I – I knew that in my circumstances, I had to prove meself a worthy mother.'

The women were all taken aback. They looked from one to the other. Julia felt so proud of Billie.

'What were your circumstances?'

'Do you mean, 'ow did I come to 'ave George out of wedlock?'

The woman coughed. 'Yes. It makes a difference to our decision. You may have been a prostitute and you may revert to that state, we do not know. But please tell us the truth, no matter what it is.'

Julia looked at Billie. Pain was etched on Billie's face, but she held her head up and looked straight into the eyes of the woman who had asked the question. Julia wondered if she was ready for the answer, or if she wanted to hear a love story, of a soldier who had to go to war not knowing he'd left his girlfriend pregnant. She held her breath.

'I – I was raped by my uncle.'

'What?'

The tone of this was disbelieving. Julia felt Billie straighten again as if taking a defensive stance. *Please, Billie, please keep calm.*

'Good Lord above, that is appalling, you poor girl.'

'Agnes! Your heart is ruling your head again!'

The small woman who sat at the end on the left of the trio had spoken for the first time, but had been slapped down by

329

the headmistress-type in the centre, who was conducting proceedings.

Agnes stood her ground. 'I am not. That is a pitiful story and something that no woman deserves to have happen to her.'

'Of course it is, but we do not show our emotions or sympathies in these situations. It isn't fair to Miss Blaider.'

'It is . . .'

Julia held her breath. Was Billie going to undo all the good she'd done? Her next words seemed to confirm she was and Julia felt a despair descend on her,

'I . . . I mean, well, I could do with a bit of comfort. I've done nothing wrong, but feel as though I'm on trial. To 'ear that said by one of you as is sat in judgement of me, gives me 'ope that you're 'uman, and that you will see me as someone that wrong was done by, not someone who sinned. I couldn't 'elp what 'appened to me, but I'm trying to not make that worse by wanting to take care of me son and make sure that he 'as a good life. None of what 'appened to me was his fault either, so why should he be punished by never knowing 'is real mum? I love 'im, and can take care of 'im and that's what I want to do.'

Julia felt heartened by this outburst, and had an urge to help Billie. Billie was right – she didn't deserve to be punished and neither did George. 'May I speak, madam?'

All three women were looking shocked and unsure, they had lost control and Julia could see that was important to them. She needed to bring this back around so they felt that it was they who were leading.

'Yes. You are . . . *Miss* Portman?'

330

'I am. I too am unmarried.'

'So we understand. What have you got to say?'

'My fiancé and I were to be married, but he was suddenly deployed two days before. I know that doesn't excuse what I did, and in my mind makes me a sinner, whereas, Billie – Miss Blaider isn't. But I can see that all three of you are married, so as women you understand the feelings that can lead you astray.'

The lady sitting in the centre coughed. All three had coloured a little.

'I'm sorry, I don't mean to embarrass you, I just want you to see how it is that some women end up in the predicament that Billie and I are in. Billie is to be admired, rather than looked on with disdain. This terrible thing happened to her, she didn't choose for it to happen, whereas I chose to do what I did, and it was Hitler who spoilt the plans my fiancé and I had. Billie not only carried her child and gave him life when, living in London, it would have been easy for her to find someone to get rid of it for her. Even her own parents were urging her to do so and would have paid the cost of the abortion, but no. Billie had the notion from the beginning that her child should have life. She could do nothing about the nuns taking her child from her, and that broke her heart. But she saw that the same was about to happen to me, and she wouldn't allow that.' Julia wasn't interrupted, and she went on to tell the women how Billie did that, and how she did war work at the munitions factory. 'And now it is time for Billie to be rewarded. If she is granted the custody of her child, I will go back to nursing, and Billie will care for George and Charlie. Once my fiancé returns, I will marry, but he and I will always support Billie and George. So please, try to look beyond thinking of us as fallen women, and see us for what we are – loving, caring mothers.'

A sob beside her brought Billie into Julia's focus once more. She put her arm around her as best she could with the sleeping Charlie taking up all of her lap. 'Don't, Billie, you have been so brave.'

'Yes, she has, I agree.' This came from the one who had been called Agnes, and had the other two looking at her. Middle-aged and with an air of being saints, they were shocked to the core by what Agnes said next. 'There, but for the grace of God, go I. Well, not poor Miss Blaider's story, but, Miss Portman's story could have been mine. I was three months pregnant when I married, but luckily nothing happened to prevent my wedding.'

'Really, Agnes, that isn't helpful.'

'Well, I think it is, Dorothy.' This from the woman sitting on the right had the effect of making the main woman powerless, which Julia didn't like to see. 'It has made me see things in a different light. It is misfortune and the sins of others that has landed these women in the situation they are in, and from what I hear, both from Miss Portman and Sister Grace, they are doing their best to put the wrongs right. They shouldn't be punished for that, but helped. I vote that George is returned to Miss Blaider on a phased plan.'

'Thank you, thank you ever so much. But what is a phased plan, madam?'

'You have no need to call me madam. I am Mrs Philcot, or, Susan, which I prefer. May I call you, Billie?'

Billie nodded.

332

'Well, a phased plan is where we work with you and George over a couple of months to ease you both into your new lives together. We do it with adoptive parents, and whilst I accept that this is not what you are, I still think it the appropriate approach. You will be able to visit George whenever you like – play with him, take care of his needs and take him for walks. And he will be able to visit you. Then, when you are both used to each other in particular, when George is used to you – he will come and live with you. How does that sound?'

Julia waited. She squeezed Billie, and smiled at her encouragingly.

Billie looked unsure. 'I – is George near to me? Can I see him after work? And in me dinner hour, and all weekend?'

'Yes, I understand that you work in Lower Darwin? Well, you are in luck because our refuge is in Darwin, too.'

Julia's heart warmed to see the happiness this brought to Billie.

'Now,' Susan addressed Agnes and Dorothy, 'what do you both think to this plan?' Agnes and Dorothy looked at her. Agnes was nodding her head. 'I agree wholeheartedly.'

'Given what you've told us, you would!'

The sternness of these words of Dorothy's put a worry into Julia. Was Dorothy powerful enough to overrule Susan and Agnes? But no, her next words showed she was just being more cautious than the other two.

'I think you are both letting your hearts rule your head. I want proper checks done of the home they have to offer George, and their financial state. It is unheard of for us to release a child to two women! We have to be one hundred and ten per cent certain we are doing the right thing.'

'I'm sure they will have no objection to that.' Susan looked from Julia to Billie. They both shook their heads.

'Good. Well, Dorothy, as soon as you have that in place and your satisfactory report, I will organise the phased handover.'

Dorothy didn't look too pleased, having had her thunder as chairman taken from her.

Julia spoke directly to her before thanking the other two. 'I don't know how to address you, but, I want to thank you. This meeting was an ordeal for Billie and for me, but you have made it less so by making sure everything is in place and in its proper order and allowing us our say. And thank you, Agnes and Susan, for being so open to our dilemma and all of you for not judging us once you heard our story.'

Dorothy actually smiled. 'These things are always difficult. And I have to keep them from getting over-sentimental and make sure that the right thing is done by the child in question. You have both given a good account of yourselves and I will do my side of things as quickly as I can. I wish you both good luck.'

All three women were smiling now. Billie thanked them as best she could as tears had overwhelmed her. Billie was a tough woman, but when she let in her emotions she was undone.

The women showed they understood with their caring expressions. For this to be so was a victory for Julia and Billie in itself. They had managed to appeal to the better nature of these women who, at the outset, had been judgemental.

Outside, Billie clung to Julia's arm.

'We won, Billie, we won! Little George is coming home!'

Billie smiled her dimply smile. 'Yes, me son, is coming to

me, I can't wait to see what he looks like, his 'air, his eyes. I know he will be a smasher. I just so long to 'old him.'

Julia felt this cut into her. The pity of it, but also the poignancy of it. She knew the longing of wanting to hold your child.

As if Billie had read her mind, she dried her tears and said: 'We did win, didn't we? I am getting me little lad back, but our job's not done, Julia. We 'ave to get Clara back too, and sharpish. Just as soon as we're settled with George, that's what we'll concentrate on. I promise.'

With their arms linked they walked to the station. It wasn't until they were on the train that Billie suddenly looked at her in a way that suggested she had something on her mind.

'What's this about you going back to nursing, then? I know you've mentioned it, but gawd blimey, I didn't know 'as it's got this far.'

'Yes, I've been planning it for a while. I worry about you in that factory, you don't look well, and you're always tired. Besides, you will need to have time at home with George.'

'Ta, mate. And that's what yer are – a bleedin' good mate.'

Julia smiled. 'And so are you. You stopped me falling.'

'I only did what was right. And that's a good way of putting it, as I've felt like that many a time, as if I was falling, and all around me were letting it 'appen. Well, we'll never let it 'appen to each other, ever again, as we'll always be there to catch each other.'

'We will, Billie. You're a friend for life. A best friend. *The* best friend that anyone could wish to have.'

Billie's eyes filled up once more, but she brushed them away. 'It were a good day when we met, Julia.'

And Julia knew that it was. Billie had truly caught her when she was in despair. In her heart she would never forget that. Now it was her turn to shore up her friend and help her get through the next few weeks. Then? Well, who knew? Maybe a miracle would happen – she'd find Clara, and Gareth would get in touch.

CHAPTER THIRTY

Clara
Justice

'Am I glad that's over, Anton.'

'I agree, *mon amour*. Now we can give our attention to all that is going on.'

'Yes, and to helping Lindsey.'

They sat in the theatre café. The last of the pantomimes had finished at the end of January, but Panda had wanted to stage a few matinees of the in-between show, which they didn't normally do. He'd thought the audiences wouldn't dwindle and said that the extra revenue would help as the theatre was short of money. But a few weeks had shown him that it wasn't worth it, and so they now had the afternoons off until rehearsals for the summer show began. Clara wouldn't be needed for the evening in-between show as there was no interval.

All of the company had been feeling the strain of not having their afternoons off at this time of year, and this had caused a bitchy atmosphere, where unpleasant comments were exchanged, which wasn't their normal way.

'So, did you take Jeannie's offer to go back into the wardrobe department in the mornings?'

'I did, but not until Lindsey is all right.'

'How is she?'

'She's doing a wonderful job of running the shop but, like me, dreading Daisy's funeral and what will happen after that.'

'Clara, you must try not to worry. It will all come right.'

Clara wasn't so sure. Everything was a worry, but she was glad that the solicitors in charge of Daisy's affairs had elected to keep the shop running while they waited for the outcome of everything. Lindsey hadn't objected and had thrown herself into making sure the shop thrived and this had been good for her.

Now, at last, Daisy's body was being released and her funeral could take place. But the thought of the trial was something both Clara and Lindsey dreaded. They feared that more would have to come out. The detective who questioned them wanted to know how they knew Tinker, and why he'd left the shop, how they had all come to be lodging in the shop in the first place, and where they'd come from and what they'd done before. For Clara's part, she had explained that she was evacuated there, leaving out the time when she'd been working for Mickey – but Lindsey had to admit to having run away from an orphanage and had skirted over her time at Mickey's by just saying she had worked in a guest house until she met Clara and lodged with her at Daisy's.

338

Sighing as all this crowded in on her, Clara told Anton that she was going to see Arnold the next day. 'I should have gone as soon as it happened. But until they caught Tinker last week, they seemed happy enough with our statements. Lindsey said that when they contacted her to tell her he was in custody, they also said that they may need to interview us both in more depth, depending on whether Tinker pleads guilty or not.'

'I will come to Arnold with you.'

Lindsey was waiting for Clara's return, even though Clara had told her to go to bed in case she was late. They hugged as always when greeting, but Lindsey held her more tightly than usual, and for longer. Her anxiety showed in the trembling of her body.

'Don't worry, Lindsey, we'll sort everything out. Nothing will happen. I told you, I'm going to Arnold. He sorted everything before, didn't he?'

On Clara's first visit to Arnold after the horror of the kidnap, he told her that he'd done his best to act as soon as he'd heard she'd been taken too, and that it had broken his heart that the takeover had taken such a long time to organise. It was strange to her that Arnold was mixed up in the gangs that ran Blackpool, but she didn't dwell on it. He was a good friend and she loved him. She knew he loved her too. What had happened to her had upset him deeply and they'd become even closer since.

'Let me make the cocoa tonight, Lindsey. You sit down, and then you can tell me what the solicitor said. Did he come today as he'd promised?'

'Aye, he got under me feet a bit. Its allus the same. You can have nowt doing, then when you're needed for sommat else the shop fills up.' As they sat down with their steaming mugs, Lindsey blew on her cocoa. 'The solicitor is going to arrange the funeral. I've to give him the names of those who would want to attend, and then he'll book a wake, too. So I've nowt to do on that score. But they couldn't say what will happen to us afterwards, only that we mustn't worry as things take a while to sort out, and it's important to keep the shop running meanwhile. Then he wanted to take all the takings to bank them. I had to explain to him that I needed a cash float. He don't seem to knaw owt about business. But it's the other money I'm worried about. I've had to keep my end of the bargain with me contacts, and them I supply, but I keep that and what I make on it to one side. It's mounting up again after Tinker went off with what we had. I can't tell a solicitor about it. Nor can I tell the detective the real extent of what Tinker took. I just said it was a cash tin that Daisy had a lot of money in. But what am I to do with it, if we have to leave this place? It ain't mine, is it?'

'I don't know. I suppose, you'll just have to hand it in. You could tell them that you found it and that Tinker must have missed it. Something will occur to us. Don't let it play on your mind.'

Mothering Lindsey along had helped with Clara's own grief. Though now the matinees were over and the funeral imminent, it all threatened to crowd her. She had to be strong for Lindsey; she had to be. Lindsey was crumbling.

★   ★   ★

340

Arnold greeted Clara with a hug, something he'd done since the incident. 'And what brings you out so early, lass. Ain't you no work today?'

'I'm worried, Arnold.'

Arnold looked up and down the prom, then told her to go around the side. Once in the kitchenette, she told him of her worries.

'You did reet to come to me, lass. That's easy sorted. A few backhanders will secure a landlady who will say that Lindsey stayed with her until she met you. But I somehow think that none of that will be necessary. Tinker knaws too much. You did well to let me knaw as the cops have him, lass. Leave it with me. And, Clara, whatever happens is for the best, and the safest for you and Lindsey. And it will serve justice, an' all.'

Clara didn't ask any more, she was just so relieved to know that it was all going to be sorted. 'You know, Arnold, I think you could fix anything for me, except one thing.'

'Bring your ma to you. I knaw, lass, that's in God's hands, or rather Hitler's. But it will happen, you mark me words. And you're all right, ain't you? You have all your friends, and Anton. You love what you do, and you have me. You'll allus have me. So, keep your chin up, lass. This war can't last for ever.'

He hugged her again in the fatherly way she loved. As always, it made her wonder what it would have been like to have her own dad with her.

'That was a big sigh, lass. I knaw, life's dealt a few bad cards to you. But you have a bright future ahead of you. I was that proud the night I came to the panto. The whole show was superb for young and old alike, but the end bit, when you sang, well, it had me in tears.'

Clara blushed. But she felt better. She gave a little giggle, said her goodbyes and left. She didn't dare to think on what Arnold had meant by what he said about Tinker. But she wasn't going to worry about him – he was a monster, a dangerous, uncaring monster. How could he have done what he did and then calmly come to the theatre to harass her? Because he did. Just seeing him put a fright into her. He was insane, and he would be better gone, as she was sure was Arnold's plan.

Two days later, a policeman called at the shop. Neither Lindsey nor Clara were shocked to hear what he had to say. 'I'm afraid I have news for you both, and given your involvement, it might upset you, but the man we have in custody, Gordon Lee, known to you as Tinker, has hung himself in his cell. I'm sorry.'

'Don't be, Officer. It's the first decent thing he's done in a long time. We won't be mourning him.'

Clara hadn't expected this of Lindsey, but she was glad to hear it, as it was how she felt too. Arnold came to her mind, but she didn't dwell on it. Whether he had had a hand in it or not, justice had been done.

'Well, if you feel like that, then I can tell you, he was for the gallows anyway as he confessed before doing himself in. So this means that you won't have any further involvement, as there's no crime for us to investigate further. It's a closed case.'

Lindsey slumped a little onto Clara's body. Her words had been brave, and she'd meant them, but Clara suspected there was a very small part of her that wished everything was different – back to how it was before Tinker betrayed her. Putting her arm around Lindsey, she gave her a squeeze.

'Well, I'll be off,' the policeman looked intently at them. *Did he suspect?* If he did his next words were a salve to her and she knew to Lindsey, too. 'And you can get on with the rest of your lives with nothing hanging over you. I hope it is a good one. You deserve it after what you've been through.'

Clara had the feeling that the policeman was referring to more than Daisy's murder with these last words. Did he know about the gang and what had happened to them? She didn't know who to trust any more, and hoped with everything in her that she never would need to know.

Holding each other, they rocked backwards and forwards. For all that they felt grown up for most of the time, Clara knew that at this moment she and Lindsey were more akin to the young girls they were – cast off from their mothers' protection too soon, hurt and damaged by other adults who should have cared for them, and not knowing how to cope with the loss of Daisy, the one person who had cared so much that they looked on her as their granny.

The gaping hole awaited. The Bearers carried the coffin, spattered with rain, towards Daisy's final resting place in the huge churchyard in Layton. Clara stumbled along behind with Lindsey. They both vented their grief. Clara knew their tears weren't just for dear Daisy, but for all they'd suffered.

At the graveside, an arm came around her and she looked up into Anton's loving face. Jeannie had been his guide. They were all there, Lofty, Panda, Jeannie and all of the cast, as well as many of the customers from the shop. As she looked along them, trying to acknowledge them, she was surprised and pleased to see Arnold on the end of the line that had formed. She'd told him the other day how much of an ordeal it was going to be for her. He caught her eye and gave her a knowing, sympathetic smile. She nodded.

Her handful of earth echoed as it hit the coffin. *Oh Daisy, Daisy . . .*

The words the vicar spoke went over her head. The rain didn't register with her. Only her loss crowded her.

Anton gently steered her away. She stood with him while she waited for Lindsey, and saw Daisy's solicitor cut across the grass and take Lindsey to one side.

'I'm here for you, *ma cherie.*'

'I know, Anton. Thank you. Soon, once Lindsey is strong again, I will turn more to you, and we'll get back to normal.'

Anton squeezed her. 'I miss you, *mon amour.*'

'And I you.'

She and Anton had been like the weather dolls in the clock that stood in Daisy's lounge. One came out when the weather was good and the other when bad. Never together. She left the theatre as he was arriving in the morning, and she spent the rest of the day helping, and just being with Lindsey.

Lindsey walked towards her now. 'We're to go to the solicitor's office with him, Clara, before we join the wake. He wouldn't say nowt about why, except to say that it's good news. He'll bring us back to the Layton Institute after. Jeannie'll see to things there for us until we arrive.'

Clara couldn't think what the solicitor would need to tell them that was good news, as she was expecting, every day, to be told that they had to move out of Daisy's home.

★   ★   ★

Mr Burridge Senior, of Burridge, Clarke and Burridge Solicitors, cleared his throat. His face gave nothing away. A thin weedy man, he was tall, with very long legs.

'Now, you two have been left the shop and everything in it, as well as a small amount of money.'

'What? Eeh, I didn't expect that!'

'No, I don't expect that you did. But Daisy's will was changed in your favour not long after the time when I understand you came to live with her. Now, there is a stipulation.' He looked at Lindsey. 'Although Daisy gave the young man who eventually murdered her a home, she didn't like him and said that you must never marry him, or the whole of her estate will pass to being owned solely by Miss Portman. However, that is now impossible, so you are joint owners for life. The actual cash sum is four hundred and twenty-five pounds, some of which is the balance of her private account and the rest is takings from the shop. All furniture and effects are yours, as is the building and all fixtures and fittings. I won't have to bill you for my services, as the sum I have quoted is the estate after debtors have been paid, myself included. However, I would like to continue to act for you both in all business matters, if I may. We have dealt with the shop for a long time, being the Brandon family solicitors when the father owned it and before it was left to his older daughter, Mavis.'

Lindsey looked at Clara. Clara saw a mixture of happiness and confusion in her expression, before she turned back to Mr Burridge. 'Aye, I think as we would like that, having got used to you over these last weeks, and if Daisy trusted you, then we will, an' all.'

Clara agreed.

'Well, then, I don't expect that Daisy thought she would die for a long time, but her misfortune has left you owning a shop and having the responsibility of all that entails when at such a young age.'

'I'm seventeen!'

'Yes, and a very sensible and capable young woman, Lindsey. May I call you that?'

'Aye, you have been doing until today.'

'Well, a will reading is very formal. But back to your ages. You are not legally old enough to sign any legal documents, and will need a power of attorney.' He explained what that meant and offered to take on the role himself.

They both agreed, though Lindsey had some conditions. 'I knaws how to run that shop. I've not been doing so for long, but Daisy gave me rein in owt I suggested, and I don't want blocking from following through me ideas.'

'Oh, no, no, no, that won't happen, Lindsey. But I will need to sign for money from the bank for you, so I think the first thing is to set up a regular weekly wage for you to draw. And I will then co-sign cheques to your suppliers. It's that sort of thing that you will need me for, until you are twenty-one. Do you both understand?'

Clara hadn't said anything till now, but she told him that yes, she did understand. Then she asked, 'But can we change the person who is our power of attorney at any time?'

'Of course you can. You are both sound in mind, so this isn't binding from that angle. Have you someone in mind?'

346

'Well, if in the future, my mother and I are reunited, or for instance, when my boyfriend Anton reaches twenty-one. He and I plan on getting married then, so he would be my natural choice.'

'You are very young to think of marriage, my dear, and you must remember that you won't be able to marry until you're twenty-one without parental consent. But I understand your concerns, though I would caution you against near relatives taking this responsibility, but let's talk all this through another time. Shall we arrange a meeting for next week? By then you will have umpteen questions for me. And you can sign the papers to make me your power of attorney. Please don't worry about anything. Oh, one last thing. Have you enough cash on the premises to cope till then?'

'Aye, the takings have been good, and I've got it on me, an' all, as I thought I'd be handing everything over to you today.'

Mr Burridge took the cash and asked how much Lindsey thought they needed. 'Right, I will bank the rest for you. Now, let's get you back to your friends, which is where you should be at such a time. I'm sorry that I kept you away from the wake, but I was afraid that you would both be very worried as to your futures. I'm only sorry that I could not disclose the contents of the will before now.'

Neither of them spoke as they sat in the back of the car. They held hands and both stared out of the window. Clara couldn't take it all in. Her time in Blackpool had been a roller-coaster of hurt, fear, love, friendship and sadness. And now, she was a part-owner of property – a shop and a home. A smile creased her face as she thought of her mum. *What will you make of it all, Mum? Will you recognise me? How did it happen that*

347

in two short years I grew up and became what I am? But I do know that just as soon as this war ends, I'll come over and fetch you, Mum. And we will live here in Blackpool. You'll never know the bad side of it. Only the good. And there's so much that's good.

CHAPTER THIRTY-ONE

Julia
Not All News is Good News

Julia stared at the brown envelope showing a crown and with the words WAR OFFICE stamped in red on the back. The summer, such as it was, had come and gone, with no news of Gareth.

A scream made her jump. She looked around the room at George and Charlie. Charlie had one of the wooden carriages of the train set he and George shared, and it seemed that George wanted it. Billie came rushing in from the kitchen at the sound of her son's cry.

'What're you boys up to, eh? Gawd, yer gave me a fright. Yer share what yer've got, but you don't 'ave to 'ave the same toy. Look, George, 'ere's another carriage, a red one.'

George made angry noises and pointed at the yellow one that Charlie held.

'Lawd 'elp us. 'Ere, Charlie, d'yer want the red one, eh?'

Charlie relinquished the yellow one and took the red one. 'Good boy. I wish you'd learn from Charlie, George.'

George's bottom lip quivered.

'Come 'ere, son, no need for that, Mummy wasn't telling you off.' As she cuddled her son to her, Billie turned towards Julia. The smile she gave faded and a look of concern spread over her face. 'What is it, Julia, luv? You look like you've seen the grim reaper coming.'

'I've received a letter . . . it – it's from the War Office.'

Billie kissed George and placed him back on the floor. In a flash she was by Julia's side and had her arm around her. 'Sit down while you open it, luv.'

Julia sat in one of the rocking chairs. Her hands shook as she opened the envelope. Shock kept her rigid as she read the letter aloud.

Dear Miss Portman

We have received a communication from Officer Gareth Maling. And on his request that we should do so, we regret to inform you . . .

'Oh God, Billie!'

'What? Not . . . no, not that!'

'No . . . but . . . oh, Billie!'

'Read on, luv, let's get the whole picture, eh?'

. . . that Officer Maling is a prisoner of war.

We hold a number of letters from you to him, as due to the nature of his work we have been unable to dispatch them to

him. However, we have noted your address from these, and hope
that you receive this communication.

Holding the letter to her, Julia looked at Billie. 'All my letters, and he hasn't received one of them. Why, Billie? Was he not a pilot after all? Have they sent him on some clandestine mission? I don't understand.'

'Well, it could be that. I mean, we must 'ave some of our blokes doing spy work, or sommat. They'd need to gather intelligence – you know, see what the others are planning – that sort of thing.'

'That's it! Gareth once told me that he spoke both German and French. He said that if he hadn't made the grade as a vet, he would have gone into a career that required a linguist. He'd be the ideal candidate for undercover work. Oh my God! If he's been caught, then . . . I – I mean, if he's a spy . . . Oh, Billie.'

Billie didn't speak, but Julia could see by her expression that the same thoughts were going through her head. *Gareth could be executed!*

Scanning the page for anything that might hint at this, Julia read on:

'"Officer Maling has asked us to put into place certain arrangements for you."' Julia's heart thudded. Every word seemed to confirm her fears.

You will shortly hear from his solicitor, as he also requested that
we give his solicitor instructions regarding your welfare, and that
of his child.
    We enclose a letter which is written to you personally.

We are sorry that we are unable to give you any further information.

The letter was signed for, and on behalf of, the secretary to the War Cabinet, E. Bridges.

The letter from Gareth brought Julia's tears streaming down her face. She didn't read it aloud and Billie didn't ask her to, but her arm came around Julia, trying to give her comfort.

My Darling Julia

Forgive me for not communicating with you sooner, it wasn't my choice, but my duty not to.

My darling, I have carried you with me wherever my travels have taken me. And I have longed for news of you and of our baby. When the time was due for our child's birth I suffered agonising heartache — missing you, wanting to be with you through the birth, wishing that we had been given time to marry, and wanting to greet our child — to hold it and tell it how much I loved it. But I could not. One day you will know why.

If you are reading this, it will mean that the fellows bringing it to you have reached home. I thank God for that, and I hope with all my heart that this letter will give you comfort, as I need you to know that you are my life. Thinking of you and the time that we will be together again has sustained me, as has knowing that will be a time of peace and our efforts to bring that about will have been worthwhile.

My darling, I cannot write all that is in my heart, it isn't possible to put it in to words, but remember that whatever happens, I loved you with the greatest love a man is capable of giving. My heart will always rest inside you, next to yours. But if anything should happen to me, I want both our hearts to go on and find happiness. Life is precious, my darling Julia. Live yours. Think of me often, but with pride, that I did my duty, and happiness at what we shared, not with distress and misery. Promise me this. I love you, my darling Julia x

Hug my child every night for me.

Your loving, Gareth. xxx

'No, no, no. Dear God, no.'

'Mama . . . Ma.'

Looking over at her son, so like his dad, and seeing his distress, Julia wiped her face, folded the letter and put it into the pocket of her skirt. As she did, she allowed the strength to enter her that Gareth had provided with his words. Standing, she went over to Charlie and lifted him up.

'You have a wonderful daddy, Charlie, a very brave, beautiful man. There, see? Let's say hello to him.'

Julia took Charlie to the framed photo of Gareth in his RAF uniform that stood on the dresser. Smiling out at them, he looked more handsome than he'd ever looked, as if the photo had come to life. Julia lifted it, kissed it, and handed it to Charlie, whilst still supporting its weight. As he did every night before he went to bed, Charlie held the picture to him. 'Da – da.'

'Yes, Daddy. Your special Daddy.'

Charlie kissed the photo, then pushed it from him and snuggled into Julia's neck. It was as if he sensed everything wasn't as it should be and that his mummy's tears were connected with his daddy.

Billie had sat quietly throughout this. Little George had toddled to her and now stood on wobbly legs with his head in her lap. As she stroked his long blond hair, silent tears found a path down her cheeks.

'Billie?'

'I – I feel so useless, Julia. I – I don't know how to help you.'

Julia sat down beside her. 'You help me more than you will ever know. You are the sister I never had. The very best friend I could ever wish to have. We will help each other, as we have always done. And we won't give up hope. I feel that hope has almost gone, but it isn't dead. Gareth tried to tell me that as he said his goodbyes.'

'Goodbyes? Oh no, Julia, no.'

'Well, he didn't exactly say it, and yet, he was saying it. I have to prepare myself, Billie. And I have to be strong for Charlie.'

Billie's head dropped onto Julia's shoulder. 'Poor, poor, Julia. Poor Gareth. I hate this bleedin' war, and the injustice of it all. Why can't it be that bleedin' waste of space, that uncle of mine? He should be the one who's killed, and very slowly, not someone like Gareth, whose heart is good and who's got everything to live for.'

Julia didn't take Billie to task about using her colourful language in front of the children, something they had agreed about, and something she had kept to so far.

Suddenly, George made a sound that sounded just like 'bleedin' thing'.

Shocked, as he hadn't yet formed many words, but at the same time seeing the funny side, they both burst out laughing.

That Julia herself could laugh at a time like this surprised her, but as the boys joined in she knew it was what she must do. At all costs, this lovely cottage had to be a happy home for these children, whose life and well-being depended on her and Billie. Her crying could be done at night, in the darkness and privacy of her room, when everyone else slept.

This resolve didn't lighten the heavy pain in her heart, but helped her to put it in a place of its own, a place where she alone could touch it.

Julia found being back in Kent a strange experience. She was in Canterbury this time, not Maidstone. Gareth's solicitor had his office here, not far from the beautiful cathedral.

Mr Redling was an elderly man who explained that he'd had to come out of retirement to keep the family business running while his sons were at war. As Julia sat down, she stretched her tired limbs. She'd left Blackburn at eight that morning and now, six hours and numerous train changes later, she felt the strain of the journey, and of all that she might learn today.

Listening to Mr Redling, she wondered if there was a family anywhere in England who hadn't been touched by war. Even those whose husbands were exempt from going to fight had the heartache of other family members being in the thick of it, or if not that, the shortages to bear, the endless queuing for basic necessities . . . and the fear. Always the fear – fear that today would be your last, that a bomb would drop on you, or that bad news would come in the shape of a telegram.

'Now, let's see. You are here to discuss the affairs of Mr Maling?'

'Yes.'

'And you are his intended, Miss Portman?'

'Julia. Yes, I am.'

'Nice to meet you, Julia. Gareth is a very nice young man. I have a great deal of regard for him, having known him since childhood. He didn't deserve what happened, but then, poor Vanda — I mean, the late Mrs Maling — was mentally ill, and wasn't responsible for her actions. I was glad to hear that Gareth had found happiness so soon.'

Unsure of herself, Julia thanked him, and waited for him to continue.

'Well now, from what I have received from the War Office, it appears that they have dragged their feet and have only acted after a recent communication from Gareth, even though it appears that he left instructions with them, along with his last will and testament and a last letter, before he left to go into action, as is normal practice. However, some of the instructions that Gareth left were for the immediate provision for you and his expected child and I wasn't notified of these. I will therefore be putting in a complaint on your behalf. Some of these chaps can be very judgemental and probably filed Gareth's instructions, thinking it was the best thing to do — no doubt seeing his unmarried state and deciding that he'd had a fling with consequences he shouldn't be burdened with.'

This stunned Julia. Gareth had put something in place for her after all? When he spoke of the arrangement they had in place already he'd thought it was to continue!

'I — I cannot believe it. How can this have happened? I have suffered greatly by not having any support. I was forced into a home for unmarried girls, and nearly lost our child.' Julia told him about Billie, and their struggle to make ends meet with one wage coming in. 'I am a nurse, but the pay isn't good.'

'A travesty, a complete travesty which should never have happened. I'm sorry to hear what this has caused you. However, I can only put it right, and I will do so by making over to you the sum you should have been receiving since the time the first agreement came to an end, and then restart the regular monthly allowance.'

'Thank you. I'm sure that is what Gareth would want you to do. And it will be a great help to me.'

'I have done the paperwork, and have instructed the bank that you are to be able to draw on the amount and your monthly allowance whenever you need to. Or have you your own bank account that I can have these payments transferred to?'

'I do. As a professional woman I have to have one, and I would prefer that arrangement, as I used to feel the disdain of the staff at Gareth's bank when I drew my allowance.'

The solicitor sighed. 'Well, a new beginning for you. I will transfer a round figure of three hundred pounds – the accumulation of the twelve pounds a month that Gareth arranged for you, and that you haven't been able to access, and from the first of next month, twelve pounds a month will be put into your bank. You will need to sign here for me.'

Julia's hand shook as she took the pen he offered. It wasn't the new beginning that she wanted, and the small relief she felt at the easing of her money problems was no real comfort.

As she stood to leave, Mr Redling stood, too, and took her hand. 'Gareth has instructed me to tell you one more thing, Julia. He wants you to know that whatever happens, your future and that of your child is secure. I am acting on Gareth's behalf in all his affairs, and that includes the winding-up of his and his late wife's estate. Should, God forbid, anything happen to Gareth, then you and his child are his sole beneficiaries.'

'Thank you, but I hope that we never, ever, realise that. I cannot bear to think of Gareth not coming home.'

'Of course, but he wanted you to know. In giving you peace of mind, it is hoped that he will find some himself.'

Julia couldn't answer this. She wanted to find a dark corner and curl up with her misery and cry out against the injustice of all that had come her way. But instead, she had to make her way back to Blackburn.

Once outside the solicitor's office, she pulled her scarf around her neck against the bitter October wind. A woman passed her, clutching a letter, her head bent, not looking or noticing anyone around her. How different the folk were down here to those in Blackburn. Whether the northerners knew you or not, they would pass the time of day. Julia wanted to call after her and ask if she knew the times of the bus to the station, but instead she put her own head down and walked to the end of the street.

Shadows crept over the buildings as the weak sun began to lower in the colourless sky. They seemed to Julia like the fingers of eerie creatures, wrapping themselves around the houses. Shuddering against the cold and unfamiliarity of her surroundings, Julia jumped as the peace was shattered by the sound of a screeching air-raid siren. Her ears rang with the assault on them. A hand grasped her arm. A muffled 'Hurry, this way' had her obeying the command and following as she was almost dragged up the street. 'Get in there. Hurry, miss.'

The air-raid shelter in the garden she'd been directed to looked like a mound in the centre of the lawn. Around her folk hurried in all directions. The woman who had hold of her arm shouted, 'Hey, you boys, get orf the street, you'll all be killed!'

Julia looked over to where a group of boys played hopscotch. She hadn't noticed them before. Her mouth opened to scream at them to come across the road, but at that moment the sky darkened with what looked like hundreds of aircraft, and the whistling sound of a falling bomb held her as if it had turned her to stone.

'Gawd love us, no! No! *Jimmy!*'

The woman let go of Julia's arm and went as if to run to where the boys' bodies had danced hideously in the air as a bomb hit the house behind them. Julia fell back under the force of the blast. The woman's body hurtled over her and hit the shelter roof.

Dazed, Julia got to her feet. To her, it seemed hell had visited earth as flames shot from houses in the next street, screams filled the air and the sound of the hack–hack of gunfire ricocheted around her.

The aircraft noise increased, but didn't drown the cheer that came from the shelter. Making her way to the entrance she saw a dozen folk huddled together. 'That'll be our boys. Take a look, miss. Can you see the RAF planes? They'll soon have Hitler's boys on the run.'

'There's folk hurt. I'm a nurse. I need bandages and water.'

'It's too dangerous. You wait . . . ' The man's words disappeared into the sound of a massive explosion that set bells ringing in Julia's ears.

'That'll be a hit. Gawd, I 'ope it's one of them that copped it.'

'We have to help now, or it may be too late. There were children!'

Turning and running towards the garden gate, Julia was through it and across the road in a flash. Three children lay in the street. Two she knew she could do nothing for, but the third one was in a sitting position. His eyes stared in shock. His one remaining leg was twisted at an angle that told Julia it was broken. A young girl stood nearby, her sobs pitiful. 'Are you hurt, love?'

She shook her head.

'Well, help me then. Can you do that? This young man needs us. Run to your house and bring me a sheet, blanket and a towel, and if you see a grown-up, tell them that I need water, hurry. We have to help him. He needs us.'

The girl turned and ran. By the time she came back, Julia was pressing hard on the boy's thigh, desperate to stem the bleeding. The girl gave her a pile of linen, then turned and vomited – as if she would bring up her stomach, let alone its contents. Julia paid her no attention, but set to work on the now unconscious boy.

Never had she known the meaning of 'saved by the bell' until now, as an ambulance drew up beside her.

'Lawd, what 'ave we 'ere, then? You 'is mum, luv?'

'No. I'm a nurse, I was just visiting—'

'Right. Come to the 'ospital with us, you can carry on what you're doing, and per'aps save the boy's life.'

Julia didn't hesitate. All around her she could see that folk needed her help, but none had injuries as serious as the boy's.

As they neared the cathedral an explosion went off in front of the ambulance. Julia felt a rush of hot air, and then her body tumbled as debris hurtled towards her.

'We've been hit!'

As this desperate voice registered with Julia, something smacked her on the back of her head. Her eyes glazed. Her stomach heaved. A huge weight landing on her took her into oblivion.

CHAPTER THIRTY-TWO

Clara
A Meeting Brings Joy and Heartache

'Clara, will you be put out if I don't spend Wednesday after-noon with you?'

'Oh? Have you something you have to do?'

Their living room was in semi darkness, lit only by the crack-ling log fire, and Clara and Lindsey had been sitting in compan-ionable silence till now, Lindsey with her beloved *People's Friend* magazine and Clara going over the script of *Cinderella*.

Nerves tickled Clara's stomach – excitable nerves – as she still couldn't believe that she was to take the lead role in this year's pantomime.

'I've met someone. Alf. He's a soldier billeted up the road. He came into the shop and we started chatting. Well, he's asked me out and Wednesday is his leave day, so ...'

'Oh, Lindsey, that's wonderful! And going by how pink your cheeks are, and you giving up our fun afternoon to spend it with him, I'd say you've fallen deeply for this one.'

'Eeh, that's the fire, it's burning my cheeks!'

Lindsey's laugh made a lie of this.

'You've really got it bad,' said Clara. 'Look at you, you're like a schoolgirl. Of course I don't mind, I'm happy for you. Look, I don't have to go in to work at all on Wednesday, as I have been given the day to really immerse myself in this script, so I'll take over from you in the shop around twelvish and do all the cleaning so that you can get ready without rushing and getting all flustered. Only, in return, this Alf has to pick you up here so that I can meet him. I have to approve of him, you know.'

'Ha! Hark at you! You've been in a relationship since you were fourteen, and now you think yourself the judge of all!'

'Well, I am a good judge. Well, I am now. Like you, I wasn't. I took folk on face value. We both did. We trusted the wrong ones.'

'Aye, we did, lass. But that's all behind us now. Since meeting Alf, I feel me faith coming back in people. I no longer suspect everyone of wanting to harm me. Alf's from a big family in Sheffield. He's kind and understanding and, well, just loveable.'

'How long have you known him? You haven't said anything before.'

'I knaws I haven't. I didn't want you thinking I was being silly. Alf's been coming in for weeks. Every day. If I'm quiet in the shop we've had a pot of tea and just talked. But well . . . on Monday, he . . . he kissed me. Oh, Clara, it was as if I was born at that moment.'

363

Happiness shone from Lindsey as she smiled over at Clara. Clara understood. Didn't she get those same feelings when Anton kissed her? And much more, too. It had been difficult being alone together. *Difficult in a nice way. I want what Anton wants to give me. I want his touches and his kisses. And yes. I want more.*

'Eeh, that was a sigh and a half, lass. I thought you'd be happy for me.'

'I am. Oh I am, Lindsey. It's just what you said. I – I, well, I understand more than you can know. I just feel so frustrated that Anton and I have such a long time to wait before we can marry. It's a stupid law. I know my own mind. If I live to be a hundred, I will want Anton by my side. It's so unfair. We were planning to marry next August, on my seventeenth birthday.'

'I knaw how you feel, Clara, I do. But, I'd say this. Don't go all the way. I reckon that once you do you'll be lost. You love each other so much that you'll not be able to control your-selves. You don't want to bring a babby into the world and not be married. You knaw what that feels like, you've told me so many times how you suffered. Anton should be helping you, not making it difficult for you.'

'It's not his fault. We try, but it just happens. Anyway, we're talking about you and Alf. Have you told him anything about yourself? About us . . . well, you know. What happened to us – what we've been through?'

'That's the best bit. I have. And he is understanding of it. He says as it hurts his heart to think of it, but that it won't make a difference, only that it makes him love me more.'

'He's told you he loves you!'

'Aye. And me him, an' all. And I do. I love him with all that's in me.'

'How come I didn't know anything about this? I'm amazed!'

'I knaw. I'm sorry. I just didn't want anyone saying owt like, be careful, or take it slowly, or stuff about rebound, or some such. I felt that would sully sommat so beautiful, that I'd keep it secret until I had to tell.'

This hurt Clara. She wouldn't have said those things. But then again, maybe she would have. After all, she would want to protect Lindsey from ever being hurt again. But just looking at her friend told her that this wasn't going to happen. She'd never seen Lindsey look so at peace with herself.

'I'm happy for you, Lindsey. Oh, Lindsey, this is the best news. I want to hug you.'

They both rose, Lindsey from the fireside chair and Clara from the sofa. Their arms were open and as they met they clung to one another. Clara looked up at the picture of Daisy hanging over the fireplace and she could have sworn that Daisy winked. The feeling came over her that Daisy was looking down at them and taking a hand in their destinies. It was a good feeling.

'Daisy's pleased.'

Lindsey broke free of their hold. 'Eeh, that's a funny thing to say! What made you say it?'

'I just felt it.'

'Well, I've felt the same, and for a long time now. It's as if she's arranging everything. Alf told me that the first time he came into the shop he felt as if he'd been led there. I laughed at him, but different things that have happened since have made me wonder.'

They both gazed at Daisy's picture. 'It's good to think it, even if it ain't right. In't it?'

'Yes. It's comforting somehow. I think I'll try asking her to make a few things right for me.'

'Eeh, does you think we should? I don't like messing with the spiritual world.'

'It's not messing. Daisy would never hurt us. I think it will be a comfort to talk to her.'

'Aye, it would, an' all.'

'Daisy, love. We miss you, and think it would be good to have you helping us. Could you try to contact my mum for me and let her know that I think of her every minute of the day, and that one day we will reunite? You've made that possible, Daisy. You've given me the means to be able to travel and that's what I'll do. I'll go to the island and bring my mum back here. Oh, and can you change the law so that me and Anton can marry?'

A breeze fluttered around the room, disturbing the curtains and brushing Clara's skin.

'Eeh, Clara.'

Clara giggled. 'You daft thing, that was a draught coming down the chimney. It's really windy out, you can hear it howling. That's always happening.'

'Naw. It were Daisy. I knaw it were. But I don't feel afraid. I feel sort of . . . well, light.'

'I know what you mean. I do, too. It's that feeling you have when a weight has been lifted off your shoulders. I think it was Daisy, but I don't feel afraid – just the opposite. I feel happy, and sort of, well, as if everything is right in our world – or, at least, it will be.'

Lindsey was the one to giggle this time. She turned and picked up a cushion and playfully hit Clara with it. 'By, you've lost your marbles, lass.'

Clara laughed out loud. It was a laugh that came from deep within her, a healing laugh, and she truly believed that everything was going to come right. Picking up a cushion of her own, she retaliated. Their laughter filled the room as they became children once more. Cares dissolved as they pillow fought until they collapsed in a heap, helpless with giggles that took all their strength.

'Oh, stop. Stop. I feel ill.'

This from Clara did little to stop them, but exhaustion did. Gasping for breath, they lay side by side on the sofa, not talking, just being together with their own thoughts. Clara's were that if she couldn't ever be with her mum and her granny again, then having Lindsey and Anton by her side would help her to get through. Unexpectedly, a tear ran down her cheek.

As if sensing this, Lindsey turned to her. 'Don't take on, Clara. It'll all come right. I knaw it will. And Daisy will make sure of it.' Lindsey sat up and cradled Clara's head in her lap. 'We've been through a lot, but our time has come. I can feel it in me bones.'

A peace once more settled in Clara. Yes, it would come right. It had to!

Clara adored Alf as soon as she met him. A good-looking young man with dark hair and tanned skin, he had a ready smile that dimpled his cheeks.

'Pleased to meet you, Clara. I've heard a lot about you.'

'And me you, considering I didn't know you existed until a couple of days ago. Lindsey kept very quiet about you.'

'Well, I'm not much of a catch, so she didn't want anyone to know of me.'

Lindsey smacked him on the shoulder. 'Don't say that! I told you why.'

Alf laughed. 'See, she bosses me already, but I love it. She's just like me ma.'

The look on Lindsey's face was a picture.

'Uh-oh, I'm digging meself a hole here. I'll go and put the kettle on. I'm dying of thirst, I left the barracks just as soon as I could to be with you, girl, and now all I can do is put me foot in it.'

Lindsey laughed at him. 'Good idea, it'll keep you out of trouble and I'm ready for a pot of tea the minute I shut up shop.'

Clara could see they wanted to be alone. 'I'll finish off here, Lindsey. You two go and have your cuppa in a café. Let someone else look after you. Oh, and take your key as I've decided to go to the theatre. Anton's going to run through a few of my lines with me, and we want to practise the couple of songs he has composed for me. Oh, and the poster is due to go up today. I can't wait to see my name up on the billboard as the leading lady.' Excitement zinged through Clara. 'It's like a dream that I didn't know I had. As if everything has led me to this moment.'

'Lindsey told me about that. So, I'm in the company of a stage star. I never thought to see the day. I just hope as I'm not deployed afore it opens. I can't wait to see you in the panto.' A silence fell. Lindsey, who'd come around from behind the counter, took hold of Alf's arm. 'By, lass, I didn't mean to put a damper on things, but we've to face up to it. I've to go overseas at some point. But thou knaws, I'll have you with me every step of the way. I'll carry you in me heart, and that'll keep me safe.'

Clara felt a warm feeling take her. What a lovely man Alf was. Lindsey looked into his eyes and smiled. His wink to her was one of love and reassurance, and Clara knew that Lindsey had found her very own Anton.

As they left the shop, Lindsey said that they would go round to the theatre first to see the poster. 'Eeh, I'm that excited for you, Clara.'

'You should go in and see Jeannie and the crew – they'd be so happy to see you, and to meet Alf. Why don't you?'

'Aye, that's a good idea. I will, an' all. I miss them. It'd be right good to see them. Ta–ta, see you later.'

When they'd gone the shop seemed very quiet. Busying herself, Clara began to refill the shelves with the weighed bags of sugar. A memory trickled through her, and she shuddered as Mavis Brandon came to her mind. Shaking herself, Clara wanted to dispel any memories of that vile woman. And as she had many times, she wondered at she and Daisy being sisters, given how different they were. This conjured up the lovely Daisy, and the dark feeling that had taken her passed. *I don't know, Daisy, I'm living with ghosts of the past again.*

As she thought this, she became still. Something brushed her face. With it, a nice feeling warmed her body. She didn't give heed to it, but made herself get on with all that had to be done so that she could get to the theatre as quickly as possible. Why that had suddenly become an urgent need, she couldn't understand, but it was such a tug at her heart that she took a chance and locked the shop door five minutes earlier than usual. Then she rushed through the cleaning chores that were always done on a Wednesday.

An hour later, her tread was light as she ran for the bus. The urgency was still with her, as if she anticipated something more than seeing her name on the billboard. She didn't even try to work out what, but she felt so impatient that the bus seemed to take much longer than usual.

Nothing looked different about the theatre, and yet, for Clara there was something that was not the same. The poster advertising the pantomime was up and there it was: CINDER-ELLA, STARRING BLACKPOOL'S OWN FAVOURITE, GRAND THEATRE ACTRESS AND SINGER, CLARA PORTMAN!

A thrill clenched Clara's stomach muscles, and tears pricked her eyes, but still she felt there was something else awaiting her. Going to the stage door entrance, she rang the bell.

It was Lindsey who greeted her. 'Eeh, Clara, we've been waiting for you. Hurry, there's someone to see you.'

'Who?'

'Wait and see. By, it's a wonderful surprise, and yet, it has a worrying side to it. Anton will tell you. He's waiting in the wardrobe room, and then you will meet . . . Eeh, I can't wait.'

Clara wanted to scream at Lindsey to stop talking in riddles, but they had reached the wardrobe room and Anton was there, standing with his arms open to her. She went into his hug.

'Let's sit down, *ma cherie*. There is some good news for you, but it is like a double-edged sword.'

This sent a worry through Clara. She couldn't think what the news was. She held her breath.

'There's a lady here. Her name's Billie. She has two children – *garçons*, with her . . . Oh, *mon amour*, I – I don't know how to tell you, but . . . it is that one of *les garçons* is your brother.'

'What! How? But I haven't got a brother. Who is this woman, what are you talking about?'

'She is a friend of your mothers.'

'She knows my mum? But . . . how can . . . ? Oh Anton, has my mum had another child?'

'*Oui*.'

Anton's arm tightened around her. His voice droned on mostly in French. His own language allowed him to express more when he was upset. Clara listened to how this visitor had travelled from Blackburn to find her, and had spent two days looking without success, and was about to give up when this morning she saw the poster going up and was shocked and delighted to see the name of the very person she was looking for on the billboard.

'But why her? Why not my mum?'

'I think it best that she tells you that. Come and meet her.'

Clara's legs shook as she walked through to the café. Sitting at one of the tables was a young woman who didn't look much older than herself. She stood as Clara entered. 'Clara! I'm so glad to 'ave found yer. I'm Billie, a friend of your mum's.'

Clara liked Billie immediately, and accepted the hug she gave her.

'I've a long story to tell, but I need yer to come with me. Your mum needs you, Clara. She's been hurt. They cannot wake 'er. They say she's given up, and something is needed to give 'er the will to live. I reckon as you're that something. She frets over yer night and day.'

Clara looked from one to the other. Her emotions flared and then quietened. All of it was beyond her understanding.

'I'll tell yer everything on the way. And lawd above, there's a lot to tell, but we need to start our journey, we've to go to Canterbury.'

'It'll be all right, lass. You go with Billie.' Jeannie looked as though she was going to cry. But she held it together. 'Me and Panda'll sort everything.'

Clara looked at Jeannie. She couldn't think what she had to sort. Her mind would only scream at her that her mum was dying.

'I've a mate who'll take you. It'll be quicker than going by train, and better for the lads. I think you knaw who I mean, Clara.' Lofty turned to one of the stage hand boys. 'Kenny, get on your bike and take a message to Arnold. He'll sort this as quick as look at you, Clara. He's got a car, and contacts who can make sure he gets enough petrol to get there and back.'

This surprised Clara. Arnold owned a car! He'd never mentioned that. But she couldn't give her mind to it. None of this seemed real. Was it really happening?

'You'll want some clothes, Clara.' Lindsey touched her shoulder. 'Look, love, you've had a shock – you sit here with Billie. Maybe she can tell you more while you wait, and me and Alf will get a cab back to the shop and pack a bag for you. Eeh, me heart goes out to you.'

Clara nodded at Lindsey.

'Well, it seems you've a whole lot of good people around you. That will more than please your mum, darlin'.'

At last Clara found her voice. 'Anton said that one of these boys is my brother? How? I mean, has my mum married?

And, which one, and . . . and how come Mum is in England? I don't understand. It's like a maze that I'm trying to fight through.'

Anton sat down beside her and took her hand. Billie called to one of the boys, who were sitting happily in the corner, playing with some coloured balls. 'Charlie, come 'ere, luv. Come and meet yer sister.'

As the little boy looked up at the sound of his name, Clara caught her breath. She could see the resemblance to herself in his pale blue eyes. He got to his feet and toddled over to her, handing her a blue fluffy ball. His smile touched a deep part of Clara's heart. 'Hello, Charlie.'

Charlie put his head on one side as if trying to sort something out in his mind.

''E can see the likeness to your mum. Yer the spit of 'er, darlin'. But I can see you're upset, and need to know 'ow it is that I'm 'ere and what has 'appened to your mum while you've been apart. The first part, I can only relate, as I didn't know Julia till just over two years ago but she came over just a few days after you . . . '

As the story unfolded, Clara's heart bled for all her beautiful mum had been through. Why was everyone her mum loved taken from her?

Charlie's hand reached for hers, and Anton still held her. Taking Charlie's hand, she squeezed it, then bent down to kiss him. As she did, the tears she'd held back flowed down her cheeks. Charlie reached up and wiped them. His bottom lip quivered. 'Mamma?'

'We're going to Mum, don't worry. We'll make her better.'

With this she lifted him on to her knee. His little head of curls snuggled into her and she knew a love enter her for her brother like none she'd ever felt.

'Everything will be all right, Charlie. I promise.' *But will it? Please, God, let my mum live.*

CHAPTER THIRTY-THREE

Clara and Julia
Love Heals

The hospital smelt of carbolic.

'You two go ahead. I'll take care of the boys. I'll keep them amused in the waiting room.'

Arnold squeezed Clara's hand. She looked up at him and went to thank him, but he stopped her. 'Eeh, lass, nowt gives me more pleasure than taking care of you. Now, get along. And, lass. Good luck.'

'Thanks, Arnold. For everything.'

His nod showed his emotion. Without thinking, Clara put her arms around him. Then she hugged Charlie. As she did, George stood by looking at her. He'd been reluctant to make friends with her, but now she could see that he wanted her to acknowledge him. She ruffled his hair. 'Be a good boy, eh, George. Take care of Charlie for me.'

George nodded and smiled. Then, as if he was ten years older than Charlie, he took his hand. 'Charlie, come.'

Charlie obeyed and both boys went over to Arnold. They'd slept most of the way, and must have been hungry, but they hadn't complained. Arnold read Clara's thoughts.

'I'll see if I can get them a drink and a bite. I'll work me magic on one of them pretty nurses.'

Clara smiled at him, though smiling was the last thing she felt like doing. Her stomach was knotted with fear, and yet there was an excitement in her. *At last I'm to be with Mum, but what will I find?*

A doctor met her and Billie as they were shown into the ward. 'I've been told that you are Miss Portman's daughter?'

Clara held her head high. She'd noticed the emphasis on the 'Miss'.

'Yes, I am.' Her answer was challenging. Billie touched her arm.

The doctor coughed. An elderly man, she didn't expect him to understand or to imagine there might be circumstances under which a woman wasn't to blame for being an unmarried mother.

'Well, the news is good. There is no physical reason why Miss Portman should remain in a coma. Her injuries were to her ribs, and the knock on her head should only have caused a temporary loss of consciousness, and the sound of the explosion only a short-term loss of hearing. But she is unresponsive. We feel that there is something holding her from coming back to full consciousness, something emotional. You could be the key to awakening her, but you have to go steadily. Don't try to rush her.'

376

'I'm 'er best mate, Doctor – maybe I could tell her that I've found Clara and see how she reacts?'

'Yes, that might be the way to proceed. But whatever you do, make this a happy meeting. Too many emotions will be too much for her to cope with. I will supervise.'

Clara could hardly breathe. How she was going to be able to contain herself enough to follow the doctor's orders, she didn't know.

When the curtain was pulled back, Clara gasped. Her mum looked like Sleeping Beauty with her hair spread over the pillow. Her face was pale and her skin looked like porcelain, but she was so beautiful. A rush of love and emotion surged through Clara. She wanted to go to her mum, to hold her, to beg her to wake up. To tell her how much she loved her.

'Julia. Julia. It's Billie. I've got someone to see you. Lawd, you'll never guess who. Clara. Yes, luv. I've found Clara.'

Julia's eyes flickered. The doctor nodded at Clara.

'Mum? Mum, it's me. Clara. Oh, Mum, wake up. I love you.'

Julia opened her eyes.

'Oh, Mum, Mum.'

'Now, now.'

Ignoring this from the doctor, Clara took her mum's hand. Her heart thumped with fear, mingled with elation. 'Mum. It's me. I'm here. Oh, Mum. I – I . . .' Nothing could stop the sob from escaping her throat, or stem her tears.

'I said, no emotion!'

'Clara? My Clara?'

'Yes, Mum. I'm here.'

Julia lifted her arm. Clara went underneath it and rested her head on her mother's breast. The rhythmic sound of her heart was so familiar to Clara. The smell of her, never forgotten, the feel of her soft skin, were a wonderful testimony to the truth. They were back together.

'I – I lost you, Clara, my baby.'

'I know, I know. Billie has told me everything. I – I have a lot to tell you, when you're well.'

'I hope it's good, my darling. I hope you've been treated well.'

Clara didn't answer truthfully. 'Yes, I've been happy.'

'You've grown. You're a young woman. How? I mean, it's only been . . . how long?'

'I'm turned sixteen, Mum. And it's now January 1943, so that's two years, six months and fifteen days.'

They smiled a watery smile at each other.

'I have to insist that you don't carry this on. Nurse, check Miss Portman's statistics. We have to be careful. This could be too much for her.'

Clara stood back while the nurse checked her mum's blood pressure and heart rate. Her mum's eyes were locked on her the whole time, and Clara couldn't look away.

'Everything is normal, Doctor.'

'Good. Very well. Another half an hour, but please don't talk about upsetting things. Enjoy your reunion. And Nurse, get Miss Portman a glass of water, and make her comfortable. I'll be back later.'

After the doctor had left the ward, the nurse explained: 'His bark's worse than his bite, that one. He's old school. All the young ones are away at war, and we have to work under old codgers like him. But his heart's good and he knows his stuff. You're mum's in safe hands.'

'Thank you, Nurse.'

'You must heed his words, though. We don't want your mum having a relapse.' This was said with a kindly smile.

As the nurse moved away from the bed, Clara told her, 'My mum was a nurse.'

'Yes, we know. She saved the life of a young boy, though Hitler had another go at killing him as shrapnel hit the ambulance. But he survived, and though he's very poorly, he has every chance thanks to your mum's actions.'

'He – he's safe?'

'He is, Miss Portman. And the crew, too. They were able to bring you here. It was the boy who fell on you, stretcher and all, and you banged your head on the other bed in the ambulance. I reckon you'll get a medal for attending a wounded person during grave conditions.'

A blush spread over Julia's pale cheeks. She reached out to Clara. 'I – it could have been Charlie. D – do you know about him?'

'I do, Mum, and I love him so much. We'll take care of him.'

'Gareth . . . he . . . '

Billie spoke then. 'Don't get upset, luv. No news is good news, and there's been nothing come through the post for you, nor one of them telegrams, so keep hoping.'

'Billie told me about Gareth, Mum. He sounds really nice. I can't believe what you have been through, or what is happening to Gareth. I'm going to look after you as well as Charlie. I'm quite well off. Me and my friend own a shop!'

'What?'

'Yes. I can't tell it all to you, but this old lady, who cared for us like a granny . . . Oh, Mum, I forgot to ask you how Granny is?'

Her mum's grip on her hand tightened. 'I don't know, love. But she was very poorly. She made me leave Guernsey. I don't think she is with us any longer.'

'Oh, no . . . no!'

'Please don't be sad. Pray that God has taken her to her rest and she isn't having to live under the Nazi regime. She was ready to go to her husband and to your dad.'

It was difficult not to feel sad. To think that she would never see her granny again splintered Clara's heart, but for her mum's sake she agreed. 'We have so much to tell each other, Mum.'

'We do. I – I can't take it in that you have your own business.'

'And, not only that, Julia, luv, but you're looking at a star!'

Julia smiled and shook her head in disbelief as Billie told her how she had found Clara. 'You mean, I only had to go to Blackpool Theatre? I can't believe it. I – I was going to look for you, my darling. It was money that was the problem at first, and then Charlie, and trying to provide . . . and—'

'I know, Mum. Nothing is straightforward.'

'I – I could have come now. I have money, too.' Julia looked over at Billie. 'We're going to be all right, Billie. Gareth left me provided for. I have back pay and a regular amount coming in.'

'Don't worry about that, luv. The rent's paid up, and I've food in the cupboard. We can manage till you come home. I tell you, that'll be a good day. We're all missing you.'

Julia smiled. 'I'm tired. Happy, as my world is almost back together again, but so tired.' As she said this, Julia tugged on Clara's hand and patted her chest with her other hand. Clara knew she wanted her to snuggle her head down on her so that she could cuddle her. Clara did more than that. She climbed onto the bed and lay down beside her mum, holding her as best as she could, hoping her love would heal her. Hoping that her mum's world would become whole again and that Gareth would somehow be saved.

How did all of this happen? How did it come about that she and her mum were torn apart and dragged through such pain and fear and unhappiness? What had they ever done to deserve any of it? But then she thought about the terrible things she'd read in the papers and heard in the news. Of the thousands of young men killed or maimed, of homes blown apart and whole families dead or left destitute, and of Gareth, and what he must be going through. She held her mum just a little tighter.

'We'll never be separated again, Mum, never.' But as she said it she knew that it was possible that they would. But not like before, not so they didn't know where the other was. And they would write and visit. Whatever else happened in their lives, no one was going to take that from them ever again.

Two days later, the journey from Blackburn to Blackpool, having dropped Billie and the boys off at their home, was a silent one for many miles.

Arnold was the one to break it. 'Lass, for a young-un, you've had a lot to contend with, but everything can only get better now.'

'I hope so, Arnold. I hated leaving Mum, but the show must go on, as they say, and I have final rehearsals and fittings awaiting me.'

'Nowt to do with getting back to Anton, then?'

Clara giggled. 'Well, I will drop by to see him!'

'Ha! Love's strong, and can't be put on the back burner for owt. But lass, I'm over the moon that you've found your mum. And she's going to be all right, thou knaws.'

'I know. She goes back to her home on Monday. That is, if she keeps making this progress. I want to be there to greet her, if Jeannie will give me the time. Like I said, the show must go on, and that's how Jeannie will feel.'

'That was a big sigh. Look, lass, I knaw as you're upset, but Jeannie is right and your mum would agree. Shows, life – it all must go on, no matter what. If it doesn't we're lost.'

'You're so wise, Arnold, and Mum would think the same. It's just that I can't get over all that she's been through, it breaks my heart.'

'And you didn't tell her what you've suffered?'

'No, it would be too much for her, she's very fragile. The doctor said that she had faced so much with hearing about her Gareth and not knowing where I was that her mind closed down. But I know Mum. She'll bounce back once she's stronger.'

Arnold tapped her hand. 'She will. I haven't forgotten what you told me about your life in Guernsey, and with what I've picked up about how she had to go into a convent to have her lad, I reckon she can come through owt. And you can, an' all.'

Clara relaxed back into the leather seat of the Wolsey and thought how lucky the day had been when she'd met Arnold. She loved him. He was always there for her. And she didn't care what activities he was mixed up in with the gangs of Blackpool. He was special.

'Arnold, you never talk about your family, or the little girl you lost.'

Arnold was quiet for a long time. When he finally spoke, Clara regretted her question.

'Clara, never ask. I liked you in the beginning because you didn't ask about things that don't concern you. Keep to that, lass. What I am to you is nowt to do with who I am, or owt else that's my business, and mine alone.'

For the first time ever, Clara felt uncomfortable with Arnold, but angry as well. 'You shouldn't have told me then, should you!'

'Ha! That's another thing I like about you, lass, your spirit. Naw, it was daft of me to say owt, but that day when I first met you, I was moved so much by you and the memories you brought to me, I just did.'

'And I just asked, so you had no need to tell me off.'

'Eeh, lass, I've upset you. Look, it's just what you don't knaw can't hurt you, now can it? You've an idea that me life ain't like the next man's, but you've had to knaw that because of what happened, and me having a hand in saving you. But ... well, I'll tell you this much, it was my dealings that led to me losing me family, and I will live with that for the rest of me life, but I've had me revenge on them as did that. They no longer rule the roost, and are eating worms. You coming along has helped me, lass, and I'll allus be there for you. You can allus come to me.'

A lump came into Clara's throat. She took hold of Arnold's arm and laid her head on his shoulder. 'And I'm always here for you.'

She didn't comment when Arnold took out a big white hanky and blew his nose. Her own tears were stinging her eyes. But she dared not let them have their way and spill over, as she knew she would never stop crying again. There was so much to cry about, but for now she had to be strong – strong enough to cope with all she'd learned about her mum, strong enough to be a really good big sister to Charlie, strong enough to live with her own past, and to be there for Lindsey, who still struggled with it all. And strong enough to be ready to stand by her mum's side if the worst should happen to Gareth.

Anton would help her, and Arnold too. That was the one thing she knew she could depend on – they would always support her, no matter what happened.

CHAPTER THIRTY-FOUR

Julia
A Visit

Getting home had tired Julia, even though Gareth's solicitor had arranged for her to be driven home in a cab. The car, with its bench seats, had left her feeling bruised and shaky. But all of that lifted when the door was opened by Clara and she stepped out of the house. Julia couldn't speak; her emotions choked her and left her shredded.

Going into Clara's arms put her back together again, as did the joyful cry of 'Mamma!' from Charlie.

'Lawd, let her get in, it's bleedin' freezing . . . Oops, I mean, well . . . I'm at it again, sorry, luv. I've been good, promise.'

Julia didn't know what was funniest, Billie swearing or Clara's reaction. Her face was a picture of shock. But Julia stopped laughing when she saw her daughter's eyes fill with tears.

'Hey, what's wrong, darling? We'll be fine now. Everything's behind us. Billie, help Clara inside. Oh, Clara.'

Clara was sinking onto her knees. The sight tore at Julia. She realised that her beautiful Clara was troubled – almost broken.

'Come on, girl. That's no greeting to give your mum. Let's get you to the sofa, eh? And you sit down too, Julia, you look all in.'

Julia accepted Billie's hand and let her guide her to sit next to Clara. The boys gathered around her, George excited and telling her something in rushed toddler speak, Charlie cautiously sidling up to her, his eyes on the sobbing Clara.

'Come on, me boys, let's get your coats on and get you to the Queen's Park, eh? We'll see if there's any ducks on the pond. Though, they'll not be getting any bread, they can feed themselves.'

Julia held Clara's hand while the commotion of the boys getting ready went on. Charlie insisted that she put his boots on for him. For the first time ever, she found herself torn between her two children. Billie saved the day by making for the door and telling him that she would go without him.

He toddled after her with his boots in his hand, screaming, 'No, Charlie come, me park!'

When all was quiet, Julia gently coaxed Clara. 'What is it, darling? Talk to me. This should be a happy day.'

'I – I am happy, but my memories . . . I – I thought I was coping, but, oh, Mum, Mum, help me.'

Alarm shot through Julia. Gently taking Clara into her arms she rocked her, just as she had when she was a child. But wasn't she still no more than a child? 'You will feel better once you tell me, my darling. I can only help if I know.'

'I – it was Billie swearing like that, it brought back to me a – a friend. Shelley. She – she was killed.'

Little by little, Julia heard the whole story. Her heart bled as the horror of what her Clara had been through unfolded. Her own tears flowed and joined Clara's as they clung together. 'We will heal, Clara. We will. I promise.'

'Oh, Mum, don't ever leave me again.'

Julia shushed her, and said over and over that she wouldn't, yet she didn't feel as if she had her Clara back – not the little girl she had waved off on the boat. That child had gone for ever. Now she had to get to know the young woman she'd grown into, who had been shaped not by her own guiding hand but by happenings that were beyond the imagination.

'Tell me about Anton.'

A simple question, but one that held all the differences she had to grasp about her Clara. How was it possible that her little girl could speak of being in love? But she saw there was no doubting it as Clara's spirits lifted.

'He's wonderful, Mum, you will love him. He plays the piano like an angel. He's kind, and funny, and . . . well, he understands. He's been through a lot himself. I love him, Mum. I love him with all my heart, and we want to marry.'

'Marry! But . . .'

'I know. I'm so young. But we have talked of waiting till I am eighteen. Would you let me marry when I reach that age?'

'Well . . . I mean, I'll have to meet Anton. I – I . . .'

'Please don't say no, Mum. I love Anton.'

Tiredness crept into Julia. Life had become more complicated than it already had been with her daughter coming back
into her life, but she was ready. She'd always been ready and
she'd face the challenges ahead. 'Then I will be right behind
you every step of the way, darling.'

Clara flung herself at Julia, knocking her backwards. Julia
laughed, but felt the bruising impact, and a gasp of pain came
from her.

'Mum, Mum, I didn't mean to hurt you. I'm sorry. I . . .'

'I'm all right.' Making a massive effort, Julia laughed. 'I
think you forgot how big you are now. That's just what you
used to do when you were a child.'

'I dreamed so many times of doing just that. Of flinging
myself into the protection of your arms. We've lost a lot,
Mum.'

'We have, but we can make it up. I promise, darling, we can
make it all up. We'll get to know each other as we are now.
Two women. We'll not dwell on the time we've been apart.
We'll remember your childhood, and build memories as you
are now. We both have to heal, and we will. We have plenty of
time, now we have found each other.'

'I can visit at least once a week, and—'

'Visit? You mean, you won't stay here, move in with Billie
and me? Oh, darling, I thought, well, now that we are together,
we'd go back to how we were.'

Julia waited. Clara's expression went through many
emotions. What she felt in her heart had always shown on her
face. And Julia could see the struggle going on inside her.
Taking a deep, painful breath, she took control and, though
her heart was breaking, accepted that she must release her

388

lovely daughter, just as every mother had to. But oh, how she wished it wasn't so early in her young life.

'No, silly me, of course we can't. You have your work, and Anton, and your life in Blackpool. And I have my work, and Charlie, and . . . Yes, as I said before, we are both women now. We will live independently, but will be bound by that wonderful link only a mother and daughter can have.' With this, she wiped away a tear that trickled down Clara's face, then drew her daughter into her arms and clung on to her. 'Right! Your first job as a grown-up daughter! Get your poor mother a nice cup of tea!'

As they went to the kitchen, the smile that lit Clara's face was reward enough for the sacrifice that Julia had made, as that was what it was – an enormous sacrifice. And it was probably almost unheard of for a mother to let go of her daughter when she was just sixteen. But then, times had changed. War had made everyone change. Youngsters were made to grow up early, and once they had there was no going back. Closing her eyes, Julia begged of God to help her through this transition. And she felt strength come into her as Clara came back into the room. Smiling with happiness, she laid the tray of teapot, two cups, milk and saccharin on the occasional table. 'I couldn't find any sugar, Mum. You should live in Blackpool, we get everything there.'

'Really? How? No, don't answer that. I'd rather not know.'

'Ha, you wait till you meet Lindsey. Like I say, she's been broken lately, but she's fighting back now she has her Alf, and she can get anything . . . or "owt" as she'd say. And if I take her to task, she'll tell me that its sommat and nowt, so leave it to her and mind me business.'

'She sounds like a right one. Salt of the earth.'

'Eeh, she is. She's a grand-as-owt lass, is our Lindsey.'

Julia laughed, ignoring the pain this caused. To hear Clara mimicking her friend tickled her. Clara joined in, her giggles prompting more from Julia. 'Oh, don't, don't, it hurts my ribs.' But neither she nor Clara could stop.

The laughter bound them back together. It started the healing process, and put them in an easy, loving place that dispelled Julia's doubts.

The sound of the front door opening sobered them.

Billie came in. 'Blimey, what's going on in 'ere, then, eh? 'Ere's me freezing to death to give you time to sort out your tears, and you're laughing your 'eads off and 'aving a whale of a time.'

'Sorry, Billie, come and have a warm. It's this daughter of mine. You were right when you said that she was a star! She's a good actress, I know that much. You should hear her take off her friend from Blackpool.'

Billie laughed at Clara's demonstration then increased the laughter by saying: 'I tell yer, this lot up north don't know 'ow to speak the King's English.'

Julia tried to calm them as she saw a look of consternation on Billie's face and heard a tone of exasperation in her voice as she asked: 'What? What 'ave I said?'

'Nothing, nothing, don't mind us. We're just happy. Very, very happy.'

'Me happy, Mamma.'

Julia scooped Charlie up into her arms. As she did, his smile fractured her heart as she saw Gareth's lovely smile in his. Brushing the thought away, she chatted to Charlie while Billie fussed over George.

After a moment, Charlie wriggled off her knee. 'Want Clarry.' She started to correct him, but seeing Clara's beaming face as she put her arms out to her little brother, she stopped herself. It was right that he should have his own pet name for his sister, it would be part of their bonding. But as she watched the obvious love between her children, Julia knew that the bond was already there. *If only you could see this, my darling Gareth. How happy you would be for me, and how proud you would be of your son.*

Billie's arm on her shoulder steadied her. 'Right, luv, what're we all going to 'ave for tea, then?'

'If we were in Blackpool, we'd have fish and chips. They all practically live on them, but they are delicious.'

'Fish and chips it is then. There's a woman around the corner, who makes them in 'er kitchen. She opens 'er window at around five, and I tell you, Clara, they'd rival any you've tasted.'

'Mmm. A good idea,' agreed Julia. 'I love them. Can you stay that late, darling?'

'If you'll have me, I'll stay the night. I've brought an overnight bag. Jeannie wants me to report by two tomorrow afternoon.'

'Jeannie?'

Julia listened as Clara told them about the folk she described as 'wonderful' and a peace settled in her. Clara would be all right. It sounded as if she loved these stage folk and they loved her. She sat back, and watched her daughter's face come alive as she told her tales. Not sad, horrifying tales, but happy tales, full of those who cared about her.

'So, Arnold runs a stall on the seafront?'

'Yes . . . He, well, he has other business interests, but that's the one he loves. He brought us to the hospital.'

''E's an all right geezer, Julia. They all are, for all they can't talk proper.'

Julia looked at Clara. Clara looked away, her face a contortion as she tried not to laugh. The action showed Julia that her daughter was still the caring girl she'd always been, not wanting to hurt Billie's feelings by laughing at her.

'Well, that's made me very happy. I'll rest easy now while you are away. And once this pantomime that you're to star in gets going, we'll bring the boys up to watch it, won't we, Billie?'

The chat took on an easy, relaxed banter between them, and Julia knew that everything was going to be all right. They'd made the transition from mother and child to mother and grown-up daughter. Everything would work out. If only . . . *If only you could come home, my darling Gareth. My world would be complete.*

CHAPTER THIRTY-FIVE

Gareth
Facing Death

The cold, dank walls ran with water, and stank of mould and mildew. But it was the clawing darkness that mocked his fear and gave Gareth images of his own death, a death he'd seen some of his comrades endure. *Was it yesterday that they had come for me, their shouts echoing like thunder as they approached . . . 'Du wirst sterben, du Schweinehund.'*

Repeated over and over, this threat to kill him had made the sweat break out of his body to run in rivulets down his back, and his limbs tremble. When they'd reached his solitary-cell door he'd vomited. One of the soldiers had kicked him as they entered.

At first they'd had to drag him, but after a moment, his dignity and pride returned and he'd steadied his body, shaken himself free of them and walked tall. With this a calmness had descended over him, and he'd faced his fate with courage, letting the beautiful image of Julia into his mind. He'd told her he loved her, and would always be with her. Then he had stood next to another man, who was not known to him previously, but who in the hour of their deaths became his friend. He was reminded of how Jesus had befriended and comforted his death companions whilst on the cross, and he'd muttered a few words to the man. 'We'll get to know one another on the other side, my friend.'

'*Halte den Mund!*'

Ignoring the command to be quiet, his comrade had shouted: 'I am David Green, a soldier in the British Army. I ask God for mercy on my soul.'

The words had earned David a vicious swipe across his face with the butt of a gun. Taking courage from David, Gareth had found himself shouting: 'I am Gareth Maling, a serving officer in the British Army, and a veterinary surgeon!'

The line of German soldiers lifted their guns and aimed them. Gareth had looked down the barrel of one and his fear resurfaced. To his shame his bowels rumbled and leaked a loose, foul-smelling liquid into his underpants.

The guns fired in unison to a shouted command. David fell to the ground, his blood forming a pool around him, but Gareth remained standing, shock holding him rigid. The soldiers began to laugh. They all aimed their guns at him and fired. Bullets ricocheted off the wall around him, and then he heard a holler that was filled with pain, and realised it was coming from himself.

When the firing stopped, tears were streaming down his face. His knees gave way, and he slumped to the floor.

Pebbles and dust had torn his skin as the soldiers dragged him away. In the far corner of the yard, they had stripped him, calling him a filthy dog. Then they had hosed him down with freezing cold water before chucking him back into this cell and throwing a pair of trousers in with him. His mind had screamed his terror, before he'd found himself on his knees, praying for David, saying sorry to him that he hadn't kept his promise of getting to know him, and of going with him to the other side.

Within a short time the soldiers had returned.

The endless interrogation and torture then began again. 'If you tell us what we want to know, you will never again face the firing squad. You will go to a better place, and wait out the end of the war, then you will return to your loved ones.'

How he'd wanted to tell them the answers to their questions: Who were the leaders of the Resistance? Who were the men in the camp who were planning and carrying out escapes? What was his roll in the Resistance? Who was his commanding officer? What did he know of British plans to bomb Berlin in the future? On and on the questions came, and each time he refused to answer he was punched and kicked or, worse, had the vice clamped to his fingers tightened until he screamed out his agony.

His mind went over how he'd come to be here. How that day, back in 1941, when he'd been sitting in a lecture, he had been sent for to attend the flight lieutenant's office immediately.

The words spoken zinged around his head. 'You are being transferred to the army, Maling. You are to leave immediately. A driver is ready to take you to the War Office for instructions. Your language skills are needed in another field, where you will be more useful to your country than as a pilot. Those are the words of the minister for war, not mine, as I can think of no more useful occupation than being a pilot. It is we who are keeping the bloody Luftwaffe at bay and saving our country from invasion. However, you are to take up an intelligence-gathering role, and I won't diminish that. We greatly need the information chaps like you can supply us with, so good luck.'

With this the lieutenant had shaken his hand. Saluting and leaving the room, Gareth had found an army officer waiting for him. He'd been given half an hour – half a bloody hour – in which to gather his personal things and write any letters he needed to, but in those letters he wasn't to give any information.

His feelings had been a mixture of excitement at what his new role may entail and devastation at the realisation that he would be taken away from his beloved Julia and forced to leave her alone. She would be left unwed and carrying his child, with their wedding plans shattered.

His role had taken him to France to work with the Resistance, to organise them and to make sure they had the equipment and ammunition as well as the intelligence to carry out their work with greater efficiency, as well as gathering intelligence by infiltrating the Germans. He'd done this by becoming a deaf-mute barman in the café they frequented. They were told that they only needed to order their first drinks from the bar, and then raise their hand when they needed refills and he would know exactly what each one wanted. None of them suspected anything and he'd been able to overhear conversations that provided valuable intelligence.

Everything had gone well, and he'd been proud of his work, but the heartache of not hearing from, or being able to contact, Julia had marred the excitement of the victories he and his comrades had. He'd often been on the raids he'd organised, or gone to meet the aeroplanes bringing in the supplies. These dangerous missions had tested him to his limits.

Then had come the night that the unit he was attached to was betrayed. And by a trusted comrade who had often been by Gareth's side.

Gareth could still hear the train rumbling towards them carrying Jews to one of the many sickening camps that he knew of – camps he'd sent intelligence about to his headquarters in London, which had seemed to fall on deaf ears.

They had been ready. Twenty Resistance workers and himself, lay low on the embankment, their intention to blow up the engine to the train and to free the Jews. Nothing had seemed different to any other raid they had carried out, until the train came within striking distance. Then it had stopped. There had been a moment when Gareth had felt his heart beat in his throat, then all hell had let loose as German soldiers had spilled from the carriages firing and throwing hand grenades.

That was when he'd been captured. The surprise element had overwhelmed his comrades, and his trusted friend, Jean Partre, had turned his gun on Gareth and told him to drop his weapon and surrender.

Gareth shuddered now as he revisited the moment, and saw the hate in the eyes in which he'd once seen friendship and

trust. In the few minutes before the Germans took him prisoner, Jean had spat vitriol at Gareth, calling the English 'dogs'
and accusing them of having the intention to rule France and
keep its people subservient.

Gareth hadn't any answers to the indoctrinated speech.
Disbelief and shock had muted him.

How long ago that was, Gareth didn't know. Time in this
concentration camp wasn't measured by a clock, only by the
coming of the soldiers to put you through torture, or the
appearance of a bowl of slop that had a few unidentifiable bits
of meat floating in it. He hadn't been without hope. But
yesterday, what hope he'd held had drained from him in that
dim yard, running with fresh blood and stained with the dried
blood of all the men who'd been executed there.

But now he was still alive, and life gave hope. His hope,
though, was centred on the message that had filtered through
to him by way of a delivery man. The old farmer hated the
Nazis and worked as a spy for the British. The message said
that there was to be a massive air raid on this part of Berlin
and that during it, he and ten others were to escape. He didn't
know the plans, just that when the sound of aircraft could be
heard, he was to be ready. He would be fetched and he was to
follow instructions to the letter.

His hours of praying were centred on that sound. *Please
God, let me hear it soon. Let the information the Germans want
from me be so important that I am worth more to them alive than
dead! Let it be in your plan that I am reunited with my darling Julia
and our child. Please, please hear my prayer!*

Two nights later the drone of many aircraft could be heard
in the distance. Gareth's heartbeat quickened. Getting off the

stone slab he lay on, he began the sequence of exercises that he'd tried to do every few hours. He had to keep the stiffness from his limbs, had to be ready when they came and to keep up, and not be a hindrance.

The sound became an ear-splitting array of explosions that seemed so close that he thought he'd die in the attack. But then a key turned in the lock of his cell door.

CHAPTER THIRTY-SIX

Clara
Courage Shows Healing

From where she stood with Anton, in the shadows of the North Station in Blackpool, Clara watched the sad scene played out in front of her as Lindsey clung to Alf.

There'd been tears by the bucketload from Lindsey and Alf since his deployment papers had been served. He was to go to Africa, where Montgomery and his German counterpart, Rommel, were engaged in battle. But now Lindsey was being brave, making an effort to send her Alf off with a smile.

Anton's hand tightened around Clara's. 'Are they still saying goodbye, or has Alf gone? Oh, *mon amour*, I couldn't bear to part with you. When you were gone for two days, my heart was lonely.'

'They are still holding one another.' Clara wanted to go on to say how many had been forced to part, and that they were lucky, but was it lucky to be born blind and unable to fight with your fellow countrymen? She knew that Anton didn't think so.

Instead, she just squeezed his hand back and gave him a watery smile. Which, though he couldn't see it, still registered with him.

'*Ma cherie*, why are you so sad?'

'Oh, for so many things. But just watching Lindsey and Alf touches my heart.'

On the way back to the shop, Lindsey was quiet. When she spoke, she said, 'I thought as I'd weep me heart out, but I reckon as I've cried all the tears that I had in me.'

They were walking down Park Road. Around them, soldiers, some with kit bags, were making their way to the station. There were always stark reminders that there was a war on. A group of airmen came towards them, and Clara thought of Gareth. In his photo, he looked like these men. He was smiling like they were, too. She so longed for her mum to hear good news of him.

'Let's not go home, eh? There's hours till you two have to be at the theatre for panto, and I can't face opening the shop. Folk'll have to blooming go without.'

'Whatever it is that you want to do, Lindsey, we will do, *mon amie.*'

'It's such a lovely day. Let's get on the tram to Fleetwood. I love it there, watching the fishing boats coming in, traipsing around the market, eating fish and chips on the quayside and walking along the promenade.'

And it was a lovely day for late January. The sky was blue and the breeze light, though the air was cold and frost still clung to the grass.

The tram trundled along, passing the Gynn and the cliffs of North Shore. By Bispham Redbank Road, when the illuminations were allowed to stay on, they stopped for the delicious fish and chips served in the corner café. Then they carried on to Cleveleys, a bustling village, and past the Rossall School for boys from rich families, and finally into Fleetwood.

This being a Tuesday, the tram and Fleetwood were packed with shoppers and holidaymakers, making their way to or from the famous Fleetwood Market. The strong smell of fish assailed Clara as she alighted. Boats were unloading their cargo, and the fish huts had their doors open. She could see men and women gutting and packing huge amounts of fish.

'This is exciting. The smells are reminiscent of many small fishing villages in France. Why is it we haven't been here before, *mon amour*?'

'It's only my second time. I came once with . . . Well, Shelley and I came here once.'

'You are feeling the pain of her loss more than ever now.'

'Yes. I didn't have time to grieve her. The shock numbed me, then all that happened closed me down inside. Can you understand that?'

'*Mais oui.* It has happened to me also. And when, what do you say – the flood gates?'

'Yes, the flood gates. When they open we are left vulnerable to the slightest reminder. I could cry now for my beautiful friend, but that wouldn't be fair on Lindsey. She is trying to be so brave.'

Lindsey was a little way in front of them. Anton always walked slowly, even when hanging on to Clara's arm.

'Let us have a distraction. Tell me what is around me.'

'On your left is the sea. Can you hear its waves crashing on the shore?'

'I can, but it isn't angry.'

'No, just choppy. In front of it are patches of fine sand, and then a green bank that stretches up to us. On your right are the fishing huts, and ahead there is a landing dock where two trawlers are tethered. Men are tending to their fishing nets. Children are playing nearby, and on the grass are bunches of flowers. They will be from the townsfolk to commemorate lost trawlers.'

'Lost trawlers?'

'Yes, many are doing war work and have been torpedoed or hit a mine.'

'That is sad. If we weren't trying to distract ourselves from sadness, I would say we should buy a flower to lay down, or at least pay our respects.'

'Yes, we should do that, Anton. A flower left there remembers all war dead, too. I could remember Shelley.'

They found a stall in the market selling silk flowers. The owner had made them herself. 'Oh, there's a red tulip, it is so beautiful. It is dark at the base and has a flower shaped like an egg when you have scooped the white and yolk out.'

'You make me see things in my mind, *mon amour*. Buy it and let me feel it.'

★　　★　　★

After laying it down with the others, they were silent. Lindsey stood next to them. She took Clara's hand. 'I bet Shelley misses you, an' all. I knaw as I would.'

At this it occurred to Clara that those who suffer are bound together more strongly than others. It is as if they have a need to offer and receive comfort through the trust that they give to each other. She held Lindsey to her and they shed a tear. Anton allowed them their space, standing quietly and not counselling them against getting upset. When they came to a peace, they felt calm. They were ready to put the hurts behind them for a short time and to have fun.

Climbing down the steps to the beach, they removed their shoes and, with Anton in the middle, they all held hands and ran along the cold sand. The breeze stung their faces and made their eyes water, and they giggled like children.

Next they went to a café but it felt hot and stuffy, so they left and bought hot scallops from a stall and ate them as they sat on the sea wall, ignoring the screaming, scavenging gulls circling above. They were delicious, though Anton cried out as he burnt his tongue. Lindsey and Clara laughed at him.

So absorbed were they in their chat and the lovely time they were having that they had to run to catch the tram that would get them to the theatre on time. But when they reached it they found that it was full and couldn't take them. Lindsey and Clara left Anton for a moment and went in search of bus times. They asked an old man who was standing at his gate puffing a pipe, and he looked at them with his head on one side.

'I haven't got my Daisy out for a run today. Hold on, she's in the yard, I'll put her trap on her and take you to Blackpool for the price of your tram fare, how's that?'

Whatever Lindsey was thinking, Clara didn't know, but any offer, no matter what it entailed, was better than being late for the panto preparations and the show.

From around the back of the house, the man appeared with a shire horse in tow. 'Here she is. I'll bring her round straight and then you can hop on. Eeh, she's fair loving the prospect – look how frisky she is.'

The ride was wonderful. The three of them sat with their backs to the old man on a bench seat in the trap.

'Eeh, Daisy, lass, I knew you'd save the day.'

This from Lindsey had them curling over with giggles. 'She has. She's always there when we need her, even if she has to take on the form of a cart horse.'

This made them laugh even more.

The progress was slow and yet they still caught up with the tram and overtook it. The wind in Clara's hair was exhilarating and blew away any remnants of her sadness. Anton was loving it. Three times he said what a wonderful experience it was, and Clara marvelled at how he never complained that he was unable to enjoy the sights around him. So, once more she became his eyes and described what they were passing.

'It is kind of you, my Clara, but are you not fed up with always telling me where we are and what everything looks like?'

'No, never. You make me see things as if for the first time.'

'Aye, and me an' all. I marvel at how everyday sights take on a different feel when Clara describes them.'

It was good to see Lindsey smiling and seeming to genuinely be enjoying herself.

* * *

It was all such a rush when they reached the theatre that Clara didn't have time to dwell on Lindsey's sadness, but only hope that when she arrived home, she wasn't too down in the dumps.

Nerves clenched at Clara's stomach as she waited in the wings for the curtains to rise. Anton would signal the moment with the opening bars of music he had composed. The set was the glittering palace and the handsome prince stood ready to declare his intention of holding a ball so that he could choose a wife. Panda always opened every show he produced with sparkle, glitz and glamour. 'Give them magic to capture and enrapture them from the beginning, and then we can get down to the nuts and bolts of the story.'

In this panto, Clara was the nuts and bolts. After this first scene, she would appear in her rags, singing one of Anton's songs as she scrubbed the floor. Then on would come the ugly sisters to taunt her. Clara loved everything about performing. For a brief moment in time she was no longer herself, but Cinderella. The tears she shed were real and heartfelt the joy she experienced when her foot slid into the slipper filled her with warmth.

It was as the curtain rose for the curtain call and a little voice shouted 'Clarry, Clarry' that she thought she would bubble over. The audience were visible now, and following the direction of the voice, Clara almost jumped for joy as she saw her mum and Charlie in the audience.

Being in her mum's hug, Clara felt whole. She'd changed quickly and cajoled Anton into doing the same, and now she waited patiently for him to arrive in the foyer.

'Mum, Anton is blind. I didn't say so before as I didn't feel

406

that I should talk about him much. I wanted you to have a chance to adjust to knowing about him.'

'Oh, no! How does he cope, will he find his way here?'

'Yes. He is wonderful. Once he knows the layout of a place he gets around as if he is sighted. And none of it worries him. He was born blind so hasn't ever known any difference.'

'Will he want to touch my face, or something? I mean, I heard that blind people see by touch.'

'No.' Clara giggled. 'Anton just makes his own mind up what you might look like by how you are. Nice people are always beautiful in his mind, and those he doesn't like are the ugly ones.'

'Hum, I like that. It sort of gives everyone a chance and means you are not judged on how you look but on the sort of person you are.'

Clara smiled, then bent to pick up Charlie, who had been tugging at her skirt. 'Did you like the panto, Charlie?'

'Liked when you were pretty.'

'Yes, poor Cinders, she is treated badly at first, but she's still pretty.'

Charlie frowned at her. It seemed beyond his comprehension that she had been Cinders. To him, she was his Clarry, who had sung and spoken while wearing rags, which he didn't like, and then in princess clothing, which he did. She snuggled him to her.

'Charlie loves Clarry.'

'And Clarry loves Charlie.'

'Oh, *mon amour*? And who is this Charlie?'

'Ha, Anton. He's my brother. You remember?'

'But of course, I was teasing you.'

'Anton, meet my mum. She looks like me, only older.'

'Thank you very much, Clara. That was a back-handed compliment!' They all laughed. 'Hello, Anton, I'm so pleased to meet you. I wanted to thank you for loving and taking care of my daughter during the last two and a half years when I couldn't.'

Clara could see that her mum's words had touched Anton. His cheeks flushed as he smiled, and his hand reached for hers. She felt so proud of her mum. Knowing that Mum still held reservations because of Clara's age made what she'd said all the more special. And when Charlie went willingly into Anton's arms, Clara wondered at her thinking earlier that her world was complete. Now she knew that it was.

After a moment she asked her mum, 'Do you have to go back today? Can you stay over? I've a couple of hours before the evening show. I'd love for you to meet Lindsey and see where I live.'

'No, I can't stay over. I have to be in work tomorrow.'

'But I thought you could give up work now that you receive an allowance?'

'Yes, I could, but there is such a shortage of nurses, I'm needed. And I love what I do, so I have continued on a part-time basis.'

'Oh, I'm so disappointed. We don't get to see each other often.'

'I know, darling, so don't let's waste a minute. Have we time to get to where you live before my train goes at eight?'

When they reached home and were greeted by Lindsey, it was obvious that she'd been crying. Clara wanted to hug her, but knew this wouldn't help. She'd warned her mum of how sad Lindsey was and why, so was shocked when her mum held her arms out to Lindsey.

'I want to thank you, Lindsey, as I have done Anton, for all you have done for my Clara when I wasn't able to. And to tell you that I know exactly how you feel. I am going through the same pit of despair at not being with my beloved, and not knowing what is happening. I'll always be there for you if ever you want a friend who really understands. You only have to write to me.'

'Ta, Julia, that means the world to me. And I will, an' all. It'd be good to put me feelings down to someone who knaws.'

'Call me Mum, as that's what I intend to be to you, if you will let me?'

Lindsey's eyes filled with more tears, but the smile she gave told that they were happy tears. 'Aye, I will. Me and Clara already think of ourselves as sisters, and have been there for each other this good while.'

Anton moved closer to Clara. She imagined he must be feeling like an outsider. 'And you'll be Anton's mum as well, when we marry, Mum, so your family just got huge.'

'My mamma.' Charlie tugged at his mum's skirt.

Julia scooped him up. 'Yes, darling, your mamma. And I'm gathering you more brothers and sisters as I go.' She tickled his tummy and made him giggle.

Although this pleased her, part of Clara didn't like sharing him so soon, but she shook this thought from her as he put his arms out to her and snuggled into her, murmuring 'Clarry'. She knew that this was his way of showing her that she was special to him, as special as he was to her. Inside, she settled, knowing that no one could surpass that bond between them.

'Well, you'll be ready for a pot of tea, Ju . . . Mum, eh? I'll put kettle on while Clara shows you around.'

Her mum loved everything about the house and the shop, though in the yard she shuddered at the sight of the shed. 'You should get rid of that, Clara. I can't bear to look on it after what you told me.'

'Don't worry, Mum, I'm over that. And Lindsey needs it for her black market stuff.'

'Don't. Don't tell me anything about that. I'd rather not know. As long as you're not mixed up in it, I can pretend it doesn't go on.'

'I'm not, I promise. And between you and me, I hate it, but Lindsey seems to think we'd lose everything without it as it means folk come shopping from a lot further afield to get their supplies.'

'Oh, this war. When will it end?'

'Mum? Are you all right?'

Julia was silent for a moment, and when she spoke there were tears running down her face. 'I try to be, Clara, love, but everything runs away from me. I lose those I love, and never get them back.'

'You have *me* back, Mum. Don't be upset.'

Wiping her eyes, her mum looked at her and tried to smile. 'I know, but you're so different to the little girl I had.'

Clara didn't know what to say. Mum was right. What she'd been through had shaped her and, of course, a thirteen-year-old would be unrecognisable after a couple of years. But in her case, living on the island, she'd been so much younger than her years, and had truly been her mum's little girl. 'I've missed you so much, Mum. I've missed having you there to look after me.'

'Oh, my Clara, come here.'

They clung together, and the child in Clara came to the fore. 'You'll always be the mum I've always known, and I'll always be your little girl.'

'You will. And I know we will have these moments, as we can never get back what we lost, but we'll get through them, I promise.'

Clara knew they would. She knew that nothing that had happened to her or to her mum had changed them, not deep inside. And thinking this made her feel better.

EPILOGUE

1944–1945

THOUGH WAR RENDERS HORRIFIC DEEDS, LOVE WINS THROUGH

CHAPTER THIRTY-SEVEN

Julia
Love Surmounts All

Julia stood looking up at the imposing building of the Royal Hospital in Whitechapel. She could feel her heart beat in every part of her body. Her mouth was so dry that she could hardly swallow.

Inside, her feet tapped out a rhythm as she walked towards the reception desk. But before she reached it, a voice called out. 'Julia!' The sound was more like a sob.

She looked up, and there he was. 'Gareth. My Gareth!'

Her body surged forward as if suddenly given wings. Gareth held out his arms but she could see he was weak. Tears streamed down his face. Going into his hug brought all the pain of separation, fear and the not knowing into focus. They didn't speak, just clung to one another, their sobs joined, their love entwined.

In a croaking voice, Gareth told her that there was a patients' room especially for officers where they would be alone. 'I have a wheelchair, it's just back there. I'm not strong enough to walk to the room from here.'

She'd known this, not only by the hollowness of his cheeks, but from the feel of him. It was as if all his flesh had left his bones.

Once he was in his wheelchair, Julia pushed him where he directed her, to a plain room full of comfy chairs and side tables, and a scattering of small round tables with chairs pushed under them. On the tables was an array of board games and playing cards.

They sat together holding hands, Gareth in the armchair nearest to the crackling fire, Julia on the arm.

'It's been so long, my darling, and yet your letters made me feel as if it was no time at all, when they finally gave them to me. Thank you for always sending them and keeping faith in me. I feel as though I know our son. Our little Charlie.'

'And he you, darling. He is almost three now, but every night he holds your picture before going to bed. And he wants to know everything that I know about you.'

Again the tears tumbled down Gareth's face, and Julia had the sinking feeling that he was a broken man.

'I've been through a lot, Julia, my darling. I can't tell you much, not yet. I am bound by the Official Secrets Act. It broke my heart not to be able to contact you. I worried about you, and our baby, but there was nothing I could do. I am so glad you managed all right.'

'I have a lot to tell you, too, Gareth. Things that I couldn't write about as they would have been too upsetting for you

416

while you were away – that is, when I thought that you were receiving my mail. But even when you weren't and I carried on writing in the hope that one day you would read them, I still couldn't tell you. One day, when we are fully healed, we'll talk.'

'Oh, my darling, I can't bear to think of you going through anything at all, apart from missing me. But yes, I am not strong enough to cope with anything yet.'

Julia put her arm around him and stroked his hair. 'You will be. I promise.'

'I was so happy to read that you at last found your Clara. But, as you said, it must have been difficult finding her so changed.'

'It is. Sometimes I still feel that I have to look for my little girl, and that I haven't found her yet. I can't accept that she has gone for ever – it is a strange feeling. And yet it is lovely, too, to have a grown-up daughter – far more grown up than her age, but she too has been through so much.'

'So much lost. We will find we have to adjust. We cannot be the same people who parted. We haven't grown together, shared things as we should, but we have to find a way of fitting it all into our new life.'

'Sharing with each other what happened to us will help, Gareth. But we have to be ready. I can give you time, my darling, time to heal in your body, and time to heal in your mind. My love is stronger than it was, and I didn't think that possible as it was already all-consuming before you left, but now I know that it can withstand anything and never die.'

'Mine, too. For now it isn't built on the feelings I had in your presence, and what we shared, but the deep feelings of leaning on that love to sustain me, of talking to you in my mind when I had to distract myself from unbearable pain, and of hanging on to the small thread of hope that one day we would be together.'

'We are now, my darling. And I will come and see you every day, and soon will bring Charlie, and then, Billie and George.'

'How? Blackburn is so far away.'

'It is, but did you read in my letters how Billie's parents owned a haulage business in London? And how her mum preferred to have her and her child out of sight?'

'I did, but how does that mean that you are able to be near to me?'

'Well, sadly, Billie's dad died suddenly and everything changed. I didn't write to you about it as I still wasn't sure if you were getting my letters or not, and I didn't want you worried about me.'

'So, there is a lot you haven't told me, darling?'

'Yes. I tried to keep my letters positive, only talking about the good things that were happening to me. Even if that meant telling a few untruths.'

'As I read them, I did wonder about a lot of things. You never really explained how you came to be nursing when you were expecting our child, and how that led to you moving to Blackburn with one of your patients. Oh, I know you wanted to be near to Blackpool, but— '

'I will tell you all, as I've promised, but it won't be easy on either of us to unburden ourselves.'

They were quiet for a moment or two. Then Julia felt able to explain without giving away too much of the real truth.

'When Billie and I met, and needed each other's support as unmarried mothers, we chose Blackburn for two reasons. One, it had munitions factories, where Billie could get work, and two, it was near to Blackpool where, as you know, I wanted to begin my search for Clara. Anyway, everything has changed. Billie's dad left everything to Billie. The business, the big house her parents had and a large amount of money. Billie's mum said if that was the case then she was off, and she took herself to Cornwall. She was going to rent a place, but Billie bought her a cottage and gave her a generous allowance and, best of all, they made up their differences. Billie will visit her mum whenever she can, and her mum wants to be a proper granny to George. As a result of all of this, Billie moved back to London and lives in her house, and I am staying with her. She did ask me to move in with her, but I wanted to be near to Clara. I would have moved to Blackpool, but I was afraid. I don't trust the War Office. Oh, I know they are acting in the best possible way for our country's interests, but they don't always take into account ordinary people when doing so. I knew they had the Blackburn address, so I determined to stay put until I had news of you – one way or . . . well, I won't say that as I never gave up hope.'

'My poor darling, you must have been lonely after Billie left.'

'I was. I miss her so much, and Charlie often pines for George, as I do. But she had no choice as she had to oversee the business. She has a transport manager, and thereby lies another tale. Tom, he's called, and she has known him most of her life, since he came as a boy of sixteen to work in the yard when she was just six. He couldn't go to war because he has

419

a withered arm. He is the son of Billie's father's oldest friend, and so was found a job in the office, and doing what he could around the yard. Now it appears that he has always loved Billie, and though she can't believe it, she has found herself falling in love with him! It's all so lovely. He's adorable, and loves George and Charlie. He's a really gentle person. I'm so happy for Billie.'

'So, it's love all around then. Billie has her transport manager, Clara has her pianist, and Clara's friend – Lindsey, isn't it? – has her Alf.'

'Well, we hope she does. Just as I did, that poor dear girl lives every day in fear.'

'This bloody war! But it is coming to an end. There are plans, darling, that should bring it to a conclusion, and in our favour. I can't tell you any more, but when I am well enough I will be involved in them.'

'What? No! No, Gareth, they can't expect . . . I mean, I thought you were going to be discharged!'

'No, darling, I am needed. I have intelligence that will help the last push. But don't worry, I won't be away from you. Well, that is if you can come and stay down here for a while until it is all over.'

'Oh, my darling, of course I can. I will miss seeing Clara on a regular basis, but you are more important, and being with you is the world to me. Clara will understand. Just as I had to when she chose to stay close to Anton rather than come to live with me.'

'Darling, I am so glad. And, strangely, as we've talked, I have felt my strength coming back to me. It is as if our worlds have joined back together, and I feel that now I can cope. I no longer feel out of control of my emotions. Instead of the animal my captors made me, I feel like a man – a husband, and a father. Julia, how soon can I see my son? And how soon can we be married?'

'Darling, let's take each step at a time. You may feel strong, and that's a huge step, but you have to give your body and mind time to catch up with how you feel.'

'Oh? So you are going to be my nurse as well as my wife, then?'

'I am. I want you back as you were, my love, and that cannot happen overnight. Let's give it a week of me coming every day, and of whatever treatment they are giving you. Then, if you are beginning to look more like the photo that Charlie loves, I will bring him.'

'Do I look that awful?'

'To me, you look beautiful, but to Charlie, well, he needs to see the father he loves, not someone he won't recognise. I want your meeting each other to go so well for you both.'

'Do I really look beautiful? It's a funny word for a man, but one you have used before.'

Julia slid onto Gareth's knee. Her head was close to his and she could feel his breath on her cheek. She lifted her lips, then drowned in a feeling she couldn't capture. All her senses came to life and were drained from her in a kiss that truly gave her Gareth back to her. It didn't last long, with Gareth being so weak, but it held a promise of the future, and filled Julia with happiness.

'We have to marry soon, my darling. Please try to arrange it.'

'I will, Gareth, I promise. As soon as you are strong enough to leave here, we will wed. Clara and my surrogate daughter,

Lindsey will be bridesmaids, Charlie and George, pageboys. Billie, maid-of-honour, and Anton will give me away. It will be a family wedding, a joyous coming together of not only us, but all the folk that I love, and know you will love too.'

'Hey! I thought, just a quick—'

'No, no, Gareth. Our love needs to be celebrated properly, as such a love should be. We have no need to do things as if we are ashamed. Not any more. God knows we have paid for our past mistakes. Now we can declare to the world how much we love each other.'

Tears filled Gareth's eyes, but Julia could see that they were tears of happiness, not pain and anguish, or fear and terrible memories. Her own tears spilled over as he held her and looked into her eyes. For a moment it was as if he could see her soul as it leapt from her and joined his. His gentle kiss sealed that joining, and Julia felt her happiness in every bone, sinew and fibre of her body.

CHAPTER THIRTY-EIGHT

Clara
A Submission to Love – A Joy Linked to Horror

Anton was waiting in the foyer of the theatre for Clara. He knew instantly that it was her tread as she approached him. His smile and greeting warmed her. The shows were over for the day, and they were going to her home for a short time together, as Lindsey was out for a couple of hours. She'd said she would take herself to the cinema. She wanted to see *Gone with the Wind*, which was having its third showing in as many years.

Anton squeezed her as he took her elbow. Inside, Clara felt a familiar twinge – part anticipation, part longing. Still, she and Anton had only ever gone as far as touching each other, but when they did, she was transported to another world and experienced feelings which she wanted to explore. *Maybe tonight we will. Maybe it's time to take our love that one step further.*

Even as she thought this, Clara felt doubt. The one thing that kept her from giving into the longings to be one with Anton was the fear of having a child, even though Anton had said that he would safeguard her against that happening. *Oh, if only we could be married!*

There was an atmosphere surrounding them when they reached her home. The quietness and the sense of knowing they were alone gave Clara a heightened feeling she couldn't understand.

She busied herself making tea for herself, and coffee for Anton. How he drank the dark, bottled liquid she didn't know, even though it was added to hot water and milk and laced with sugar. Ugh! She couldn't stomach the thought.

As she handed his mug to him, Anton caught hold of her hand. '*Mon amour*, we are wasting what time we have.'

She managed a smile.

'Do not be afraid. I know we are rarely alone, but everything will be as if Lindsey is in the next room, or we are catching a moment together in the wardrobe room of the theatre. I just want to hold you close, and make love to you in the way we normally do.'

'Oh, Anton, it isn't you that I am afraid of, it's me. I want more and my body may betray me.'

He placed his mug on a side table then, without saying a word, took hers from her hand and put it with his. 'They can wait. *Mais moi? Non*, I cannot.'

In his arms Clara felt her resistance weakening. She went

like a lamb with him to the sofa. There, he kissed her. At first it was only a gentle joining of their lips, but then a deepening of the kiss had her letting go of all her doubts. Her response shook Anton. He pulled from her and looked deep into her eyes, unseeing yet seeming to read her soul. 'Is it that we . . . will we finally come together, *mon amour*?'

'Yes, Anton, my love, yes.'

'Oh, Clara. I have waited for this moment for so long. I will take care of you.'

As he kissed her again, all Clara knew was that she wanted him. She wanted to give herself to him.

When the moment came, she felt nothing but joy wash over her, taking her to a place she'd never thought it was possible to go. Love carried her, letting her leave behind any fear and only surrender to the ecstasy of becoming one with her love, her life, her Anton.

She didn't hear Lindsey come in later. By then she and Anton were in bed together, drinking in each other as if they were to die by the morning.

It wasn't until morning came that they finally slept. When they woke, the hustle and bustle of the street drifted up through their open window. Clara shot into a sitting position. 'Anton, Anton, we're still in bed!'

'Ha, my funny one, where did you think we were? Come here, let me love you again.'

'Anton, be serious. Lindsey's been back and slept in the next room. She must have heard us, and now she has the shop open. Oh, Anton, I feel so embarrassed.'

'Don't, *mon amour*. We are one. We couldn't hold out any longer, Lindsey will understand.'

'Oh, Anton, I love you. I love you even more than I did before. But we must get up now. I'll go to the bathroom, then help you.'

With this, Clara jumped out of bed, not trusting herself even to look at Anton, let alone letting him catch hold of her arm as he was trying to do.

When she ran downstairs, leaving Anton in the bathroom, Clara was shocked to see Lindsey at the bottom of the stairs. Her head was bent and her shoulders hunched. 'Lindsey, what is it? Are you all right?'

'Naw. Well, I don't knaw. I've had a letter from Alf's mum. Oh, Clara, Alf's injured. They're bringing him home.'

'But that's wonderful, I – I mean. Not that he is injured, but that he is safe, and you will see him again. Does she say what has happened to him?'

'Y – yes. He has shrapnel inside him. In his leg. They . . . well, she says, that they don't knaw if they can save it.'

'Oh, Lindsey. I'm so sorry. I – I feel terrible now for even thinking that it was good that he was coming home. Hang on, I'll just see that . . . well, I – I . . . '

'Eeh, lass, spare your blushes. I put me head under me pillow. But I was that glad that at last you're a proper couple. Don't be embarrassed or owt. If me and Alf had the same chance that would have been us. Give us a hug. We both need one.'

The hug felt good. Coming out of it, Clara said she would make sure Anton was all right and then take over the shop for a while to give Lindsey time to take in the news and get her head straight.

'You can write back to Alf's mum, too. She'll be worrying as to whether everything's going to be all right for her son when he does return. It's hard to believe, but some girls are turning their backs on our returning wounded.'

'I knaw. But I could never do that.'

'Well, I know that, but maybe Alf's mum doesn't.'

'Ta, Clara. I didn't think of that. Aye, I'll take you up on your offer.'

Clara rushed back upstairs to be met by a fully clothed Anton. 'Oh, you managed.'

'Of course I did, *mon amour*. You had no need to worry, though I was trying to remember the number of steps from the stairs to your room. I was so engrossed with making love to you when we came up that I forgot to make a note.'

Clara burst out laughing. 'Oh, Anton, stop it. Here's me feeling all embarrassed and you're making it sound as if it was every day we did what we did last night.'

He smiled with her, but then, when she told him what had happened, he showed his sadness. 'That is very bad, *cherie*. Injuries like these can change a man, make him feel a lesser person than he was. We have to pray that it doesn't do that to Alf.'

'I'm going to take care of the shop for an hour, but if you want to get to the theatre, I understand.'

'I want you, and then breakfast, and then you again, *mon amour*.'

She laughed at him and hit him playfully. 'That isn't on the menu. So be good.'

'I'll get to the theatre, but you know, I'm sure Jeannie and Panda would give you the time off next week. Your

427

understudy could take over. These in-between shows are not that important. That's if you need to take over the shop.' His eyes twinkled, just as if they were seeing. 'Then we can pack Lindsey off to Alf and have the place to ourselves.'

Again she laughed at him, but she didn't miss the implication and an answering message tingled through her. 'Yes, Anton, my darling. Yes, yes, yes. I'll go and see if Lindsey would like that . . . I mean . . . Oh, Anton, you get me all in a tizzy.'

'Tizzy? Is that good?'

'Very. Now, let me help you. And behave!'

After she'd guided Anton to the top of the stairs, Clara ran down in search of Lindsey. 'I'm ready. Lindsey, have you any idea when Alf will land in the UK and where they are taking him?'

'Yes, his mum said they would have him in the Sheffield Hospital by the weekend.'

After Clara told her of Anton's suggestion, Lindsey threw her arms around her. 'Would you? Would you really do that for me?'

'Selfishly, yes. I mean, I would do it if there wasn't any gain for me, but there is. You will be out of the way, and me and Anton . . .'

'Clara! You devil! Here I am worried sick and upset and all me best friend in all the world can do is take the opportunity to get rid of me so she can have a love nest all to herself!'

Clara hung her head. Did love do this to you? Shame washed over her. Now Lindsey had put into words what she and Anton were doing, she didn't know what to say in answer.

'Eeh, I'm only kidding. I knaw the pair on you better than that. And I'd be the same. But, Clara, I'm scared. Really scared. Me poor Alf.'

The reality of it all hit Clara then. She took Lindsey into her arms. 'I'm sorry. So sorry. You and Alf least deserve this. But, if I know Alf, he'll cope. With you by his side, and us supporting you both, he'll be fine.' Holding Lindsey at arm's length she told her: 'And, Lindsey. Me and Anton want our own place when we're married, so you and Alf can have this. You can rent my half. Just think, if Alf can't go back to the work he did before the war, then he can help you to run your business. He was good in the shop, the customers loved him.'

'Eeh, Clara, you've just given me hope. Alf worked in the steelworks in Sheffield afore the war, and he often said that he'd love to do sommat like run a corner shop. He talked about how we could expand the delivery service, and extend into the stockroom and sell a more varied range of goods. We used to get that excited about it. Let me get to him, and see how the land lies with him, and no matter if he has to lose his leg, I can give him a future, as nowt can change our love for each other. Being together is all that matters.'

Panda and Jeannie agreed to Clara's request for time off, and by the following Monday Lindsey was on a train to Sheffield. That night and the next two were magical for Clara and Anton, but always at the back of her mind was the worry about what Lindsey would find, and how she and Alf would really cope if he had to lose his leg.

Yawning, she wearily filled a large jar from the small sack of toffees, and felt glad that it was half-day closing. At least she wouldn't have to face the crowds of kids when they came out of school. They could get you flustered at times, and would try to get more than their ration coupon allowed them.

The sound of the shop bell ringing broke into her thoughts. Turning, her mouth dropped open at the sight of Janet walking through the door.

'Hello, Clara.'

'What're you doing here! I mean. Janet! Is it really you? You look different, but . . . I . . . '

'Ha, so do you! It's been a long time. Clara, I – I'm, well, has your mum been in touch with you? Mine hasn't, and well . . . '

Clara drew in her breath. *Oh God! How am I to tell her?* Avoiding the issue, she asked: 'How did you find me? You're the last person I expected to walk through the door.'

'I saw you at the theatre. I've been a couple of times, but, well, I – I felt ashamed of how I'd been with you, and I didn't know if you'd talk to me. Then today I went in and asked for you and they told me you were here.'

Janet looked so like her mother. Her chestnut hair hung in waves to her shoulders, and her hazel eyes, though full of worry, were just as beautiful as Rhoda's had been – large and framed with long dark eyelashes. They set off her oval face, making her look almost doll-like with her rosy full lips.

Clara's heart sank. What was she to do? She imagined how devastated she would be if the tables were turned, and without her bidding, a tear plopped onto her cheek.

'Clara?'

'Let me close the shop. Hold on a mo. It's nearly lunchtime anyway, and this being Wednesday, I've the afternoon to spend with you.'

As the click of the lock resounded in the silence, Clara wiped away the tear and took a deep breath, before turning and ushering a frightened-looking Janet into the living room.

As she watched Janet sit on the sofa, Clara's legs turned to jelly. She wanted to delay the moment as long she could. 'So, where have you been billeted, Janet? Have you been happy? Are you working?'

'I was put with an elderly couple in Bispham, Mr and Mrs Elder, Sarah and Ronnie, as they liked me to call them, but Ronnie has a bad heart and has been taken into hospital. Their daughter came and took Sarah to live with her. She shut their house up, and so I had to get lodgings. They're fine, the landlady's a good soul. I work in a hotel on the front, though every day I think I might receive a call-up letter. Have you had one? You're a bit older than me, aren't you?'

'Only a couple of months. No. I hadn't even thought about it, but now you say . . . Though some theatre players are exempt, as they are judged as keeping the nation happy, or they go on tour to entertain the soldiers. I'll have to deal with it if it happens. Can I get you a cup of tea, Janet?'

'I – I . . . Clara, are you avoiding telling me something?'

Clara sank down next to Janet and took her hand. Janet didn't resist her. Her face showed tension, but she didn't speak.

Nor did she move or utter a word during Clara's telling her of all that happened, until Clara reached the awful part about the fire. Then a moan came from Janet that cut into Clara's own pain. Janet's body slumped onto Clara. Clara held her and cried with her, while begging and begging of God that Janet wouldn't blame her mum for the death of Rhoda. Yes, her mum did wrong, but Clara understood now. Love can make you act in ways you shouldn't, and no one could have predicted the terrible actions of Gareth's wronged wife.

431

Patting Janet's back, she told her: 'We're here for you, Janet. Me and my mum. We'll help you. My mum and yours promised each other that if anything happened to either of them, they would look out for each other's daughters. My mum was going to look for you, just as soon as she could.'

'Why? Why does your mum do these things? She hurt you. I mean, none of us were allowed to mix with you because your mum had you out of wedlock, and now she's caused the death of my mum. Why?'

Clara held her breath, but could feel no hostility in Janet's words. She tried to explain. Janet listened. Whether she took it in or not, Clara couldn't say, as her sobs increased, becoming a wail.

'Don't. Oh, Janet, I'm so sorry, I'm so sorry. I wish I could put it right, but I can't. Come with me next week, when Lindsey, my friend, is back. We'll go to my mum. She'll help you, I know she will.' Janet let Clara hold her, and her tears wet Clara's jumper. 'We have lost so much, Janet. When they tore us from our mums and our homes, they tore our souls from us. We were nothing to them, they didn't take care who they put us with, or help us to stay in touch with our families. We have to help each other, Janet. Please, let us help you.'

Janet came out of the hug. She nodded, her face a pitiful sight. 'I – I'd like to go to your mum. I'm sorry about what I said. I . . .'

Clara held her once more. All the hurt of her past rejection by this girl and others left her. She would do all she could for Janet, as she knew that her lovely mum would, too.

CHAPTER THIRTY-NINE

Clara and Julia
Their World and That of Those
They Love, Comes Right

Clara wasn't a bridesmaid after all on this lovely September day in 1945, when happiness clothed not only her and her mum, but the whole country.

This was their wedding day. Hers and her mum's.

For her mum, it had been an agonising time in coming, as once more, she and Gareth had been separated. Not that Gareth had been in danger this time, but he'd travelled back and forth across Europe in his new post with the War Office, which he'd taken up after his involvement in the planning of D-Day.

But now he was discharged, and to Clara's great happiness had bought a house and land just outside Blackpool. He and

Julia now lived there and were setting up a veterinary practice. She was planning on building a home for unmarried mums who didn't want to give up their babies. Clara was so proud of them both. And she loved Sister Grace, who came for regular visits, staying with the nuns of the Sacred Heart, and helped with the planning of it all.

The service had been wonderful. It was held in the beautiful Sacred Heart church on Talbot Road, a church dear to the heart of all theatrical folk, no matter what their religion. It had been packed with friends and well-wishers.

She and her mum wore rose-pink dresses. Mum hadn't wanted to wear white, afraid that she may offend as everyone knew she had two children. This saddened Clara, but she understood, and so stood solidly with her mum, and didn't mind not wearing white herself.

Now they were in the church rooms for their reception and the moment had come for the speeches. Anton's was beautiful, though short, and told of how much he loved Blackpool, and how they had become his family. 'And now, it is that I have a family for real. My lovely mum, Julia, and her new husband, Gareth, and a little brother, Charlie, who I am teaching to play the piano.'

Charlie blushed, but had a beam on his face. George pushed him in a way that said, 'Don't get big-headed.' The pair giggled.

Then Gareth stood. By the time he came to his last line, about how Julia's love had kept him alive, most in the room were dabbing their eyes. 'And now, I must echo Anton, in saying how wonderful it is to have a new family. My wife, Julia, who has my undying love, my daughter, Clara, my sons, Charlie and Anton, and my surrogate daughters Lindsey and

Janet. Oh, and if he'll let me, once we are acquainted, Alf too, will be looked on as a member of my family. A man we are proud of. A hero. I give you Alf.'

The room stood as one. The applause was rapturous. Alf stood, supported by Lindsey at first, but then on his own, balancing on his good leg and his false one. He looked as if he would cry, but an encouraging tweak of his arm by Lindsey made his face light up. 'Only if you will promise to buy all your groceries at L & A stores of Hornby Rd, sir.'

Everyone laughed at this and at Alf taking a bow. Cries of 'good man' and 'well done' came from around the room.

'And now, may I ask you all to stand and toast the beautiful Mrs Maling and Mrs Auxier.'

As all stood and raised their glasses, Clara glowed inside. Clara Auxier. It had a beautiful ring to it. Anton took her hand and whispered: 'My Mrs Auxier. At last, *mon amour*, it is that my world is complete.'

Clara looked around the room. *Yes. All our worlds are complete and have come right and we are all filled with hope.*

Hope for the future, not only for her and her mum, but also for Lindsey and Alf – Mr and Mrs Potter. They had wed soon after Alf returned, a bedside wedding in the hospital. It had been hastily arranged as Alf was failing but, thank God, he pulled through and was going from strength to strength.

Her eyes fell on Billie and her Tom, also wed, and so happy. And Janet, and her dad. It was such a relief when he had been found. That had been down to Gareth who used his influence through the War Office. Though discharged from military duty, Uncle Roger, as Clara now called Janet's dad, still went to sea as a merchant seaman. Janet hadn't gone back to

Guernsey when the island had been liberated in May, but planned to visit her grandparents regularly. She was living and working with Billie now, and it was as if she was Billie's younger sister, such was the love between them.

Gareth had been right to welcome Janet as a surrogate daughter, as Clara and Janet had become as close as sisters too. They liked to talk about Janet's mum and Clara's granny, as only a daughter and granddaughter could remember them – sometimes with laughter, sometimes with sorrow, but each time with healing.

Clara would never forget her lovely granny, and though she hadn't known Rhoda very well, she had made a space for her in her heart. A lot of heart-space was occupied by the very special Shelley, and dear Daisy. She would always love and miss them. A part of her felt sadness at this, but then she realised they wouldn't want that of her today. They would be rejoicing for her.

'Penny for your thoughts, but first a hug.'

Coming out of the cloud she'd gone into, Clara smiled as Gareth took her hand and tugged her so that she stood. His arms came around her. 'My beautiful daughter.'

'Thanks, Dad. For everything.' It was the first time she'd called him that, but suddenly she knew that's what he was – her dad. She would always keep her own dad close to her, imagining him eternally as he looked in the photo – so happy, holding her mum and smiling down on her. And she knew, he too would be watching her today, and be happy for her.

'Hey, let us in.'

Her beautiful mum came into the circle of arms, and moments later Clara felt a tugging at her skirt. She unhooked her arm from around her mum and picked up Charlie. 'You're getting heavy, my lovely brother. Clarry's very proud of how you conducted yourself today. You were a proper little man.'

Charlie laughed and clenched his other arm around his dad's neck.

Enclosed in this love circle of her family, Clara knew that, though they all still bore scars, they would heal. With each other's love to help them, they were almost there.

At this, Clara looked over her mum's shoulder. There watching them, was Jeannie, Lofty, Panda and Arnold. She smiled at them. How lucky she was to have them in her life, caring for her and being there for her.

Being a Blackpool evacuee had turned out well in the end for her. Though now she wasn't just a visitor, a stranger thrust into the midst of the lives of these Blackpool folk. She was one of them. A Blackpudlian, as they called themselves. None of them were Sandgrownians as those born here were called, but Blackpool had embraced them and taken them into her heart, and was now embedded in theirs.

A peace settled in Clara at this thought. As it did, a hand touched her shoulder. She released Charlie to his dad and turned to look into Anton's face. There she saw his beautiful love for her, and she knew for sure that life was going to be good. How could it not be, with her beloved Anton by her side?

Together, they would all travel the journey to a new and good life, where bad things belonged in the past, and love, deep friendship and, above all, happiness, awaited them.

Letter from the Author

Dear Readers

I hope you enjoyed *Blackpool Evacuee* as much as I enjoyed writing it. If you did, I would be so grateful if you could take the time to leave me a review on Amazon, Goodreads, or any other platform you may use. A review is like hugging an author.

If you would like to contact me, you can do so at www. authormarywood.com or through Facebook: www.facebook. com/HistoricalNovels or by tweeting me @Authormary. I would love to hear from you and will answer any questions you may have about this book, or any of my books.

Blackpool is my home town and has been since 1984, and I love it. It is a place that can get right into your heart, and I am finding so much out about its sometimes notorious, sometimes bleak, but mostly colourful history through my research.

The way it was controlled by gangs as infamous as the Kray twins before, during, and after the war really surprised me. This information was given to me by my son-in-law, Richard Gradwell, a Sandgrownun – the name given to those born in Blackpool – and led me to finding a wealth of information to help me with the gangland activities in this book. So my thanks to Richard.

Other research came from a little gem of a book: *Blackpool History Tour* by Allan W. Wood & Ted Lightbown. The book is full of interesting snippets about Blackpool and some wonderful historical photographs of the seaside resort.

But the real inspiration for *Blackpool Evacuee* began quite a while ago when I read *Guernsey Evacuees* by Gillian Mawson. This book is a moving true account as told to Gillian by evacuees who experienced being sent to England at the beginning of the war. Their story is heart-rending as many never saw their parents or their home again. Many were treated badly too. I would recommend this book to you if you are interested in real-life stories of wartime.

Many evacuees came to Blackpool and one little boy, like poor Shelley, was killed by a tram. May he rest in peace.

Blackpool had a good war. A thriving war, fed by the aforementioned gangs who were black-marketeers. The town was barely touched by Hitler, who it is said had set his heart on making the resort his playground. But for this notion, things could have been so different. The town housed the Vickers Armstrong Factory, which built twin-engine Wellington Bombers. There were two airfields, one at the site of Blackpool Zoo, and one which is still operational today, Squires Gate Lane, which was used as a fighter squadron base and an RAF training base. All targets that could have greatly disrupted Britain's defence.

Of course, like the rest of the country, its people suffered loss of family members and my heart goes out to them; my heartfelt thanks goes to the young Blackpudlians who lost their life to the cause and those who fought just as valiantly but were lucky enough to return home and to help to build Blackpool as it is today – a wonderful cosmopolitan seaside town that is inclusive of all and has the greatest lightshow in all the world. I think so – do visit the Blackpool Illuminations one year to see what you think.

Much love to you all
Maggie Mason x

ACKNOWLEDGEMENTS

There is always so much help given to authors when writing a book and my heartfelt thanks go out to all who contribute their special talents to the creation of my novels:

- My editor, Maddie West, for your support, your faith in me and your enthusiasm for the Blackpool books
- Thalia Proctor and her editing team for the wonderful work you do on my books
- Millie Scaward, my publicist, and her team for all the hard work promoting the Blackpool books
- My agent, Judith Murdoch – simply the best

You all enhance my work and make me feel that I and my books are in safe hands. Thank you.

My thanks, too, to my family and friends, always supporting me – especially my husband Roy, who lovingly takes care of me and our home to free me from the domestic practicalities of everyday life. Our son, James Wood, helps with the many edits, social media and advising on my manuscripts. Our girls – Christine Martin, Julie Bowling, and Rachel Gradwell – are always ready to support and encourage me. And all my grand-children and greats, and our Wood and Olley families. You all surround me with love and help me to reach the top of my mountain. Thank you.

And no acknowledgement is complete without sending my thanks and love to all my readers. Your support, the trouble you go to to leave me a review, and the help you give in promoting my work by sharing social media posts is invaluable to me, as is the lovely interaction I have with you. You make all the hours I sit at my desk so worthwhile.

And, already mentioned in my letter, my thanks to Gillian Mawson for the invaluable help your book *Guernsey Evacuees* was to me, and Allan W. Wood and Ted Lightbown for your book *Blackpool History Tour* and the amazing historic photo-graphs you share in it.